MERINDAH

ROSS HUDSON

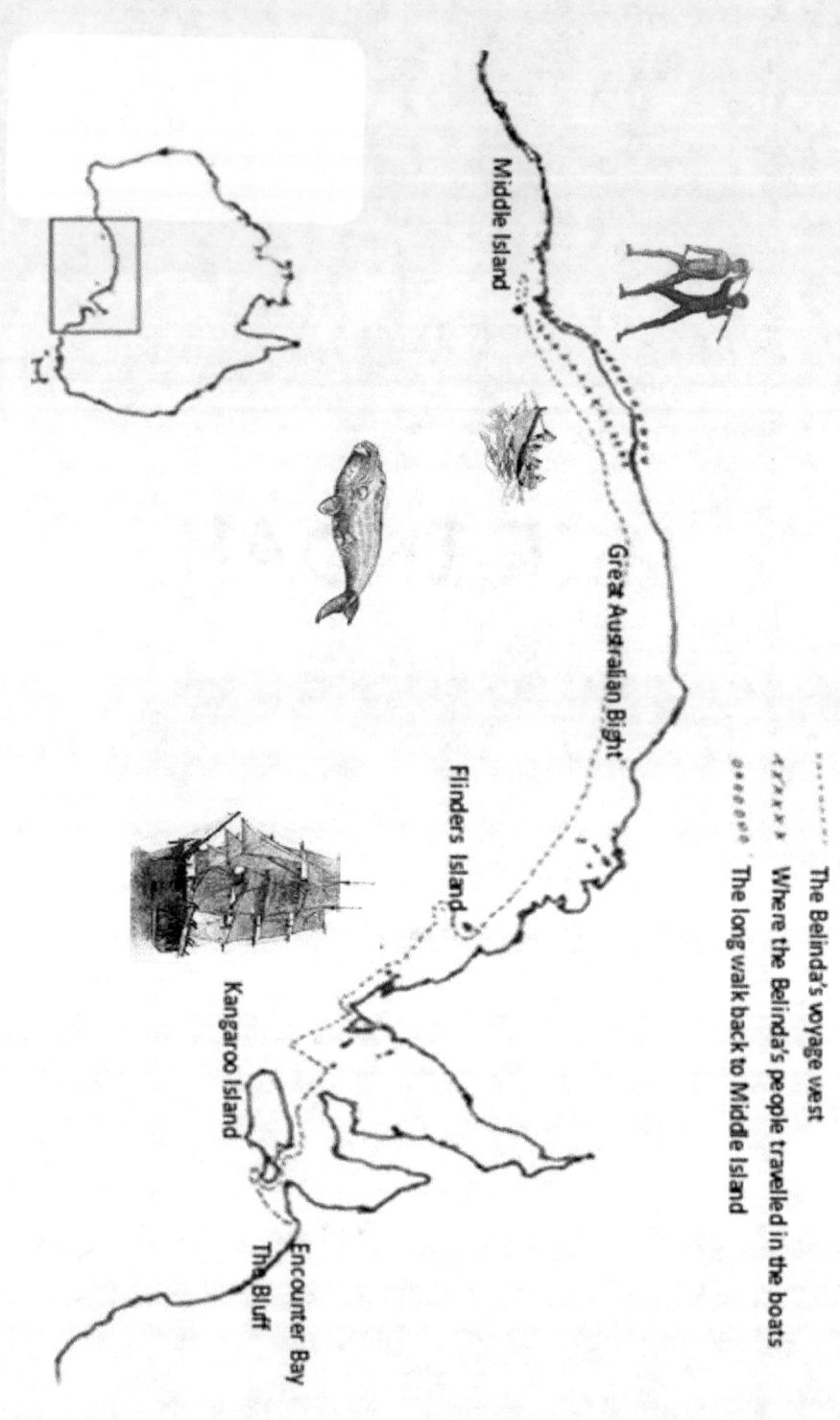

Middle Island

Great Australian Bight

Flinders Island

Kangaroo Island

Encounter Bay
The Bluff

··········· The Belinda's voyage west

××××× Where the Belinda's people travelled in the boats

°°°°°° The long walk back to Middle Island

This book is dedicated to all the girls who were taken and to the
mothers who cried their tears.

Paperback ISBN-13: 978-0-9925318-7-4
E-book ISBN: 978-0-9925318-6-7

Bailing piggin

Wooden bucket

Water breaker

ACKNOWLEDGMENTS

It would have been impossible for me to tell Merindah's story without the encouragement of my family.

Jack Casanova's books created my interest in Bryant and Charlotte.

Cherrie De Leiuen's theses, *The power of gender,* gave me more inspiration and information; without her work I would not have found Charlotte's hut and well. (or Merindah's pendant).

Spending time on Flinders Island with Peter Woolford and our discussions about the area gave me more encouragement.

Hours of reading about sealers and their activities was by no means a difficult chore, and helped me imagine how they lived and what they expected from their harsh lives.

Even if I read all that was available, it would still be impossible for me to understand all of the culture of the Encounter Bay Aboriginal Nation, but I have tried to get some perception by reading. — *The Conquest of the Ngarrindjeri.* —Graham Jenkin. *Manners and customs of the Aborigines of the Encounter bay tribe.* —Edward Meyer, and various other works.

Perhaps I feel an extra connection with the Encounter Bay people and their story, because my Great Great Grandfather was a whaler/sealer there in the 1840s. He certainly would have had contact with Ramindjeri people and did know Edward Meyer.

My learning the basic writing technics, and starting to make sense of the art of story-telling has been assisted by the Eyre Writers group.

I also appreciate the assistance of Eric Kotz who has also written briefly about Charlotte and Bryant.

Most importantly, I trust that all my effort has been made readable with the patient editing of Mary Gudzenovs and Odette Applebee. Thank you both.

FOREWORD

I first became aware of the story of Black Charlotte twenty years ago when I read the late Jack Casanova's wonderful book *When Grass Was Gold*. Her story has fascinated me ever since.

The early history of South Australia involved rough whaling and sealing men who were here thirty years before the first settlement of Adelaide. These men from all over the world lived very rough, and pillaged the coast line and coastal waters.

Thousands of years of Aboriginal culture was wrenched away, the white men brought disease and disruption. The women and girls who they took away by various means were South Australia's first stolen people.

Ironically some of those women, and many Aboriginal men and boys, who were taken, became an important part of the white men's endeavours. I am sure that without their labours, voluntary or forced, the white men would not have been able to prosper, and in many cases would have perished without Aboriginal assistance.

Of course her Mother did not call her Charlotte: I have named her Merindah. Hers is only one of many stories, but it has been reasonably well recorded, and shows how these women survived against great odds. By telling this story I hope to show how these women were treated, how they protected their children that the white men let live. And I wish to show the bonds that would have been formed between these women, even though at times they came from different places and cultures far away from each other.

It is certain that Charlotte was taken to Flinders Island by an Irish man called Brian, or Bryant, and that she was taken from Encounter Bay. Authorities stated that she may have left a daughter from a white man there.

This book is about Charlotte (Merindah) growing up at Encounter bay, and her early life before Flinders Island.

There are only a few characters based on actual people, the story is fictional but based on actual events and ships that were here at the time.

I have used the true story of the brig Belinda becoming stranded at Middle Island, and the subsequent fate of her survivors. In the written accounts of this ship wreck there is no mention of Aboriginal people on board the Belinda, but I am sure that that would be most likely. I have changed the names of the Captain and crew.

I needed to tell this story about Charlotte's, (my Merindah's) young life, before writing about her later amazing life which I will relate in another book to follow shortly.

Wind, waves, sand. The ocean swell building and falling. The hills and creeks, the big river forcing out through the sand hills from the lakes. It had been that way forever.

For a short time, people lived among these things, they adapted with the flow of seasons; changed little, were part of it all, and it seemed things would always be that way.

Not briefly, like their time, but in a flick of time, much has been altered. The animals on the land, and the fish in the sea, the bushes, the trees and the grass on the hills; all changed. Even the big river; people tried to change that. They blasted half of the island away.

The people have changed, or have they gone?

The swell still rises, the waves keep rolling in; the wind still blows. The sea mist is still there in the morning. But who now watches the sun come out of the surf at the end of the beach?

Chapter 1 – Footprints
Southern coast of South Australia, 1820.

The large fly stood high on long stick legs. She flew low along the sand looking for flesh; landed on a dead shell fish searching for a break in the shiny dry shield. Huge black spotty eyes turned left, right, up and down. Wings flashed, gleaming the colour of the sun setting into a smoky sky.

A young girl lay stretched out on the beach, the sun warming her as she slept soundly.

That same dream returned.

Her dreams were always alike. The rhythm of the waves became the rhythm of the camp when the old men told their stories.

An old man danced; children crouched behind their mothers, with wide eyes peering through smoke and dust.

Men chanted. Fire glowed in dark mesmerised eyes as the stories were told once again. Each time the children grasped more of the meaning.

As the old man danced with his body covered in white stripes he seemed to float in the smoke from the fires. His feather-covered feet moved with the rhythm of chants and beating sticks. He kicked the sand, fire squirted from his feet. People chanted.

The old man's dance suddenly stopped; he lurched, stumbled, Blood gushed from his body onto the sand. He ran to the sea and fell into the waves.

The young girl stared. The old man had become a whale, but his face remained the same; painted stripes, white hair and spindly beard. Piercing eyes stared at her through the mist of the surf. His giant black body and tail thrashed the water in fury.

It was always the same face, the same dance and the whale with the old man's head, swimming away.

The talk around the fire had been different; of men without skin, men who came across the sea on white clouds. They had huge knives to cut up the whales.

The girl slept on. The man-whale lay lifeless on the beach. The power of his face had vanished, and his story destroyed. The skinless men were standing on his body hacking into his shiny flesh.

The fly jumped from the shellfish onto something alive. Long legs gripped young flesh as they stepped along the girl's leg.

The girl moved; her skin shuddered. A skinless man lent over her; finger nails gripped her leg. He raised a huge knife ready to thrust.

The fly pierced deep, seeking blood.

The skinless man drove down his knife.

The girl woke suddenly. She screamed.

Afternoon winter sun flashed off blue sea; the long sandy beach shimmered far ahead. Low tide; surf tumbled, waves collapsed, slapped and rolled across hard flat sand, hissed in, drew back. Birds ran and darted after small creatures before the next wave would roll them away.

The two young girls could have been the only people on earth as they walked with the afternoon sun on their faces. Toes dug into clean white sand as they stepped carefree and invigorated by the fresh salty air, the smells of the ocean, freedom and close friendship.

'Look Merindah, here are our footprints from yesterday; the waves did not come up this far last night.'

'No Yara and now we've reached the rocky place again. Our mothers forbid us to go past here; other people live that way.' She pointed west. The two girls hesitated, peering curiously ahead down the barren beach. They glanced at each other, and then walked on slowly.

Yara glanced at her cousin. 'This is further than we've ever been Merindah; our footprints have never been here.'

Cool wind blew sand along the wide beach. Grains of sand stung Merindah's bare legs. She sucked in the cool air that kept a shock of wavy black hair away from her bright eyes. She scanned warily ahead; this was other people's area. 'There's nobody here, let's walk further.'

Tumbling seaweed and dead fragments from the ocean had made erratic patterns on the sand. Amongst those random patterns were familiar bird footprints.

Yara stopped suddenly. There were human footprints, clearly made since the tide had receded that morning. 'Other people have been here today Merindah. I want to go back.'

Merindah hesitated. She could see tracks coming east, and then disappearing into the low bushy scrub on the sand hills hugging the beach. 'Yes, and they walked up there into the bushes.'

Merindah examined the footprints. 'They are small like ours, children's. And see, over there somebody has drawn in the sand. It's a whale Yara. Shall we draw too?'

A fish, and a bird; they pressed their open hands into the sand; hand prints. As they drew, they kept glancing uneasily back down the beach.

Something moved in the low bushes above the beach, a flock of small birds rushed skyward.

Yara stood quickly, 'What's that Merindah? Is someone

watching us?'

Suddenly they remembered their mother's warning; other people's place, keep away. Both girls turned and ran.

'Here run close to the water,' Merindah exclaimed. 'The waves will wash our footprints away.'

Young hearts thumped as young legs sprinted on hard wet sand. Busy small birds darted momentarily away, disturbed.

Merindah stopped and waited for her cousin.

Both girls stood panting with chests heaving. 'Were you frightened Merindah?'

'A little; I don't know why, but when we ran I became more frightened. The waves are washing our footprints away, like we were never here. Every night the waves bring things in and sometimes they take them away again. The waves are always here, and will be long after we're gone.'

'Will we go somewhere else Merindah?'

'Yes, one day. Perhaps we are like the things that wash up here every morning; we come, and then we go.'

They ran again.

'Wait for me Merindah; I can't keep up with you.'

The taller girl ran slower. 'You're a bird Yara, your mother named you after the seagulls; you should be flying.' She stopped. 'Shall we swim?'

'Yes, but don't go out too deep,' Yara pleaded. 'I'm a bird not a fish.'

'I'm a fish,' exclaimed Merindah as she ran and dived into the waves. Yara walked in and stood in small breakers as she watched Merindah swim out, turn and surf in on a wave.

'Come out with me,' Merindah called.

'Oh! You make it seem so easy.'

'It is; come on I'll show you.'

* * *

Still a young girl, Merindah had spent twelve seasons growing up, running along the beach, through the sand dunes, coastal shrubs, and among the trees further inland. Each plant and animal had its place. Dark bright alert eyes revealed her intelligence as she absorbed her clan's basic, but intricate lifestyle.

Merindah loved the sea, always confident among rolling waves, diving with the fish amid the rocks and seaweed. The sea was part of her. Every day Merindah swam. As her shock of black curly hair dried and glistened in the sunshine, she studied the world around her. Other young girls regarded Merindah as their leader; the smartest in her group, the one who led the way and helped the younger children. Tall, alert and strong, destined to be a leader.

Yara, born to be a mother, steady, always ready to help, but never in the front. A shorter girl, she was quieter, never needing to push ahead, because the taller girl was always there, so confident.

*   *   *

Exhausted from their swimming, the two girls lay on a flat rock that had been warmed in the afternoon sun. They both dared to glance toward a prominent black rock that stood defying the waves.

Yara turned to Merindah, 'Have you seen men walk out there?'

Merindah stood and brushed sand from her long legs, 'Only when we are far up the beach, that's a special place; only for men.'

Yara stood; she shook her mass of black curly hair. 'Yes, I know my mother told me. Do you know why Merindah?'

'No that's not for women. Let's not think about that.'

Relaxed, happy with their world they gazed up at the blue sky. They studied shadows creeping across the low cliffs. Together since babies, when at times they drank from the same breast, the two girls had rarely been apart. Although they did not talk about parting, deep in their minds they knew that day would come. They could never imagine their future and the dramas that lay ahead.

They watched the sun setting next to the Bluff and wondered where it went each night.

'We see it come out of the mist at the end of our beach each morning,' Merindah told Yara. 'It warms us all-day before going into the ground, over there, each night.' She pointed west toward the Bluff.

'Where do stars go during the day?' Yara asked. 'And the moon, sometimes it's in the sky during the day, other times at night, like a child, trying to catch the sun, who is its mother.'

With the sun behind them they stepped silently on their shadows toward their home; a small bay, protected on both sides by rocky headlands.

At their home bay, they could see people from their clan walking around in the shallow water. They stood for a few minutes gazing out to sea. They had heard the elders talking about the strange crafts that people had seen in the ocean in recent seasons. Neither spoke but both were aware of an uncomfortable feeling.

Merindah turned to her cousin, 'Our clan are at Kangjeinwal. It's low tide; our fathers will be spearing fish in the traps.'

'Yes,' Yara agreed. 'We must hurry to help them.'

Their mothers greeted them at the beach. Men walked in shallow water spearing fish caught in the stone traps. They put them into woven reed baskets that balanced on small rafts which women dragged through the water. It was a peaceful scene, people chatting, laughing and working together, as they had for generations. Small children were on the beach playing, others watching. Older women sat minding the younger children.

'We must catch many fish,' Yara's mother said. 'The hot time is ending. Soon we will move inland to our cool season camp; not far away. The men will hunt; we will be eating different food.'

'Yes,' said Merindah's mother. 'We'll soon need our skin cloaks and rugs for the children.' Women carried the baskets of fish up to the sheltered camp close to the beach, the older women and children followed. Dogs woke from their lazy places in the afternoon sun; they yawned, scratched and then sniffed and trailed behind the baskets of fish. Women wrapped fish in seaweed and placed it in hot coals to cook.

Smoke draped the cool evening air as the sun set over the land in the west. After the clan ate, men sat and talked, women tended young children. The older children played with the small yellow dogs.

Hot coals glowed, the smoke drifted away, stars glimmered in a clear sky. Young children and babies were sleeping. People sat quietly discussing the day.

'Did anyone see white clouds floating on the sea today?' an old man asked.

An old woman pointed toward Merindah and Yara. 'They've been walking on the beach, and out the rocks.' People turned toward the two girls sitting together.

Merindah kept her eyes down. 'We saw nothing different today.'

Small clusters of people resumed talking; the elders in serious discussion, they knew that the white clouds were sails on the white man's ships.

A few seasons before Merindah and Yara's birth, Aboriginal people had seen the first of the white man's ships sailing near the coast. The clan had watched for two days as two mysterious craft remained stationary out in the sea beyond the big river.

Within three seasons, they were aware of the white men and their ships. Ships had anchored at the sheltered cove by the large headland the people called Longkuwar. White men used small boats from their ships to chase whales, kill them and drag them up to the flat rocks. They cut up the whales and cooked the flesh with a hot fire.

Aboriginal dreaming told stories of the Southern right whale. Historically, if the clans found a whale stranded on the shore, several adjoining clans, Lakinyeri, gathered, making use of the valuable food and other products. Huge rib bones sometimes became the frames for huts. Blubber was melted into oil and rubbed on people's bodies and also used in other traditional ways.

*   *   *

Merindah and Yara listened to the adults talking; each had their own troubled feelings as they slipped quietly off to their own family shelter.

The weather became cooler, and the clan moved inland to their traditional winter camping place.

Women recovered the possum and wallaby skin cloaks and rugs.

Although they had moved inland, they still occasionally collected food from the sea.

At the western end of the big bay white men and their ship had returned.

Merindah listened to the adults talking. One old man at the fire said that clans from the place or ruwe, where the white men brought the whales ashore, were neglecting their traditional hunting and culture. Aboriginal men helped to melt down the whale blubber. People remained at that place, living off whale meat, ignoring their age-old traditions.

'The white skin men are taking their women,' a man stated angrily.

'We must keep away, there is sickness there,' declared an old woman.

'Yes, we will keep our children in our own ruwe,' said another.

Another woman shook her head. 'I fear that the sickness will come to us whatever we do.'

Merindah's mother was concerned for her daughter's safety and health. 'Keep away from there,' she warned. 'Stay near our beach.'

*   *   *

The white men and their ship had gone.

On a sunny day at the end of the cool season, Merindah and

Yara walked westward along the beach; they were curious and came to the place where the small reef came right onto the beach; the place their mothers had forbid them to go past.

Yara pointed west, 'Merindah, there's somebody coming this way along the beach.'

Merindah lifted a hand and shaded her eyes from the sun, 'They're children, like us. Let's talk to them.'

Merindah and Yara waited and watched warily as three young people approached. They were from the Longkuwar clan.

At first both groups regarded each other cautiously, but soon talked timidly.

The oldest girl in the group from Longkuwar shook her head, 'We're hungry; our men have not been hunting.' She wiped her nose with the back of her hand; then sniffed, 'Some girls are sick with disease from the white men. The white men took girls away.'

When Merindah told her mother what the young people from Longkuwar had told her, she became upset and concerned for those people and the future for her own clan.

*   *   *

Three cycles of the seasons passed. The white men and their ships had not returned to the place by the Bluff. Traditional life resumed, except for the unexplained incidents of new disease in the clans. Merindah and Yara noticed changes in their young bodies. They were growing into young women. Their mothers talked to them about their future. Other women would prepare the girls for their future life.

Older women had taken Merindah and Yara to a special place where they received instructions and teachings. Traditional markings were placed on their bodies, preparing them to become women. One day in the future they would leave the group and go to a man in another clan.

When they returned to their mothers as young women, the two

friends were sad and afraid.

But Merindah's mother remained firm, 'You must not be with a man from our clan. My brother, your uncle, will arrange for you to go to a man that he will select.'

Merindah wept, 'I don't want to go.'

'Women never choose,' her mother answered. 'Others decide, you must accept, it's always been that way.'

Distraught and weeping, Merindah ran off. She hid alone in the scrub for the night. Next morning she found Yara, also alone, crying. Her mother had given her similar news. Devastated, the two friends clung together, terrified to leave each other or their families.

*   *   *

A ship had returned to the far end of the bay in the shelter of the big headland. The white men were killing whales again.

Men from Merindah's clan talked to men from there, they asked, 'Where did the white men come from, where did they go?'

Men from Longkuwar answered, 'They came from America, they told us; wherever that is? When it's the warm time again they will go to a big island. It is two days sailing away; they kill seals there, like they do here sometimes. No clans of our people live there, and white men have made it their home. They have taken some of our women there. There are other women like ours there, taken from different places. Our kind of people call this big island Karta, the white men from America call it Kangaroo Island.'

Whalers bargained with the Aboriginal men to help them work on the whales. They also used them to collect the vast amount of firewood, needed to melt down the huge carcasses. In return the Aboriginal people were allowed all the whale meat they could eat. The white men used and abused The Aboriginal women.

The days became warmer; Merindah's clan moved back to their beach living place. The warm time had returned, the ship and the white men had left, again taking away young Aboriginal men and girls.

Young men from Merindah's clan had been working with the white sailors. Some of them had lost interest in the traditional ways.

Dismayed, old people wondered what was going to happen to their community in the future.

One of the older men waved his hands, 'Well the white men have gone again.'

Another shook his head anxiously, 'Well I hope they don't come back.'

Many people agreed.

'Merindah I want to talk to you.'

'Yes Mother.' This was the conversation that Merindah was dreading. She did not want to hear.

'Your uncle has made an exchange with the clan at Longkuwar. You will be going to a man there; you'll only be here with us for one more cool season.'

Merindah was heartbroken, she knew this must happen, but she did not want to leave her family and her friends, especially Yara, who was also upset. She was promised to a man at a different place. The two girls hugged each other, cried and ran away. They hid together in the scrub for days, but hunger and love brought them back to the clan.

'What is this man like?' Merindah asked her mother. 'Is he old? Will he be kind to me?'

'I don't know, that's our way,' her mother said. 'You must accept the decision.'

The two girls worked with their mothers learning the skills and crafts they would need in their future lives. They swam and enjoyed each other's company, spending days together on the beach, knowing that soon they would separate.

Merindah became more aware of the world around her; she watched the signs of the plants, the patterns. Events that she had remembered from her childhood became more important.

Incidents such as the changing place where the sun rose each day, and how the moon was not as regular. Sometimes the moon was shy like a woman, peeping with her eye half closed. But then she gradually became bold and proud, opening her eye, lighting up the scrub, the beach and the waves in the night.

Merindah studied the stars and noticed how they moved and twisted across the sky each night. They reminded her of the way myriads of tiny fish swirled around as she swam with her eyes open under the water. But the stars were in slow motion, performing the same dance each night, changing slightly with the seasons; always returning to their starting place again.

The girls spent many hours together, looking at the birds in the water, the skimmers, the divers, the waders and the runners on the beach. They watched birds feeding, scratching in the seaweed; scavenging from a dead animal or fish. Seasons changing taught them to expect some birds to leave; then return with another season.

Merindah and Yara stood gazing at the pelicans floating in the sky; so elegant. They watched as the big birds landed, collapsing into the waves. When the pelicans flew from the surface of the water, with their huge wings flapping, the girls thought they resembled children splashing with their hands.

They sat together on the sand, drawing images of birds, fish, the sun, and the moon. They discussed their world, and their future.

Merindah hugged her best friend. 'We will never be apart. We'll both see the sunrise each morning. The moon will sometimes show us the way while stars dance across the sky.'

'Yes Merindah,' Yara replied. 'Now I have decided that the sun is a man, and the moon is his woman. The moon needs to be on her own some days, as we do, then she tries to catch her man again, who is the sun.'

Merindah smiled and nodded, 'Oh yes, and the stars are her children, when she tips over she's trying to catch one.'

'So many children, I wonder which are ours,' Yara said. 'No, they are all our children; we will both be looking at them long after we part.'

Their eyes met, 'Yes!'

Toward the end of the warm time, the two friends strolled along the sandy beach on the big river side of their clans little cove.

Yara stopped, gazing out to sea. 'Merindah! A White man's big boat is coming from that way.' She pointed east.

Previously, the white men's ships had come from the west, not the east. Little did the two friends realise how this ship would change their lives forever.

Chapter 2 - The Ship Arrives

Some things are not forever.
Events may occur that change all we have known.
One unexpected incident may lead to a series of life
changing outcomes.

Two young men sat toward the bow of the Southern Sky, a small whaling ship. When the brig left Hobart Town ten days earlier the captain told the two friends this would be a longer voyage, they would be away for at least six months; maybe longer. It would not be like the short trips they had experienced around the coast of Van Diemen's Land, and trips to Sydney.

James Miles and Jacob Bennet, both sixteen years old but quickly growing from boys to men, joined the ship at Hobart Town. Originally from New South Wales, and sons of convicts, they had found their way to Van Diemen's Land, seeking adventure on a whaling ship.

Unexperienced, the lads kept away from the older sailors on the ship. When not working they spent their time together talking, or sitting quietly watching waves slide under the bow.

The fairer of the two young men, James tucked his short light brown hair into a felt cap. He wore loose fitting sailcloth pants and a sun-bleached cotton shirt. The more friendly older sailors teased him about the soft fair whiskers that were starting to grow on his chin and cheeks.

'When are you going to learn to shave lad?' They would ask.

James was still growing, life at sea hardening him. Twelve months hauling on ropes and climbing rigging had made his young hands tough and callused. His bare feet were fast becoming like the leather soles of those boots that he left in his sea chest.

There was little privacy aboard the ship, and the two young men saw the way that the sailors treated their Aboriginal women. Most of these women had been taken from their home places in Van Diemen's Land. Occasionally fights would break out over the women.

Growing up in Sydney Town James had seen squalor and loose morals, but here on the ship he lived among it. He heard the stories of how men got rid of babies and what sailors did with women when they had finished using them.

Living and working amongst this group of men, James recognised how diverse men could be. He was shocked at how some men treated their Aboriginal women. Other men were calmer; he soon sorted out which group of men that he would rather mix with.

James had never been with a woman, and other sailors teased him about that.

'Come on Miles,' rougher men told him. 'Take this woman, she'll teach you. There's nothing she doesn't know.'

James would turn away. The way these men treated the women disturbed him.

Jacob was a shorter thickset young man, his olive complexion becoming darker from the wind and the sun. He weekly shaved off his thickening black beard and wore a canvas cap over his long black hair. Like his friend James, time aboard the ship had hardened Jacob, but he still turned away when sailors took their women. Jacob worked with Bill Bryant, who was the blacksmith on the ship.

15

Captain Harris had been whaling along the coast southwest of Sydney and around Van Diemen's Land for years, but this would be a longer voyage. The men who chartered his ship wanted him to find new whaling places further west.

The Captain had taken on an American sailor as third mate. He hoped to gain information about places even further west than where the Southern Sky would sail on this voyage.

Whaling companies in eastern Australia were aware of the Americans working in the west, and they were aware of the American base on Kangaroo Island. American whalers had been in that area for years and occasionally ventured east, often taking Aboriginal men and women from Van Diemen's Land. The whalers based at Hobart Town did not welcome the Americans around their grounds, they wanted to set up more permanent bases in the west and discourage the American whalers. The Negro's experience and detailed knowledge of distant whaling grounds would be valuable.

Captain Harris was not interested in the shady past of his crew men. He would take on hard workers provided they kept their past indiscretions to themselves and pulled their weight. Although he and his company bosses weren't sure about the American, they engaged him hoping to use his knowledge of these new places.

'My name is Ned,' he told Captain Harris: no other name given.

The ship sailed nearer to the area where Captain Harris wanted to investigate; he called the American to his cabin.

The Captain had charts spread on the table. He nodded to the American, 'Can you show me where you sailed?'

Ned glanced at the chart. 'At the bottom of that peninsula, Eastern side I think.'

He pointed, 'Yes, it would have been here. They called it the Bluff.'

'Well do you know where the reefs are, and the best shelter?'

'Course I do,' snapped Ned.

Captain Harris ignored the tone of that remark; he needed to put up with this rude American. 'What about seals? Are there many there?'

'Yes, but more to the south around the rocky points, the ship that I sailed on mainly chased whales, and then we spent the summer months at Kangaroo Island. We camped there and did some sealing.'

'Yes, I've heard about your people at Kangaroo Island.'

The Captain rolled up the chart and placed it in a water tight cylinder. 'That's all for now, I'll need you tomorrow. If this east wind keeps up, we'll be at your Bluff in the morning.

The Southern Sky was not a large ship, actually a brig. A small wooden sailing ship one hundred and twenty feet long, with two masts. The crew and the ship were prepared to go shore whaling. On board were four whaleboats, two small dinghies and all the equipment for whaling and sealing. The ship had supplies to stay away for twelve months. Barrels for whale oil, tools and timber and hoop iron to make more barrels, salt to treat sealskins and many other items for the quest.

Among the crew were men from all different parts of the world, including those with shady pasts that the Captain did not ask about, but expected them to do their job.

Aboriginal women from Van Diemen's Land also lived aboard the ship. Taken from their traditional land, these women were virtual captives. Although this was brutal life among these men, at least they were fed, and alive. There were also young boys, the sons of sailors and the Aboriginal women. The Captain tolerated women and children aboard his ship for various reasons. Women could do most of the work that men did and sometimes work that many men would not do. Women aboard encouraged men to stay on the ship, and the sons that these women bore created a source of seamen and whalers.

There were five young half-caste boys, ranging in age from one to ten years old. Some older boys or young men in the ship's crew were also part Aboriginal. The women and the young boys lived in a separate area from the men on the ship. When sailors wanted their women, they would find a place, not always easy on a small crowded ship. However, privacy never bothered sailors, they even shared some of the women, not caring whose sons they bore. There were forty-five souls aboard counting the crew, women and children.

But there were no baby girls.

Captain Harris had his own young Aboriginal woman on the ship. But he kept her well away from the other men.

Bill Bryant, an experienced whaler and sealer, also worked as the blacksmith on the Southern Sky. He had learnt that trade while on other ships. An Irishman, maybe twenty-five years old, Bryant had a native woman on board, he called her Sally. Captain Harris tolerated Bryant's two huge hunting dogs, they would catch game from the land; a welcome change from fish and seal meat. No other man shared Bryant's woman, his dogs never left her side.

Levi was a native of Van Diemen's Land, a tall lanky lad, only about eighteen years old. Abandoned as a small child, he never knew his parents, just followed one of the native women who may have been an aunt or even a sister. Captain Harris had noticed the lad alone on the wharf at Hobart town and brought him aboard the ship. One year later Levi had become a handy worker.

Addis, the sail maker, slept with his sails and ropes. He was a large man of mixed race, aloof with a strange manner. He took no notice of the women.

First mate Hugh Byron an Englishman had a wife and family at Hobart Town, he tried to ignore the way sailors treated their women.

Second mate Owen Muller, an older German man, claimed not to be interested in women.

'Too old,' he told the other men.

Possibly one of the most important men on the ship, the carpenter and cooper lived in separate accommodation with his young apprentice. They could have been father and son, but nobody asked.

Another important man on the ship was the cook, an American, part Negro, part American Indian, a large man, very friendly and respectful of the women and children.

'Just call me Chief,' he would say, chuckling.

Late March; the ship sailed along the south coast toward the place Matthew Flinders named Encounter Bay. Whaling season would start within a month and Captain Harris wanted to be ready when the whales came. He also knew the American whalers had been at this place before, and he hoped that they would stay away if he set up there first.

Early in the morning, the Bluff that the American had mentioned became visible in the west. The Captain called for Ned. Although he did not like him, he needed him now. At that time the American's local knowledge was more valuable than the Captain's pride.

A south -east wind blew steadily and miles of surf rolled into white sandy shores east of the Bluff.

'Always south- east in the summer,' Ned remarked. 'But mainly from the south and west during winter. Also bloody cold and miserable here when it rains.'

'Where did you anchor the ship?' The Captain asked Ned.

Ned pointed to the biggest island, 'There, behind that big island. We called it Granite Island.'

He pointed toward two other islands. 'Seals are on those two smaller islands but we took most of them from this bigger one.'

Although the Captain's main objective was whale oil, seal skins would add to the ship's profits, and give the men work before the whales arrived.

Once the ship was securely anchored, the sailors lowered a whaleboat and first mate Byron took a crew off testing the water depth and reefs in the vicinity. The Captain was cautious until he knew where his ship could swing safely.

'We need to have a strong anchorage here,' the Captain told the mates. 'There's protection from most wind, but not an easterly.

That's when it would be difficult to get out of here.'

The Captain had decided, 'Right, this is where we'll set up.'

During the next week the men used whaleboats to ferry equipment from the ship to the island. Poultry, pigs and goats were taken in, shut in cages, pens, and tethered. It was obvious that white men had been on the island before. There were signs of fire places, walls made with rocks, and scraps of sailcloth, broken glass and other rubbish. There was not enough firewood on the small island to fuel the huge fires needed to melt down the whale blubber. That would have to be done on the flat rocks on the mainland beach.

That's where the natives waited.

Aboriginals had watched the ship sail into the bay. A group of men gathered on the beach and waved toward the ship. Days later, they remained camped on the beach. They had seen ships before and were waiting for the whales to come, and the white men to kill them.

Most of the ship's crew, the women, boys and Bryant's dogs went to live at rough camps on Granite Island. The cooper took ashore timber and equipment to make more barrels, and he set up a separate camp and workshop nearby.

James and Jacob shared a rough shelter on the island. The camp was established, and the older men were anxious to kill whales, but the two young men were content to relax when their work was done. They walked around the island, exploring the small beaches and interesting caves in the rocky cliffs, where they caught small penguins that laid eggs in burrows.

The cook welcomed the tough little birds to cook for the men at the camp. Chief's large stomach shook as he laughed, his plump face turned crimson.

He sucked in fresh air, 'These are tough, but I'll boil them for hours. They'll make a nice change from salted pork, or greasy seal meat.' More shaking and giggling as he wiped his eyes with a dirty white apron.

During the day, James could see, and often smell smoke from the Aboriginals fires on the mainland. Each afternoon he could see smoke rising from fires in the distant hills.

Levi pointed, 'They're burning. Our people used to do that before white men came.'

James watched people moving on the beach, and at night he, Jacob and Levi sat and watched the glow of small fires. On calm nights voices, and occasionally natives singing drifted across the water.

James's skin shivered as he heard the shrill voice of a woman singing. The sound echoed across and bounced off the island's small cliffs. He stared as the glow from a fire on the beach reflected and shimmered on oily calm water. 'Things are changing here aren't they Jacob?'

His friend sat quietly thinking; then answered, 'Yes, we've seen how it is at Sydney and Hobart town.' Both young white men remained quiet. Levi stared across the water at the black men's dying fires.

Clouds silently moved through the black sky, they blocked out and then liberated a myriad of stars. Glowing fires withered to dull red smudges, the only sound was waves slapping the beach, and an occasional cry from a bird.

Captain Harris was satisfied with the preparations, now he wanted whales. Although seals would keep his men busy until the whales came, he wanted to be prepared. 'We'll go to the beach and talk with the natives, let's find out what they're excited about.'

James was in Ned's whaleboat as two boats with twelve men were rowed toward the mainland. Aboriginal men were waiting and talking excitedly amongst themselves when the boats glided onto the beach.

The Captain expected Ned to talk to the Aboriginals, 'Ned, you've been here before, can you talk to them?'

'A little,' Ned said. 'But I'm sure they want us to bring them a whale.'

The Captain knew the Aboriginals would always come when the white men killed a whale. But would they help work on the whales or just wait for the easy meat? He did not want the meat; he wanted the blubber to melt into oil.

Although the Captain had used natives to gather firewood and help with the boiling down at other places, he did not know these people. They had obviously seen whalers before, and he could see signs of white man diseases.

James stood back as the Captain and Ned talked to the Aboriginals. He saw Ned peering further into the bushes; he seemed to be more interested in something else rather than talking about whales. James noticed that there were no women on the beach.

The Captain wanted information. 'Well Ned, will they help with the whales?'

'Yes, they're just waiting for us to kill one,' Ned said.

'Have the Americans been? Will they come back?'

Ned's eyes were still on the beach and bushes, 'They've been here alright; that's why these men are hiding their women.'

The Captain understood what Ned wanted. 'We're here for whales. Not women.'

Ned turned and spat on the sand.

Whaleboats went out to kill seals. The women helped, two in each boat. Two women and two men were put ashore on the coast a short distance from a colony of seals. The other men rowed the boat quietly along and anchored a safe distance from the rocks where the seals gathered. The people on shore would come upon the seals and quickly cut them off from the sea. The slaughter began, seals were clubbed to death and the women expertly used knives to remove the skins from the still heaving animals. Soon the skinners walked on slippery rocks covered in blood, slime and raw bodies. A good swimmer, usually a young Aboriginal boy would take a rope into the rocks. The skins and best pieces of meat were tied into bundles before the ropes hauled it out to the waiting whaleboat, to be taken back to the island. The women and men ashore would be picked up later and taken back to the camp.

Then the work began, scraping and salting the seal skins. Seals could also be melted down for oil. Seal meat was not always wasted, not as tasty as pig or kangaroo, but it could be eaten. The dogs needed food. Pigs would eat almost anything, certainly seal meat and offal.

Although they were killing many seals and treating their skins, the Captain's main purpose for being there was to kill whales. He wanted barrels full of whale oil.

The crew would receive their share when the skins and whale oil reached Hobart Town. They wanted whales. As the weather became cooler, they became impatient.

Meanwhile, native men showed interest in helping the sealers, and some went on sealing trips. They had obviously worked with the Americans before; cooperation began between the two groups.

Jacob and James both worked with the other men sealing. Jacob always worked in Bryant's crew, and James in Ned's.

Captain Harris had his eye on young James, the stronger of the two and perhaps the brightest. The Captain moved him around in different jobs, training him to take on more responsibility.

A small river ran into the bay north of the island. Until rain filled rock holes on Granite Island, men made trips there to bring fresh water back to the island in barrels.

James pulled on his oar; another young man sat rowing next to him. The other two rowers were Ned's mates, or men that Ned controlled. Ned stood in the stern holding the larger steering oar, he studied the shore; they were going to the mainland to get water from the small river that ran into the bay.

The boat was awkward to row with empty barrels between the rowers. The young man nearest James turned to see where they were heading, 'Hey the rivers up that way.'

Ned held the oar firm; he chewed on a wad of tobacco. Without taking his eyes away from the shoreline, he spat a blob of green slime into a wave. 'You just row, I'm in charge here.'

James watched Ned's face. The big man shaded his deep-set eyes with a huge hand, then steered the boat further away from the direction of the river.

James turned around on the bench and noticed the Aboriginal children playing in the shallows; that's where Ned steered the boat.

Ned became excited, hissed quietly through his yellow teeth, 'You blokes ready, they haven't seen us yet. Be ready to jump as soon as the boat touches the bottom.'

The two men toward the bow shipped their oars and stood. 'We're ready.' one muttered.

The whaleboat lurched to a stop as it hit sand. The two men standing were hurled forward into the shallow water.

Ned was not quiet now. 'Run you bastards. Catch one of those girls each. I want one; you two can share the other.'

Children screamed as two eager sailors rushed toward them. Young children turned to older ones for help; some fell as their legs tangled in panic. Two older girls hesitated to help younger children out of the water. Ten children reached the sand hills; two men close behind concentrating on the two older girls.

Ned stood urging his men on, but he wanted the boat ready to leave that place quickly. He yelled at James and the other man. 'Stop gawking, get out and turn the boat around, get ready to leave.'

James held the boat steady in the surf. He was stunned when the men dragged the two oldest girls out of the bush. They were only children, perhaps thirteen years old.

Ned cheered, 'Bring them here. Tie them up.'

James felt sick.

Suddenly the beach filled with screaming black women. Young women, old women. Sticks, stones and wild curses rained down on Ned's thugs.

Ned urged them on, 'Don't let them go. Quick get them into the bloody boat.'

A twirling stick hit one man, he released his captive and swore, 'Bloody hell let's get out of here.'

The other man clung to his prize, but the women advanced fearlessly. He dropped the girl and ran.

'I'm not fighting those bloody women, for a couple of kids.' the man said as he flew into the boat. 'Let's get out of here.'

They rowed away dodging stones and sticks.

Ned was furious, 'You useless bastards; let women beat you?'

He ordered James to keep guard as the other men filled the kegs with water from the small river.

Ned fumed as they rowed back to the island; he wanted one of those girls.

Increased activity ashore meant more contact with the Aboriginals. This caused unrest between sailors and the native people. The Aboriginal people were divided, some wanted the white men there; some did not. There were sick people and people showing the signs of previous disease.

On the ship the sail maker appeared busy, but he had other things on his mind. A young half-caste boy from Van Diemen's Land, Tari, fourteen-year-old perhaps; nobody knew or cared, had been left there to help him and maybe learn sail making. But that's not what Addis had in mind to teach him.

Only a few men still lived aboard the ship, including the Captain and his woman.

May; the whales would come soon, and perhaps the Americans. Crews selected for the whaleboats practiced.

Bill Bryant was the headsman on the boat that young Jacob always worked on.

James manned an oar in Ned's boat.

The boats continued practicing, competing against each other. Sailors were keen to do well, each wanting a generous share of oil at the end of the season.

More west wind; cooler weather with rain, the season changing, soon there would be whales.

Sealing trips went further west along the coast where there were rocky points, rough water, and fewer sandy beaches where a boat could land on the shore. When the wind blew off the land, the days became more suitable for sealing. Because they travelled further from the camp and the ship, it became necessary for two whaleboats to work together. After the killing, while one boat picked up the killers and skinners, the other, loaded with skins and meat sailed, or was rowed back to the camp.

On one trip Bryant's boat moved in to collect the skins. Jacob watched Bill Bryant skilfully steer, and direct the whaleboat near to where the killing and skinning had begun. A native boy from Van Diemen's Land prepared to dive into the water to take a rope to the rocks.

'Off you go lad,' Bryant ordered. Jacob handed a rope and a pulley block to the boy. The boy swam, reaching the rocks with ease; he fixed the block and began swimming back to the whaleboat.

'Sharks!' Jacob screamed. 'There are sharks.'

The killers and skinners were busy, but Bryant and the men on his boat saw the boy disappear under water. Thrashing water and an explosion of pink foam showed where two sharks fought over the naked slim black body. Jacob turned away and vomited over the side.

They left the seal skins on the rocks that day; they would not reach the boat with sharks still there. They picked up the killers and skinners away from that place.

Bill Bryant decided that he would be placing a line before the killing and skinning started in future. But sharks could still attack the meat and skins as men pulled them toward the boat.

Fatal accidents on whaling ships were always possible, but that night the women howled in distressed. Most of the men ignored the death.

A more sensitive man, not as detached as most of the other men, Bryant felt the loss. He had seen it happen, there right next to his boat.

Jacob told James about the shark and the boy. They sat quietly together at the fire contemplating their own mortality. Coals became ash as the cool sea air seeped around the camp.

Rough weather interrupted the sealing; the men wanted different meat. The natives were restless. They were waiting for whales, and expecting a feast.

Captain Harris asked Bryant to take his dogs and two men to get game from the bush neighbouring the bay. Bryant convinced three of the local Aboriginal men camped on the beach to go with them on the expedition.

The men led Bryant through stumps of small trees that had been cut down for firewood to melt the whale blubber. On a slope protected from the wind and amongst a belt of trees, there was the Aboriginals main camp. Old men and women sat around small smouldering fires in the middle of a circle of well-built huts. Children scampered through the small openings into the huts when they saw the white men coming.

This place was much like the small village where Bryant grew up in Ireland. Not stone cottages, but circular huts built from branches and some with whale bones, dirt placed on the walls made the huts wind and rain proof. There seemed to be a larger central building, a meeting or special place.

'Why do you stay at the beach when you could live here?' Bryant asked one of the Aboriginal men who could understand his Irish- English.

'Cool time place.' the man answered. 'Old people, young ones.' He pointed to the huts. 'Hot time we go near the beach, now whales there, we stay there cool time too.'

Bryant understood that they stayed at the beach for the whale and seal meat. When he observed the Aboriginal people in their camp, Bryant recognised how contact with men from his, and previous ships had affected them. Many Aboriginals showed the scars of smallpox. The old people, women and children seemed neglected.

'Men don't go hunting now. They're always at the beach, waiting for whale meat.' An old woman told Bryant. She told him there were fewer people in her clan now than before the white men arrived in their ships. But more people lived at the beach now. People from other clans had moved there for the whale meat, food and goods from the white men. Traditional way of life was dying.

In the past when the winter months approached they would move inland to the settlement and then hunt and eat foodstuff from the bush.

'But now they just wait for the whale meat.' She shook her head and walked away.

Bryant had brought Argus, the male dog and Dina the bitch ashore. These dogs amazed the Aboriginals; compared to their small native dogs, Bryant's dogs were huge.

'Wolfhounds from Ireland,' Bill Bryant called them. They had small flat ears and long grey coats with white stripes, making them almost invisible when lying on the seaweed. Long hair on their faces shaded their bright eyes. Their long gangly legs and gaping mouth made these dogs look as if they could kill and eat a man without encouragement.

Tea- tree grew along the creek lines and the flat coastal verge. As they walked up the slopes they came to belts of small twisted gum trees with white bark. Soon they walked into more open country with scattered She-oaks and Yackas; there they saw the first signs of game. A mob of kangaroos grazed on a grassy hillside.

An Aboriginal man waved his hand, 'Old men light fire here two hot times ago.' Bryant struggled to restrain his dogs until the right time. He let them go. These dogs had hunted kangaroos before, and soon caught one each.

'Emus!' A native explained awkwardly. Yes, the white men understood at last. The Aboriginals led them further inland; there were fresh shoots of bushes, regrowth from mallee stumps, and green native grasses growing. Aboriginal men had also obviously burnt this area two or three years earlier.

Men and dogs quietly crept around the edge of the burnt area. A large emu lifted its black head out of the clumps of grass. Two excited dogs ran at the bird, legs and feathers exploded; a violent kick sent one dog backwards. The other dog pounced, grabbed the emu's long neck and dragged the bird to the ground. Bryant needed to pull his dogs off to stop them ruining the meat.

The Aboriginal men demanded a share of the days hunting, and the different meat was shared with them and over forty people on the ship and at the island camp.

The Aboriginal men wanted big dogs like that.

There were rainy days with wind blowing from the west. A man was stationed permanently at the top of Granite Island watching for whales. Men from the ship worked on the beach gathering wood ready for the fires to melt the whale blubber. Captain Harris knew that there would be friction about women, between his, and the Aboriginal men. He wanted to keep his men busy and away from the mainland when they were not working.

He wanted whales. 'Whales! Where are these bloody whales Ned?'

It was the second week of May; the man at the highest point of the island rang a ship's bell. Crews sprang into action, three whaleboats headed swiftly out. When they were away from the island and the rolling waves, a westerly wind filled their sails, and flattened the waves.

The boats surged forward, loaded with water, biscuits and ropes and gear to get whales. Men aboard could not see whales, but they rowed, and the wind pushed the boat ahead in the direction ordered; dipping and rising in the ever-present swell.

Bill Bryant's boat led the way; he stood at the stern hanging on to the big oar that steered the boat. There were older experienced men, and new lads hoping for their first kill.

Jacob and Levi had become friends working together in Bryant's crew. Both young men were excited, this would be their first whale chase. Jacob sat pulling on an oar; he watched Levi standing high in the bow, scanning the sea ahead for any sign of whales. This was not practice; they were after a real whale.

The boat lifted on an extra-large swell.

Levi lent forward, stretched out and pointed with his long wiry right arm. 'There!'

His other arm held onto the weapon that he hoped to attach to a whale; this would be his first kill. The four men rowing pulled harder. Rowing and sailing, the boat turned toward the whales.

The other two whaleboats followed. Three adult whales and two young ones swam together in a pod, disregarding the boats that closed in on them.

Bill Bryant's boat neared the first whale. He urged his crew on. 'Pull in the sail and pack away the mast. Tidy up those ropes.'

As the boat neared the whale, Levi stood tall and placed the harpoon in his right hand preparing himself. Jacob pulled on his oar, determined to match the older men. Rowers stretched out as the boat pulled alongside an enormous whale.

'Now!' Bryant yelled. Levi was a knot of nerves and excitement as he thrust the weapon toward the huge whale, twice the length of the boat. He aimed for a place behind its head. 'Anywhere,' he thought. 'Stick it in;' the harpoon struck the whale but glanced off its black shiny back.

Levi's shoulders slumped, he studied the limp rope in his hands, 'Sorry, Mr Bryant.'

He heard and understood Bryant's curses, and did not lift his head as he pulled on the rope to retrieve the harpoon.

 Ned was in charge of another boat and James Miles one of the crew, this was also James's first whale. Ned moved his boat alongside of the whale that Bill Bryant's crew had lost. James sat toward the front of the boat, next to the man who stood ready to throw the harpoon into the animal. The man stretched; he heaved the weapon; it struck and became fixed into the giant animal's side. The whale dived and the rope tore from the tub in the middle of the boat. James poured water on the line as it whirled through that special groove in the bow. The men knew that the whale would soon surface and swim away. They secured the rope and Ned's crew prepared for their first ride of the season.

Bryant steered his boat toward one of the smaller whales, possibly one of last year's calves.

'Now Levi!' He yelled.

Levi hurled the harpoon; the rope spun out, and stopped when the harpoon stuck fast into the whale's flank. The young whale began swimming back toward its mother.

'Pull that bloody rope in again,' yelled Bryant. 'Don't let it tangle.'

The whale swam around confused, men worked quickly to let the rope out and then bring it back in again.

'Keep that rope neat in the tub.'

The whale's mother sensed trouble and swam away, the calf followed and the rope spun out again. The mother pushed at the calf, and both whales dived.

'Let that rope out again.' When the rope stopped moving out Bryant urged his crew to stay alert.

'Be ready when she comes up, keep that rope neat again,' Bryant told his crew. The men sat searching the water, minutes later the young whale surfaced. 'Right, now let it pull more rope out; then fix it,' he ordered.

With the rope fixed, the small whale pulled the boat for half an hour before tiring.

An older man shrugged. 'This'll be easy.'

'Watch out for its mother,' Bill Bryant warned. 'She may cause trouble; then it won't be easy.'

Levi coiled the rope into the tub as the others rowed up to the whale. After swapping places with Levi, Bryant thrust a long deadly lance into a place where he knew it would kill the animal. Blood gushed into the sea around the boat. Bryant attached another rope to the whale's body, and the long row back to shore began.

Ned's crew had won their battle with their whale. James sweated as he heaved on a huge oar. The third boat came to help. Two boats worked for hours dragging the huge creature back toward the Bluff.

Late in the evening, men helped drag the two whales up onto the flat rocks in the sheltered water north of the Bluff. Aboriginals stood around talking excitedly. They were eager for a feast.

Work began at first light, testing the weeks of preparation. A high tide assisted a winch haul the whale carcasses further up onto the smooth rocks.

Fires were lit under the huge cauldron. Men started work on the whale bodies, stripping huge chunks of blubber off the carcase and slicing them into smaller pieces to fit in the huge pots. Aboriginal people worked with the white men, they knew there was a massive quantity of meat on the whales, enough for everyone. A few pushed in, impatiently, getting in the way of the workers.

As the day progressed the black smoke and smell brought more Aboriginals, and word had spread to neighbouring clans. As the whale blubber melted, the skim that formed on the top was thrown into the fire, causing it to burn fiercely; foul black smoke rolled around and up the sides of the huge try pots. Beneath the blubber was whale meat; food for whalers, natives, and dogs.

Men scooped the molten blubber from the try pots into copper vats to cool before putting it into barrels. The barrels that held forty gallons of oil each would be taken out to the ship and stacked securely in the hold.

The long day rowing and bringing in the whales, and then another day cutting and carrying blubber, sharpening knives and axes, had left the two young friends weary. James and Jacob sat on the beach discussing their first kill. They were waiting for a boat to take them back to Granite Island.

James rubbed his right arm, 'Shit, my arms still hurt, it was hard pulling that whale in against the wind last night, and I've been carrying knives and axes back and forth all day.'

Jacob nodded, 'Yes I know what you mean, and now we've still got more days of cutting up this whale and boiling the blubber.'

The two young men had been working alongside naked Aboriginal women during the day. At Sydney, Hobart Town and on the ship they had seen Aboriginal women wearing scanty old clothes. But there on the beach these women wore no clothes. There were children there and older boys, but no young girls.

James grinned at his friend. 'Hey, did you see those women? Bloody hell, there're not shy.'

'Yeah! I had trouble keeping my mind on the job today.'

'Shit I reckon, me too. But they're mostly old women, where were the young ones?'

'Their men keep them away.' Jacob said. 'You can't blame them with this lot here.'

'Ned and his mates find them. There's always a way.'

'Our turn will come mate, we just need to wait,' Jacob told his young friend.

James thought about the women on the beach.

'She'll be young, but I don't think she'll be from here.'

The two friends slept soundly that night, dreaming of young women.

Early next morning, the fires were stoked up and work continued; smoking hot fires, greasy whale blubber and many human bodies moving on, and above the beach. Jacob and Bill Bryant toiled sharpening knives and dealing with other tools that men used. Barrels of whale oil stood cooling on the beach. Men skilfully cut the baleen from the whale's head.

It took four days to process the two whales. More Aboriginal people arrived daily.

Three boats dragged the bare carcass of the large whale out into the water. While they waited for another whale, native people continued scavenging meat from the smaller carcass left on the beach. There would be more bones left scattered on the beach to add to those that previous whalers had left for the Aborigines to scavenge on.

Captain Harris was keen to get more whales, he knew now that he could rely on the Aboriginals help. He urged the watch on the high point of Granite Island to stay alert.

Aboriginal families waited for the next whale. Before the whalers came and killed whales, the clans would leave the coast and move inland for the winter period. There they hunted traditional game and collected food from the surrounding countryside.

Extended contact between the whalers and the natives began to cause problems. Aboriginal men sometimes tolerated white men taking their women, but this caused friction between the two groups. Captain Harris tried to keep his men either on the ship, or at the camp on Granite Island. He needed more whales to keep the men occupied, and that did happen. Crews captured more whales and dragged them into the beach.

Captain Harris was satisfied; the enterprise was going to be successful.

A change brought in a strong wind from the east. Captain Harris became worried for the safety of his moored ship. The strong gale tested the anchors that his men had placed weeks before. The entire bay was a mass of white water and lines of foam streaking into the beach. Wind ripped and howled through the rigging. The Captain stood on the deck for hours, nervously watching the lines strain as the wind threatened to blow the small ship across the reef and onto the beach.

Two days after the storm the bell rang, the crews rushed to their boats, but there were no whales. Another ship approached from the west. It anchored in the sheltered cove next to the Bluff. As Captain Harris watched it swing around in that small refuge, he wondered if that was a safer place to anchor. Men lowered a boat from the new ship, and sailors rowed over to the Southern Sky.

The new ship was an American whaler. The American Captain said they had killed whales there before, and he did not seem pleased to see the English whaling ship there.

'This is our territory,' he declared. 'We've been coming here for years. We've just come from Kangaroo Island where we have a base.'

Captain Harris was not going to be intimidated. 'Well we're here now,' he told the American. 'And we are going to stay here for winter, maybe longer.'

'And I'm going to set up here again,' the American whaling Captain replied. 'If you keep your crews away from mine, and my whales, things may work out.'

The little bay became crowded with two ships and over seventy whaling men. The Americans set up a camp on shore in the shelter of the Bluff. They renewed contact with the Aboriginal people and began preparations to bring in whales. Captain Harris worried about possible friction between the two whaling crews; for whales and the local native women.

Two days after the Americans arrived, Harris's men caught another whale and towed it in to their usual place. They began to strip another huge carcass. The Aboriginals helped; and ate more whale meat.

The American whalers set up a lookout stationed high on the Bluff. Within a week they had dragged a whale onto the beach.

Industry and disorder came to the Bluff. White men working with help from Aboriginals; white men disrupting their traditional ways. Firewood needed to melt the whale blubber became scarce close to the beach; men had to walk further inland to gather it. Many people, white and native, working and living in that small area with the remains of whales made it a messy, putrid and unsanitary place.

Even though it was cold and bleak living close to the coast, the natives remained close to the whale meat.

Life at the camp on Granite Island carried on, the women and children from the Southern Sky keeping away from the action ashore. They grew vegetables in the winter rains. They collected water from rock holes and run off from canvas catchment at the camp. There was no permanent fresh water on the island; men took barrels into the mainland creeks to fill with fresh water for the animals.

Captain Harris considered moving to the mainland, but decided it was more secure on the island. He had instructions to leave a group of men there when he returned to Hobart Town at the end of the whaling season. The company who sent the ship there wanted to set up a permanent base there for whaling and sealing before the Americans.

Sail maker Addis and the young Native boy who worked with him still lived aboard the ship, but Addis had little work to do there.

Captain Harris ordered him to take his turn on the summit of Granite Island.

No more than fourteen years old, when taken from Van Diemen's Land, Tari had never known any family. Addis knew that he would be an easy target for his needs. During the voyage from Hobart Town and while anchored in the bay, the big man had steadily been gaining the boy's trust and dependence.

Sleeping together in the sail room gave Addis the opportunity to cultivate this bond with young Tari; he soon became dependent on the rum that Addis gave him each night. The boy became confused and began to accept the older man's demands. Tari had little contact with the other boys or men; he did not understand the distorting feelings that tangled in his young head.

The Captain often sent Addis to Granite Island to watch for whales, he took young Tari with him. This gave him more opportunity to be alone with and exploit the young boy.

Tari became more confused. He sought the company of the sailors' women camped on Granite Island, but he could not tell them of his distress. Addis knew where to find the boy and dragged him back to the ship, and the privacy of the sail room.

One afternoon at the lookout Addis was particularly demanding of the boy, causing him to run off down the rocky hillside in tears.

Two days later Captain Harris's woman commented that she had not seen Tari on the ship. When Harris questioned Addis about the matter, he became elusive and uneasy. A man spotted a body at the bottom of a cliff, but the tide washed the body away before it could be retrieved.

Addis told the Captain that he required a new boy to help him. He would recruit a native boy from the mainland.

James Miles and Jacob worked with the older men, learning skills and becoming part of a team. Captain Harris studied the younger men, to select future leaders. Each man had particular skills that became noticed. There were men who merely did their work to receive their food and money. Other men showed that they could handle extra responsibilities. James was growing into a tall strong man, shy but sensible.

The Captain talked bluntly to James, 'I'm going to leave you in Ned's crew young man. He's a hard man, but he'll toughen you. Keep your mouth shut and learn. When you get the chance, grab a harpoon and practice; you'll be in the bow of a whaleboat before you know it.'

James knew Ned worked his team hard. He understood the challenge of working with experienced whalers, he wanted to learn more, and accepted the Captain's order.

Jacob remained in Bill Bryant's crew, happy on an oar, not tall or strong like James, never to be the man at the bow throwing the harpoon. But Bryant recognised the young man was always going to be a reliable part of his team. Jacob showed he was reliable, good with tools or a knife, and skilful at sharpening the tools the men used to cut up whales. That became his job at the beach working with Bill Bryant.

Chapter 3 – Abduction and Gentle Meeting

Some men take what they want.
Innocence destroyed, taken without guilt.
Someone or something can change a life with one swift
action.

Although their families had moved to their winter camp, Merindah and Yara still came down to the beach to spend time on their own, and sometimes collect seafood for their families. They were cautious, aware of the two ships and the activities not far south of their small cove. More people in their clan had gone to the place where the white men killed whales, and some had not returned.

The man that approached Merindah one morning was her uncle. She noticed him talking to her mother earlier that morning, and when he approached her she stood trembling, staring at the ground. She stared at his feet.

He placed a hand on her shoulder, 'You are a woman now; your future has been decided.'

'Yes,' Merindah replied timidly.

'You'll be going to a man at Longkuwar after the cold season.'

Merindah struggled to stand; her legs became waving branches. 'Yes.'

Although she had warning it would be difficult to leave her family and friends. She did not want to go nearer to the whaling men, or the Aboriginal people who lived there.

Merindah and Yara became even closer; they knew their time

together would soon end.

The friends sat together on the cliff overlooking their home cove.

Merindah gazed out across the sea; she held Yara's hand.

'What will become of us?' Yara sobbed, then remembered that they were supposed to be collecting oysters, 'Come on, we should go down to the beach Merindah.'

'That will nearly be enough for today,' Yara suggested as Merindah put another handful of oysters into the woven basket.

Merindah turned, 'Just two more dives.' She swam a short distance away and dived.

It was late in the afternoon; they were gathering shellfish from the water in the bay behind the cliff that obscured their view to the south. Two boys from their clan, Yoola and Warri were with them talking and playing in the water. The girls stood in chest deep water, intent on their own activity, and ignoring the boys playing in shallower water

There had been no whales sited for days, Captain Harris had sent a whaleboat with six men on a trip to the rocks at the small cove north of the Bluff. Perhaps there would be seals there worth chasing.

Relieved to be away from the smell of the rotting whales and the filth on the beach the six men used the sail, cruising as close to the shore as the surf allowed. The leader in the boat was the third mate, the surly Negro Ned, with him four other men and young James Miles.

A fine August day with a light cold southerly, the sun glinting off the surf. The whaleboat glided quietly through calm water as they rounded the rocky point at the southern end of the cove. The white men noticed two Aboriginal boys playing in the shallows but the boys did not see the boat coming toward them.

'Quick! Catch those boys,' Ned said quietly. 'We'll take them back to the camp to work.'

The boat came alongside the boys. Two men jumped out of the

boat and grabbed them before they could react, they screamed, but were soon in the boat with ropes around them.

Yara heard cries; she spun around to see the boys being pushed down into the boat.

She turned back. 'Merindah! Quick!'

But Merindah was further out, diving for more oysters. Yara dropped the basket and swam towards the shore. When in knee deep-water she stood and ran toward the beach.

'There's another one,' Ned yelled. 'No it's a young woman; I have other work for her. Get after her.'

Two sailors jumped out of the boat and chased after Yara. Ned and the other men let the sail down and anchored the whaleboat. It was then that he saw another Aboriginal behind the boat swimming for the beach.

He pointed in the direction of Merindah; 'there's another one!'

Merindah had surfaced and seen Yara running through the water toward the beach with two white men chasing her. She dropped the oysters out of her hands and swam.

Merindah stood naked with her back to Ned and then ran through the shallow water.

Ned thought that she was another boy. 'Look at that big strong, tall boy. Quick Miles, get after him, he'd be a handy worker on the boats.'

As James jumped out of the boat Merindah reached the beach. She stopped to pick up a net bag with her belongings in it, turned and glanced quickly at the boat.

'Jesus, did you see that?' Ned exclaimed. 'It's a bloody girl, and I want her. Move Miles!'

James reached the beach as Merindah disappeared into the low scrub; he ran along the path where she had disappeared into the sand hills.

James was a very fit sixteen-year-old lad and he could run. Merindah was surprised when she heard him still running through the bush behind her; she changed direction and ran along a different path that led inland towards a small hill. She ran faster; then stopped to listen. It was only luck, but James had taken the same path and she could hear him getting closer. She ran again.

Merindah's father and her uncles had placed a net made of strong vines in a strategic place; put there to capture emus when they were disturbed and run up this particular pathway. She did not see the net as she ran through the gap in the low trees.

James heard the noise of branches falling, a quick scream and then nothing; silence. When he came upon her, Merindah lay unconscious on the ground, blood oozing from a cut on her forehead and tangled in strong vines. He quickly tore a strip off his shirt and tied it around her damaged head. He untangled the vines from her body and dragged her out to a grassy area. He picked up the bag that she had been carrying and opened it, finding a water pouch and a small skin cloak, a few shells and some small tubers.

James realised that he stood there looking at a particularly handsome young girl; and she was naked. 'That's why Ned wanted me to catch her.'

James knew she was sleeping and breathing steady, he tried to make her more comfortable by covering her with the skin cloak from her bag.

*   *   *

The two men brought Yara back to the boat.

'Did you see Miles?' Ned asked them.

'No,' they answered.

Yara was in shock; trussed up with rope and pushed cold and shaking with fright into the bottom of the boat next to the two boys.

'Well let's get out of here. It will be dark before we get back to the island. But that's good. I don't want Harris seeing what we've got on board; he'll be on the ship with his woman.'

'What about young James?' one of the other men asked.

Ned was not going to wait for James.

'He'll find his way back to the whale camp,' Ned answered. 'I don't think that he would've caught that big girl. Did you get a look at her?'

'No,' said the two men who had brought Yara back to the boat.

'Well you missed something,' one of the others said. 'She would've been handy back at camp.'

'That's if you could handle her,' said the other.

'I would have lots of fun handling her,' Ned boasted.

That night Yara and the two boys spent their first night on Granite Island huddled together in fright not knowing their fate; although Yara had some idea what hers would be.

*   *   *

It was beginning to get dark in the bush; with the darkness would come cool night air. James had nothing to light a fire, so he searched for something to make shelter. He broke off branches and placed them so that they would make a simple wind break. Unsure what to do next; he sat alongside the unconscious girl. As darkness came James moved closer to her, keeping them both warm as he held her.

After two or three hours Merindah started to regain awareness. In the darkness, she did not see who held her, but felt secure and reasonably warm. As soon as she stirred, he had helped her drink from her water pouch. During the night Merindah slipped in and out of consciousness. James slept a little.

As daylight came Merindah started to regain more composure; she opened her eyes. When she realised who held her she pulled away quickly. But the pain in her head caused her to faint again. When she woke James was talking softly to her.

This was not the skinless man in her dream, he had smooth pink skin on his face, his hair was the colour of dry grass, his hands and arms and bare feet were tanned. His gentle words meant nothing to Merindah; but they were calming.

Merindah needed water. She could not stand, but James gently sat her up against a tree trunk in the warm morning sun. He took the now empty water pouch and walked away down the slope where he soon found a small winter stream. He drank himself, then filled the pouch and returned to Merindah. As she sipped water she seemed more alert, so he tried speaking to her again. Alas, his efforts were futile; she did not understand a word. She had had no contact with the whaling men and knew nothing of their language.

'Where is your camp?' he asked.

'Yara!' she cried, 'Yara!' Then there were lots of other excited and frightened ramblings that James could not follow.

James wondered if the girl wanted food, 'I must find food somewhere,'

He picked up the bag that Merindah dropped when she fell; he found tubers and gave some to Merindah. She tried to take the outer skin off one, but her hands seemed too weak. He realised what she wanted to do and used his fingernails to skin one, and as he did more, she slowly ate them all.

James went back to the creek for more water. In a bare patch of ground he spotted bunches of long thin spindly leaves that triggered a childhood memory of digging yams out from the dirt in Sydney Town. He picked up a stick and by digging, found that under these tufts of grass were tubers like those in Merindah's bag. Feeling pleased with himself he took the yams, and more water back to Merindah. She managed a small smile when he showed her what he had found; they sat and ate.

The day warmed; Merindah gradually recovered her strength

and later stood with James's assistance. He helped her walk toward the small creek where Merindah showed James some small plants, he dug those up, and together they ate the roots.

They sat quietly together out of the cold wind in the shelter of low bushes. The girl slept, but James sat listening to the sounds of the scrub. He heard voices and remained very still as the unseen people passed by. A small yellow dog came trotting past; it stopped and examined James and the sleeping girl, the dog's ears stood erect, his tail hung down to the sand. Alert eyes scrutinised; he moved closer, stopped and examined. The cheeky native dog turned away without making a sound.

As night came, they remained together by the creek. Merindah was still unsure about James. Although she had never seen a white man before, she now sat eating with this young man and would soon lie down and sleep alongside him. James treated her gently, helped her eat and drink; she became more relaxed and soon slept. When she woke the next morning he was still asleep, holding her for warmth. Slowly she eased herself away, and watched him sleeping, 'He has helped me.'

When she came back from behind a bush, the young white man woke with a start.

James's eyes focused on the tall black girl. 'I am not taking you back to those men. They're bad men; you must keep away from them.'

She had no idea what he was saying, but relaxed, as his gentle manner soothed her.

Her mother told her many times, to stay away from the white men. At the beach she did not see the two boys in the bottom of the boat, or hear their cries. But she watched the other men from the boat chase Yara. And then this young man chased her.

Merindah was confused. Now this young man had helped her. She remained there sitting next to James; together they drank water and ate more of the yams.

Later when they stood together, James sensed that the girl aroused him. Merindah became aware of his attention; she pulled the skin cloak firmly around her body; he watched her do that and smiled. Merindah returned a shy smile. Together they walked back towards the beach. James climbed the small cliff so he could see the coast going back to the camp on the island. When he turned back, the girl had gone.

He started walking back along the sandy beach with the surf rolling in on his left; he stopped often to glance back. The empty beach and the small cliff where he left the girl became more distant as he walked. He climbed up a sand hill and scanned the miles of sand and never-ending surf. As always, a mist came from the waves as they tumbled into the shore. He wondered; should I go back to find the girl? But he knew that he would never be able to find her in that huge expanse of sandhills and scrub.

* * *

'No, I didn't catch her,' James told Ned when he got back to the island.

'We thought you must have, and stayed there with her,' remarked another man.

'Where've you been then?' Ned asked.

'I got lost in the scrub and took two days to find my way out.'

'Sounds like bullshit to me, I bet you got onto something and you aren't telling,' Ned alleged. James glanced across at the women's camp, where the sailors' women lived, and he was pleased that he had not brought the tall girl back there.

'What was it like there; did you find any other people?' Jacob asked his friend when they were alone.

'Only one girl.'

'Ned has one at the women's camp, and two boys.'

'Shit! That's why he left me there. What's he done with the girl?'

'What do you think? But she fights.'

'What about the boys, do they work?' James asked Jacob.

'No, Bill Bryant has tried to talk to them, but they can't

46

understand anything.'

James shrugged his shoulders. 'Bastards, why won't they leave them alone? That girl I chased hurt herself; I didn't want to bring her back here.'

'Wanted to keep her for yourself, did you?' Jacob probed.

James recalled the tall girl's naked body; he blushed. 'Be good, but I guess I'll never see her again.'

Chapter 4 - Yara

A world of dreams, childhood innocence shattered,
abruptly gone.
Alone, unprotected, defenceless.
Violently abused. Cast off.

Yara, Warri and Yoola spent their first night on Granite Island in
terror, huddled together in the camp with the Aboriginal women
and children. Although these women were obviously aboriginal,
they had different features than Yara's people. They kept their curly
black hair cut short and wore a decorated band pulled tight around
their head. Their children were all boys, with lighter skin colour.
The women gave the three young Aboriginals some sailor's old
shirts; then ignored them and sat talking together in a totally
different language that the children could not understand.

As the sun came up out of the ocean the next morning, Yara and
the boys clung together in shock. The ship lay anchored close to the
island. People moved around on the beach across the water. They
stared northward, toward the headland of the small bay where they
knew their home camp was.

At first the women and children ignored the three new people
there. They sat around a small smoking fire, eating strips of dry
meat and chunks of flat bread. Two large dogs lay placidly around
with the children, snapping up any food thrown towards them.
Yara and the boys sat huddled together, away from these huge
dogs, much bigger than the native dogs back at their camp.

Gradually the women acknowledged the three newcomers; they indicated that they should eat. Yara and the two boys shyly took small pieces of the food and accepted a drink of water that the women took from a wooden cask. Everything was strange, the cask of water, the tin cup that they drank from, the distant, aloof way of the women and the inquisitive shy glances from their children.

Yara sat terrified, trying to conceal her face while she watched the white men moving around the island. Men working on the whaleboats, men loading other wooden casks onto boats.

A group of men walked past Yara, a man pointed at her, laughing and talking a different language than the women.

'She'll be Ned's tonight.'

'You best keep away from her, or Ned will be onto you in a flash, he is a nasty bastard,' another man said.

Yara cowed away, she did not understand their language, but she knew they were talking about her.

'The sail maker would like one of those young boys,' another man sneered.

'If you drink enough of that rum you may want one too.'

'Piss off you prick.'

Suddenly Yara heard a loud ringing sound coming from above her somewhere on the hill. Men rushed towards the whaleboats. The big black man who had pushed her into the bottom of the boat the previous evening ran past the women's camp. He stared at her with a lustful smile. His features were different from other black men, not like the strange talking black women either. A tall man, strong body, with tight curly black hair kept short, little or no facial hair.

Most of the men left on the whaleboats. Yara and the boys moved closer to the women and children. The women began to scrape skins. Yara saw many sealskins; skins stretched out on frames drying, skins tied in a line hanging in the sea water in shelter of rocks. Stacks of skins tied in bundles. The women's camp was next to the beach, their shelters built from rocks, branches and skins. Children played on the pebbly beach, two big dogs sprawled on the sand.

A fire smouldered at a similar cluttered camp where the men had been. More wooden barrels and other strange objects lay there. Another man and a young white boy stayed together at another camp, working with pieces of timber and strips of a shiny black material she didn't recognise. They were using another fire to heat the timber. Yara later understood that they were making more barrels.

During that first day Yara kept staring back toward those small cliffs where her family lived. Where was Merindah? She had not seen her since she ran from the two men. She had not seen Merindah in the water, or on the beach, as they dragged her back to the whaleboat.

The boys kept close to Yara; often crying and asking her when they would return to their families. Yara tried to reassure them, but she felt it was not going to happen soon. She scanned the stretch of water between the island and the mainland. Reefs and currents made it plain to see why they were not tied up, or shut in.

Yara and the boys walked away from the women and climbed the hill behind the camp. From there they gazed back toward their home area. Endless waves rolled in from the ocean to white sandy beaches where the three friends had played and spent much of their short and sheltered lives. Confused, they knew that it was all going to change.

It had started that day the first ships arrived. They were babies in their family's shelters when things began to be different, disrupting age old traditions. The new diseases started then. As they grew, the changes to their clan increased. Even though their families tried to keep away from the white men, and their influence, they had become more drawn toward them.

Life was about to change for the three young friends, but not how their clan had imagined. Yara was soon to leave her family and go to live with a man in a different clan. Both the young boys were due to be taken away soon to be prepared for manhood. But now these three young people stood in terror, prisoners on an island where their people never visited.

Out from Granite Island, or Kaike their parents called it, waves crashed into another small island surrounded with white water. Yara could see seals there on the rocks. Toward the Bluff, Longkuwar, waves circled another smaller island. A different ship lay anchored there in the shelter of the Bluff. Other white men were on the beach there.

The three young Aboriginals had been told dreaming stories of this place, but now everything seemed out of place. They walked down the sloping rocks to the ocean side of the island; sat and held each other wondering about their future.

'Can you take us home Yara?' Yoola asked.

'I don't know how to,' she said. 'We need to find food here.'

Shellfish was abundant there amongst the rocks; they gathered all they were able to carry.

What could they do? Reluctantly they returned to the women's camp, where there was water and fire. They took the shellfish to share with the women.

At sundown the white men returned to the island. Most of them went to their own camp; some came to the women's fire, paired up with women and took them off into the bushes. One man, the one with red hair, sat with a woman and the two dogs by the fire. The dogs came up and nuzzled him affectionately as he lit and smoked a pipe. Yara smelt the strange soothing smell of tobacco. She noticed that none of the young children seemed to belong to that woman.

As it became darker, women came back to the fire, men returned to their own camp. The white men became noisier at their camp. Yara considered sneaking off into the bushes to hide, but she did not want to leave the two boys alone. They sat on their own, eating pieces of food that the women offered them. Men came back to the women's camp, scuffling started as others came and dragged them away from the women. Men began to talk louder at their fire.

Yara dozed with the two boys asleep on the sand next to her. She woke abruptly when the big black man grabbed her arm. The other woman turned away as Ned easily encircled Yara's young body with a huge arm and dragged her away from the group.

Yara had barely screamed before the man put one large rough hand over her mouth and carried her away. He had his intentions well planned, and took Yara a long way from the camp, to the other side of the island. Very excited and in a hurry for what he wanted, he pushed her to the ground and with one swift motion pulled off the single piece of clothing that covered her trembling body.

The big man smelt different, his breath hot and strong. He was chewing something. Spittle ran from the corners of his mouth as he groped all over Yara's young body. Brown saliva dribbled on her nakedness as he spat the wad of tobacco out across the sand.

Yara screamed and scratched with her nails; she tried to bite and kick him; she pounded her fists into his taught body. But she was no match for this big man. The more she fought, the more determined he became. He struck her on the side of her head with an open hand. Dazed, she had not recovered, before he started to have his way. She fainted with shock and pain. When Yara regained consciousness minutes later the man still lay across her young body sweating and breathing slower.

'You're a little fighter,' he mocked. Not beaten, she leaned her head into his neck and bit him fiercely. She tasted his blood as he pulled away from her.

'Fucking little bitch,' Ned yelled as he hit her harder.

Yara knew it was much later when she opened her eyes and saw stars. Those stars were the clock that her mother taught her. But her mother did not warn how a strange man could harm her. The big man had gone. She sat, with head aching, one eye feeling wrong, face swollen, body hurting and blood stuck to her legs. In shock, terrified and confused, Yara covered herself with the scanty garment that Ned had torn from her. It was cold. She spent the night lying on the ground shivering and sometimes sleeping. When the sun rose she realised which side of the island it was. Yara needed a drink of water.

Later she heard someone coming through the bushes. She waited, terrified.

It was not him again. A woman from the camp came to her, the one who sat with the red headed man and the two dogs. She came up quietly to Yara, offering her a drink from a skin. Yara cried into the older woman's shoulder as she consoled her. After a time they returned to the women's camp. The other women knew what had happened to her and displayed their concern. Yara slept, often waking in fright, but the dog woman was always close.

There were no men at their camp during the day. When they returned that evening Yara did not see Ned. The white man with the red hair came and sat with his woman. They talked quietly together.

'He's a bad man,' Bryant told his woman.

'It's happened to all of us,' she said.

'Maybe not as violent.'

'Not all men are as kind as you,' the woman answered. 'I have had that done to me many times before you took me away.'

Bryant slept with his woman and his dogs that night. Yara had a sense of security while he sat there, and she and the two boys slept close to them.

Yara and the boys remained anxious and pined for their families. They could not understand the women's language, but were gradually accepted around the fire and almost relaxed in their company. Yara could still feel the pain in her swollen eye and face. She feared the man would come again.

The food that the women offered the three friends was unusual; mainly meat and a type of bread that they had not tasted before. There was an abundance of fresh meat, each evening men came to the camp with large pieces of flesh. Women and children sat and ate meat as it cooked on their fire, but the women did not gather fresh plants or seafood from the rocks.

Two days after the night Ned abused her, Yara noticed two

different men in cleaner clothing come to the island from the ship. They came to the women's camp and talked to the dog woman. Yara had no idea what they were saying.

'What are these three young natives doing here?' Captain Harris asked.

'Ned and other men brought them here from that beach up there.'

'Well if they stay here, they must work.'

'We can't talk to them,' explained a woman.

'Well there'll be natives here from the whale camp later; they may be able to talk with them and teach them what to do with the sealskins and other work.'

Bryant came to the women's camp and tried to take the two boys away with him, but they would not leave Yara.

'You can work on the whale boats,' he told them as he pointed, but they did not understand.

Frustrated, Bryant went back to the men's camp. 'Why did you bring them here?' he asked Ned.

'We need more help here, and those two boys will learn.'

'What about the girl?'

'She's mine.'

'You'll cause trouble,' Bryant warned him.

'Not your problem,' Ned snapped.

Bryant left it there; Ned was a senior mate on the ship.

Next morning the sail maker, Addis, came off the ship. He walked past the women on his way to the whaler's camp. Yara shuddered, 'Another different-looking black man.' She knew that Addis was staring at them, but she realised he was watching Warri and Yoola, not her.

That night the men in the camp became noisy again. After sunset men came to the women's camp and took their women away. Bryant came and the dog woman left with him. Yara and the boys felt insecure there alone; the young children were sleeping or ignoring them.

Alone with the two young boys, terrified and feeling exposed, Yara feared that the big man would come again. She tried to hide in a stack of seal skins.

'There you are.' Ned grabbed and held her. 'Time for more lessons!' She felt his hot strange breath on her neck. Impatient, this time, he threw her on the ground not far from the camp and started to grope her. Yara scratched at him. He was far too big and strong, but as he lay across her having his way, she was once again close enough to bite. This time she latched onto his upper arm with her teeth and used all of her strength to remove a piece of flesh. Ned yelled and hit her, but the blow did not knock her unconscious this time. She twisted away from him and ran off into the darkness.

*   *   *

Addis had been drinking rum with the whalers; he watched men going to their women. He had different desires. The other men in the camp merely desired their rum and payed no attention to anything else.

Addis walked back in the direction of the ship, but he was not going there. He walked into the women's camp deliberately. It was quiet, the women with their men, and children asleep. He spotted what he wanted, the two boys sitting, drowsing together by the fire. They did not see him coming. He did not care which boy, but he grabbed one and dragged him away from the fire. The other boy ran off into the night.

Addis dragged Warri away from the camp. He had no time to groom the boy as he did with Tari. He had an urgent need. As soon as he pushed Warri to the ground, he was on top of him. The boy had no chance to fight back; his struggling and fighting made him even more exhausted. He was no match for the big Negro. Addis groaned and relaxed, but he did not let the sobbing boy go. He waited until his urge returned.

Warri fainted with the shock and pain when the man took him again.

Yara hid in bushes until the first morning light, and then she crept back to the women's camp. All the women were back there, with men sleeping nearby. The dogs heard her coming; they opened their eyes briefly, ignored her and made no noise. She went to the place where she and the boys normally slept. Only one boy sat there shaking, he cried when she sat down beside him.

'Where's Warri?' she asked.

'A big black man dragged him away,' Yoola told her.

When the dog woman woke, she went across to Yara and Yoola, she could see fresh bruises on Yara's face; she knew that it had happened again. As she talked soothingly to Yara and held her as a mother would, she saw that one boy was missing. With difficulty Yara tried to tell the woman that a man took Warri away during the night. Yara pointed to the ship. The woman realised what happened. She woke Bryant and explained.

'That Addis is a bad bastard,' he said. 'But there's nothing I can do. Just keep away from him.' Bryant left and returned to the men's camp.

The woman called the two dogs; she let them smell the place where Warri and Yoola had slept, then urged the dogs to follow the scent. Yara and Yoola followed the woman and her dogs into the bush and rocks. They found Warri hiding under a rocky outcrop. He sat with his head down, knees drawn up to his chest, dried blood on his legs, body bruised. At first he did not want help. Yara sat with Warri, and in time she convinced him to walk back to the women's camp.

The white men realised that Yoola and Warri could not work with them.

Yara and the boys spent three days with the women without being bothered by the whaling men. It was another noisy night at the whaler's camp. Yara became terrified again when men came for their women. She woke the boys; they moved back away from the fire into the shadows. But he found her there.

Ned appeared without warning. He grabbed her. Yara fought,

but the man was too strong he held her firm as he dragged her away. This time he was prepared, she would not bite him again. He covered her head with a rag, threw her to the ground before violently using her young body to release his urge. He did not release her when he'd finished.

'Now you can come with me, I'll teach you how to behave.' She sobbed as Ned dragged her to the whaling men's camp.

'Who reckons they can handle this one?' Ned said. He pushed her toward the group of drunken men. Three men stood and rushed at Yara. They were far too strong for her. She screamed as they dragged her a short distance away and fought each other as they took her in turn. Then they began pushing each other, fighting over who would have her a second time.

Yara grabbed her torn shirt as she stumbled to her feet and ran off trembling into the darkness. The men staggered back to the other men drinking, talking and laughing.

Hours later, Yara stumbled back to the woman's camp. The women, children and dogs were quiet. The two boys were hiding, but came and stood alongside Yara as she sat there sobbing.

She wanted to leave that place. 'We are going to get away from here,' she told them.

They walked in the moonlight to the beach closest to the mainland camp. There across the water they saw Aboriginal fires burning.

Yara considered the calm water and receding tide. 'We can swim to that reef soon,' she told the boys. 'We can walk along the reef toward the other beach and swim across the channel. It won't be as deep when those stars go across the sky. We will wait.'

As she gazed at the water Yara thought of Merindah. How she wished she could swim as well as her friend. She knew the boys were not strong swimmers, but they had to get away from the island and the ship that floated nearby. They waited as the fires across the stretch of water burnt into small red glows. The moon was low in the sky above the mainland before Yara decided that the tide was at its lowest.

'Now we will leave here,' she told the boys. 'Follow me and keep together.' The three cautiously walked into the water. They reached the rocky reef walking and bouncing on toes to keep their heads above water. They carefully walked along the reef, sometimes slipping and hurting their feet on the sharp rocks and shells. Yara stood in knee deep water at the end of the reef. She watched water moving through the deep channel between them and the beach.

'I need you now Merindah.'

'We will rest,' she told the boys.

'I'm afraid,' Warri said. He had not recovered from his traumatic ordeal with Addis.

'We must go soon,' Yara urged, 'the tide is turning.'

The three slid off the rocks into the water; soon it became too deep to walk.

'Keep together,' Yara cried out as they started swimming. The current took them along parallel to the beach, dragging them away from the shelter of the island and toward rolling waves. Yara and Yoola swam together but Warri had been swept away, taken further toward the breakers and the undertow.

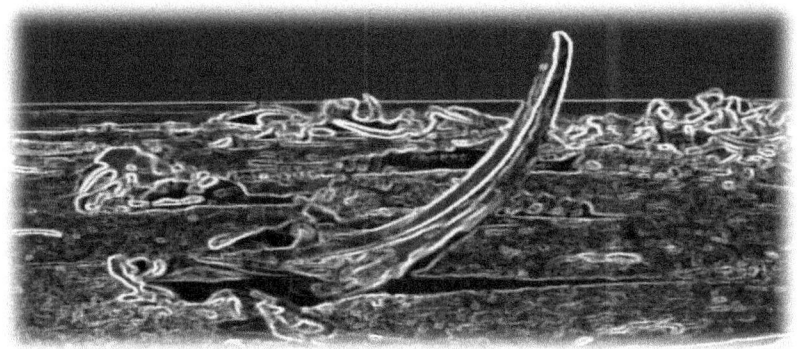

Chapter 5 - The Beach of Bones.

Every entity ceases, day, night, trees, men, the fish and
the animals.
Sometimes things are finished before they get a chance
to live their time.
Watch their stars grow into babies, or even become
aware of the stars that one day will become their babies.

Yara and Yoola sat on the beach, the moon had gone; the tide rising
and new stars appearing low in the eastern sky. An orange glow
hovered out behind the ocean's edge at the far end of the beach.
They sat and waited for Warri, but he did not come out of the
waves.

'We must leave the beach before sunrise,' Yara said. They knew
Warri would not be coming out of the sea and reluctantly turned
away. As they slowly walked along the beach toward the Bluff, the
smell became overpowering. They could sense shapes in the
darkness in front of them. Like a forest of burnt trees, there were
great bones piled up on the sand. Some single, curving, sticking
into the night sky, while others lay tangled together in the sand. As
they neared the whaling camp dawning glow exposed more of the
killing scene. Complete, but stripped carcasses of whales lay strewn
on the flat rocks. Wild dogs sulked around. Above the tide line

there were fire places built of rocks, also large pots, and stacks of firewood. There were ropes, pulley blocks and other equipment. Most of what they saw was strange and new to the pair of frightened youngsters. The mess and destruction shocked them most; even the trees above the beach were gone.

'We won't stay here,' Yara murmured, 'let's go inland and find help away from this place.' In the low scrub back from the beach and away from the whale bodies, the two found a track leading toward low hills.

'Why don't we go along the beach toward home?' Yoola asked.

'We can't,' replied Yara, she did not explain it to the boy, but she could not go back to her family yet, not after what happened to her on the island. She just wanted to be away from those men.

They came across a small creek, drank and rested. From the morning shadows there appeared two Aboriginal women, carrying skins to collect water. These women were not surprised to see strangers in their area. Since the whalers came, different clans started coming to the locality, attracted by the chance to get the abundant food from the whales.

Yara did not know these women, but she did understand their language. She did not tell them all the details of their ordeal, but the women shook their heads and shuddered when Yara pointed toward the rocky island; they took them further inland to their camp.

When Yara and Yoola walked into the women's camp they saw that there were mainly women, children and skinny dogs. Yara became aware that more than half the children had lighter skin and different features than their mothers.

'Why don't you stay at the camp by the beach?' Yara asked.

'We're not welcome there; we collect bush food and small animals to eat. Sometimes we get meat from there.'

Yara was not ready to go back to her mother's camp; she was ashamed for what happened on the island.

'We'll stay here now,' Yara told Yoola; but the boy did not understand why; he wanted to go home. Yara was not ready to go back to her family after her abuse.

*   *   *

The women at the camp on Granite Island had not seen the three young Aboriginals for two days.   The whalers had killed a whale and dragged it to the beach; that night there was extra rum. Ned was pleased; his boat won the whale; giving him an extra share of reward for the oil.

'Pass that rum here,' he ordered. 'I'll need it to wrestle that girl again tonight.'

'She's gone, and those two boys,' Bill Bryant told him.

'What do you mean gone? Where could they go? Someone's taken them.'

'My woman told me last night that they have disappeared. Maybe they swam to the mainland.'

Ned eyeballed the other men through a haze of smoke from the fire and tobacco. 'Can any of you tell me about this?'

'We thought you'd finished with her,' a man said.

'So did I, but now I want the challenge; and the girl.'

Jacob and James sat in silence listening to the men talking. They knew how callous Ned was, they remembered how he had left James ashore to find his own way back to the beach of bones, and to the island.

Ned was furious, he had got himself worked up; he wanted that young girl.

'If I find that any of you have taken her off, hid her somewhere on this island, you'll pay.'

'Perhaps they swam,' Bryant suggested.

'Bullshit!'

'Swam; then drowned,' another man said.

Men continued drinking.

As he watched others leave to visit their women, Ned became enraged. He drank more rum.

Jacob, James and Levi sat quietly, sipping their rum and keeping to themselves. James sat thinking about that tall girl he had helped. He realised what would have happened to her if he brought her back to Ned.

'Shit I'm glad I didn't bring her back here.'

'What did you say?' Jacob asked.

'Oh nothing, I'm going to my bed.'

Next morning as the men pushed their whaleboat into the water to go across to cut up the whale, one of the women came running. The body of a young black boy had been found washed into the rocks by their camp.

'They swam; then drowned,' Bryant told Ned.

'I'll get another one.'

* * *

Days passed at the outcast women's camp. Yoola became friendly with the oldest boy in the group. Wandura was older than Yoola and Yara; tall with lighter-coloured skin. His mother asked him to see if there was a whale, she did not want him to go near the beach, but the group needed meat. Yoola agreed to go with the tall boy. Afraid for the boy's safety, the women told them to come straight back.

Wandura's mother sat and talked to Yara, she sensed what had happened to her on the island. During a long and painful conversation the woman told Yara about their lives.

Most of the women in the group had been treated in the same way by white men. It had begun many seasons ago when ships first came to get the whales. At first the Aboriginals kept away, but the opportunity of so much meat attracted them to the whale carcass. Sometimes the white men took the women by force; occasionally the Aboriginal men traded their women to the whalers, for rum and other things. Soon the diseases came, then disruption to the traditional ways.

The ships and the white men did not stay. Sometimes they did not return for two seasons. But they were here more often, and now there were two ships and more men.

'Most of the children here are from women being with white men,' the woman told Yara. 'We have been sent away from our own clans. We are not wanted there.'

Yara stared at the women and their different looking children; would she be like that now? Would she be accepted if she returned to her home place?

Yoola and Wandura left early, walking carefully down the track to the beach. When they came to the camp Yoola grasped the disarray and filth clearer in the daylight. It had now become a permanent camp, both for Aboriginals and some of the white men. There were a few native women there, but very few children. Further around the bay he noticed another camp and more bones and stripped whale carcasses.

The boys talked to Aboriginal men who told them that both groups of whalers had gone out in whaleboats that morning. Perhaps there would be whales later that day.

The boys decided to wait. They spent the day at the camp talking to the men there. Aboriginal men were helping white men go inland to get wood for their fires.

'We need to go further each time,' one man said. 'But there will be meat for us when they bring in another whale.'

Yoola saw white men from Granite Island, but they did not recognise him. He gazed back down the beach towards his home area. He knew that he could walk back there before sundown; what should he do? He glanced out toward Granite Island and the water that was so calm in the channel; he thought of his friend, Warri, who did not come out of the water, just a few mornings earlier.

Later that afternoon two whaleboats hauled a whale onto the beach.

'Come back tomorrow,' the boys were told. 'There will be a lot of meat.'

Back with Yara that night Yoola asked her when she was going home to her family.

'I can't yet,' she answered.

Yoola looked at the women and their children; he knew what had happened to Yara. He understood her apprehension.

'I will help get meat tomorrow,' he told Yara. 'Maybe I'll stay at the camp at the beach, I talked to men who are there from our clan, they are staying; they say there's always lots of food.'

'What will you do when the white men leave?' Yara asked.

'Will they leave?'

'I don't know, everything is changing.'

Yoola and Wandura returned to the whale camp the next day.

White men and black men worked together. Yoola stood back watching; he had never seen such activity. He recognised more men from the island; the man with red hair, the big black man who had seized himself, Warri and Yara from their beach; the man who dragged Warri away from the fire that night was there.

Aboriginal men talked to the white men and seemed accustomed to their ways, willing to help them. White men wanted the blubber, not the large amount of meat that came off the carcass. After the white men removed the blubber Aboriginals scraped meat off the giant bones. A continual procession of people moved on the beach, some going down to the whale, others coming back.

Yoola walked along the beach where the last whale lay rotting, its bones now stripped, guts pulled away and spread around the sand and rocks. As he walked closer, scavenging birds rose up, annoyed at his disturbance. Yoola noticed another procession; large black ants coming to the carcass; then going back up to the beach with meat. 'On the next high tide or rough weather it won't go, just be spread out along the beach with the other bones.'

Yoola and Wandura took as much meat as they could carry back to the outcast women's camp. When Yoola told Yara about the men who had come to the whale camp from the island she shook with fear.

The days became longer; the rising sun changed position. Yara knew warmer weather would come soon.

'The ships will go soon,' Wandura's mother said. 'The whales are not there during the warm time.'

Not all the white men were going away, and Yara was not going back to her people.

Chapter 6 – James and Merindah

To know love for the first time; a short time.
Will it always be like this? Knowing each other, but not
knowing each other at all.
Things that were never in your dreams may reshape all
your dreams forever.

Merindah missed her friend whenever she walked on the beach
alone. But at night she sat looking at the stars and knew Yara was
too.

Both ships were still in the bay. The Americans were preparing
to leave; their ship was loaded with sealskins and whale oil. They
said that they may not be back the following winter.

'Possibly the next one,' the American captain remarked.

The men who would stay at Granite Island for the summer
months killing seals, would need salt to treat the sealskins. The
American whaling Captain had told Captain Harris about the good
supply of salt on Kangaroo Island. Harris had his ship ready to sail
there as soon as the weather became suitable, but he wanted one
more whale.

The man on the hill rang the bell.

'This will be your last chance this season,' Captain Harris told his men.

It was late in the afternoon; three whale boats sailed away from Granite Island.

James Miles sat holding an oar.

'It's going to be a late night,' big Ned grumbled as he took out a wad of tobacco and stuffed it into his mouth.

'Probably all bloody night,' one of the crew remarked.

Three boats closed in on two whales.

'A mother and calf,' the man at the bow yelled. 'I reckon it'll be the last ones we'll see this year.'

'Let's get on her before Bryant's crew can,' Ned yelled. 'Bring the sail in, and mast down.'

The men rowed swiftly toward the mother whale.

'Now!' Ned yelled from the stern. The harpoon stuck fast. As the whale swam away the rope sped out of the tub; a man poured water on the rope to stop it burning. The whale stopped.

'Now she's going to dive,' Ned yelled as he swapped places with the man in the bow, ready to lance the whale when she rose again. 'No, she's coming back toward us. Get that rope back in the tub.'

Clouds came in from the southwest hiding the setting sun. The whale had swum back towards their boat, still with the harpoon firmly attached.

'She's trying to find her calf,' a man shouted.

'Here it is, right by the boat,' yelled another.

The wind had come with the clouds.

'It's coming up rough,' James said as he watched the mother whale circling the boat.

She dived.

'Keep that rope tidy,' Ned yelled. 'Watch it, she's coming back up.'

But the rope had become tangled around the bow. The whale began to surface. The boat pitched sideways, and the bow plunged into the sea.

Ned knew they were in trouble. Reluctantly he grabbed the axe ready to cut the rope.

He hesitated; he didn't want to lose this whale, and his bonus.

The whale surfaced completely. The huge tail thrashed against the boat. Wood splintered. Six men were hurled into the water.

Levi and Jacob could only sit and watch as the giant whale surfaced under Ned's boat and smashed it to pieces with her tail. Shocked, they helped row Bryant's boat across to the mess of rope, sails and floating timber. Bryant's crew pulled three surviving men aboard their boat and franticly searched amongst the wreckage for the three missing men. As the weather became rougher, and night came across the cold windy sea, Jacob and Levi feared that James was lost.

The two young men were devastated; their friend James was one of the missing men. The two white boys had left Sydney Town as young lads, probably to never see their mothers or siblings again. They had become close friends; the two youngest white men amongst the crew of hardened and sometimes violent sailors. Perhaps a few years older, Levi the tall wiry Aboriginal from Van Diemen's Land, was a lost soul before Captain Harris took him aboard the ship; he had become attached to the young white men.

'That's all we can do,' Bryant said as he instructed his crew to head back to the camp.

'Who's missing?' Ned asked as he recovered.

'Two of your older men, and young Miles,' Bryant answered.

'What about the whale?' Ned asked.

'Bugger the whale, what about your men?'

'There are plenty of men,' Ned answered, 'I wanted that last whale.'

Jacob and Levi both glared at Ned in disgust, their friend had drowned, but Ned was upset because he lost his whale. Both were growing into young men, hardened by the rough life, but they sat rowing in the darkness with their heads low, tears in their eyes. Ned would have a new boat the next day, and new men in his crew.

There was no whale that day. Three men lost; young James Miles was one of those men.

Despite the loss, early the next morning conditions were good and Captain Harris decided to sail west to Kangaroo Island to collect salt. Ned and other men remained on the island. Jacob and Levi went on the short voyage to Kangaroo Island.

'If you two are staying here when the ship goes back to Hobart Town, perhaps you should come on this trip. I want to check out this island and see what these men are up too,' Bill Bryant told the two young men. He had heard about the men who lived on Kangaroo Island, and he had a plan.

Jacob and Levi stared back at the coast as they sailed away on the ship. Somewhere on that white sand their young friend's body would lay wrinkled and lifeless.

*   *   *

A group of people from Merindah's clan came from their winter camp to the beach. They found two bodies washed up; some of the men approached cautiously.

'They're both dead,' someone said.

'Are you sure?' another asked.

Many of these people had not been near white men before. The two bodies lay on the sand with wrinkled white skin, seaweed tangled in their clothes and hair. Several of the braver men prodded the bodies. Yes, they were dead. They dragged the two men up into the sand hills, removed their clothes, and buried their bodies, shallow in the sand.

Other people from the clan found rope and timber on the beach.

Merindah walked alone. She ambled aimlessly on the beach toward the big river. A cold, cloudy morning, damp from the previous night's rain, columns of the early morning sun streaked through the clouds at the far end of the beach.

'Is Yara looking at the sun like I am?' she mused as she wandered along on the hard sand, unaware of debris that a high tide left on the beach; the shells, the crabs and things on the sand that she and Yara used to find.

She peered ahead, something strange lay high on the shore line where the tide had risen to earlier that morning. As she approached, she realised that a body lay in the sand; a white man. Merindah stood staring at the body, lying motionless alongside tangled rope, seaweed and a strange object the length of her forearm. Unsure what to do, she cautiously prodded him with her bare foot. Warm, and not stiff. Merindah knelt; held her face away and nervously peered at the man's face; sand moved as he breathed, he was not dead.

She quickly glanced back down the beach, and then back at the man. Alone there with this white man. What should she do? Merindah cautiously rolled the man over, and then she recognised him. It was the young white man, who had chased her into the scrub, but helped her when she hurt herself running away. She knew that although he could have taken her, as the others took Yara; he did not.

James's arm twisted out of place when Merindah moved him. A searing pain woke him from a deep sleep. He was exhausted after his struggle to stay afloat for hours. The water breaker had saved his life. He could swim, but not for hours in that rough water.

James had a broken arm where a timber from the boat hit him, bad cuts on his face and a deep gash in one leg. Somehow the rope attached to the water breaker had become wrapped around his body, or perhaps he held it as the whale smashed the boat. The half full water breaker with the cork stopper firm had kept him afloat until the waves washed him up onto the beach.

As he opened his eyes bright sunlight flooded in. He squinted, aware that someone had moved him. But he lay still, his head hurt, and he had a bad pain in his right arm.

There was no one to help. Merindah dragged James up into the bushes above the beach. He groaned with pain when she moved him; that's when she noticed his badly injured arm. She made him more comfortable. She returned to the beach and recovered the rope and the cask. When he saw the water breaker, James tried to get a drink; impossible with his broken arm. At first she didn't understand him asking her to lift the small cask to his mouth to drink. He demonstrated with hand movements. She understood and helped him drink from the strange wooden water container.

After he recovered enough to stand, the girl helped James further inland to a more sheltered place. James soon saw how smart the girl was when she found a shell to use as a cup and poured water from the breaker. She used a length of rope from the beach to stabilise his arm with a stick and pieces of bark and tie it against his body. She gathered berries and roots, strange food, but James was still hungry.

He needed to relieve himself and found that awkward with her there. She helped him remove his sailor's pants and put them on again after he roughly wiped himself with a hand full of leaves. James realised that the girl was shy, but understanding and smart. As his mind became more focused, he studied the tall girl closely, suddenly he recognised her, *That's the girl that I chased into the scrub.*

James remembered how he was glad that he didn't take her back to Ned. 'Hell, it's you again. I would only have been able to take you back when you were hurt. You're strong; I would never have been able to handle you on my own if you weren't injured.'

Merindah stared blankly; she had no idea what he said. 'I will help you now.'

James did not understand what she said.

It was going to be a cold night, Merindah wore only a skin around herself, the white man needed warmth, and he needed something to help heal the cuts on his face and legs. They needed fire and food. What was she to do?

James slept in the shelter of the tea-trees with the afternoon sun providing some warmth. He woke with his arm paining but secure. The girl had gone. He could hear waves rolling in, close to where he sat. *That noise never stops here.*

There were other noises; she-oaks sighing nearby, perhaps whispering he imagined. He sat there feeling at peace; different from being with a bunch of rowdy whaling men. He watched a line of small sand ants going back and forth, and honey eaters darting in and out of the flowers on the different trees and bushes. They argued amongst themselves, all wanting the same flower. When they suddenly became quiet, the shrill bell-like whistle of a single bird higher up in a tree startled James. Two black and white birds, Willy Wag tails he remembered his mother calling them, sprang and darted around him, they appeared to be bouncing in the air. Then they told him, 'get up- get up- get up.'

The girl returned at sunset. She brought two skins, food and a burning fire stick. James sat warming himself by the small fire and watched her singe the piece of unfamiliar meat that he ate cautiously. She placed something that smelt bad on his cuts. As night came, the unlikely pair sat gazing into the small fire. The clouds had gone, and the moon appeared through the trees at the far end of the beach. A clear cold night; neither talked, what was there to say? Even sign language difficult in the light from the fire. The girl gathered more wood and fed the fire.

'Sleep now,' she said, indicating that he should lie down. He did not grasp the words, but did understand the gesture in the extra light from the new branches on the fire. Sleep came quickly as James lay on the ground with the wallaby skin covering. He needed to lie carefully to avoid hurting his arm. When he woke later in the night, the moon had moved across the cloudless sky. James was alone. He stood and walked away a short distance and urinated into a small bush.

Finding it difficult to hitch up his pants again, he exclaimed,

'Hell, how would it be with no hands? You'd need help with everything.' The coarse material dragged across the gash on his leg as he struggled with his pants and he realised how bad his injury was. James understood then that he would not survive without the girl. His right arm pained terribly whenever moved or bumped. Carefully James moved back to the fire, he used his other arm to put on more wood and was soon asleep again.

Merindah walked alone, watching the sun rising through the mist, made by the never-ending surf rolling in as far as she could see. *I wonder if the beach goes on forever that way?* She knew of the big river, she had been to the edge of it sometimes with her family. But had never been across it where the big white sand hills were, and the waves still rolled in beyond them. It did seem that the sand and waves went on forever.

She remembered one particular visit there with her family.

'We don't go any further,' her Father had said. 'That's another clan's area; we only mix with them at special times.'

'Sometimes we trade young girls with them,' Merindah's mother said quietly.

'Did you come from over the big river Mother?' Merindah asked.

'Let's go back to our place now,' her Father said. Her mother glanced across the river; then they had turned and walked toward home.

Merindah found James still sleeping by the fire, gathered more wood and stirred the coals into life. He woke when the fire began to crackle.

'I have some food here,' she showed him the shellfish before she wrapped it in seaweed and placed it amongst the coals. There was water in a skin bag, she removed the cork from the water breaker and poured it in, then put some in the shell and he drank. James needed to urinate; when he came back from behind a bush Merindah noticed him struggling to hitch up his pants with one hand.

'Why don't you leave them off?' she asked. He had no idea what she said, but became embarrassed when he realised that she had been watching him.

'I'll have to do the other thing soon,' he said. 'I hope you are not going to watch me then.'

Merindah smiled at him.

'Shit, I think you understood me,' he said.

She smiled again.

Merindah took the cooked shellfish out of the seaweed, broke the shells with two stones and passed some food to James.

'Good food, my family eats a lot of this,' she told him.

'Food,' James said in English, as he held up the shellfish meat with his good hand.

'Fod.'

'No, food,' James said.

'Foood,' tried Merindah, pushing out her lips.

'You are a smart one,' James said. 'You'll learn quickly.'

She answered James with another jumble of words.

Simple things; food, water, trees, fire, they soon made each other recognise.

He anticipated Merindah's visits each morning. Gradually they started to understand each other more.

She tried to ask him about Yara but he did not understand.

Merindah did not know what to do with James; she knew that he was not ready to move. Should she take him to her people to get help? Should she keep him hidden from them? How long could she do that? Somebody from her clan would find him there.

For five days she nursed him, going back to her family in the evenings. She always brought James food, but it was different from what he usually ate.

Her Mother did not notice Merindah's absence; she was always busy with other children. Besides, Merindah had become a woman, ready to move away, her Mother expected her to be more independent. Soon Merindah would leave her to go to a man at a different place.

James lost track of the days. Each day he slowly walked the short distance to the edge of the bushes at the beach. As he sat in the early spring sunshine one morning, James watched the Southern Sky sail east. They were going back to Hobart Town; he presumed they believed he had drowned. He had no idea what had happened to the rest of the crew on the whaleboat, perhaps he was the only survivor.

James knew of the plan to leave a group of men on Granite Island to continue sealing until the ship returned, but he was not well enough to go back there yet. He needed the girl's help to do most things, even walking was difficult. James painfully limped back to the smouldering fire. His groin ached; he pulled up the leg of his baggy sailor pants and examined his wound, the deepest cut swollen and red, his leg was beginning to turn black above the gash.

'That looks bad,' he said to himself. He had been on ships long enough to hear stories of damaged and infected limbs needing to be amputated.

When Merindah returned that afternoon James showed her his inflamed leg.

'I will need help,' she said.

'I don't understand what you are saying,' James said. 'But my bloody leg hurts.'

Now James grasped the concern in Merindah's words when she pointed to his leg and shook her head. He was concerned when the girl suddenly left because she usually spent most of the day with him.

'I need your help,' Merindah pleaded to the old woman. 'It is a young white man, he has injuries, and he needs your medicine.'

'We need to stay away from the white men,' the old woman said.

'This one is not much more than a boy, and he's helped me before, please come and look at him.'

'Take me to him then, but I'm not happy about it, the others won't be either.'

When the old woman inspected James's leg, she frowned, and then hurried off into the bush, returning a short time later with roots and unusual leaves. She sat close to the young white man, chewed the roots and spat the resulting mouthful into the cut. She placed the leaves over the wound, holding them in place with vines wrapped around his leg.

The next morning James could barely walk, Merindah realised that she had to tell the rest of her clan about him.

Reluctantly, the people agreed to have the young white man moved closer to their camp.

'He must not stay long,' men told her.

'He will need to,' Merindah thought, but did not say.

'He may die anyway,' the old woman said.

Four of the older boys helped bring James back to the camp where they settled him in front of a small domed shape shelter and lit a small fire just for him. The hut where they left James was a short distance away from a collection of other similar tidy huts that were in a row sheltered from the wind by a band of trees. He saw fires smouldering in stone hearths and small shelters that must have been storage places for food; this was an ordered community. There were people going about their normal tasks. The older people did not want to see him, but the children stared from a distance.

That first night at the camp was uncomfortable for James.

'Where do I go to do it?' he asked. Merindah remained puzzled; James made obvious movements and actions, when she understood, she pointed toward a path. He noticed boys leave in that direction and used a stick to limp to the place.

The old woman continued to dress the injury with the same treatment. She checked his arm that Merindah had bound with rope; it needed to be kept firmer. She called three boys. After what seemed to James merely a babble of noise, they ran off, soon returning with wet red clay. The old woman stripped bark, like paper, from a nearby tree. She took the rope off James's arm and packed the bark and clay firmly around it. As the clay dried, his arm was far more stable. Merindah watched, learning as the woman tended James.

The men ignored James; they did not like him there.

James became delirious and drifted into restless, perspiring sleep. When he was fully aware again, it was morning, and someone had shifted him into the hut. When his eyes adjusted to the dull light, the same old woman, and another one, were squatting near him holding food and water, obviously meant for him. James looked down to his legs; his pants were gone, only a skin covered him. He quickly pulled the skin up to cover himself better.

The old women smiled and giggled to each other. 'White man has all the same things as a black man,' one of them chuckled.

'We will take his strange skin that he fouled and clean it in the sea water,' the other woman said.

'What the hell are you talking about?' James asked.

'We have food and water for you.'

James had some idea what that meant as they passed him food. He ate the food, but felt uncomfortable there.

'I need to move further away from the camp,' he said to himself, but he realised that he would not have lived without the women's help. The tall girl had been missing for three days. When she returned, she seemed pleased that James had improved. She noticed his pants missing, pointing to his bare legs, smiling she said, 'That will make it easier for you.'

'I wish I could understand you,' James said.

'We are moving to our beach camp for the warm time,' Merindah told him. 'We will take you to a different place, nearby, where we can help you recover.'

The next morning it was quiet, no children and no dogs.

'They've left me,' he said to himself. 'What now?' Later in the day the girl and two young boys came, they indicated that he should go with them. They helped him along a track which he realised led back toward the beach.

Away from the track and in shelter of Tea-trees they showed him where he should stay. That became obvious when they lit a small fire and put his water breaker on the sand next to him. James spent weeks recovering at that place near the beach. He realised the Aboriginal's camp was near, because he often heard children playing and sometimes dogs from the camp visited him.

As James recovered, the old women did not come as often, but he was still unable to walk far. Merindah brought him food and helped him get wood for the fire. Although his arm was healing, it was awkward and heavy with hard dry clay packed around it. Merindah came to see James during the day and remained with him late into the night. By drawing pictures in the sand she soon learnt the English words for many things.

James pointed to himself. 'Man,' he said, and then he pointed to her. 'Woman.'

'Woman, Man,' she understood.

Names though, were more difficult; he pointed to himself again and said, 'James.'

Puzzled, Merindah did not understand at first. It took time, but when she at last understood she smiled and pointed to herself saying, 'Merindah,' then touched him. 'James.'

They both laughed and hugged. Suddenly a wall fell from between them.

James had never been with a girl before; he became more aware of Merindah's young body, becoming more attracted to her each night.

Merindah also felt an attraction. 'Should I stay with this man?' she wondered.

The fire had burnt down. As they lay together on the sand James moved his body next to hers, his uninjured hand touched her skin. She did not resist him, suddenly they embraced.

'I haven't done this before,' he said as he nervously explored her body.

'You will be my first man, yes this is right,' she told James.

They were each unaware what the other said, but it did not

matter. Neither hesitated, there was no turning back. Afterward as they both lay gazing at the stars; they knew it would not be their last time together.

As Merindah studied familiar designs, the stars seemed even more remarkable. Her blissful thoughts changed when she remembered Yara. 'What about Yara? What events are changing her life?'

Merindah's visits each night became more dynamic. James had mixed feelings; he knew that he should go back to the sealers on Granite Island when he recovered. But could he leave her there? Perhaps he would take her with him. *No, I won't do that, not with those other men there. Especially Ned.*

Ned. He remembered the boat. *Did he survive when the whale smashed the boat? It didn't matter either way, he did not want this girl; no, she is a woman, near those men. Any of them.*

Longer days; living by the beach Merindah's people could see that both ships had left.

'But there are still small boats at the island,' one person said.

'And they still come to the beach up there,' another said. 'There, where the small river comes to the beach.'

'Yes, I think they come to get fresh water.'

James lost track of the days, he did not know how long he had been with the group of Aboriginals. He became extremely attached to the young woman; she and the other women had saved his life, he understood that. The wound on his leg healed, his arm was stronger. The women replaced the clay and paper bark. In time his arm would be strong again, but he knew he would have to treat it carefully until then. 'No rowing for a while.'

He started to visit the Aboriginal's camp. Most of the people began to accept him there, but he did realise that they expected, maybe wanted him, to go soon. James wore his sailor's pants again; he noticed two of the native men wearing sailor's pants, and two other men each with a shirt.

'How did they get those clothes?' he wondered.

James realised that his time with the group, and the girl, would end soon.

'This may be our last night together,' James said to Merindah. 'I will walk toward the island tomorrow.'

'What's troubling you?' she asked, not understanding him.

'Come here to me,' he said. She understood that.

Next morning James started walking toward Granite Island, Merindah understood that he was leaving, but as she followed, he tried to stop her.

'You mustn't come with me,' he said. Merindah started to understand. 'There are bad men there; I will not be able to keep them away from you.'

She understood 'bad' and 'men'. Merindah quickly grasped some of James's speech.

During the morning they walked along the beach together. In the afternoon they sat, he tried to explain to her what would happen if she followed him. Eventually she seemed to understand. She understood that he was trying to tell her about her friend Yara, and that white men mistreated her.

While he lived with the Aboriginals, James had watched from a distance as the sealers came in their whaleboats to the beach where a small river ran into the bay. That's where they collected fresh water; he would wait there and meet them the next time they came.

Merindah and James spent two more nights together at the small river waiting for the sealers to come for water. On the beach together during those two days, James and Merindah talked and grew more attached to each other. They each drew images in the sand. Those pictures and signs would stay in each of their minds all their lives. This became their special time together. James realised the images that Merindah drew held great meaning for her. He carefully memorised each symbol.

'This is our special time,' he said pointing to himself and Merindah.

She said, 'Yes,' plainly in English, and pointing to a symbol in the sand she clearly said, 'us, our time, our camp.'

James understood what the illustrations meant.

'They're coming,' he told her, pointing to the sail as a whaleboat came toward them from the island. 'You must go now, before they see you here with me.'

'I not forget you, ever,' she said in English, as she merged into the scrub.

'I will come back to you one day,' he answered.

*   *   *

Jacob assumed that his friend James drowned when the whale smashed Ned's boat. It had been two months since the ship left, leaving ten white men and four Aboriginal women on Granite Island. When the weather was suitable, they sailed and rowed the whaleboats south where they killed seals and brought the skins back to the camp to scrape and dry.

Ned had gone on the ship back to Hobart Town. Levi and Jacob worked with Bill Bryant in his whaleboat killing seals. Jacob also helped Bryant work in the basic blacksmith shop on the island. Bryant repaired equipment and sharpened knives and tools that the men used.

The youngest white man at the rough camp, Jacob now became closer to Levi the young tall wiry Aboriginal from Van Diemen's Land. When the older men became rowdy and unruly after drinking rum the two younger men sat together, or walked away from the camp.

'Bloody hell, look who it is,' one of the men on the whaleboat said as they pulled into the beach by the river. 'We assumed you were long dead and had fed the sharks.'

It was obvious to the other men in the boat that James must have been living with some Aboriginals, but he would not tell them all the details about his ordeal.

'Did you get a little one of their women?' They kept asking him as they rowed back to Granite Island. He told them about his injuries and how the Aborigines helped him. But, no matter how much they dogged him, he said nothing about the tall girl.

Jacob could not believe his eyes when James stepped off the whale boat. The two friends hugged and laughed with tears in their eyes. Levi joined the unexpected reunion.

James continued to recover doing light work at the camp. The other men went sealing when the weather allowed.

The Aboriginals at the beach of bones gathered their own food, there were no whales now. Sometimes they got seal meat from the white men in exchange for other things; perhaps women.

Merindah returned to her family. It was more than two months since she found James washed up on the beach. She had spent every day with him apart from the few days that first month when she needed to go away to be on her own. That hadn't happened again. Something different was happening to her body.

Merindah's uncle came to her; he told her a man would soon come to take her away to his clan.

'It must happen, it's an exchange. You will be going to the clan close to Longkuwar.'

'But that's where the white men are,' she said, alarmed.

'It's been arranged,' he told her. 'I can't stop it.'

Chapter Seven - The Voyage of Life Begins

We cannot know where life's journey will take us.
You may believe that you can plan, that you may steer
it, that there may be a choice.
But sometimes there is no choice. Someone else will
guide your journey.
The passage may be rough, and you will be swept along
on the voyage.

Merindah followed him. Not a young man; neither handsome nor strong, withered before his age. Other exchanges had been suggested, they had not eventuated. Now this was the final decision; Merindah's journey had begun.

Merindah did not look back as she walked along the sand. With her head down she followed the wrinkled man, unaware of the things on the sand that used to fascinate her. She did not hear the waves as they rolled over and slapped the sand. Did not watch the seagulls as they searched in the water as it ran back to meet the next wave.

As they approached the beach opposite the island, Merindah stepped through giant whale bones lying everywhere. On the island across the calm channel men moved around and two whaleboats lay anchored in shallow water.

Merindah stared, contemplating her future.

'We take this track,' the man said. 'My camp is up here, away from the beach, but close enough to get meat from the white men.'

When they arrived at his camp, Merindah saw two children and mangy dogs. She gazed at the whale bones. Old white bones, small bones, and large bones. Even larger bones formed the main frames of the two shelters. The dogs had bones, the children played with bones.

A woman, who may have been twice Merindah's age, sat on the ground grinding seeds between two stones. In the dirt close by a baby lay sleeping. Merindah noticed a much older woman sitting in front of a shelter doing something with an animal skin. Both ignored her

The wrinkly man indicated a place for her to go; a place for her to put the few things that she had carried from her mother's camp, so close, yet so far away.

He did not come near her for days. It appeared as if he was letting her become part of the assortment of things that were, maybe not his, but under his control.

The other two women gradually accepted Merindah as part of their group. The everyday chores were familiar. The man left the camp, sometimes for the day, other times for a few days. Probably to the beach, Merindah supposed, because sometimes he brought seal meat back to his women and children.

'There will be whale meat when white men return in the big boat,' he told his women.

He always wanted meat; he brought seal meat to the camp from the white men and hunted only when the white men brought their huge dogs ashore. His women gathered other food from the bush, but they had been told not to go near the beach or the white men.

The man spoke only sparingly to Merindah. More commands than discussion, usually merely a hand gesture and a grunt. But he did speak clearly when he told her.

'You are not to go near the beach where the white men are. Your place is here with my other women.'

Merindah did not lift her head, she nodded. 'Yes, I understand.'

The first time he took Merindah, he had his way quickly, grunted and left before she was ready.

'This is my life now.' Merindah thought as the old man walked away, 'Only for his needs. Nothing to do with me, well that's the way it will be. Obviously I am not here because I want to be. I'm here because it's my journey.'

Sharing the man with the other woman did not concern Merindah. She helped with children, gathered food, prepared and cooked it, and collected firewood; all the usual tasks. As time passed the relationship with the man did not change, Merindah was there to serve his desires; that was her place. As the days became shorter and cooler she still had not needed to go away on her own for three or four days. She knew now that she was expecting a baby, and certain that it was James's baby, not the wrinkly man's.

She became anxious. 'The man may not want my baby. He will realise that the baby is not his because it will be too soon after coming to him.' What could she do?

The sealers still came to the beach of bones. They brought seal meat; sometimes they came to hunt with their big dogs, and Aboriginal men went hunting with them.

The days were cooler, but it had not rained. Aboriginals carried water to their camps. There was no water on the island now; sealers needed to come to the creeks often to fill their water casks. Whale bones on the beach became dry and bleached. The Aboriginal's dogs were hungry and skinny.

Merindah swam in the sea early each morning, noticing the place where the sun rose; she understood the shorter and cooler days were coming. She stayed away from the place where the white men came to the beach and went to the beach far away from there to swim. Although aware that James was there with the other white men, Merindah was not sure if she wanted to see him.

'Perhaps the big boat and more white men will return soon,' she said to the younger woman.

'Yes, but that will bring more of our people back here,' the woman said. 'More problems with white men and our women.'

'Are there problems here now?' Merindah asked. 'I haven't seen many children who may be from white men.'

'There has been more of that happening than you think; it's hidden.'

'How and why?'

'The women involved are not accepted back to their families, not part of the clans. The children are not always welcome either. White men sometimes accept the children; they will use them as workers, and keep young girls for themselves, or to take away to other men. Like those women they keep out on the island; white men have taken them away from their families, stolen or traded.'

Merindah shuddered as she thought of Yara with the white men.

'Is Yara on the island?' she said aloud, starting to understand how the white men treated Aboriginal women.

'Who's Yara?' the woman asked.

'Oh, a friend of mine who the white men took away from us, she must have been taken away on the ship, or she may be on that island.'

'I may know something about her,' the other woman said.

'Please, I need to find her,' Merindah pleaded.

'Later, we need to gather food, or the wrinkly old man will be furious.'

Soon it became obvious Merindah was going to have a child. The wrinkly man did not notice, but the two other women at his camp could see the change.

'Too soon for you to be like that,' the older one said to her. 'He will know soon and realise that it's not his baby.'

'How will he take that?' Merindah asked.

'Possibly not bothered. He would kill any baby from a white man, but you came from a place where there are no white men, didn't you?'

'Yes, I did,' Merindah answered. She turned away, hiding her face.

The old woman had seen Merindah's reaction, but she kept her suspicions to herself. Merindah turned away, panicked, wondering what she should do. She wanted to keep James's baby safe.

If the wrinkly man did realise, there was a baby, it made no difference to his visits to Merindah's sleeping place. But she knew that each time he lay with her, he eyed her belly. He said nothing about her changing condition, but she could feel his suspicion. Merindah continued to wear a long skin that covered her waist.

The place where the sun rose showed the seasons changing, but the cycles of the moon gave her a sign of the days passing. Merindah accepted her place, thankful that the man did not stay after he had satisfied his need, but she remained concerned at the way he avoided her increasingly obvious condition.

'We are going to shift our camping place,' the younger of the two women said.

'Further inland now that it's cooler and rain will come soon?' Merindah asked.

'No, we will be closer to the beach.'

'Why?' Merindah asked, puzzled.

'Because the white men will return soon and he wants to be near the whales.'

'We used to go inland and eat different foods during the cold time,' Merindah told her.

'Yes, people here did that, but now we just wait for the whales. Easy meat. But too many people come here, it becomes crowded and soiled.'

Merindah agreed. 'Yes, even this little camp of ours is becoming dirty, look at the dog's droppings, and ours is just over there. We need to walk further each day to get firewood. Yes, we should move.'

Their new camp was closer to the beach of bones, but still a distance away from the main camp of Aboriginals.

'He wants to keep us away from the white men.'

'I am happy to do that,' Merindah said. She wondered what would have happened if the white men had taken her with Yara. But James was a white man, he did not hurt her. Although she believed James was different, she was not sure if she wanted to see him again. Perhaps he was just like the other white men. She may be wrong about him.

Soon after the move, a ship returned. It lay anchored in the same place behind the island. Merindah noticed the increased activity. White men came to the beach of bones and collected firewood, preparing for their big fires.

'They need to go further each season to get the wood,' the wrinkly man told his women. 'I will help them, you women must stay at this camp, don't go near the white men.'

As darkness fell, a child ran into camp. 'They have a whale!'

Well before sunrise the next morning Merindah stole away to the deserted beach to swim. She ventured closer to the beach of bones.

The whale lay in shallow water next to the flat rocks. Merindah remembered her recurring dream of the whale with the old man's face.

The huge black body shocked Merindah. Sadness overwhelmed her; she realised it may have a calf, a baby, still out there now, in the sea, swimming around alone, searching for its mother. There were gaping holes in the whale's side where men had lanced it to death. Dried blood stuck to shiny skin.

The dream of the skinless men flashed through her mind. She thought about James, *No they do have skin*. Another dream returned; of time alone with the young white man.

She was fascinated with the whale's huge mouth hanging half open, a cave; the entry to a mysterious other world. *Why do those nightmares about the whale-man always return?* Fading morning stars reflected in the whale's sad eyes. 'Oh, it has babies!' She turned and ran away sobbing.

Now the wrinkly man brought whale meat to his camp.

The days became shorter and colder; white men killed more whales. Merindah kept well away from the beach of bones, swimming even earlier in the mornings.

Occasionally she stole away from the camp during the day to peer through the bushes; Many Aboriginal people were coming and going to the dead whales on the beach.

Soon the rotting whale smell spread everywhere in the area. Birds, wild dogs and rats came like the people, to get the easy meat. The beach became chaotic once again. Merindah had seen wild dogs, crows and other scavenging birds fighting over a carcass. *It's the same. Each scavenger waiting for the other to finish or be chased away, and then it's their turn at the prize. After the last foragers leave, the maggots and the ants will come.*

While gathering wood one afternoon, Merindah discovered a well-worn track going inland leading away from the whale beach. As she stood wondering whose camp it must lead to, she heard somebody coming. Two young men carrying whale meat came along the track from the beach. They stopped and stared at Merindah, one Aboriginal, and another man, black, but different.

Suddenly Merindah recognised the young Aboriginal; he was one of the two boys who were taken from her beach that day when Yara also disappeared.

'Yoola!' she cried out. The young man dropped the meat and ran to her in tears.

The other young man, who Merindah could see was a little older, watched shyly, waiting as Merindah and Yoola slowly relaxed and began to talk.

'Tell me, do you know where Yara is?' Merindah asked. 'Is she alright?'

'Yes, I do know where she is,' Yoola said. 'And she is alright, now.'

'What do you mean, alright now?'

'Yara can tell you herself, she's not far away. She lives with some other people, this man is Wandura and he has helped us.'

Merindah believed she would never see Yara again, but all this time she had been living close.

Yoola and Wandura led the way further inland to the outcast woman's camp. As they approached, there were children playing and the predictable dogs lolling around. There were women working preparing food, and women minding babies. Merindah recognised at once that most of the children had lighter coloured skin, and sandy or brown hair.

One young woman sat in the sand, breast feeding a newborn baby.

'Yara!' Merindah exclaimed. 'You have a baby!'

Many tears and hugs later the two young women settled and told each other their respective stories since that day on the beach. Yara's baby girl was not like the other children; her skin was gleaming-black. She had different facial features and tight black crinkly hair.

'You're going to have a baby soon too,' Yara patted Merindah's belly.

Merindah began to cry. 'I don't want him to kill my baby,' she sobbed.

'We can help you,' agreed the other women who understood Merindah's distress.

When Merindah returned to the wrinkly man's camp, she did not tell the other women where she had been. She realised that the children where Yara lived were clearly the result of relationships between Aboriginal women and white men. Merindah understood that James's child would most likely look like those children.

She was not going to let the wrinkly man hurt her baby.

The wrinkly man was always away getting meat during the day; he only came to her sleeping place for a short time at night. But he knew there was a baby coming; even Merindah's animal skin could not hide that.

'That baby, it's not mine, it's too soon. What are you going to do about it?' he challenged her.

Merindah's heart thudded. She stared at her feet, dreading what might come next.

'When I made the deal with your uncle, I was not told about that. I'm not happy. Perhaps I will send you away or exchange you; get another woman without someone else's baby. There are too many babies around here now. Even white man's babies. We don't want them.'

Merindah did not move, her eyes searched her toes for an answer, but there was none.

The man grunted and walked away.

The place where the sun rose each morning changed as always; the days would soon become longer and warmer. It was obvious that Merindah's baby was due soon, but she had a bold plan. She was determined to hide her baby from the wrinkly man.

'I'm going back to my Mothers camp to have my baby,' she told the other two women.

'That's unusual,' they said. 'Have you told him?'

'No,' answered Merindah. 'It's the custom at our clan,' she lied. 'I want you to tell him when I've gone. He may not like it, but I think he will be happy when I return with a baby. He may not even miss me; he is busy eating lots of whale meat, and his stomach is big now, like a wombat's.' The other women agreed and said they would tell him.

Chapter 8 – To Love May Be to Leave.

Love may mean leaving.   A brief time of love is a memory to hold.
But the love need not be just for that brief time, it can remain constant after the leaving.

Merindah and James's baby was a girl. Merindah named her Alinta. She held the baby constantly for the first twenty days of her life; that would be the only time she would be hers.

Yara was nursing a young baby, and could provide ample milk for two babies, especially now that there was whale meat. Merindah knew that although she may see Alinta again, she would now be Yara's baby. She was heartbroken, but relieved and thankful because she was afraid the wrinkly man would most likely kill the light skin baby with James's sandy hair.

When she returned to the wrinkly man's camp, he was not there, but at the beach eating whale meat.

'He doesn't look like a wombat now,' the women said. 'He is a big fat whale.'

'But where is the baby?' one of them asked in alarm.

'My baby boy died,' Merindah cried. She did not need to fake the tears; tears of happiness for Alinta, and for sadness because she had to leave her with Yara.

Merindah's breasts hurt as her milk dried up.

The wrinkly man accepted that the baby had died, and he soon returned to Merindah at her sleeping place. It was the same as always; when he had satisfied his desire he left; always back to the whale meat, seal meat or hunting with the white men and their dogs.

'You'll be having another soon, because you are not nursing,' the older woman said.

'Another what?' Merindah asked.

'Baby, silly girl, didn't your mother tell you how it works?'

'She told me lots of things, but maybe I did not understand that bit. Can you help me; is there a way to stop it happening until I'm ready?'

'Yes, there are ways, I can tell you how, but it may be too late. He has been with you many times since you returned. All the whale meat has made him a big male whale, even some wrinkles have gone.' They all giggled.

Merindah learnt a lot from the older woman, she grasped their knowledge eagerly. But her lessons about preventing a baby may have been too late.

She knew that there was another baby, the other woman suspected. The wrinkly man did not, but he would expect it soon. Merindah sensed him study her body each time he released his need. He was often away from his camp getting meat, and during those times his women were left alone. Although his camp was away from the beach of bones, there were many other men about, both Aboriginal and White men.

The wrinkly man still did not trust his new young woman, and Merindah noticed his suspicions.

Soon another whaling season would pass; Merindah had rarely been to the beach of bones. Although she had been told to keep away, she wanted to find James and tell him about their baby girl. Yoola and Wandura would be going to get whale meat; she waited for them on the track that they used to come to the whale beach.

'Can you find the young white man with the sandy hair,' she

asked them. 'His name is James, two names; Miles I think.'

James did not realise that Merindah lived close to the beach of bones. He often thought about the tall girl who he had spent many weeks with. When young Aboriginal women came to the whale carcasses, he wondered where Merindah was, and if he would ever see her again.

Wandura could speak a little English; the white men were cutting up a whale. A young white man with dark hair stood sharpening knives. Wandura approached him shyly.

'Young white man with sand coloured hair?' Wandura asked Jacob.

'James,' Wandura said.

Jacob looked at the two Aboriginal men. 'Why do they want James?'

Jacob spoke and used his hands, 'Wait here. He will come here.'

Yoola and Wandura understood, they settled on the sand to wait.

Soon James came from the whale carcass with tools to be sharpened.

Jacob pointed. 'Those two boys want to talk to you James. Do you know them?'

'No, why would I?' James nodded to the two young Aboriginal men. He pointed to himself. 'I am James Miles.'

Wandura understood. 'Woman needs you.'

James did not understand. Was the man offering him a woman? He shook his head, waved his hands at the Aboriginal.

'No, I don't want a woman now.' He hesitated; maybe he could use the company. 'What do you want for this woman?'

At that moment James remembered the only woman that he had ever been with and changed his mind. 'No, not now.' He turned and began to walk away.

The Aboriginal youth stood talking, saying words which were strange to James. Amongst those words James caught, 'Woman, Merindah.'

James stopped. He had not heard her name spoken since the day he left her on the beach almost a year before, but during that time he had pronounced that name many times to himself.

James turned back to face the young man. 'You say Merindah.'

'Yes, Merindah wants talk to you.'

Nervous and excited, James followed the two young men into the scrub.

Merindah stood timid, trembling and silent as she tried to remember the words that James taught her.

'James!' she said shyly.

James hesitantly stretched out a hand; first their fingers touched; next bodies hugged awkwardly. Merindah pushed away; she nervously glanced around.

'Our baby,' she cried in English, pointing to James, herself; then away. 'You must go and meet her.' Merindah said in her own language. She pointed at Wandura and Yoola. Then in plain English she said. 'Man take you.'

James understood.

Merindah stood anxiously, with her head down, but she glanced up at the young white man through her eyelashes. She wanted to stay longer with James, but was afraid for her baby, their baby; afraid for herself and the white man.

'I must go now.' She turned and ran crying into the bushes.

'When will I see you again?' James called out, but she was gone.

James was nervous but excited to see his and Merindah's baby girl when Yoola and Wandura took him to the camp of the outcast women. He was sorry for what had happened to Yara, and for the loss of Warri. James talked to Yara with Wandura's help and told her he would try to come again and help as much as possible. Although unsure if she understood, he said he would send simple things like knives and needles, small things which would make her life a little easier. There were other things that Yara could use; things like rugs, cooking pots and an axe. Later he would get these and send them to her with Yoola and Wandura.

When James returned to the beach of bones, Jacob knew that he had been with the two Aboriginal youths and guessed it was about a girl. James went about his work again, confused. The baby was obviously his and Merindah's, but why didn't Merindah take him to the baby herself? He had tried to ask Yara but the language barrier was too great. Why did Merindah run away? And why didn't she care for the child herself?

Merindah did not go to visit their baby again for a long time; it would be too upsetting to leave Alinta again. Like tearing something from her body, leaving an ache that would last forever. It would explode into agony if she prodded it again. There was no choice; she had to leave her child with Yara. Alinta's future was more important to Merindah than her own pain. But what would that future be? She had seen the changes, and knew there would be more.

Merindah did not talk to James again, although occasionally she slipped away from the wrinkly man's camp and stood unseen in the shadows, watching James as he worked at the beach of bones.

Sometimes Wandura worked alongside James while they cut up whales. He awkwardly explained how Merindah lived nearby with a man who would not have accepted her baby. He made it clear that Merindah's man had told her to keep away from the crowded beach.

James watched the men, both white and Aboriginal working. He hated to imagine Merindah with another man.

He wanted to talk to her again and ask questions. He asked Wandura which man Merindah lived with.

Wandura pointed, 'Old man there.'

James had seen that man before, always standing amongst the bones of a whale. His screwed up, pock-marked face, half hidden under thin white whiskers and a chaos of grey hair. A tight round black ball for a stomach; scars on his hollow chest and skinny arms and legs. His greedy eyes were fixed on the whale as he hacked lumps of meat away from the carcass.

'Why is she with him?' James asked.

'Because it had to be,' Wandura answered. 'That is our way.'

James shook his head; he recoiled as he thought of Merindah with that old man.

Jacob watched James talking to the two young Aboriginal men; he suspected James had an Aboriginal girl out there somewhere. When James fetched tools back to him to be sharpened, Jacob asked. 'What aren't you telling me? Those boys, have they got a girl for you?'

James flushed, the fair skin on his face turning red. He would like to have told Jacob about the tall girl, and about their daughter, but he was cautious.

'No, they're just some blokes I've gotten to know,' he said.

But Jacob was not convinced. 'They were the two who came looking for you. They must have wanted you for something.'

'Yes, that was them, and there is something, but it's a bit awkward to tell you now.'

James turned to take tools back to men working on the whale. He saw the old wrinkly man standing knee-deep in mess as he cut meat off the carcase.

He frowned in envy. 'Fuck!' He felt sorry for that girl. 'Yes, it's difficult now.'

Occasionally James helped Jacob and Bryant work in the blacksmith area on the island where there were tools and material to make and repair things.

James and Jacob were leaving with the ship at the end of the whaling season and did not know if they would return. James wanted to give Merindah something to remember him by. When Bryant and Jacob were working ashore, he took the opportunity to make her something from the soft metal that Bryant used. He asked Wandura and Yoola to take it to Merindah.

Merindah's life continued to be a cycle of gathering, preparing food and helping to mind children; what the man expected her to do. Although she did it all without hesitation, her daughter remained in her thoughts constantly. She needed to see her again.

The white men brought in the last whale of the season; Merindah's wrinkly man went there for the whale meat. He would be away for two days. Merindah took the opportunity to visit Yara and Alinta.

When she held Alinta, she knew leaving her there was the right thing to do, but the tears flowed when she handed her back to Yara, who was now her Mother.

As Merindah prepared to leave in tears, Yoola hugged her briefly. And then he remembered; he had something for Merindah.

'James asked me to give this to you,' Yoola passed her an object wrapped in a piece of sail cloth.

As she walked back to the wrinkly man's camp alone, Merindah opened James's gift. She gasped with delight; James had made her a pendant from the heavy soft metal. It was suspended from a strip of leather so she could wear it around her neck. Merindah sobbed with joy when she noticed what James had engraved on the pendant. It was the signs that she had sketched for him in the sand, those symbols told of their friendship and time together.

Merindah knew then that she would keep it with her forever.

Merindah was afraid that the wrinkly men would take her pendant from her, she hid it away. The other two women did not understand why Merindah was so upset, but of course she could not tell them.

The man knew there was another baby on the way.

James, Jacob and Levi stood on the deck watching the beach and Granite Island fade in the mist.

'Do you think you'll come back here Levi?' Jacob asked the wiry Aboriginal youth.

'Dunno. I reckon I'll go wherever the Captain takes me.' Levi glanced at the Captain who was talking to the first mate. 'I'm better off here on the ship with him than trying to live back at Hobart Town, there's nothing, nobody there for me.'

'What about you James, do you want to come back?' Jacob asked.

James thought about Merindah and the baby. Should he? Would it be better to forget the girl and stay away?

No, he wanted to return. 'Yes I'll come back. I need too.'

'Oh do you, do you want to tell me now?'

'Well, yes, there's a girl. No, she's a woman now, but I can't have her. Perhaps things will change. And there's something else, I can't tell you about that now.'

'Right! Alright James, I knew you were hiding something. I won't tell anyone, I know how these men can be.'

James gave Jacob a friendly jab. 'Thanks mate; I'll tell you the rest one day.' He recalled the beach of bones. Somewhere behind that place, Merindah lived with an old Aboriginal man. James's baby girl would grow up amongst all that disruption. He wondered how long before he would see Merindah again, and if he could take her and their baby away.

I will come back. But can I take them away from that place?

'Stop dreaming Miles; get up there with the other men,' the mate yelled.

'There'll always be another one when we come back boy, they're all the same,' an old sailor told James.

'No, they're people, same as us, can't you see what we're doing to them?'

'I just do my work boy and get some pleasure when I can. Most times from a cask of rum; sometimes from one of those women. That's our life, we can't change that.'

Only a few men were left on the island, killing seals once again. Men made trips to the mainland to collect firewood and water. Trips to the whale beach when they brought seal meat to the Aboriginal people.

The red headed man was the leader of the white men now.

Sometimes he brought his dogs across to go hunting for different meat.

Aboriginal men marvelled at the strength and capabilities of these two huge dogs. They wanted dogs like that to hunt with and possibly breed with their smaller native dogs. Merindah's wrinkly man wanted one of those dogs; he knew they could get meat for him even when the white men did not.

Only two women remained on the island; Bill Bryant's and another man's woman and two children. The rest of the white men did not have women; not unusual for sailors, but distracting when there were women so close. This made it difficult for Bryant to keep the few men that he had there, focussed on the sealing. Men were always keen to go ashore for water or to take seal meat across to the Aboriginals.

Bryant's bitch Dina had four pups. Other sealing men wanted a pup but it would not be practical to keep more dogs to feed and control at the sealing camp or on the ship.

'We'll just keep one pup, a bitch,' Bryant told his woman. 'We'll need a new breeder for the future. I'll exchange the other pups at Kangaroo Island. Those men there will have pigs and goats to trade.'

When he went for the next hunting trip to the mainland, Bryant left the bitch on the island.

'Where is the other dog?' the Aboriginals asked; a simple question to understand; language no longer a barrier after so much association with the white men at the beach.

'She has pups, I couldn't bring her today,' Bryant told them.

Merindah's wrinkly man heard and understood. He wanted one of those dogs, and he had a woman that he did not trust.

'What have you got to trade?' Bryant asked.

'A woman,' said Merindah's wrinkly man.

Chapter 9 – The Value of a Life

What is the value of a life? A woman for a dog.
Leave your baby for love.
Be a slave so you can live. Try to block it all out; just to
continue to breathe and survive.
What is the value of a whole race of people?

Merindah kept her head low, but out the top of her eyes she
managed quick glances and studied the white man as he took her
out to the island in the whaleboat. She sat on a wooden bench in the
bow with her small parcel of belongings wrapped in a net bag.

The man sat in the rear of the boat as four men rowed. She
glanced briefly at the clay pipe in his mouth. He had lit it from a
fire on the beach before they left. Each time she lifted her eyes, he
was analysing his deal, sucking and blowing smoke from his
mouth. Blue smoke clouded his intense blue eyes before the wind
blew it away. His red hair shone in the afternoon sun; the red
whiskers on his face, and his dirty cotton shirt flapped in the breeze.
He took the fire from his mouth and talked briefly to the men
rowing the boat.

Merindah tried to remember some words that James had taught
her. She recognised only three. 'Woman—Dogs —Mine.'

The man pointed a finger to his own shoulder and said
something else to the rowers. Merindah noticed heads nod and

heard muted grunts, 'Yeah.'

The man put the fire back into his mouth. He sat, still looking at Merindah as smoke curled upward.

She wondered what the white men's shirts were made from. She had heard James call it a shirt. Their sail cloth pants, another type of material, or was it a skin. Merindah sat and remembered her dream about the skinless man. What would happen to her now?

The man with red hair took her to a camp on the island. This camp was untidy and dishevelled, as if more people had lived there recently; not just the two Aboriginal women and two grubby, shy, clinging children. Two huge dogs and three pups lay next to a smoking fire; their hairy coats the colour of the seaweed on the beach, black ears hung down over their piercing bright eyes.

Merindah fell in love with the three pups.

'Now I have three babies.'

The other two women at the camp appeared unlike any Aboriginal people Merindah had seen before, their features sharper and hair closely curled. They spoke together in a language totally different from Merindah's. They could not understand her language, but they also spoke words that James had used, and they were surprised when she understood a little of their jerky English.

Merindah was soon able to have a patchy conversation with the two women.

'He swapped you for a dog,' one said.

'They just took us,' the other told Merindah, her hands and face expressed violence. 'And then they gave us away when they were finished with us. We wondered if that was better than being thrown off the ship, or even jumping off as others did.'

Merindah did not understand all that the women told her, but she was fast remembering words from her time with James. She had spoken those words to herself and in her dreams many times. Hand movements and expressions hastened the process; soon she could understand more of what the women were saying.

The women gave Merindah a faded old shirt.

'This will be better than that heavy skin,' one of them said.

When Merindah unhooked the skin from her shoulder and stood naked, the women saw she was tall and strong. They noticed the pendant Merindah had, just that day, hung around her neck. She had not worn it when she lived with the wrinkly man, because she was afraid he would ask questions, and would take it away from her.

'Look at her; she's worth all three of those pups.'

'Yes but I can see, she is worth even more. She's got a baby in that pretty belly.'

The woman with the dogs next to her told Merindah that she was the red-headed man's woman. She pointed to the sun, her hair, stroked an imaginary beard, held an imaginary pipe; then she pointed to the men's camp.

'They call him Bryant,' the dog woman said.

Merindah looked toward the other camp.

'Yes,' she nodded, 'Bryant.' She remembered the other men saying that name as they rowed her and the man to the island in the whaleboat. Then she remembered the breakthrough moment with James all those months ago. She put her hand on her chest.

'Me, Merindah.'

The woman smiled and nodded. She pointed to Merindah. 'You, Merindah.' She said slowly.

Merindah smiled and nodded.

'He calls me Sally,' the woman said. 'Sally.' She put her hand on her chest.

'Sally,' Merindah repeated.

The woman smiled and nodded again. 'Yes, I did have another name, but the men who took me a long time ago, called me Sally, and that's my name now. This is Jilly.' She pointed to the other woman there. 'She is another mans and the two boys are hers; but we are not sure who their fathers are.'

'Jilly, yes.' Merindah understood that, but not all that Sally had told her.

Merindah had been on the island for three days. She became relaxed with the two women and started to work with them on the sealskins.

Sally told Merindah how another sailor had passed her on to Bryant.

'I don't know what he gave for me,' she shrugged. 'But the other man had finished with me. He took a younger woman and was glad to be rid of me. If Bryant didn't take me, he probably would have thrown me overboard, like he did my babies.'

Merindah watched the other woman's hand gestures and expressions, she understood. Shocked, she tried to grasp what the older woman said. 'Babies, you had babies?' she asked.

'Yes, I had babies. Three baby girls, white men don't want baby girls, there are plenty of bigger girls there when they want them.'

'What about baby boys?' Merindah asked.

'Sometimes they let us keep them; perhaps they think they'll grow up into sailors.'

'Will you make more babies?'

'No more babies for Sally,' she said. 'Sally nearly died last baby, and baby died, sailor threw her overboard, dead. A lot of blood. I was sick for a long time. Lucky they did not throw me over too. Then, I wished they would.' Sally sighed. 'After that they gave me to Bryant.' She put her finger to her nose; 'I didn't smell too good. I am much better now, but no more babies.'

Merindah stood still; she put her hand on her stomach.

Sally pointed to Merindah's stomach. 'You will have baby soon.'

Merindah nodded. 'Yes,' she said quietly.

The other two women talked to each other in the white man's language, 'Maybe it's going to have light skin, that's why the man swapped her for a dog. No, he would quickly knock it on the head.'

'That may happen here anyway, likely if it's a girl.'

Merindah understood enough of this to panic.

'No,' said the woman next to the dogs. 'Bryant's different. But I wonder if he knows?'

'I think he'll know soon,' the other answered.

Merindah tried not to think about her baby. She watched the bitch feed her pups.

'Will he kill these baby dogs?'

'No, he's going to keep one, and trade the other two,' Sally answered.

'I want to keep this one, it's a girl, its name is Yarinta,' Merindah said with tears in her eyes as she picked up the only bitch puppy.

The other two women did not understand why there were tears.

'He wants to keep the girl pup,' Sally said.

More tears from Merindah.

Merindah sat dreamily gazing up at the stars. *All those babies, there are so many. Perhaps the babies that sailors threw off the ships are up there searching for their mothers.*

She did not notice him come to the fire; the man with the red hair disturbed her fantasies.

It had been five days since he had brought her to the island.

He spoke and used his hands to tell her, 'I want you to come with me.'

'Yes, I will come now.' Merindah answered him in plain English. She did not see his reaction in the light from the coals of the fire, but her answer shocked Bryant.

'How did you know what I said?' he asked in amazement. 'He told me where you came from, and where you've been, I didn't expect you to understand me, or answer me as clear as that.'

Relieved that he could not see her face in the dark, Merindah sat with her head down, shaking, expecting trouble. She did not answer, just sat biting her lip. She glanced at the other women; they had their eyes to the sand too. They also had questioned how she understood their broken English. They knew where she had come from and wondered how she could speak and understand their English.

'Well if you can understand me, I shouldn't need to explain. Come with me now.'

'Yes I will come now.' Merindah stood and followed Bryant away from the other women.

Bryant took off her shirt, carefully studied her young body in the moon light, but did not seem to be as hasty as the wrinkly man. He gave her back her shirt and told her to sit down.

'Where did you get that thing you wear around your neck?' he asked, pointing to James's pendant. Merindah had prepared an answer; she had practiced the words in English.

'My father gave it to me, when I was a baby,' Merindah lied. 'I think he got it from a white man who killed whales here, long time ago.'

'Bloody Americans,' Bryant said. 'You can keep it.' He waved his hands, 'you will do me just fine. Yes, fine.' He sounded a little different than James, but she understood.

'Can you understand what I am saying?' he asked.

'Yes,' she said sheepishly.

'Well you're mine now. Mine now, do you understand that?'

'Yes.'

'Good. No other man is to go near you, do you understand that?'

'Yes.'

'Good. Perhaps it's for the best that you can understand; for the best. I won't ask how you can understand, but you just do as I say.'

'Yes.'

'Now go back to the fire. Tomorrow you can help get seals. I'll see how else you can surprise me.'

Merindah found her way back to the woman's camp.

'That was quick,' Jilly said, giggling.

Merindah lay down to sleep.

Merindah had not been sealing before, but she soon became part of Bryant's sealing team. She could swim; and better than any boy that Bryant ever had. She dived to get the anchor out of the rocks when it got snagged. She soon learnt how to skin a seal.

Bryant would never let her swim when there was blood in the water.

'I think you're too good to feed to the sharks; too good,' he told her.

Killing, skinning, drying, scraping; that became her life. The smell of blood, the slippery rocks, the race to kill the slithering beasts before they reached the safety of the water, all became a way of survival for Merindah. She blocked out her feelings for life each time she clubbed a seal to death, knowing it may have a baby somewhere amongst the bloodbath.

'The stars,' she told herself. 'The babies will be up in the stars.' She clubbed another mother seal to death.

Although Bryant did not rush her as the wrinkly man did, it was not passion as with James. He indulged in the pleasure of a younger woman, and she responded with, perhaps not affection, but satisfied tolerance. When he had finished, he did not rush away; sometimes they talked. In her broken but improving English, she told him about her life at her mother's camp. About her friend Yara, and how she herself had been sent to live with the wrinkly man. Merindah did not mention the time with James, or their baby. Alinta was her secret.

It was inevitable; Bryant noticed that she was going to have a baby, and he knew that it could not be his. As her time came closer Bryant told her to stay at the camp; she need not go sealing.

Then one day he questioned her. 'This baby,' he said. 'What are you going to do with it?'

'What you mean, do with it? It's not one of your dogs.' She mumbled with her head low.

'Well, a baby was not in the deal that I made with that old man.'

Merindah understood deal, like trade; living amongst the other women she had learnt the English words quickly. She remembered what they had told her about the sailors and Aboriginal babies and started to panic.

'I want to keep this baby,' she cried, 'not---,' then stopped.

'Not what?' Bryant asked.

Merindah hesitated, calmed herself. 'Not hurt the baby,' she said.

'We'll have to wait and see,' Bryant told her.

This left Merindah with a shadow of fear. She left him and went to be busy with a seal skin, but her mind was on her baby.

The dogs became Merindah's way of coping with her situation, her distraction to keep her mind off the fear of what may happen to her baby. The fear was always there, but she pushed it away. Wherever she walked on the island Dina and the three pups followed her; they walked together on the beach they swam together in the sea, were by her side as she worked on the seal skins. At night they slept together. Merindah was pleased when Bryant told her that he wanted to keep the female pup.

'You train her up. She's your dog now, but I want to breed from her one day.'

'Her name is Yarinta,' Merindah told him.

'That sounds a bit strange,' Bryant said. 'Bit strange, can't you shorten it?'

Merindah considered for a few seconds. 'Inta.'

'That'll do.'

Merindah gave the bitch pup even more attention now that she knew she would not be taken from her.

The days turned cooler; the south-east winds blew more often.

Merindah sat gazing at the mainland and the hazy blue hills in the distance. The beach wrapping around to the Bluff at the end of the bay was a mother's arm holding it all. The knob of the Bluff was the mother's closed fist, that small island there, a mother's thumbnail, shining in the sun. The rocks out on the point the knuckles of her fingers.

Dreaming became real when she remembered Alinta, but no one heard or would have understood her ask. 'What is my baby girl doing? I'm sure Yara is minding her well. I wish I could just see them again.'

She realised that Alinta would soon have lived for one cycle of the seasons.

*　　*　　*

'A ship! A ship is coming!' Jilly was running down to the beach. 'Is it ours?'

Merindah watched as the ship sailed across the bay. *James, I wonder if James is on this ship? It will be difficult if he is living here on the island, and I am here with Bryant.*

'What are you dreaming of?' Jilly asked. 'There'll be changes here now, more men, more trouble.'

'Yes, I know.'

FOR FREIGHT or CHARTER, the superior Fine Fast-sailing Brig BELINDA, THOMAS COVERDALE Commander, Coppered and Copper-fastened.—Stands A.1. at Lloyd's.

For Particulars apply to Messrs. BERRY and WOLLSTONECRAFT, George-street.

Chapter 10 – West into the Setting Sun

Perhaps it is best not to see lost loved ones again.
Perhaps that which was once torn apart should not be
reunited. It would only mean more painful memories
of another parting.

The ship that sailed in and anchored at the usual place was not the Southern Sky.

This was a new ship, fitted out for a longer voyage.

The Belinda had only the year before, sailed out from England to Van Diemen's Land and suffered much damage on that voyage. After major repairs, a whaling company chartered the brig to travel on a voyage to the southwest coast of Australia. Captain Harris's instructions were to investigate whaling and sealing opportunities further west.

The Captain, the mates and most of the crew from the Southern Sky were aboard the new ship; including Levi, James and Jacob; they were fast growing into strong young men. Hugh Byron the first mate, Owen Muller the second, and the American, Ned still the third mate. Captain Harris expected Ned to have knowledge of the western areas. Chief, the cook had followed the rest of the crew aboard the new ship.

While unloading stores from the ship, James walked past the women's camp. When he glanced over at the women, his eyes met Merindah's.

James stared, hesitated, surprised to see the girl there.

But Merindah turned away, remembering Bryant's words. 'You're not to go near the other men.' She thought of the baby that she carried and did not dare glance back.

James walked on.

'What were you gawking at?' a sailor asked. 'She'll be someone's; you won't get her.'

'Yeah, I s'pose,' James answered gloomily.

Each time he walked past the camp James would look for Merindah.

A sailor told him how Bryant had exchanged that new woman for a pup.

'And she's probably going to produce a black baby soon,' the sailor said. 'The Irishman may not like that.'

*   *   *

Captain Harris had instructions to leave three whaling teams at Granite Island and then sail west in the Belinda to investigate other areas. If possible, he would leave men sealing at other places. His orders were to sail west as far as Recherche Archipelago and get, trade, or buy sealskins from there. It was possible there would be sealers working there; maybe Americans. After returning to Granite Island, the whale oil and seal skins would then be taken back to Hobart Town or Sydney.

'They think this should only take about six weeks,' Captain Harris said, 'but they want me to investigate a large strip of coast. I reckon we may be away longer. On our way we'll stop at Kangaroo Island to get salt to cure the sealskins.'

'Where will we leave men sealing?' Bill Bryant asked.

'I don't know for sure yet, but I have some places in mind. Come to my cabin tonight Bryant, I want to talk to you about that.'

'Good, I want to discuss something with you too,' Bryant said.

Ned overheard and wanted to be included in that discussion. He stormed off, muttering. 'Bastard, I'm the one he should be talking to.'

Later, as he walked past the woman's camp, Ned noticed Merindah cooking at the fire. 'Who's that new woman?' he asked a man who had been there sealing.

'She's Bryant's,' the man said, 'you'd better keep away from her.'

'Looks like he hasn't been keeping away.'

'Rumour is, it came as a package.'

'Shit! I wonder what he's going to do about that.'

'There's talk that it will be as black as its mother.'

'Well I know what I would do with it then,' Ned snarled, as he walked away.

He intended to stay on shore for the few nights before the ship left. 'I'll be going over to the black's camp for a little recreation.'

Addis also returned on the ship; still in charge of the sails, and in charge of the stores. He did not mix with the other sailors, other than a distant relationship with his fellow American, Ned. Although they seemed different, they shared a common manner of arrogant self-assurance. Addis had enlisted a new apprentice to work with him. Rebus, a young boy; perhaps fourteen years old, came from Van Diemen's Land. His parentage was questionable, mostly Aboriginal, but that did not bother Addis, he preferred young boys to mould in the way he desired. His hidden resource of rum in the sail hold helped his nurturing of young Rebus.

*   *   *

When Bill Bryant told Merindah that she would be going on the ship, she had many questions in her mind. Should she try to escape from the white men? But where could Merindah go? Not back to her mother's camp, or back to the wrinkly man. Should she try to see Yara and Alinta before she left?

After much deliberation she decided to stay with Bill Bryant. He did not mistreat her, and she had become attached to the other women and the dogs. It would be too traumatic to visit and then leave Alinta again.

Merindah did not know if James was going on the ship; they had looked at each other from a distance, but not spoken. Merindah was worried about the consequences for her unborn baby. *He must realise that I am the red headed man's now. He must keep away. It would be better if he did not come on the ship.*

'What about the baby?' Merindah asked Sally. 'It may come while we are on the ship. Who will help me this---?' She stopped, almost admitting that she had a baby before.

'We'll be with you,' Sally said. 'We've helped with lots of babies on board ships, haven't we Jilly?'

'You'll be fine, even though it's your first,' Sally assured her.

Merindah cringed and turned her face away.

'Something about her,' Sally whispered to Jilly.

'Yes.'

Preparations continued for the voyage west, and for the men to be left at Granite Island. Barrels of flour, ships biscuits, and other food unloaded, the salted meat left on board for the trip. Barrels filled with fresh water were secured below decks. Men made trips to the mainland to cut, gather and bundle dry grass; feed for the goats. The pigs ate scraps; anything thrown at them, and sparingly a little grain soaked in fresh water, so they could digest it without waste.

'There'll be plenty of fresh meat here on the island,' said the man organising the stores.

'Bryant is going on the ship, taking those dogs of his,' commented another man. 'There'll only be whale and seal meat, perhaps those tough little penguins; no roo or emu.'

'We're going to leave some pigs here,' the storeman said. 'Oh, and a couple of goats.'

Regardless of her feelings, Merindah did not have a chance to get off the island, and within a few days the ship was ready to leave.

Ned returned from the mainland with a spring in his step.

'And maybe something else that he caught,' a man commented.

'More like they caught something from him,' another said.

Other women had returned on the ship with their men; they were staying on the island.

Jilly and her two boys were going aboard with Sally and Merindah. Sally told Merindah that another woman lived aboard the ship, she was the Captains woman and she lived in his cabin. She had no children, or none with her. Merindah remembered what Sally had told her, 'Or none who had not been thrown overboard.'

'We'll pick up more goats from Kangaroo Island,' Bryant told them. 'I hope to do a trade with those other two pups.'

Merindah would miss the other pups when Bryant traded them, but she had become attached to Inta, and the young pup to her. Dina was Sally's dog, but she had also become fond of Merindah.

'They are both your dogs' now,' Sally told her, 'The old-man dog Argus, he will always be mine.'

'No,' Merindah said, 'they're our dogs. They're all part of our clan; they follow Jilly too.'

Although they passed each other often as she prepared to leave the island, Merindah tried to avoid James. Each time he looked toward her, Merindah turned away or searched the ground. She wished that she could talk to him, but was afraid for herself and for her baby, she didn't want Bryant upset.

Merindah didn't know whether James was going on the ship or staying on Granite Island. As she watched the men preparing the ship she wondered. *Will James be on the ship? Perhaps it's better if he is not here when I am with the other man. It would be awkward with him close, and me there with the red headed man.* There were so many questions in her mind. *Will James go to see Alinta again?*

'I have a plan,' Bryant told Merindah and Sally when they were alone the night before they left. 'I can't tell you two yet, but I have discussed this with Captain Harris, and he agrees. But first I need to check out some things. We may not come back here for a long time.'

Although she did not understand all of that, Merindah realised what a long time away meant, she trembled and thought about Alinta. *Perhaps it's for the best, she's Yara's daughter now.*

Merindah noticed a young tall Aboriginal youth often with Bill Bryant, and he seemed to talk freely to Sally and the other women.

'Does that boy belong to one of you, a brother, or perhaps a son?' she asked Sally.

'No,' Sally answered. 'But he comes from our place. He is one of us, like a brother, his name is Levi. Bryant likes him around.' Merindah smiled at the tall Aboriginal youth as he walked past her. Levi shyly returned the smile, but he knew that she was Bryant's woman.

A whaleboat took Merindah, Sally, Jilly, her two boys and the dogs out to the ship. This was where they would live for weeks. Merindah gazed at the huge wooden craft with all of its fittings and strange things.

Another Aboriginal woman stood on a deck above them as a sailor showed them where to go. Sally gave the woman a wave and a small smile.

'Who's that?' Merindah asked.

'She is one of us, but lucky. She's the Captain's woman, she lives on the ship; better food and better clothes.' Merindah realised that the woman was looking at her and her large belly.

'He calls her Sarah; that is her name now,' Sally told Merindah. 'She came from the same place as Jilly and me. Sarah has no babies yet, I don't know why.' Merindah noticed that the woman wore a clean shirt and a pair of trousers, and she had short curly hair with a colourful head band just above her eyebrows.

'Sarah will come and see us when she can,' Sally told Merindah. 'But the Captain likes her to stay in his place on the ship.'

Merindah marvelled at the holds that disappeared down into the ship, she peered through openings in the deck at wooden barrels and boxes. They walked past another opening where below there were ropes and sails. Wooden cages stood fixed to the deck with poultry in them, and a pen with goats and another with the strange animals that Sally called pigs. Sally put the dogs in another wooden cage. They whined softly when she shut them in.

'Bryant will let you out when he's ready,' she murmured, as she stroked the bitch's huge shaggy head.

'There,' the sailor indicated a square opening in the deck.

Merindah's eyes strained as she peered into the dark hole. *Is this where we live now?*

She followed Jilly down; the dark sides of the box closed in and trapped her. When her eyes adjusted to the dull light, she realised how small the space would be for the three women and Jilly's two boys. Everything smelt different; the animals so close, the damp timber, tar, oil, ropes and canvas.

Jacob and Levi were on the ship, but James was not going on the trip west. The Captain had asked him to stay at Granite Island and work with the whaling teams.

As the ship sailed away, Merindah saw James standing on the shore. She knew that he was watching her; she glanced around for the red headed man. He was busy. She looked back but James had gone. Merindah stood by the railing, wondering when she would return.

Merindah had handled sailing and rowing along the coast in the whaleboat without feeling sick, but on the ship it was quite different. Out in the swell the ship rolled, pitched, rose up, and seemed certain to dive under the next huge wave. Merindah's stomach seemed to rise, then fall, before coming up again, threatening to explode right out of her mouth. She swallowed with her mouth shut, hoping that that would hold it all in. She stood holding her belly tight with one arm while the other hand gripped the railing. The baby moved up and down. Merindah had watched the sea all her life, thinking that there were only waves, but now the ship climbed hills and plunged into gullies.

'You'll get used to this,' Sally told her.

'Wait and see what it's like when it gets rough,' Jilly warned.

Merindah stood on the deck and focused on the horizon, she held her mouth shut tight. The ship seemed to be a huge gum nut tossing in the sea. She was amazed at how many things were crammed into the small space. You could not be tossed around because everything and everybody leant on and into each other. All the different smells, some good, some very bad, seemed to fuse together and bounce around as the ship moved in a thousand different ways.

As the ship sailed west along the coast, Merindah gazed at the land in the distance; hills with trees and grass, hills that tumbled right into the sea. During the night, sitting on the wooden bench in the women's dark enclosure she listened to new noises. Instead of the constant swish and slap of waves that she had heard all her life living close to the beach; now there was the noise of sea as it slapped against the side of the ship. The sound of the rigging, creaking, groaning as if it wanted to be released, rarely ceased. Occasionally the sails flapped and cried out for the wind, but were happy, almost silent, when the wind filled them again. She listened to the noises from all the living creatures on board, the pigs snuffling, the goats bleating, rats scurrying about. Sometimes a rat would poke its nose and whiskers out and stare at Merindah as if to say; 'What are you doing here? I was here first.'

In the crowded space of the ship there were over thirty humans. When most of them slept and the cool night breeze pushed the ship gently through valleys and rises, Merindah lay on her bench listening to the many sounds; people snoring, moving and sometimes crying out in their dreams. There were always men walking on deck, moving around, smoking, waiting for the next bell. Occasionally, when it was calm the ship drifted, the sails resting, and then it became almost quiet. During those times she could hear the personal noises of those people; a sneeze, a cough, a fart, or a sailor standing on the deck above her, urinating into the sea. Sometimes alongside of her she smelt and listened as one of the women or a child used the bucket they kept in their space. That's what it was, not a cabin, a room or a cell, just a tight space where they had to spend most of their time.

White sails filled with wind as the ship sailed west; scrubby hills on the right, countless waves moving into the land on the left. Three Aboriginal women sat in the sunshine out of the cool wind. The two huge dogs walked on the deck but kept close to the women. A young pup stood next to Merindah who held a rope attached to the pup's neck. The pup gripped the deck with her young claws each time the ship rolled; her dark eyes looking questioningly up to the woman holding the rope. From the other side Sally smiled and patted the pup's head.

'Don't let her loose yet, let her watch the old dogs. She'll get used to the ship soon.'

'Will I get used to it too?' Merindah asked as another green slope of water approached.

'Soon.'

Merindah breathed in sharply; something moved in her tight belly. Both anxious and excited, she put a hand to the spot.

The ship anchored off the north side of Kangaroo Island. Men took two whaleboats into the shore and returned with bags of salt. It took two days and many trips with the boats to bring the salt aboard and find space to store it below decks. Everything and everybody leaned in a little closer to each other.

Merindah heard the Captain talking to Bill Bryant.

'If you and some men stay somewhere killing seals Bill, you'll need salt. There's not always salt where there's seals. Now we're prepared.'

'We've got to find the right place first,' Bryant said. 'For my plan to work we must have water and soil to grow stuff.'

Merindah glanced at him, *What does he mean?*

As the ship sailed further around the Kangaroo Island coast, the women looked across at the mainland. Small cliffs and hills came right down to the sea; that's how it had been since they left Granite Island. In places great wide trenches reached down to the waves.

'Look! Smoke,' Merindah cried. 'And there's more; there must be people there.'

'None of your lot on the island though,' said a sailor who heard her talking. 'Only women that the white men took there. Those men aren't very nice.'

Merindah noticed Ned further along the deck, remembering what Sally had told her about him and Addis. She thought of Yara and Warri. *And you're all nice men?*

'No, you're not all nice men either,' she muttered as the sailor walked away.

Four sailors rowed Captain Harris and Bryant ashore in a whaleboat. Men on the island had seen the ship and met them on the beach.

'Some of us have been here for twenty years,' one man told Bryant. 'Come to my place I'll show you what we have to trade.'

The wild man reeked like an old stale animal skin.

Bryant kept his distance, *Looks and smells as if you haven't had a wash or changed your clothes for twenty years.* He carried the two pups and followed the ragged clothing, filthy scruffy hair, black stained teeth, and that awful smell.

The man walked barefoot along a track leading Bryant and the Captain to his rough camp. Two untidy Aboriginal women were moving about, and three grubby half-cast children sat playing in the dirt.

'Most of us keep two or three women each. Got some from the mainland over there, and we brought others with us when we first came.'

'Are the Americans still here?' Captain Harris asked.

'Not now, they come and go, been coming here for twenty years. They even built a small ship here once. They sail right back to America, take the oil and skins back. One ship here last year headed off to China with oil and skins.'

The men living on Kangaroo Island were more like farmers than sealers and whalers. They grew vegetables and crops on their small farms scattered along rivers and creeks where there was fresh water. They kept animals to trade with the whaling and sealing boats that came to the area, and killed many wallabies and kangaroos, trading their skins to passing ships. The Captain and Bryant traded the pups for goats. They purchased more pigs, grain and vegetable seeds.

'What would they need money for?' Bryant asked the Captain as they were rowed back to the ship.

'Buggered if I know, they seem to have all that they need, even make their own grog one of them told me, and three women each.'

'Not sure about the three women each bit,' Bryant said. 'But it could be a good life, that's what I was talking to you about.'

'Yes, but you need to find the right place, it's got to be somewhere where our ships go past.'

'Yes,' Bryant nodded, 'but it must be an island.'

'Be best, I agree.'

With the new goats, pigs, seeds and grain loaded, the ship sailed along the east coast of the island; it was then that they realized how big that island was.

'Look here at Flinders chart,' the Captain showed Bryant. 'This is where we're going.'

'Imagine the seals that would be there,' Bryant commented.

'We may find that there're men at some of these places already. We'll check out those islands, may leave men there, and pick them up on the way back.'

'How'd it be, if we left that bloody Ned here somewhere?' Bryant suggested.

'I know what you mean, but my bosses seem to want him around; they think he has knowledge of these waters because he was with the Americans.'

'The Americans were probably glad to get rid of him.'

'Yes.'

The ship left the shelter of Kangaroo Island and once again sailed into the ocean swell. Captain Harris told them that land on the starboard was the mainland, then a large gulf before more islands and then the mainland again.

Merindah marvelled at the expanse. She watched as dolphins escorted the ship. They darted and dived, only to reappear in a different place.

'Wherever we are going,' she said, 'they are coming too, they must be; they are always with us.' As it became dark on the second night out from Kangaroo Island, Captain Harris had the ship steered out to sea away from the reefs and small islands that he could see on the chart. The sky went black in the west as the sun slipped towards something that Merindah could not clearly identify; more clouds, an island, or hills on the land? Whatever it was, the Captain wanted to keep away; the ship turned and headed south where the chart showed clear ocean.

'Why don't we stop here tonight?' Merindah asked Sally.

'The ship can't just stop like that, it must keep moving.'

The wind turned and blew strongly from the west; they needed to steer almost directly south.

'We are heading out into the Southern Ocean,' the Captain told first mate Hugh Byron. 'There'll be big seas, but at least we know that there're no islands or reefs.'

'That's what the charts say,' the mate said. 'I hope they're right, it's black as a dog's guts out there now. Can't see a bloody thing.'

'You just keep her up the right way and we'll see where we are in the morning,' yelled Captain Harris as the wind shrieked through the riggings.

'I had sail brought in, only left enough on to keep her stable,' the mate yelled back.

'Good, keep her like that, this is going to be a rough night.'

As the ship heeled over and tossed in the ferocious weather, Merindah recognised the pain.

'I think it's started,' she told Sally.

Sailors had secured the hatch shut above the women's place. As the three women and two boys sat in their small damp, dark wooden box, light from the small oil flames flickered and made faint eerie shadows on the timber planking. Each time a wave broke over the ship, water washed along the decks, seeping into even the smallest openings.

'You've picked a bad time,' Sally said. 'I don't think we can even get out of here to get fresh water.'

As the ship headed south away from land, Merindah felt the familiar rhythm of labour pains. Her baby was on its way, she had experienced it before; she prepared herself. Sally tried to open the hatch to get fresh water and other things to help. But sailors had fastened everything and made all the hatches as watertight as possible. All the women had there with them, was a little drinking water, skins they slept on and a few rags, which were their clothes. There was the bucket for their body wastes, which was in danger of tipping over into the already soaked floor of their cramped space.

This is where Merindah prepared to give birth to her baby. Two candles each burning in a clay pot of whale oil jammed into a wooden ledge threw a dull light around the damp and heaving space, now their prison. Jilly tried to calm her two children, she huddled them both together on sealskins stretched out on one small bench, only knee-high above the floor where water sloshed about as the ship rolled, rose up, then slid down the swell.

The water that Sally and Jilly stood in attacked them from every angle. Merindah lay on another wooden bench. The skin under her became wet from water splashing around; one moment over the women's ankles, next rushing away to the other side, before coming back around their feet again. Cracks in the floor allowed some water to escape and go down further into the dark spaces below where boys would work the pumps to lift it out. Sally dragged the waste bucket into a corner and tried to jam it there.

'Perhaps this may drown some of the rats,' Sally tried to relax Merindah as she caught a gasp of the foul air between sessions of breathtaking pain.

'We must keep those candles burning. Jilly, you kneel here by her, don't let her fall off the bench, the floor is dirty, and wet.' Sally tried to push all their tattered clothes and skins into higher places where they would not become soaked in the sloshing water. A huge wave washed right over the ship as it drove down into the black angry sea. Merindah shuddered when streams of water found their way through the cracks in the deck timbers and the hatch.

Hour after hour the ship ploughed on. The few scanty sails that they had set allowed the helmsman to keep the bow pointing in the best direction to avoid the ship lurching over on its side.

Although Merindah felt cold, she was perspiring.

Jilly knelt; her knees in the water as she held Merindah on the bench. Her children were at last asleep with a piece of old rope around them, securing them onto the bench that they shared.

In the early hours of the morning the storm eased off a little, the wind screeching through the rigging became marginally quieter, and the women heard the ships bell for the first time in many hours. Soon weak rays of the morning sun seeped through the cracks instead of cold sea water. Merindah used the last of her strength to help her baby arrive in a world of slopping water, spilt body waste, wet skins and countless stenches. Sally and Jilly had no choice; they had to clean up Merindah with the dirty sea water that moved back and forth across the floor. And then wipe her and the baby with their old clothes that they had kept a little dry.

Tears of joy and fear ran down the young woman's cheeks as the baby suckled from her breast. A damp animal skin covered mother and baby.

Jilly's two children had woken with the noise of wind in the rigging and the young woman's cries. In the dull morning light, they watched their mother and Sally shivering together, hunched over an animal skin that moved and sobbed. They heard the sound of a baby with an uncertain future, testing its lungs for the first time.

Suddenly a sailor opened the hatch. Weak sunlight fell into the wet space like a bucket of water pouring into a hole in the ground. All the little hidden spaces came into the morning. Dark corners seemed to sulk away and hide, waiting to return again the next night. Someone passed food down to the women. Merindah hunched across the skin on her lap as if she were hiding something. She was.

'Will they take my baby away?'

'We don't know,' Sally answered. 'They're all very busy now, putting things right after the storm. But you can't hide the baby here for long; we must get you out of here when the sun warms up. Get you dry and try to clean up the mess in here or it will make you and the baby sick.'

Jilly stood on the ladder with her head and shoulders above the swaying deck. 'Captain Harris is coming this way,' she said.

Merindah cringed; she pulled the skin over her baby again and hunched forward.

Chapter 11 - William Bluff

What is the value of a life?
To preserve a life is to give hope.

After being forced out of Spencer Gulf by the strong storm front that came from the west, the Belinda sailed southwest with a brisk south-east wind.

Captain Harris sent Sarah out and called the four mates to his cabin. 'If you look at this chart, you'll see that the storm blew us out of the gulf. I had instructions to investigate these islands and other places at the bottom of the peninsula. But we are well past those islands now, and the wind is favourable to take us west. West is the main aim of this trip. We could examine those islands on our return, or another time. But, if the wind is favourable, we may still be able to check out these bays at the extreme south tip of the peninsula.'

The Captain pointed at the chart again. 'We will be passing there tomorrow or the next morning at the rate we're travelling now. I also have instructions to investigate these other islands on the west side of this big peninsula. We'll do that before we head across the Bight to Middle Island.' He checked if his mates were paying attention, 'Is there any questions? Well, that's the plan, but as you all know, sailing depends on the winds.'

The Captain also reminded them of his instructions to leave a gang of men at a suitable place to carry on sealing. These men would be picked up on the return from Middle Island. If the place seemed promising men would be left there for a longer period.

Back at their respective tasks the mates got the ship in order after the storm. The wind changed, and the ship sailed northwest toward the tip of Eyre Peninsula. Without the charts drawn by Matthew Flinders that had only been available for about ten years, the ship would have been sailing into unknown waters.

A cold windy day with periods of sunshine allowed the women to clean out their cramped space. Sally and Jilly washed the floor with clean salt water and carried buckets of dirty water up the wooden ladder to throw over the side. They hung the skins that they needed for warmth up on deck; they would take days to dry, taken up and down the ladder each day. Their scant clothing, which was really rags cast aside by sailors, dried quicker after being washed in clean sea water then rinsed in a little fresh water. All the men were too busy with tasks on the ship to even notice the baby.

Jilly's man came to visit. He peered down the hatchway and saw the women were busy and went back to his duties. The Captain walked past several times during the day, but as usual took no notice of the women.

Merindah did not have the strength to climb the ladder that first day, but she moved cautiously around the space as the other two women cleaned and dried things out. Whenever she heard a sailor walking near the hatch, she covered her baby with whatever skin or clothes she had at hand.

Bryant talked to Sally briefly when she was on deck. The Captain's woman, Sarah, came to visit the women; she stayed and

126

comforted Merindah and held the baby.

'No need to tell the Captain yet,' she said. 'He's too busy with other things now,' she assured Merindah.

The cook had the stove going and for the first time in two days there were hot drinks. There were still fresh vegetables and a little fresh meat from Kangaroo Island. Everyone aboard the ship enjoyed a hot stew.

As Sarah left the galley with a pot of the stew for the other women, Chief commented. 'We'll be back on salt meat and ship biscuits soon. Oats for you and the Captain in the mornings though, and a little milk that the boy gets from the goat each day.'

Sarah knew that the Captain and the mates received better food than the rest of the crew, and the other women sometimes had even more basic food than the sailors. She was privileged to be living in the Captain's cabin. Although, she had to keep well away when he had other men come there. She would go out on deck, sometimes to the other women.

Late that evening Sarah came back to visit Merindah, she brought some oatmeal with a little hot milk that she persuaded the cook to give her.

'I told him I was feeling ill. He's easy to fool,' she smiled. 'I will bring you more in the morning. I must go back; the Captain will be looking for me.'

As they ate Sally and Merindah chatted quietly. 'I worry they'll hear the baby crying tonight.'

'Try not to worry. You need to eat this; you need more of this better food,' Sally told her. 'Perhaps we could ask Bryant for more of those vegetables that he got from that island, that's what you need now.'

'I don't think I want to see Bryant, or him find the baby. I'm afraid he'll take my baby away, I couldn't bear that again--.'

Sally nodded.

'Again. Yes, I thought you may have had a baby before, something about the way you knew what was happening last night.'

'Oh, please don't tell him, or anyone else,' Merindah cried.

'Don't worry, it'll be our secret. You may tell me about it another day, but not now. We'll keep this baby dry, warm and healthy, and when Bryant sees it, he may decide not to take your baby away from us.'

That then became Merindah's goal; to have the baby looking well, clean and dry before Bryant came. She now had a goal, and she was going to succeed.

The ship sailed on into the night through a big swell, but rode sound and dry. Merindah fed the baby whenever it woke; she did not want it to cry during the quiet of the night.

At first light, the lookout spotted land in the northwest.

'We'll sail closer, there are places to check here,' the Captain ordered. Another day of watchful sailing past outlying islands brought the ship toward the mainland.

Hugh Byron observed cautiously as the man at the wheel steered the ship closer. The Captain, mates, and sailors stood on the deck. They saw large cliffs and scrubby hills, many wide sandy beaches without shelter. A few small coves sheltered by white or orange limestone cliffs, with occasional granite headlands. As they sailed toward a prominent cape with a high granite outcrop amongst white cliffs, they noticed a snug cove.

'I want to stop here, it looks fairly sheltered for small boats, but I am not sure about ships anchoring here,' the Captain said. 'We're going to inspect this small cove and others in the vicinity. We'll put a boat off, and then sail the ship out to sea if need be, while some of you men investigate with the boat. I want you, Ned and Bryant to take four men and assess what's here. I need to know if it's a suitable place to set up a sealing camp, or perhaps shore whaling in the future. I've been told that whales come along this coast. That right, Ned?' The American just nodded.

'He was meant to be here to help,' Bill Bryant commented to Hugh Byron.

Bill Bryant realised that something was amiss in the women's sleeping place; he guessed there was a baby. Before he left on the trip in the whaleboat he came down to visit the women.

Merindah watched and trembled as his legs, then his body descended into the small damp space, she covered the baby and stared at the floor.

'Let me see what you've got there,' he demanded. She slowly pulled back the skin showing him the babies face.

'Well, what is it?' he said as he lifted the baby out of a cocoon of animal skin. 'It's a boy then. Looks all right to me, alright to me.' Bryant's habit of repeating the last lines of some of his speech was confusing to Merindah at first, but now she had become accustomed to it.

He handed the baby back to Merindah. 'No doubt about his father then. Well, what are we going to do about him?'

Merindah held the bundle of skin and baby tight, tears welled in her eyes.

Bryant did not answer his own question. He started to leave, then turned to Merindah and spoke again. 'You'll need better food, I'll tell the cook to send you some. I need you to be fit.'

Merindah watched his bare feet on the wooden ladder as he climbed out of the woman's place.' She did not understand all that he had said, but wondered if Bryant meant that she needed the better food for herself, or the baby's health.

'Of course he wants you healthy,' Sally said. 'He needs us women to help with the seals, and he just wants the other whenever he feels like it. The children too, they put them to work as soon as they can walk. Jilly's oldest is up on deck now, cleaning out the dog's pen.'

The three dogs remained shut in their enclosure on the deck; Merindah had not seen them since the storm. 'Oh! How did the dogs handle the storm?' she asked Sally.

'They're alright now, but they must have been wet and cold. I gave them some of the last kangaroo bones from that big island.'

'I want to go up to them,' Merindah said. 'I forgot about Inta.'

'You had other things to worry about; she's fine and growing fast.'

'Yes she's already as big as the dogs at my family's camp--.' Merindah stopped when she remembered her family. 'Will I ever see my family again?'

'I don't know. I've never been back to where they took me from. I don't s'pose I ever will. Not much to go back to anyway.' She turned away with tears in her eyes. 'Everything has changed; perhaps we need to forget. We're your family now; this is our life, we just need to make it bearable.'

Merindah sniffed back tears. 'Sometimes it all seems like a bad dream, and I'm lying in the sun on the beach with Yara, I'll wake up soon and take fish back to my mother's camp.'

Sally moved closer to Merindah and the baby.

'No it's not a dream, but I hope things will be better for you than they were for me.'

Flecks of dust sparkled in a stream of sunlight spearing through a gap in the deck. 'It's warmer up there now, I'll hold the baby while you go up and get some fresh air, and visit the dogs.'

'Thank you,' Merindah said and climbed up into the winter sun. The coast was near; she stood gazing at cliffs and long sandy beaches with waves rolling into white sand. The morning sun shone on a headland where two huge pieces of the cliff had fallen into the sea which circled around claiming them. *Now you are mine; you don't belong to that cliff anymore.*

The ship lay anchored out from a small cove; there was protection from the west by the high cliffs, and from the east by a less prominent point. One of the whaleboats from the ship was now sailing into the small sheltered beach.

Sarah came up to Merindah. 'Some men may stay here,' she said. 'We saw lots of seals on the rocks as we approached here this morning.'

'It's very open to the ocean; those waves are big as they roll in,' Merindah said. 'I thought no one lives here, but look, other people are there on the beach. Are they white men, or like us? They are walking along to meet our boat.'

'I don't know.'

After talking to the dogs, she returned to her baby and once again began to agonize over his future.

Late in the afternoon the men in the whaleboat returned.

'There are nine men living in there. Damn Americans,' Bryant told the Captain. 'Some of them recognised Ned, but they didn't seem pleased to see him. I think he may have been trouble when he was with them.'

The Captain glanced at Ned walking down the deck.

'What are they doing there, are they getting seals?' he asked.

'Yes, and whales too, 'til they lost one of their boats and three men.'

'They've got oil then, and skins?'

'Yes, and they're expecting a ship to come soon. I think the one that was at the Bluff. They're short of flour and biscuits and sick of eating seal meat.'

'Tomorrow you can go back there with your dogs, get them fresh kangaroo meat and bring some back here for us. Tell them we'll be back here in a few weeks and we'll check if they're still here. We may trade skins or oil for more food. I bet they would like some of that rum we've got down in the hold. You better take them a taste tomorrow; and some tobacco too.'

Then the captain asked: 'Now, what are you going to do about this baby? I don't want the ship cluttered with any more children. The rumour is, it's as black as its mother. Is that right?'

'Yes, it's black alright, black alright, but it's a boy and I want to keep him. Yes, a boy, and if he grows up to be as smart and strong as his mother, I would like to have him around. Besides, I will be taking my two women off the ship if my plans work out.'

'OK, let's see what we find around the coast to the west. I'll need you to stay on the ship until we come back from Middle Island. But if they're both still on the ship when we get back to the Bluff, we'll leave them there.'

'Now.' The Captain said, 'I want this ship away from this coast, we will sail out and come back first thing in the morning. You can get us meat and see those Americans. I like the look of this coast for whales, but I wouldn't like to leave a ship anchored here for too long, it's very exposed. Perhaps I'll send another boat in with a lead line and check that cove while you are away. These small coves worry me, not much room to move if things get difficult.'

Now Bryant had the Captain's permission to keep the child for a time he felt relieved. If the baby was going to be fed to the sharks, it should have happened straight after birth; something that he knew he would never have been able to do. 'Bloody Ned would though. He probably would now if he had a chance.'

If Bryant's plan did not eventuate, he might be forced to leave Merindah and the baby at the Bluff when they returned there after the voyage to Middle Island. But Bill Bryant was determined not to give up his new woman.

Merindah had eaten well; the baby slept quietly in his warm animal skin. The ship was sailing again, away from the exposed coast, to be safe until daylight. Jilly's man came and took her off to a quiet place they knew well; her two boys were sleeping.

Bryant came down into the dark space, lit by just one oily wick, burning and smoking in a small clay pot. Although Sally was normally part of whatever Bryant did or decided to do, he ignored her. He spoke to Merindah.

'If you, Sally and I don't stay here somewhere, you can keep the baby on the ship until we return to the Bluff, then he must go. Do you understand?'

'Yes,' Merindah said. 'If he stays there, I will too.'

'No you don't understand,' Bryant said. 'You are my woman now and you will stay with me.'

Merindah's eyes searched the bare boards, 'I want to keep the baby with me.'

'Yes, well, that may be allowed, if we--, you, Sally and me, get off the ship. I'll talk to you about that later. Now, what's the boy's name?'

Merindah was confused by all the talk and options, but she understood she could keep the baby for now and would face the challenge when it arose again. She was not letting this baby be taken from her. From his manner she realised that Bryant could be firm but compassionate.

'No name yet,' she mumbled, still searching the rough boards with her eyes. 'I just want to keep him.'

'If I'm the one who decides his fate, I'll name him,' Bryant decided. 'His name is the same as mine, William. Yes, William Bluff. That's where he came from, the Bluff. He will be called William Bluff.'

Feeling satisfied with himself, Bryant turned to Sally and said. 'Now you can come with me, I need company tonight and I don't suppose she's ready for that just yet.'

After two more days in the vicinity of the small cove the Belinda set sail for the west, with fresh meat, and much information about the bays and islands in the area.

Captain Harris wanted to find a place to leave a gang of men killing seals, and then sail to Middle Island. 'I am satisfied with the stop,' he said. 'But it'd be better if the Americans weren't there. When they leave, it will be there for the taking. Although I still wouldn't leave a ship anchored in that small cove, it would be shore whaling without a ship to back them up. You'd need to leave men and boats there and come back for the oil. There may be better places further west.'

The first morning sailing west they came across a pod of whales.

Ned was excited. 'We'll be back here boys,' he said to the men working with him. 'I'll have my own ship one day; you just watch me.'

'You'll probably cut some throats to get it too,' one brave sailor said.

'Yes no doubt, and yours may be the first — no not the first, it's already happened to men who crossed me.' The sailor walked off;

he would say no more.

Fresh meat, vegetables and a little goat's milk that Sarah had sneaked off the Captain's table, were helping to make Merindah and her baby bloom.

'He's a fine baby,' Sally said. 'Even the rats are smiling at him.'

'Yes he is,' answered Merindah 'but do you know what Bryant's plan is?'

'No, but we are both part of it,' Sally said, 'I don't know about you Jilly. Has your man said anything to you?'

'No,' Jilly answered. 'But he doesn't want to be with Ned.'

'Do any of them want to work with him?'

'There are some, but they're like him; bad.'

South and then west that's how the Belinda needed to sail to clear the southern tip of Eyre Peninsula. Ned and Bill Bryant scanned other islands, more areas where seals would be climbing out of the sea onto rocks.

'They are there for the taking,' Ned said, 'but it's a wild exposed coast.'

'Yes,' Bryant said. 'It's wide-open; and I agree there would be a lot of seals around here. Difficult to get at though; difficult to get at. You'd need small boats and brave men and need a sheltered base here somewhere.'

'Must be some protected bays here about,' Ned pondered, 'I'll come back one day and find them.'

'Not this time, we are heading west, got to get to Middle Island and then bring oil and skins back this way.'

'Seems to me oil and skins should be heading west to be sold, not east,' Ned commented.

'We just do what we're told.'

'Not me, I'd like to get my own ship.'

'Who'd you use for crew? Black women?'

'I would certainly have some on board. Anyway, you seem to be set up now with those two you have.'

'You need to treat them right.'

'No you need to train them, keep them in their place, and throw them overboard if they misbehave or get too old. You just go and get another young one and break her in,' Ned announced as he walked off down the deck.

Chapter 12 – Flinders Island

There is so much more than the beach, the big river, and
the Bluff.
We have sailed past the place where the sun goes down.
Will we ever catch it?'

With a south wind the ship made progress along a coast continually
assaulted by huge seas from the unrestricted Southern Ocean. They
sailed for two days without sighting islands or sheltered coves.
Captain Harris had Bryant and the other mates in his cabin,
studying the chart again.

'In a few days we'll be coming to this group of big islands, that
Flinders named the Investigator Group. We'll spend time looking
around there; maybe a week, perhaps longer. If it's suitable, we
may leave men there until we return from the west.'

'What if the Americans are here too?' Ned asked.

'Well I was hoping you could tell me about this area Ned. That's
why we've got you aboard the ship. You said you've been to
Middle island, what about these islands?'

'Nup, haven't been here, I don't think.' The American answered
vaguely.

The Captain moaned, 'Well that's not much help. I think the
Americans are more interested in whale oil than messing around
after seal skins. We need to find places where we can set up
permanent bases to do both. That's what we'll be looking for in this
area, and I'd appreciate your help.'

'Okay.' Ned walked off.

*   *   *

The women and boys stood on the Belinda's deck, captivated as they sailed around a group of islands. Even the hardened sailors were fascinated by the rugged beauty of the small group of islands. The largest island rose straight out of the ocean; great sheets of rock sloped straight into the sea. Seals climbed and lazed on flat rocks and black reefs pounded by waves. The mates searched the coast for a place to anchor, but only found one small sandy beach. Even that had very little shelter.

Captain Harris ordered the ship sail out into open ocean. 'There's another island east of this one, the chart shows that it will have more sheltered bays.'

Next morning they investigated a large flat island; waves surged over reefs and around small rocky islets as they cautiously circled what the Captain said was Flinders Island.

'We need to find a sheltered place on the east coast, that's where the most protection will be from the ocean,' Harris told the mates.

They sailed warily along the east coast again where they had seen two sandy bays.

'We'll anchor in here. Take the sails down, this bay seems promising.'

They anchored in a bay sheltered by striking yellow cliffs to the northeast that protected it from ocean swells.

'I'd leave a ship anchored here for weeks,' Captain Harris said. 'Although this bay would get rough with southeast winds, there's room to move around and get out of here. It's not like those small coves that can trap you in a storm.'

The first morning after arrival men lowered two boats into the water and sailed and rowed along the shoreline. Ned wanted seals; he took a boat northward toward the cliffs where he had seen seals on rocks. He sailed around the point of the cliffs and followed a long beach which was not as protected as where the ship lay anchored.

Ned was keen to find the best places to get seals and discover another sheltered cove. He continued to sail and row close to shore around the island.

Bill Bryant was not in such a rush; he wanted seals too, but had other plans and was interested in this island. With four men rowing, he and Captain Harris took the other boat and explored the two bays south of the yellow cliffs. The smaller of these two bays appeared to be the most sheltered. That's where they landed their whaleboat; in a small cove protected by a rocky point. An exposed rugged coastline continued south from the point.

'This could be the spot.' Bryant told the Captain. 'But water; we must find water before we leave men here.'

A short walk around ashore had satisfied Bryant.

The Captain seemed interested. 'Right Bill, you'll need to come back here tomorrow and have a good look around.'

The company that had chartered the Belinda had other ships. Some would be sailing regularly from Hobart Town, or Sydney to the west, where they planned to set up shore whalers and sealers. These long voyages would need places like this to get provisions; water, meat and vegetables. The bonus at this place was the opportunity to get many seal skins, the main reason to leave a gang of men here. And whales would be here in the winter months.

Bill Bryant knew of those plans, and he envisaged that other companies, other ships, would be sailing through this area. He sat in the whaleboat as it took him and Captain Harris back to the Belinda. *This may be the right place; but I need to find water.*

Bryant went to see his two women. He told them he would be going ashore again the next day; he wanted to investigate the island thoroughly.

Merindah and the other women sat on the deck in the winter afternoon sun.

'How long are we going to stay here?' Sally asked Bryant.

'Don't know yet, maybe a week. If there's water near that beach over there this may be the place to leave men killing seals.'

'Be good to get off the ship,' Sally said. 'Too many men here now with less to do, if they start drinking too much rum we don't want to be here with them.'

Bryant agreed, 'I see what you mean, yes, yes.'

He didn't want to leave his women on the ship with unoccupied sailors. The dogs normally protected them but he wanted to take his dogs to the island. He let the dogs out of the pen; Argus went straight to where the women sat, the bitch and pup followed.

'I'll leave Argus and the pup here with you tomorrow,' he said. 'I need to take Dina to the island, we need fresh meat, and she'll easily catch those small wallabies. They're so fearless I reckon I could walk up and club them to death.

Jilly sat quietly with something on her mind. Many men abused and shared their women, but her man, Olath, shielded her, and her two young boys. Olath was a large, strong man, an experienced whaler and sealer, originally from Scandinavia. The Captain wanted him to stay and be the leader of a group of men left somewhere to set up a sealing camp. Jilly wondered if this was the place. Olath mentioned the Captain's intention to Jilly, but she was not to talk about it to anyone else yet.

Ned returned to the ship. He had seen many seals as he went around the island. He wanted to stay there; be in charge and pick the men to stay and work with him. Like Bryant, Ned also had plans. But the Captain did not intend to leave Ned in charge. He knew Ned could be trouble and he certainly wouldn't leave him with men and the company's boats, besides he needed the Negro's information about Middle Island.

Merindah gazed at the white sandy beaches, the snug little bay sheltered by a rocky point where spray burst up into the evening sky as wave after wave crashed into the rocks. *Those waves are trying to tear those rocks away. They charge the point, like a dog with its tail up in the air. Then when the rocks smash it, the wave runs away across the bay. Like a dog when you yell at it, and it scurries away with its tail between its legs, not as brave as it was before.*

Merindah wished to be off the ship. She felt as if she was one of a hundred seeds in a gum nut, bursting to escape, away from the other seeds, to be alone; grow on its own, sprout its own leaves and have its own smells. Not stay there with a hundred different smells all pushed into the rotten gumnut together.

Now the gum nut had stopped and the smells of all the rotting seeds just wafted around. Pigs in their pen were getting fat waiting for a sailor's knife; the goat's skinny kid wanted its mother's milk, but the cook's boy took most of it. The fouls were shut in their coop on the deck; the wind had ruffled half of their feathers out, the waves rolled their eggs away.

Merindah scanned the beach; she would have liked to walk on that sand. *I may get off this ship one day, but if those hens and pigs do, it will be through a sailor's stomach.*

It was a different sensation that night as the ship quietly rose and dipped with the bow into the swell that came around the island. The furled sails were not talking to the light wind; the rigging hanging loose. All the ship's life was at rest, but could spring back ready to meet the wind when asked. Merindah heard the familiar music of waves slapping the beach, and in the distance the boom and crash as bigger waves fought with the rocks.

Once again Merindah recalled her home and the beach where she and Yara used to run; the rocks where they found shellfish. She remembered the morning when she found James washed up on the beach, the days when she nursed him, and the time they had together. Merindah held onto the pendant that James had sent to her, it hung there on her chest to help her remember Alinta and James. – Alinta, what was she doing now? She would be running around playing in the sand, but what of her future. What of all their futures?

Merindah lay quietly on her shelf, with baby William sleeping next to her. *Who knows where each person's voyage will take them?*

Olath came and took Jilly away to the place they knew well. Bryant came and sat with Sally, Merindah and the baby; then he took Sally away. The sailors were noisy because a cask of rum had been brought up on deck; not just the nightly mug that night.

*   *   *

Five men, a dog bursting with excitement, and Bill Bryant anxiously wanting to explore this place landed on the beach in the small bay. They pulled the whaleboat up on the sand and took note that the tide would leave it high, but would float it again when they needed to return to the ship.

'First, we must find water,' Bryant said. 'Although it's winter now, and there may be some water in hollows after rain, we need to find permanent water that'll be here during summer. Those wallabies must drink water, we'll follow their pads.'

After many hours of searching, Bryant became frustrated. Perhaps they should dig? But if they did find water there was no guarantee it would last the summer. He couldn't take that chance. As the short winter day came to an end, he took Dina into the trees away from the coast. Soon each man carried a wallaby back to the boat.

Bryant reported to the Captain. 'Finding this meat was much easier than finding water. The only water now, is on the surface from recent rain. We need to find places where water will last all summer.'

Bryant had been getting water from Aboriginal wells for years when he was working along the east coast. There were no natives living on this island, no signs; no wells or soaks that had been used for thousands of years. Natives inadvertently led white men to water on the mainland, but not here. The women and a few half-caste boys on the ship came from a place where their customs had already been disrupted by white men's intrusion. Then he remembered the only Aboriginal on the ship who may have those skills.

Chapter 13 - Merindah's Island

Alone? Not quite alone.
But so different than being on the ship.

The baby had made Bryant's plan to take Merindah to the island difficult. He wanted Merindah to help him find permanent water, but she did not want to leave the baby on the ship for a day, or perhaps longer. The baby needed milk from her breast.

'No, there's nothing else he can drink yet,' Sally told Bryant. 'You can't take his mother away for a day, what if she can't come back? No, the mother must stay with the baby.'

'Well,' Bryant said. 'He'll have to come with his mother, I need her. You'll need to come too to look after him.'

Merindah stepped onto the small beach. The eager pup ran around in circles as soon as Merindah set her down on to the sand.

Dina was already sniffing around the low bushes, she had jumped from the boat the instant it touched the sand, keen to catch more wallabies. Bryant called the bitch back.

'Not yet,' he told her. 'Later, we'll do that later.' He reached down and patted the dog's head and pulled one of her small black ears. 'You just settle down.'

When Merindah took those first few steps on Flinders Island, she had no idea how a large part of the voyage of her life would be affected by this isolated island, far away from her Mother's camp.

'I'm glad to be off the ship, I wouldn't mind if we stayed here,' Sally commented.

Bryant seemed distracted; he hesitated, 'That may happen, but I need to be sure of some things before I decide, yes got to be sure, be sure.'

The two women glanced at each other, uncertain what he meant.

Bryant pointed to some bushes; he turned to Sally. 'You stay here with the baby.'

Sally carried the baby up to a sheltered place and gathered branches to make a windbreak. The men at the boat secured it with an anchor; they would be making many trips to and from the ship with firewood which was easy to collect nearby.

Bill Bryant used a flint to light a fire next to Sally's shelter.

He was impatient; he made a gesture to Merindah, 'Now you come with me girl, I want you to show me where the water is.'

Merindah followed Bryant into the scrub. She had water in a skin, and her net bag that she always carried, containing small tools. Bryant took her into the huge Tea-trees behind the beach. Dina sniffed the ground in anticipation. 'Not today.' Bryant ordered the bitch.

'These wallabies,' he suggested to Merindah. 'They must find water in the summer; we need to find where.'

Merindah had been hunting for small marsupials with her mother. She knew there should be trails here now even though they may be faint.

The pup bounced about between her mother and Merindah, Dina kept sniffing bushes and patches on the ground; Bryant was constantly calling her back. There were wallaby droppings, scats from small rodents and many tracks of small lizards and beetles. Merindah recognised them all.

'No big kangaroos; no emu here,' she told Bryant. 'But lots of small animals, there'll be lasting water here somewhere. See here, these are the tracks you and other men left yesterday, and there's Dina's mark. No footprints of other men; nobody here, just us.'

Bryant and the dogs followed Merindah for hours; through Tea-trees and She-oaks. They saw many wallabies; the dog whined when Bryant held her back, the tiring pup followed Merindah's heels. Birds moved away only when they walked close.

They walked inland onto a rise that gave them a view of the two bays; the odd shaped cliffs to the northeast and the Belinda hanging from its anchor out from the smallest bay. Two whaleboats were being rowed across the bay. Men busy collecting firewood; men fishing.

'Seals,' Bryant commented, 'They should be killing seals. 'Ned said they're all around the rocks out there just waiting to be taken. Well I reckon that'll happen soon, but you've got to find water here before we can leave men here.'

Merindah grimaced when she relived the frenzied killing; the baby seals swimming around in the blood-stained water to find their mothers. She knew it was going to happen here. She had been part of that killing and knew she would be again.

Merindah's breasts were tight; starting to hurt. 'I must go back to my baby, he needs me.'

'You must find the water,' Bryant said. 'Everything else here is good for what I need, but I must have fresh water.'

'After the baby. I must go to him now.' She walked quickly, taking the shortest way back to the beach. Bryant had been following Merindah for hours, her feet were tough; she had not noticed the sticks and odd stone that she had stepped on. Bryant's sailor bare feet were tough after years of walking on hard timber decks, climbing rigging and walking on rocks when he killed seals. He only wore boots when he worked as the blacksmith, with hot coals and iron. But walking briskly to keep up with Merindah had made his feet tender. He let her go quickly back to the baby. The dogs followed her while he made his way alone.

Sally and the baby were next to the fire. The shelter that Sally had built made a cosy space, out of the cold wind. Merindah recognised the smell of shellfish wrapped in seaweed and cooking in the coals that Sally had pulled away from the fire.

Sally was pleased with her cooking, 'That girl Ned brought to Granite Island showed me how to do this with shellfish.'

Merindah frowned and turned away to hide tears. She remembered Yara's ordeal. James, Alinta. The smallest things would revive the memories.

Merindah fed William, wrapped him snugly in a skin and put him in Sally's shelter. They ate the shellfish, and a piece of cold wallaby that Chief had cooked on the ship the previous night.

'Now!' Bryant said. 'Let's go, we must find water today. Captain Harris is getting anxious; either we set men up here, or go on. He wants to know.'

Merindah walked south. Along the coast were low cliffs, and inland was white stony country; less soil, mostly sheets of the white rock with sharp edges jutting out.

Now Bryant's feet were becoming tender; he lagged behind trying to find smoother places to walk.

It was difficult to find animal trails, but she followed one through the low bush. The sun was getting low over the interior of the island; Bryant was becoming anxious, and he wanted to get away from those sharp stones.

'We can't dig a well here,' Merindah said. 'Nor can the animals. There would be no water up on these rocks in the summer.' She stood and studied the area. 'The water must go into and through these rocks when it rains. Where does it come out?' She answered her own question. 'Water might come out of the rocks into the sea. The soil here is different from where we walked this morning; it would not hold the water.' She walked across to the edge of the low cliffs.

'Let's walk back along the water's edge,' she said.
The dogs ran down the small cliff after her; they sniffed around rocks at the tide mark.

Bryant gingerly climbed down the low eroded cliff. He stood watching the dogs. 'We don't want sea water,' he said impatiently.

'I know. See how those rocks are a different colour,' she said to

Bryant. 'I don't think water would go through them, it would run along on top of them and come out somewhere. Look, there's a wet patch in the side of the cliff. There, under that ledge.'

Bryant stepped on round boulders that had been polished by the waves, he walked to the place. Beneath the ledge, water had left a stain as it slipped across a smooth black rock into a small pool. Another trickle of water slowly drained out of the pool and vanished into the sand. Small plants grew in the sand. Not plants that grew in the rocks where the seawater came in, they were obviously growing with fresh water.

He scooped water up in his hand and brought it to his lips. 'Tastes good. Can you find more places like this?'

'I think there'll be more along these cliffs,' Merindah said. 'It's the water seeping through those white rocks. If you look carefully, you'll notice where the wallabies climb down to drink. Not now maybe, but they do in the hot time.'

They followed the rocky shore, back toward the point next to the small bay where Sally and the baby waited.

'There!' Merindah pointed. 'This one's running out faster, and see those animal tracks; this one's well used.'

'You're bloody marvellous!' Bryant exclaimed. 'Bloody marvellous.' The dogs ran up to the pool under a ledge and drank. 'O'kay, It's good water alright, good alright. Empty that skin you have and fill it with that water.'

On their way back to Sally and the baby, Dina ran down two wallabies; Inta joined in the chase.

'She'll soon learn,' Bryant said, pleased with the way that Merindah had trained the pup.

Sally was becoming anxious; there was no boat on the beach.

'Cook that wallaby,' Bryant told her. 'We'll stay tonight. See how you like it here.'

Sally looked at him, unsure what he meant. Merindah did not hear what Bryant had said, she was absorbed with her baby.

Later Merindah lay back and scanned the sky. 'The stars are the same as those at my beach,' she reflected. On the ship it was difficult to see all the stars at once, the masts and sails hid more than half the sky. Lying there on the ground she was able to gaze at them all again, the many groups that her mother had shown her.

Merindah did not remember all the names, but the shapes and the narratives, she remembered them. *I'll tell my children those stories,* she promised herself, as she placed a hand on the little bundle of skin wrapped up snug in the shelter. *Alinta? Yes, I know Yara will tell her the same stories.*

At first she just noticed a glow. Soon Merindah watched the jagged edges of the cliff change shape as the moon rushed into the sky. Moonbeams found the water in the bay.

Merindah's mind was far away, she talked in her mother's language, 'There's a pathway across the water over to those cliffs. It looks like I can run right over there.'

She sat on the beach at that small bay, so far from her home, so far from the ones that she loved. She held on to her pendant as the coals in the fire hissed and made strange ever-changing shapes.

Slowly and quietly at first, the strong haunting sound of the young woman's voice carried across that lonely bay. Her voice grew stronger as the echoes bounced off the cliffs.

Sarah, Jilly and the Aboriginal boys on the ship listened; there was something powerful in those chants, those words. They did not understand Merindah's lyrics, but they could feel the power. Even the sailors stopped to listen.

*   *   *

When men brought a whale boat back to the beach the following morning, Bryant hurried out to the ship to talk to Captain Harris.

'I will come and see for myself. I need to be confident about this water supply before I leave men here.' The Captain announced. He considered for a minute then continued, 'We'll take the other two women and those two young boys to the beach when we go. I'll organise another boat to come and pick up some of this water of yours. Now if we are going to leave men here, we have a lot to do.'

Bryant took the Captain along the rocks under the small cliff. They found more places where water ran out of the low cliff.

'Shit, check this out!' Bryant exclaimed. 'Someone's been here before.' A small rock wall had been built up to hold water in. 'Wallabies didn't do this. And here's an iron peg, and this is a piece of sail cloth and rope. We're not the first ones here.'

'Bloody Americans again,' the Captain said. 'Probably camped in these caves when they were getting seal skins. There are seals here now on the rocks. I think they just camped here, did the killing and dragged the skins out to a waiting boat.'

The Captain did not have the experience that Bill Bryant had working in the small boats around the rocky coast. He asked Bryant, 'Do you think we'd get a boat in here; close enough to load barrels of water?'

'No it's too rough, always too rough! Too risky to bring a boat in here. The water will need to be carried back to the beach, loading a boat will be simpler and safer back there.' Bryant said. 'That's what we can do; water in small kegs that a man can carry, full, back to the beach. We need to find a good one of these outflows as close to the beach as possible. I'll get some men organised. And we need to decide about leaving men here.'

'I've decided,' the Captain said. 'This is the place. We'll leave men and boats here; I'll expect a lot of seal skins when we come back in a few weeks. Now, about that little plan of yours, we need to decide.'

'Yes it might suit me, I'll decide in the next few days. Need to be sure. Yeah, be sure.' Bryant answered.

'Seems to me this is a good spot, now that you've found permanent water.'

'I didn't find the water, my young woman found it, she's bloody smart.'

'Looks fine too, and strong. You got a good deal there. Didn't you swap her for a dog?'

Bryant didn't answer. He was considering all the things he had to organise if he was going to stay here when they returned from

Middle Island.

The Captain announced that two boats and about six men would stay. The ship would return in about four weeks.

Now provisions had to be unloaded and stored on shore to supply the sealers during that time. It was possible men would be left on the island for many months even after the Belinda returned to the Bluff; this could become a permanent base. They unloaded the salt to treat seal skins, barrels of flour, barrels of ships biscuit, dried peas, and of course casks of rum. Then the tools, the knives, axes, canvas for shelters, and other things to sustain the camp.

'Who's staying?' Bryant asked the Captain.

'Olath will be the leader; he can pick out the men he wants. I don't want Ned to stay here; he'd cause trouble and I need the other two mates on the ship. I don't expect these men to be getting whales yet, need more men for that. They won't need a cooper or many barrels.'

'Sounds good to me, good to me.' Bryant agreed.

'Now, what about your plans Bill?' the Captain asked. 'I need you to come west with me now, but have you decided about staying here when we come back?'

'I'm willing to stay here indefinitely; yes, for a long time,' Bryant said. He was normally a reserved man, but now he became a little excited. This place seemed ideal and Captain Harris would assist him. 'I'll need help to set up, and a handful of men left here for sealing. I'd like to keep young Levi with me. If that's all agreeable to you we need to leave more things here now.'

'Yes, the men that chartered this ship want a base along this coast somewhere, and I think this is ideal. We'll take off the things you need, it's no sense taking equipment and animals west to Middle Island, that's not needed there. We're just going there to get seal skins, perhaps oil and check the area out.'

Ned was not happy, he wanted to stay. He approached the Captain.

'Why is Olath in charge of the men? I should do that. He's just a seaman, I'm a mate.'

Captain Harris was firm. 'I make the decisions here Ned. We put you on to show us around those islands in the west and you're coming with us.'

'Hmph.' Ned sulked away. He would make other plans.

The following days were a flurry of activity aboard the ship and adjacent beach. With thirty men working, it didn't take long to build stone yards for pigs, bush timber goat pens and rough poultry shelters. Bryant knew winter was the time to grow things in Australia; he organised men to dig up a piece of ground and planted potatoes, turnips and grain. Most of this he had traded or bought from the men on Kangaroo Island. Those men had also given him advice about what to grow and when to plant.

He also organised men to dig a ditch at the base of a small gully; this would hold water briefly after rain. He placed some large barrels there ready to be filled.

'When it rains,' he told those men staying on the island. 'You'll be able to fill these barrels from the ditch. You'll need to get water from the springs most of the time though.'

Then there were more busy days of unloading stores, equipment and animals. Most of Bryant's blacksmithing equipment was taken ashore; that wouldn't be needed for the short trip to Middle Island.

Merindah, Sally, Jilly, Sarah and Jilly's two young boys camped on the island. With the other women there, Merindah could leave the baby for short periods. Usually herself and one of the other women went exploring in the scrub, and to the beach far from where the men worked. For the first time since she had left her mother's place, Merindah swam without having to avoid white men. She encouraged Inta to swim in the waves. Inta became Merindah's constant companion and the young bitch soon came to love the sea like her keeper. Merindah found bush food which the women enjoyed; she took some to Chief, he was amazed at all the different things that she told him they could eat.

Bill Bryant became more aware of the talents of his new woman. He would like to have been able to stay on that island straight away, but he had other things to do.

He had been spending the nights on the island with the women. At the camp the night before the ship left he decided to tell his two women his plans. He tried to explain. 'We're going on with the ship,' he told them. 'Jilly and her two boys are staying here with Olath. When we come back we're going to stay here, probably with just a few men. We might stay here for a long time. This is going to be a permanent base.'

Although Merindah was not entirely sure what he meant, she did understand that they would come back and stay on the island; she just nodded and nursed her baby.

Merindah remembered what Bryant had said about her baby. 'If we go back to the bluff, you must leave the baby there, but you will stay with me.'

Soon the baby slept in his warm skin on the ground; Bryant went to Merindah. 'Come on, it's time we got together again, I've waited long enough.'

'I thought that would happen sooner,' Sally muttered to the other two women as Bryant led Merindah off.

Merindah relaxed, pleased to get away from the restrained life on the ship.

'Why do we need to go back on the ship?' she asked Bryant.

'I've got other things to do; perhaps get more animals and seeds. Then we'll come back here.'

'When will we go back to the Bluff?'

'Maybe a long time, a very long time,' Bryant answered.

Merindah lay quietly, thinking of Alinta, Yara and James. *Why do I think about James?* Once again, she thought about what Bryant had told her. Did she want to go back to the Bluff, or did she want somewhere safe for herself and William, away from that disorder? Merindah knew that things would never return to the traditional ways.

Stars glimmered in the clear night sky. The four Aboriginal women sat on that peaceful beach, feeling that this could be their last time together. As the moon rose, showing a pathway across to those craggy cliffs, the women started to sing. The men on the ship, seals on the rocks, birds in the trees, the small wallabies, and every living creature nearby stopped and listened as haunting songs reverberated around the bay and into the trees and bushes.

Chapter 14 – Further West

Blue sea; giant waves. Such a small thing this ship is,
bobbing around.
Such a small space, is it possible for men to live pushed
in together like this?
The wind says which way we go each day.
The wires, ropes, and the sails; all talking to the wind.
'Where are you taking us today?'
Is that the land? No, just another island.

They had left in the evening; the sun setting across the island.

Merindah stood on the Belinda's deck clutching William to her
breast as they sailed north. 'What stories you could tell your sister.
Where will this ship take us now, my beautiful boy?'

The island grew smaller as she studied the high cliffs
silhouetted against the orange western sky fade into the evening.
Seals lounged on the rocks, unaware of the ship passing and
ignorant of their waiting doom.

'Bad things will happen here too,' she told Sally. 'Things are
going to change, it's been like this forever here, but I know it'll
change. What can we do?'

Sally stood next to Merindah. 'We can't do anything, this is our
life; we're part of this now. We can't go back. I've helped with the
seal killing; so have you. I'm sure you just block it out, like I do.
Mothers and their babies; we shut out those feelings and help with

the slaughter. We cry the tears of blood but we keep killing because that's our life now. We can't go back.'

Sally stood quietly staring back at the fading cliffs. 'I have nothing to go back to. Have you?' Merindah felt her baby on her chest and thought about what Bryant had told her. Tremors of fear surged through her body, tears came to her eyes.

Sally continued, 'Perhaps we are both better off here. I hope Jilly's' alright left there with those men.'

Merindah's eyes cleared, 'She's got Argus with her. He's her dog, as much as yours,'

'I miss having him with me.'

'We have Dina and Inta. Inta loved helping to catch all those wallabies before we left.'

'Yes, we'll be eating wallaby meat for days, and we'll salt some.'

'And we still have the goat; just that little milk is good for me and the baby.'

Days passed slowly. The Belinda was a very small lonely speck on the ocean sailing across the Great Australian Bight. The sailors had seen other islands as they sailed west, but did not stop to investigate. Captain Harris had decided they needed to sail straight to Middle Island. There was more room on the ship now; six fewer men on board and fewer animals. Only three whaleboats remained on board; the other two were left at Flinders Island with Olath and his team.

Without Jilly and her two young boys, Merindah and Sally had extra room in their space, but Merindah did not like to be shut down in that cramped damp place. Between the periods of rain and small storms that buffeted the ship she took William up on deck in the winter sunshine and fresh air. She often took the baby to the galley and proudly showed him to Chief. The cook was always pleased to see them; he was a very friendly man and gave Merindah extra food.

Bryant regularly took Merindah away to a quiet place on the ship. Sally now out of favour with the younger woman over her pregnancy and childbirth. Merindah did not resist Bryant; she accepted it as her obligation. He was much more understanding and considerate than the wrinkly man.

The ship made slow progress, having to tack in different directions, to make use of the west wind. There were no islands but occasionally they could see cliffs shrouded in haze.

'We'll keep away from there,' Captain Harris told the mates.

'Have you been across this way to Middle Island?' he asked Ned.

'Not this way, we stayed at Middle Island for a while. After that we sailed further south than this, straight across to Kangaroo Island. Later I got to Hobart Town on another ship.'

The Captain assumed that that was all the information he would get from the American at that time. He addressed his mates, 'We should be at Middle Island in a few days. We may find men already there, if there are, we may be able to buy skins, or trade for flour and rum. I know it's been a rough trip west, but when we come back across here, sailing should be better with the west wind behind us.'

Hugh Byron gestured toward the north. 'It's that south wind I worry about. We need to keep away from those cliffs.'

'Yes,' they all agreed.

Captain Harris continued, 'There's a hundred islands and hundreds of reefs where we're going, that's my biggest concern, we need to be extra careful.'

'Sounds interesting, who counted them?' first mate Hugh Byron asked.

'Well, Flinders did, so I hope these bloody charts they gave me are reliable. I'm not taking any chances.'

The Belinda tacked across the Bight. The little ship dipped and rose; the sails were soaked. Rain ran down onto the deck and slopped around as the ship rolled. Even on the days when it did not rain, the wind remained bitterly cold. The weather kept Merindah in the small space below deck, but she and William were both well.

They had eaten the fresh wallaby meat days ago, now they ate salted meat and ships biscuits again. Once a day, a stew of sorts, with salt meat and the smallest amount of vegetables, boiled until the cook judged it edible.

Fifteen days after they had left Flinders Island, they sighted a pod of whales, and soon after small islands appeared on the horizon in the west.

'That's the start of the Recherche Archipelago,' the Captain told the mates. 'Now we need to find our way through to Middle Island. It's the largest of this group, and the chart shows that it has a good anchorage. But we need to be cautious everywhere here.'

'What are the chances of men being here already?' second mate Muller asked.

'It's possible. These islands have been known about for a long time, even before Flinders. I've no doubt that there has been activity here, sealing and possibly whaling. What do you think Ned? You've been here before.'

'I told you, we just spent a short time here, and then sailed straight across to Kangaroo Island.' Ned said.

Bryant wondered why the Captain had Ned aboard if that was all the information he would give. And what did a 'short time mean, or why?' Bryant knew if there were many seals, the Americans would have left men there.

Captain Harris ignored Ned and talked to the other mates. 'Well we've already seen whales, now we need to find out where there are good places to set up a shore party. Must be fresh water and fire wood close by. We also need to know about the local natives. But first we'll find a safe place to anchor the ship.'

'One good thing about islands; at least sometimes they give shelter from the wind. But, the surrounding reefs are usually the problem,' Muller commented.

They anchored the ship in relative shelter behind a small rocky island without any beach.

'Most of the islands here are like this,' Ned uttered, but the Captain had flinders chart; he ignored him.

Early next morning, Bryant stood in the stern of one of two whale boats that had been lowered; first mate Hugh Byron and Ned were aboard the other.

The ship remained secure at anchor. Captain Harris did not want his ship moved until they found a passage to Middle Island and the safe anchorage.

The whale boats easily scouted around the islands, rowing and sailing with the usual cold brisk south to southwest wind.

Hugh Byron enjoyed the chance to get away from the ship; Ned was steering that boat; he took a different course than Bill Bryant. Ned seemed to be searching for seals and small coves. Hugh had inspected the Captains charts, he wondered if Ned was going the right way. But Hugh was also interested in the possibilities of the area.

'I can see there could be a whaling station here, Ned. And seals, look at the islands, reefs and rocks. Just need a sheltered bay and this place would be ideal. But it's a long way from Hobart Town. Now where's this big island and the place to anchor the ship?'

'Not far now, I must've took a wrong turn back there.'

But Ned was scheming; he stood steering the boat, thinking. *If I get some men and a couple of boats, I would stack up seal skins to sell. Soon ships will be coming here to trade. I bet there are women on the mainland in there. Bring some out here, a man would be set.* All Ned needed was one or two whale boats, and men to join him and he would be gone, off the ship.

Hugh watched Ned; he seemed preoccupied. 'Which way you taking us now, Ned?'

Ned continued to gaze about but waved his hand vaguely. 'That way.'

Ned pulled the big oar across to steer the boat in that direction.

Hugh shook his head. *Yes, that way. - Arrogant prick.*

Bill Bryant had studied the Captains chart too and sailed his whaleboat directly to where he considered the big island would be. Early in the afternoon he noticed a sail. It was not Hugh, but another boat similar to theirs, sailing toward the largest island. Bryant followed the boat in to shore.

Surprised to see Bryant's boat sail into the bay a straggly group of men gathered on the beach.

'Where the bloody hell did you come from?' one of the men asked.

Bryant explained that his Captain had sent them to find a safe passage into the shelter of the bay.

The men told Bryant that a ship had left them there to kill seals. The small group of men lived at a rough camp in shelter above the beach. They had two whaleboats.

Bryant spotted native women at the camp. 'How long have you been here?' he asked the scruffy men.

'Lost track of time, not really sure,' one answered. 'But there's been two summers. You know when the seasons change here. We struggle for water in the summer months.'

'Do you want to buy or trade seal skins?' another man asked. 'We've got a stack of skins.'

'Possibly,' Bryant said. 'We could trade for flour and rum. I'm hoping to get some pigs somewhere. You got any?'

'Did have, ate them all the first summer; too hard to get water for them. Now we eat seals or wallaby if we can catch them in a snare.'

'Well, if there are wallabies here I'll catch them with my dogs.'

'When we first got here, they were easy to catch, but now they're more cunning. I guess they worked out we weren't going to just scratch their ears,' a dirty sealer smirked. 'The flour sounds good, the rum even better. Since our flour ran out we've been grinding up roots and berries, I reckon we'd all be dead, or sick with that scurvy thing if the women here didn't show us how to do that.'

The Belinda's other boat sailed into the beach; Hugh Byron, Ned and their men came ashore. As the groups of men met and talked, Bryant noticed some men from the island were ignoring Ned. Ned seemed edgy.

'Yes they look good,' Bryant said when the sealers showed him their heap of skins. 'I'm sure our Captain will be willing to trade. How did you salt them?'

'There's all the salt we'd ever need,' one of the men said. 'Just over there in a big dry lake; well, it's dry in the summer.'

'That's ideal, ideal. There're trees here too; this place would be good for shore whaling; just what our Captains' looking for. The thing is, we need to check out the anchorage. Yes the anchorage.'

'Yeah, the ship that left us here, told us it was coming back to do whaling, but it hasn't returned. It was a Yankee ship, and there was trouble with the crew. That big Negro on your other boat; some of our group recognise him. He might be trouble. How'd he come to be with you?'

'Our Captain put him on, to use his knowledge of new places, but we'd sooner not have him around, he makes trouble.'

'Maybe more trouble than ya think!' the other man suggested.

Next morning the Belinda carefully sailed into the bay on the north side of Middle Island.

Captain Harris was pleased. 'Okay, this is a good anchorage. It would be difficult getting in or out of here if the wind was against you, but I guess that's the same in many places, just got to know what you're doing.'

A whaleboat took Merindah, Sally, Sarah and William into the island; the women were pleased to be off the ship. The native women at the sealers camp were very timid.

'Just like the other places,' Sally said. 'Same as us, taken from their people, shared amongst these white men. Come from the land over there, I s'pose, it's not far. I can't see any babies here though.'

Merindah held her baby tight and grimaced; she tried to talk to the Aboriginal women. The women talked timidly in their own language, which was different from Merindah's or Sally's. Merindah tried to talk to the women in her broken English; she asked them where they had come from. The women shrugged. 'Long way, long way.'

Captain Harris arranged to trade barrels of flour, tobacco, kegs of rum, and money for sealskins. He wondered what these sealers would do with money.

Bryant took Dina and Inta with him and soon had wallaby meat for the ship and the sealers.

The Captain had instructions from the men who chartered the ship to examine the islands further west. Although reluctant to leave the safe anchorage, he told the mates to prepare to leave in two days; or sooner if the wind was suitable to sail.

Bryant had seen Ned talking intently to some of the sealers on the island, and three men on the ship seemed uneasy. He reported his concerns to the Captain.

'Ned's trouble, we'd be better off without him,' the Captain said. 'And Addis seems different, as if he has something on his mind. We've needed him to work on sails and keep order with the stores. He does his job, but doesn't get on with the rest of the crew. And I'm afraid he has too much of a fondness for young boys.'

Captain Harris lay in his bunk, worrying about the trip further west. Blurred stars glowed softly through a small frosted glass skylight.

'I'm going out on deck,' he told Sarah, who had shared his bunk. 'It'll be light soon and we'll be leaving here first thing.'

As he walked out on to the deck he saw two men at a whaleboat lowered level with the deck. At first he assumed they were sailors on watch doing some maintenance, but something seemed amiss. They were talking quietly and putting things into the boat. Further along the deck in the misty morning light, more men sat quietly smoking and seemed to be unaware of the others. Two more men approached the whaleboat carrying a large sea chest between them.

'What are you doing there?' Harris demanded as he came closer. Surprised, the two men dropped the chest and turned to see their Captain standing there in the morning gloom.

Captain Harris recognised his third mate. 'What are you doing Ned?'

'We're takin' this boat and we're stayin' here.'

'You can go. But you can't take that boat, and I need those other men on this ship.'

'They're coming with us, and we're takin' this boat,' Ned declared.

Addis came out of the hold where he lived with the sails; he dragged young Rebus by an arm.

'I don't want to go with you,' Rebus cried.

'You're coming.'

'What's going on here?' The Captain demanded. 'Are you in on this too?'

'Yes, and I'm taking the boy.'

'I won't let you do this,' Captain Harris shouted.

'I think you will.' Ned pulled two pistols from his sea chest and pointed them at the Captain.

'This is mutiny!' Harris fumed. 'Leave the boy; you can't force him to go.'

'The boy's mine,' Addis growled.

But Rebus broke free from the big man, he ran to the other side of the ship, and jumped overboard.

The yelling woke Merindah; she stood in the shadows watching. She ran to the side, jumped into the water, and kept Rebus afloat against the side of the ship.

On deck, Addis had lost his prize; he sulked behind Ned and the other three men.

'I told you, this is mutiny, and you'll hang for this,' the Captain warned.

'Never,' Ned replied. 'We're joining some of the sealers on this island and we're goin' to take one of their boats. Those other men in there are lucky we're leaving them a boat.'

The Captain couldn't stop the five men. They put Ned's sea chest in and lowered the boat into the water. They hastily climbed down the rope ladder; Ned went last, still with the pistols pointed at the Captain. The men started rowing the second Ned stepped aboard.

Hugh Byron and Bill Bryant had heard the yelling and rushed up on deck.

Hugh shook his head. 'That bastard! I knew he was up to something. What are we gonna do now?'

Harris considered what action to take next. 'They've got at least two pistols. We've got muskets, and two cannon, but we can't take the ship around these shallow beaches; it's too risky to move the ship until daylight. Anyway a whaleboat can go many places that we can't. Those other men on the island know their way around here, and he may have powder and other weapons in that chest. I don't really want Ned back, and we don't want those others, now we know that they're with him. I do want that bloody whaleboat back though.'

In breaking daylight on a misty wintry morning, Hugh Byron, Bryant and the fittest four sailors were in a whaleboat, far behind Ned and Addis. They watched as the stolen boat sailed towards the sealers camp. As the boat approached the camp there appeared to be an argument on the beach. Four men ran to one of the two boats there, pushed off and rowed out toward Ned's stolen boat.

With their sails raised, the two boats turned and sailed toward a rocky point.

As the deserters' two boats passed Hugh Byron's boat, Ned pointed both pistols at Byron and his crew. He fired them both. The birds in the peaceful bay rose, screeching, from the beach. Bryant only had time to fire one musket shot back, but it was hopeless. The whaleboats soon sailed out of site.

Bill Bryant, Hugh Byron and their crew went into the beach. Hugh spoke to the remaining six sealers.

'We couldn't stop them,' Hugh said. 'Where d'you think they're going?'

'There's so many islands west of here you'll never find them,' one of the men said. 'He's been organising this ever since you got here. He tried to do it when he was here before, but couldn't get men to go with him. Those others joined him now because they think we're never going to be picked up from here. First thing they'll do when they find a place to hide out is, go to the mainland and get some women; cause trouble in there with those guns.'

Then another of the men said. 'His name isn't Ned; it's Jack, and he's no good, you're best rid of him.'

'Yes,' Bryant said. 'But we want that boat. Now we've only got two.'

'And we've only got one,' a sealer said.

Merindah had helped Rebus back onto the ship. Addis had been molesting the boy; he had kept him in the sail hold away from the other men. He would need careful treatment to recover from the big man's abuse. Merindah took the young boy to the women's place on the ship.

Captain Harris accepted the loss of the whaleboat and still wanted to carry out his instructions. To sail around the group of islands, search out safe anchorages and features like firewood and fresh water; and assess the number of seals there.

The sealers told him about another large island further west. That island would now be the ships most westerly destination after which they would return to Middle Island and pick up sealskins before heading back east across the Bight.

A steady east wind blew, ideal to sail west again. Men set the sails, raised the anchor, and the Belinda sailed further west.

'Only a few more days,' Captain Harris announced. 'Then we'll be out of this bloody maze of islands.'

Merindah and the other women saw more rocky islands, few small sandy beaches, and waves breaking on the many reefs. A beautiful but treacherous place.

Merindah would sooner be off the ship, tired of sharing that smelly hole with the cockroaches, the rats, and the bugs in the skins. She welcomed the fresh meat and different berries from the island, but she knew that the trip back across the Bight would start soon.

She went to check on young Rebus. He wasn't in the women's place where she had settled him. She found him at the place where the sails were kept. Rebus was agitated and seemed to be searching for something amongst the rolls of canvas.

'What are you looking for?' she asked the boy.

'Oh nothing, just some things that Addis may've left here.' Merindah suspected he wanted rum. She went to find Bill Bryant, but the mates and the sailors were far too busy to be concerned about the boy.

The east wind strengthened, and the ship moved too fast into unknown waters.

Merindah studied the sky as she walked along the moving deck on the way back to William and Sally. 'There is something bad coming from that way,' the smart young woman said to herself, she checked the dogs.

As she climbed down into the women's space she heard men yelling. 'Take sail off; let's take it easy.'

Black clouds stacked up on the western horizon. The Captain ordered the ship to be anchored on the sheltered side of a small island. He was nervous. Although the wind suddenly dropped, threatening black clouds continued to build, completely blocking out the sunset.

The Captain stood on the deck watching with the mates. 'It's calm now, but something's brewing; look at that sky.'

The sun rose scornfully; a narrow band of blue in the east, the wind had returned, blowing strongly from the north-west. Black storm clouds blanked out the rest of the sky.

'Let's get out of here,' the Captain ordered. The wind increased as he spoke, swinging more to the west. With little sail the ship moved away from the island into clearer sea, sailing freely, but forced back toward Middle Island.

By midday the wind had risen to a gale, the black clouds swallowing the sun. The wind flattened the waves to streaming lines of foam but the swell came from the south-east, as always.

Captain Harris was watchful and helpless as his ship sped toward Middle Island; far too fast; the tempest from the northwest kept increasing, and the ship charged ahead. He studied a small island to the west of the sealers camp and considered the best action to get into shelter.

'We must get to the other side of that small island. We'll have protection from this wind. When we go past the east end, come about straight away.'

As they rushed past the end of the small island the mate ordered the ship to come about and turn sharply back to the south. Three men at the wheel forced the rudder across; the Belinda began to turn and then heeled over, the tips of the yardarms touching the water. With so much lean on the ship, the rudder lost its control and the wind drove the ship directly ahead towards the northern tip of Middle Island.

'Bring her back! Bring her back!' the mate yelled.

Even with no sail, a gale like this would have pushed them ahead; they were trapped in the sandy bay; nowhere to go. The ship drove toward the breaking surf and the beach. Then slowly, the brig turned south and came around.

Too late.

The keel dragged on the sand. She ploughed through the surf, each wave taking her further in, harder onto the sand. Suddenly the Belinda ground to a halt, the waves pushed the hull towards the shore, and she tipped back with her deck facing the oncoming waves.

Chapter 15 – Shipwreck

In this foul hole, moving again, tossing and rolling.
Will we die, down in this hole?

Merindah, Sally and William were shut in their foul wooden warren under the deck when the ship struck the sand.

The previous evening, when Merindah was looking for Rebus, she knew that they were sailing towards the setting sun, and past more rocky islands, more sand, and more reefs. She noticed towers of charcoal clouds on the north-western horizon as the sun set. 'The weather is going to change tonight.'

That night as the ship lay at anchor in the lee of an island, Merindah took William up to the deck. The wind had dropped to an eerie quietness. The only noise, waves on an adjacent beach, and the creaking of the ships rigging. The moon and stars above Merindah were hiding away as the clouds moved across, blanketing the entire west and northern sky.

Lightning started; sheets of light first; next angry cracks fractured the burnt sky. Merindah watched; it was like a tribesman's spear gashing through the black sky, it seemed as if her world would split apart. She went back below deck and wrapped William up in his warm animal skin. The two women huddled together with William between them. They were aware of sailors moving about on deck, tying down, or moving loose objects to more secure places.

Later large threatening drops fell, and soon the rain came in quick heavy sheets. With each period of rain, stronger wind came. Rain poured in through the cracks in the deck. The women heard the groans of the cables straining against the anchors and felt the ship rise and fall.

As the first weak rays of morning appeared through gaps in the deck, the two women realised that the ship was moving again.

Shut in, with the hatch closed to keep out sea water as it rushed across the deck, Merindah and Sally could sense the ship charging through the sea. The gale had flattened the waves, but the ship still rode through ocean swell. Their small space leaned over as the men tried to steer the ship, but the wind in the rigging screamed, 'No, you will go where I say.'

The rain eased, but the wind strengthened. Sometimes the women heard men shouting above the shrieking noise. Suddenly their little space turned and leant over further, they fell forward as the rush stopped, then rolled and fell over to the opposite side. The side became the bottom, the hatch on one side and the other side the roof. Their small enclosure lifted then dropped as sea water came in through deck timbers that were now the side of their trap.

Somebody opened the hatch; more water poured in each time the ship rolled before another wave lifted it. As that wave passed, the ship fell on its side again.

Merindah held screaming William firm in his soaking animal skin. She crawled out of the hatch onto the deck which had become the slanted and slippery side of the ship. She clamped William to her with one hand and used the other to clamber up to the railing at the high side of the deck.

Sailors perched on the edge, hanging on to the rail. Some men panicked, others yelled, asking what to do next. Waves kept pounding the timbers as the ship lay with the deck facing the onslaught.

The two remaining whaleboats swung from their davits. Hugh Bryon pointed. 'We should get those boats down.'

'No! Wait!' second mate Owen Muller shouted above the wind.

'If we get them down now, they'll be smashed to pieces. This ship's going nowhere. If we can ride it out, we might be able to get them off without any damage.'

Hugh frowned; then nodded. 'That's makes sense. Let's just get everyone up here and wait.'

The Captain had gone to his cabin to help Sarah. When he and Sarah clambered up the swaying deck to relative safety, he stood holding on and muttering, 'Christ, this is my ship. These people are all in my care. How did this happen? What will the owners think? How are we going to get off the ship?'

Sally had crawled up after Merindah and she now held William. Rebus had somehow scrambled up the sloping deck, he moved across to the women.

The cook had found the women. 'Here let me hold the young fellow?'

Captain Harris left Sarah with the other women and worked his way along the rail to where the first and second mates stood holding on. He held on to the rail and looked back down to the deck of his ship, at the mess of sails and rigging amongst foam and green water. Devastated, he let the mates take control.

Second mate Owen Muller was by far the oldest of the three men, and this was not his first shipwreck.

'What do we do now?' the Captain shouted over the howling wind to Muller. 'Can we get those boats off and everyone in them?'

'Not with these waves. They'd be wrecked in minutes. This storm can't last. See that beach, the tide is high now. When it goes out these waves won't hit the ship as hard. We should wait.'

'But the ship will be left without water to float off.'

'Afraid she's stuck fast Captain,' Hugh Byron said.

Harris grimaced. Perhaps Hugh was right. Although probably not damaged yet, the hull would fast be filling with water; pounding waves weakening the deck. He acknowledged that his ship was doomed. He gaped at the mass of rigging, sails, canvas and debris, all moving back and forth with each lift and fall.

'Is everyone up here?' he asked Hugh Byron.

'I've counted twenty-four Sir, don't think young Jacob is here.'

'What's that woman doing down there?' the Captain yelled.

The dogs were still shut in their wooden box that was fixed to the deck. Merindah climbed back down one of the many swinging ropes. Water washed over the box each time a wave hit the sloping deck and Merindah could not get to the door. The dogs whimpered and begged for help with dark searching eyes. She gripped the top edge of the box and smashed the framework apart with her heels. Dina and Inta crawled and scratched their way up the sloping deck. Bryant and another sailor grabbed each dog by their scraggly coats and held them safe.

'There's someone in the water,' the first mate yelled. 'It's young Jacob. He's in trouble.'

Still half way down the deck, Merindah heard the yelling and noticed men pointing into the thrashing waves. She steadied herself with the rope to see what they were pointing at. She could see the young sailor Jacob being hurled against the deck with each wave. Without hesitating she let herself slide back down in to the churning water and swam across to the drowning boy.

Merindah used her feet to keep herself and Jacob from being buffeted against the deck as she held his head above the surface. She bounced their way slowly across to a rope that hung thrashing around. Merindah held Jacob there while he spewed up mouthful's of sea water and recovered his breath. He was still too weak to climb up to the others, she tied a rope under his arms; men pulled him up the sloping deck.

Merindah climbed alongside Jacob. Nobody noticed the irony of the near naked young Aboriginal woman saving the white sailor.

It seemed like forever that they sat on the side of the ship's hull. Slowly the tide receded, the wind abated and the waves no longer lifted the ship each time they struck. The hull became full of water and sat solid on the sand. But with no movement the waves began to do even more damage to the deck.

Sailors carefully let down the two whaleboats and pushed them around to the sheltered side of the hull.

The three women and William were amongst the first boat-load of survivors taken to the beach. When everyone and the dogs were safely ashore, it seemed that the only casualties were the goat and some ships cats.

One boat returned to see what else could be saved; they found the poultry soaking wet perched miserably in their cage. The pen was unlashed from the deck and brought to shore with the six hens and the rooster still inside.

It was late in the afternoon before twenty-five shocked, cold and wet survivors made their way back to the sealers camp that they had left two days earlier. They found the six men enjoying some tobacco from the Belinda as they sat around watching another seal cooking over sizzling coals.

'What're you all doing back here so soon? We thought you'd be gone longer than this. Did the storm blow you back?' one of them asked.

'It blew us back alright,' Hugh Byron said. 'And now we're here to stay. There may not be any more of that tobacco.' Then he told them about the ship stranded on the beach.

A sad site greeted Captain Harris and the mates when they rowed out to the doomed ship the next morning. Although it was low tide, the ship still lay in ten feet of water. Water and sand filled the hull to the level of the sea. A tangle of rigging, ropes and torn sails still attached to the ship moved back and forth with each wave. Storm waves breaking against the deck had smashed in large parts of it.

'We should be able to salvage some stores from the hold,' the Captain said. 'We'll bring more men and the other boat out; see what we can get off her. Some barrels of food may still be alright.'

Hugh Byron considered the waves still swirling into the deck. 'Most will be spoilt,' he said. 'And it'll be difficult getting anything out with those waves still coming into the deck constantly. It may be days before the sea is calm enough to get a boat alongside there.'

'Perhaps there's another way to get gear out,' second mate

Muller said. 'We could cut a hole in the lee side of the hull; that's sheltered.'

'What! Cut a hole in the side of the ship?' Captain Harris asked; shocked.

Muller shrugged his shoulders, lifted his bushy eyebrows, and opened his hands in expression. 'Well, this ship's never going to float again. And that would let us get stuff out. That's if it's any good.'

'You do what you must. But I'm not going to be here when you cut a hole in the side of my ship.'

Bill Bryant took Merindah and Levi back out to the ship.

As the boat circled around the doomed wreck; Merindah was amazed at how big the ship seemed to be. *Before it was a living thing, but now it's just lying there like a beached whale; dead, never to be free in the ocean again.*

Merindah watched the limp sails being tossed and tangled in the waves. She knew they were the ships heart, its soul. When those sails spoke to the wind, the ship became alive. Now all of that life lay writhing and swirling around in the water.

The wind had talked to the sails; now the sea had drowned them.

They needed Bryant's tools. If they were still where he stored them on the ship, he knew that Merindah would be their only chance of recovering them. Bryant explained where the chest of tools should be. He told her how to open it and explained the most important things he wanted her to get.

Merindah sat in the stern of the whaleboat alongside Bill Bryant, Levi stood in the bow directing the boat away from any floating danger still attached to the wreck. Four sailors sat rowing, facing Merindah and Bryant.

Bryant steered the boat closer to where he hoped his tool chest would still be; the waves lifted and turned the boat sideways. 'Keep those oars in the water, keep the bloody boat straight.' Bryant yelled. He turned to Merindah, 'Are you ready to go?'

Yes, she nodded as she stood and removed her shirt and dropped it on the bench. Two of the rowers gaped at the naked young woman, Bryant yelled again. 'What are you bastards gawkin'at? Watch those bloody waves; keep your eyes on the job.'

Merindah slid over the side and held onto the gunwale.

'You better take that thing off your neck girl; you don't want it tangling up in something down there.' She hesitantly lifted James's pendant over her head and passed it to Bryant.

Merindah breathed deep; then dived.

Bryant examined the metal ornament hanging from a leather strip. It was the first time he had studied the engravings. 'Don't look American to me,' he said as he tossed it onto her shirt.

Constant wave surge pummelled Merindah as she found her way along the submerged deck that lay facing the ocean. Her eyes quickly adapted to the salt water, now she needed to familiarise herself, and find her way into the place where Bryant kept his tools. She had been there alone with him and seen his large wooden toolbox. Now it lay on its side against timbers which had been the side of the cabin but now were the bottom of a water filled cavern.

She surfaced and swam across to the boat, 'I'll need Levi to help me.' She called out to the red headed man waiting anxiously.

Bryant waved a hand, 'Off you go boy, be careful down there.'

Merindah and Levi dived together many times before Bryant was satisfied. 'That's good, yes, good. Leave it, we'll go back now. I'll bring other men out here, but I may need you again later.'

With an axe that Merindah had fetched up from the chest, men cut their way through the hull of the ship, gaining entry to the drenched and flooded stores.

Dull, eerie light shone through the broken deck, and the hole that they had smashed through the side of the ship. The men could see rats scurrying around on the higher places, still above water. Other drowned rats and cats floated amongst debris washing back and forth as water surged in and out. Timber from broken barrels moved in the water. Many barrels were broken, others damaged. Men worked in difficult and dangerous conditions to recover whatever they could. They took the barrels that were still above water level out first. The smaller casks were easier to handle. The large barrels of flour and ships biscuits were more difficult to recover. A sailor was excited when he found a crate of tobacco above the water and reasonably dry. That crate was nursed on the way back to shore.

Merindah and Bryant sat alone on the island that night. Bryant was proud of his young woman, but he still had unanswered questions. Examining her pendant had renewed his doubts.

'That thing around your neck,' he asked. 'You told me it came from an American. It doesn't look American to me. You sure your father gave it to you?'

Merindah stopped breathing; she gulped and swallowed air. He didn't see her face in the moonlight as she held her head low.

'Well.'

'Yes, my father gave it to me, he told me American man.'

'Shit. Did he trade you to the American for the Pendant? Is that where you learnt to speak English? From an American?'

Merindah jumped to her feet, she yelled at Bryant, 'No American, I was the old mans; where you got me from. He gave me to you. I got English words from Sally and Jilly, now from you.'

She started to walk away.

Bryant stood and grabbed her arm, 'Whoa there, calm down. But don't you forget that you're mine now.'

'Yes.' Merindah knew that Bryant would never give her to another man. And now she had also learnt that she would not always be controlled by him. She was finding her strength.

The next day Merindah dived again; she found her way into the Captain's cabin and recovered charts and some of his personal items.

'Although water damaged, they may be of use later,' the first mate told the men. 'Especially the navigation instruments.'

Merindah needed Levi to help drag up the Captain's strongbox; it contained gold coins that belonged to the company. Money to pay sealers for skins; skins that now would remain on the island waiting for another ship to come. Hugh Byron helped another man lift the box onto the whaleboat. 'This box has important instruments that the Captain may need.' Harris had told him to keep quiet about the coins.

Merindah and Levi dived again into the hull of the ruined ship. They got into the sail loft and brought out undamaged sails, needles, tools and twine from Addis's store.

Each day the Belinda became more damaged as the tide rose and waves smashed in more of the decking. Stores and other things became loose and were tossed around in the hull, eventually to be washed onto the beach. The crew gathered whatever was still useful.

A man found the goat's bloated body on the beach.

'No more extra milk for my baby,' Merindah said. 'The dogs will get us all the meat we need, but now I need to find other things.'

Men built shelters with sail cloth to get out of the cold wintry weather. They collected fresh water and killed seals. Bryant's dogs caught wallabies; the women found shellfish and berries. But now, with the Belinda's crew, the six sealers and their Aboriginal women there were almost forty people on the island. The food resources would be tested.

Idle men became bored; it was the still intact casks of rum that kept men patrolling the shoreline, searching for liquid booty. Another crisis threatened the fragile situation.

Captain Harris and the mates had unruly men to deal with.

Each morning Owen Muller and four of the most level-headed men walked the shoreline to recover flotsam from the wreck. Any food that may have been still edible was collected. Timber, ropes and other items washed ashore were heaped to be sorted. Even weeks after the wreck the last few potatoes, pieces of salted meat, ships biscuits and broken crates of ruined tobacco were being washed ashore.

Men occasionally still found a cask of rum on the beach. Merindah and Sally kept the dogs near them; Bill Bryant stayed close to his women, and the Captain to Sarah.

The Captain issued an order. 'Any rum found on the beach is to be brought straight to me. A cask of rum found open will be smashed and the man or men with it will be punished.'

Now men were hiding the casks of rum.

Captain Harris asked Bryant to organise four men to row him over to the small island across the bay.

'There are large birds circling that island, I need to take a closer look,' he told Bryant. 'It may be too early in the year yet, but there may be eggs there.'

Once on the island they could see where the big birds nested. They knew that it would be worth coming back when the geese began to lay their eggs.

Captain Harris sent the men off in a different direction to explore. He took the heavy box of gold coins that Merindah had recovered from the ship. It was wrapped in a wallaby skin, so the other men would not know what he had. Quickly checking again that he was alone, the Captain buried the gold. It was easy digging amongst the loose, smelly sand where the big birds had been scratching. He made a mental map of the place where he had buried the gold coins. Later he would make a sketch on the back of one of Flinders' charts.

Hugh Byron had been keeping count of the days. 'We've been here for three weeks,' he told Captain Harris. 'If these men keep finding rum there's bound to be more trouble.'

'Yes I know. I want to leave here as soon as we can.'

Whenever Captain Harris went to the beach, it was impossible not to see the wreck of his ship being slowly broken up. Each day more pieces washed up onto the beach.

He wanted the wreck out of his site. 'We're leaving this island,' he told the mates. 'We don't know of anybody or any ships to the west of here. The only way out, is to go back east in the whaleboats.'

'Shit, that's a bloody long way to go in those whaleboats,' Hugh Byron commented. 'And it's across the Bight. We all remember what it was like coming west.'

'Yes, but what choice do we have? With the prevailing wind behind us those boats will cover a big distance each day.'

Bill Bryant did some quick calculations as the Captain spoke. 'Shit! It'll be crowded if we all go on those two boats. We can't take the sealers boat; that's all they've got now that Ned, or whoever he is, and those other runaways, have taken their other.'

'Does everyone want to go back east?' Muller asked.

'I'm responsible for everyone aboard my ship,' the Captain said. 'Nobody's staying here.'

Hugh Byron had been counting too. 'What about the women? Will they be coming? That's three more to fit in the boats.'

The Captain wanted to take his woman, Sarah; so he could hardly leave the other two.

'We'll all be going. I want you to get things ready, any flour that's good, and ships biscuits. You'll need to salt down wallaby meat, and load casks of fresh water in each boat.'

'Surely we're not going to take those two dogs,' Muller exclaimed.

Bryant stood firm. 'If I'm going, so are my dogs; they'll get us food from islands or the mainland.'

'Or we could eat the dogs when we run out of meat,' Hugh said.

'Or perhaps we'll eat you; it's happened before. Yes, happened before.'

Preparations began. Anything not needed was taken out and essential stores carefully packed in each boat: One cask of rum, four casks of water, a water breaker full, ship biscuits, salted wallaby meat, half of the precious tobacco, a flint box, a bailing bucket (piggin), another wooden bucket, knives, needles and twine. The Captain's charts and instruments were stored on his boat; a bundle of Bryant's tools on the other. There was little room for men, women, a baby and two dogs.

The remaining casks of rum, damaged food and equipment from the ship were stacked by Captain Harris's shelter.

'The sealers can take what they want from that lot,' Harris told the mates.

Men wanted to take more rum. 'No, only one cask on each boat.'

Merindah watched the preparations with interest, and unease, she remembered the trip across the Bight in the ship; long and rough. Now they were going to attempt to go back in those two little boats. She didn't want to stay there on that island with all those men, or with the sealers. She realised more than anyone, how the food would soon become scarce.

Chapter 16 – Impossible

Too many people in two small boats.
Two specks on an immense sea, following a hostile shore.
This is madness.

Two open whaleboats sailed east following the chain of islands off the coast. Twenty-five people, one baby, two dogs and scant provisions. All this crammed in two small boats, which would each normally hold six men and their gear to kill whales.

Merindah, William, Sally and the two dogs, were in the boat with Bryant and Muller. As always Levi and Jacob were amongst Bill Bryant's crew.

For four days the two whale boats wound their way through the islands. It was still winter, with occasional showers of rain and a biting wind. Pieces of sail canvas salvaged from the shipwreck covered the bow and the stern of each boat to help keep water out. The boats were open only where men would sit to row, steer, and work the small sail. Often, the wind blew from the southeast, not the west as the Captain predicted. During those times, men needed to row continually to keep the boats away from the coast.

They needed more water. Each time they came close to an island the Captain ordered the boats closer to search for a sheltered place to rest. But every island had rocky coasts; far too rough to attempt a landing.

Merindah sat in the bow; canvas was stretched over her and William, Sally sat leaning against her. Somehow the two dogs also squeezed in with the two women. The hopelessly over-crowded boat sat deep in the water.

They had eaten the last of the fresh cooked wallaby meat two days ago; now they ate ships biscuits spoiled with sea water and a few strips of salted wallaby meat. The men thought that the rum would help them keep warm against the cold weather, but they all sat wet cold and irritable. And worse, the Captain barred them from smoking on the crowded whaleboats.

Bryant's dogs had only seal and wallaby skins to eat.

Second mate Muller even complained about that. 'Bloody dogs. We should've left them on that island.'

Bryant challenged Muller, 'Do you want to eat the skins? You'll change your mind when they get you fresh meat.'

The young sailor Jacob sat in the bow of the boat beside Sally; he had become closer to the two women since Merindah saved him from drowning. Six other men took turns at rowing, or just sat trying to keep warm when using the sail. In the stern, also covered with canvas sulked the young boy Rebus. Bill Bryant and Muller took turns steering the boat with the large oar. Whichever man was steering would have to stand out of the canvas, but keep out of the way of the rowers.

Water constantly slopped over the sides of the overloaded boat, and salt spray blew into the faces of the rowers and the man steering. The piggin was continually being used to bail out water.

Bryant knew that it would be impossible to reach Sydney or Hobart Town like this.

'This is madness,' he told Muller. 'We won't get far like this, be better to walk along the beach that's over there somewhere. What's going to happen when there's a storm?'

'This east wind won't last, it'll change to the west, then we'll sail,' second mate Muller said. 'Sailing will be better than rowing two thousand miles.'

Bryant shook his head. 'Madness, bloody madness.'

Bill Bryant was certain that the two boats would never get to Hobart Town or Sydney. He imagined that if they got as far as Flinders Island, they could stay there until a ship found them. But he understood why Captain Harris wanted to get away from the place of the shipwreck.

The Captain now relied on the experience of his first and second mates to get his crew back east. Sarah sat with him in the other boat, also overloaded with men and provisions.

Progress was slower than the Captain expected; the water in the casks would soon be used. They knew that they would need to stop soon to get more water and food. Because it was winter, they expected to find surface water; even on a small island after showers of rain.

The men had been rowing day and night; surely the wind would change soon. Ghostly islands slipped past them as they rowed in moonlight. With no moon to show the way the Captain used the stars to guide them east, while the noise of breakers warned them all of islands and reefs.

On the evening of the fourth day the captain signalled from his boat.

'He wants us to go ashore; there, on this island,' Bill Bryant told Muller. 'I'll run the boat in between those two points, it's sheltered in there.'

That night they dragged both boats up onto the sand in a small sheltered bay. Bryant used a flint to light a fire. For the first time in days they were dry. They dried out their clothes, their rags and skins. The small bushes on the island made it difficult to find good wood to keep the fire burning. But it was fire, warm and drying while it lasted.

'This is the last of the islands,' Captain Harris told them. 'We'll stay here tonight and try to find water in the morning.'

Sitting by the fire, the men were allowed to light their pipes and smoke.

'How'd we keep this tobacco dry?' a man asked.

'That was my job,' said another, 'and I made sure that I did it right.'

It had been four days since they could stand and walk, or even relieve themselves in private, not in a bucket while squashed against another man. They were relieved to be off the boat, warm and dry by a fire. This felt so different from sitting in a crowded wet pit in the sea, continually being blasted with cold salt water, while sitting alongside of another wet stinking body. None of them wanted to get back into the boats.

Each man received a measure of rum, there were only a few metal mugs, and they needed to wait for their allocated portion. On the moving crowded boats, that had been difficult to manage, but at the beach that night each man received an extra measure, a small celebration of having got so far in four days against the wind.

Young Rebus tipped down his extra rum and then became agitated; he needed more. Addis had methodically primed him with rum; it had blocked out the things that happened in the sail hold most nights. The young boy's mind had become a mixture of guilt, confusion and fear. He had soon learnt the best way to deal with that was to drink more rum.

He kept asking Muller for more.

'No, that's your draft boy, no more tonight, sleep while you can. Tomorrow we'll likely be crammed back in that bloody boat. Bodies, shit, piss and dogs.'

'But Mr Addis always gave me more,' the boy protested.

'He gave you too much boy, now you've got a craving for the stuff. Perhaps I won't give you any in future.'

'Please sir, I need it, I can do things for you. Addis taught me.'

'I don't know what you mean boy, go away. I want a good night's sleep.'

The Aboriginal women sat by a small fire, they stared into the small coals and watched the flames dancing. They sensed something exceptional and seemed to mould into the same belief. Perhaps this was the first time any man, black or white, had been on this island.

None of them spoke. Past lives, past people, past places were remembered as they stared into the fire. Dreams, sounds and visions; brief crackling of light branches thrown onto coals, Soft hissing of dying flames, Fizzing squirming embers. Nearby, small waves rolling and slapping sand. Further away, the distant boom of surf on reefs.

Stars glimmered down on the women as they began to sing softly. Haunting rhythm drifted across the calm sheltered bay. The white men sat quietly; they also felt the isolation and the desperation.

Another cold misty morning greeted the forlorn group, damp but not wet. Small puddles of brackish water were nearby, but they needed more and better water to refill the casks.

Men searched for water, Merindah and Sally, carrying William strapped in a sling made from wallaby skin, took the dogs and found food. There were no wallabies on the small island, but bird nests with eggs, shellfish on the rocks, and small bushes with berries. Back near the boats, other men kept a fire going. Someone had killed a seal.

That night Merindah and Sally helped Chief make a hot meal for everyone.

The second night on the island, Bryant took Merindah away from the group. Captain Harris allowed each man an extra measure of rum and some men became rowdy. The rum made Jacob sleepy, and he was soon asleep by the fire. The baby slept in his warm skin next to Sally who sat looking into the coals, with the dogs by her side as always. She didn't see the two men who approached her.

'Bill Bryant has two women, and we have none. You can come with us tonight.'

One man grabbed Sally by the arm and dragged her away from the fire; the other quickly pushed her down and pulled off her shirt.

Sally yelled. 'Dina! Here!'

The dog had stirred when the men first came to the fire. The man above Sally shouted as Dina's claws and teeth found his flesh. 'Get off me, you bastard dog,' he screamed. The other man let go of Sally and ran.

'Stop. Come here Dina!' Sally ordered as she pushed the man away. She fumbled for her shirt in the darkness.

The man held his bleeding arm, 'I'll kill that bloody dog.'

'You're lucky she didn't kill you, I would if I could, I've had too many men like you. You should wash those wounds in sea water, or they'll become bad.'

The man sulked away as Dina followed Sally back to the fire. Jacob sat holding the baby who had woken; he passed William to Sally and put his arm around her. She shook as she leant against the young man.

'I don't want to be taken like that anymore. I'll decide who I'll go with now that Bryant has Merindah.'

She felt Jacob's young body next to hers. *He's young, but perhaps I would have him. I wonder if he'd have me?*

Sally said nothing about the incident when Merindah and Bryant returned to the fire. The group settled for the night.

Next morning there was a man sitting by a fire with rags wrapped around one arm, and deep scratches down his back.

'There must've been a fight last night,' Muller said to Bryant.

'No, perhaps somebody learnt a lesson. Lucky he's from the other boat, it'd be awkward if he was from ours. Dina wouldn't like him with us.'

'What d'ya mean?'

'See the way the bitch is eyeing him.'

'I see what ya mean. Something must've upset that dog.

Wouldn't want her looking at me like that.'

'Might be something to do with Sally; she hasn't said, but I don't think the bastard will bother her again.'

'Talking about bothering,' Muller said. 'That young Rebus is offering himself to me if I give him more rum. Addis certainly trained him. I don't want that from him, I think I'll stop his rum altogether.'

'Perhaps you should. The rum must be nearly all gone any way, and then we can fill that cask with water.'

Captain Harris wanted to prepare for the next stage of their trip.

'We'll stay here one more day,' he told the group. 'Kill another seal; that may be the last fresh food for some time. I don't know if there're any safe places to go ashore along those cliffs on the mainland, and it's a long way to the next island.'

Men found a small supply of fresh water in a rock hole and refilled the casks and breakers. Merindah and Sally found more bird eggs and gathered shellfish. The first seal was almost all eaten; men from the Captain's boat killed another. They cut the meat into strips and placed it on rocks to dry. There would not be time to dry it properly in the cool weather, but it would be all eaten within a few days anyway. The two dogs cleaned up any meat left on the seal bones, and they would have fresh skins to chew on in the boat.

At first light the next morning, with everything prepared for their journey east, men dragged and pushed the two grossly over loaded boats into the waves, the same people in each boat. Raised sails filled with the steady, cold, south-west wind, they headed out into the Great Australian Bight leaving the islands behind. On their port side, stretched an expanse of white beaches with surf rolling in; there was no chance of taking the boats in through those breakers.

That first day they covered a significant distance without rowing, but the wind stopped at night and the rowers started their shifts. Even with no moon the stars provided enough light to show the distance from the shore. When there were clouds, the noise of waves breaking warned them how close the beach was.

The Captain ordered, 'Keep out far enough for safety but close enough to see a place to land.'

Merindah sat squashed in the bow of a small overloaded boat, listening to the dip and splash of the oars, the groans of the men as they pulled the heavy boat through the water. She felt the surge of the boat with each stroke. William slept on her lap as she lay back against the timber side of the boat, gazing through a gap in the canvas stretched across the bow. Her stars all performed in their own position, so familiar, but she could not comprehend just how far she was from her home. She sat quietly nursing her second baby and not yet eighteen years old.

Soon she dozed, imagining she had never left her mother's beach, this entire journey just a dream. Soon she would wake and run along the beach with Yara, or would she be running along with James, Alinta beside them.

Dozing became deep sleep, Merindah dreamt about things she knew; her family, the whale–man of her childhood nightmares. She dreamt about her babies, her time with James, the dead whales, killing seals and blood on the rocks. That was Merindah's life. No horses, no pretty dresses, no printed material, not even a wheel. She had never seen a white woman. Her existence was what she had seen and done in the few seasons of her short life. However, she could never dream what life had in store for her.

Suddenly Merindah woke, the boat rocked about. The men had stopped to change rowers. Men were talking, men were spitting, urinating into the water. Somebody used the bucket, then threw their business over the side. William woke; she put him to her breast.

Only one day back on the boat, and it already stank with bodies and waste. Although she was dry, that would not last; an east wind would bring the spray into the boat again, wetting skins and the rags that were her clothes. Filthy water would again be sloshing around the bottom of the boat. Merindah peered out from the canvas at the eastern sky and the glow. Presently her familiar moon greeted her; a nightly companion coming up amongst the stars that she knew so well. She sat there reflecting as she held James's pendant. 'No it's not a dream, it has all happened.'

The rowers pulled. The boat surged forward another boat length, many thousands more to go. Impossible.

Chapter 17 – No More Islands

The Great Australian Bight.
Two small boats.
Two splashes among millions of white caps.

The moon sat high in the sky as the sun rose in the east. Another day; another east wind, the spray cold and wet and the piggin always bailing out water. The sandy beach had been left behind; now there were huge cliffs, a giant step that separated sea and land.

'There's nowhere to take a boat in there,' Muller told Bryant. 'We'll need to go in somewhere to find water and food soon.'

'We need to find a break in the cliffs; that may be days, I think we should reduce the water rations,' Bryant suggested. 'We should be ready to catch water in this canvas if we get some rain; every bit will help. The men can't keep up this rowing without fresh drinking water, but I've got a feeling rain is scarce along this coast. I reckon the further east we go, it's more barren. There were only bushes along that beach back there, and I can't see trees up on these cliffs.'

East wind blew spray into the boat all that day; the men grew tired, rowing continually. They needed to keep the boat away from the cliffs and continue to move east.

Another night, Bryant steering with the large oar, and Muller and Rebus under the canvas. Rebus was still asking for more rum; he put his hand on Muller's groin.

'I want more rum, I can do this.'

Muller hit him. 'No, boy! That's not going to happen. No more rum for you.'

'I'll jump off the boat,' Rebus blubbered.

'That'd help us all.'

Bryant heard the yelling, 'What's going on?'

Muller told him of the boy's suggestion; his desperate act to get more rum.

'It's Addis's fault,' Bryant said. 'Keep him busy.'

'I am not letting him touch me,' Muller exclaimed. 'I might throw him overboard. You got any suggestions?'

'Get him to bail!'

A forlorn calm; the men were rowing steady through the never-ending swell of the Southern Ocean. As the night became darker, the wind blew gently from the northwest. The rowers rested with the small sail set. They could clearly hear the waves breaking on the rocks at the base of the cliffs.

'We must keep together,' Captain Harris called out, as his boat drew up alongside the other. 'How much water have you got left?'

'Only one cask,' Muller answered.

'We'll need more in two days, but we should find a break in the cliffs before then.

'We could sail right past during the night, without seeing it,' Muller said.

'I've got Flinder's chart, there's no break for another hundred miles or so,' Harris answered. He seemed confident. 'That's where we will go ashore. When these cliffs finish there is a beach.'

'We're nearly out of rum.'

'Ours is almost empty too, but that may be a good thing. We can fill those casks with water when we find some,' answered the Captain. 'Be prepared to catch moisture off the canvas in the morning, I think it may be damp. Loosen the ropes so there's a dip.'

Merindah and her baby were asleep in the bow with the dogs.

Sally and Jacob sat pushed together. Sally was much older than him; maybe twice his age. Jacob had never been so close to a woman since his mother. He had seen the other sailors with the Aboriginal women; he remembered those naked women on the beach of bones. He pushed timidly in against Sally. Her breasts pressed against his head.

It was dark, the boat being pushed along by the sails. Most of the men were sleeping. There was just enough star light for Muller and Bryant in turn to steer the boat and keep a safe distance from the coast.

Jacob became aroused with his groin against Sally's leg. As usual, Sally wore only her old sailor's shirt, but skin covered herself and Jacob. Jacob's hand slipped under her shirt, he put his other hand between her legs, and then pushed up her shirt. His face soon found bare breasts and his mouth found a nipple. Sally had not been with Bryant for weeks, now that he regularly took Merindah. Although he was not much more than a boy, she did not push Jacob away.

Willingly Sally held a breast to his mouth with one hand, like she would a baby. Her other hand went down to his groin and held his hardness as he sucked her breast. Sally had never experienced the sensation of being in control before. She would never forget the violent abuse of other men before they passed her on to Bill Bryant. Even with him it was when he wanted it, not violent but only to satisfy his own urge. This was different, Sally was in control, Jacob pushed into her legs; she held him tight and felt moisture on her hand as he quickly but quietly reached a climax. Jacob's face fell away from her breast as he relaxed and fell asleep against her body.

The boat steadily sailed on while the men who were awake and the man steering watched a phosphorescent glow trailing from the tip of the steering oar.

Sally sat quietly thinking to herself that she could have a son as old as this young man, if sailors had not killed her babies. 'I'll have this man for myself. It will be my choice what happens.'

As the sun appeared in the fog on another cold damp morning, men carefully swabbed water off the sagging canvas at the bow and the stern of the boat; barely enough moisture to give each person on the boat a sip. That morning they ate salty ships biscuits, and a little dried seal meat. The fog drifted in with layers of cold air, but no wind.

'Right, let's get rowing,' Muller told the men. 'We need to get further east before our water runs out. Captain Harris says that there should be a place where we can get the boats in safely tomorrow. Let's hope we find water there.'

Bill Bryant was certain that young Levi had the best eyes. He told him to stand and watch for any break in the cliffs. He did not want to miss something in the fog.

Merindah sat up in the bow, her head out of the canvas; she lifted William out and washed him with a little sea water and a rag.

Sally used the bucket and threw her business over the side; no privacy aboard the crowded boat. Jacob emerged from under the canvas and used the bucket too. He did not look at Sally, unsure what to think of what had happened between them during the night.

Men kept rowing. There was very little wind and those cliffs still mocked them; kept them away from the land where they may have found water and food. Just one day's water remained on each boat. The rum was gone; now there were more kegs to fill with water. But what water? Slowly the two boats edged along, keeping a safe distance from the cliffs. It was still calm and four tired men rowed steadily ahead.

The salted meat was eaten, now they ate only ships biscuits damaged with salt water. The dogs still chewed on the seal skins, but they were thirsty. Inta sat against Merindah and William, the pup like another baby. There was no doubt that she considered herself to be part of Merindah's pack. The young pup wanted to drink. She kept licking at the filthy sea water in the bottom of the boat.

'No, Inta!' Merindah cried out. 'Stop! You can't drink that, it'll make you sick.'

Dina lent against Sally; she never left her side unless Bryant called her. She sniffed the sea water but did not lick it.

Determined, Muller still would not let the dogs have any of the precious water.

'We need to save the extra water for the men rowing, not for the dogs. They'll have to wait.'

Inta could not understand; she licked at the bilge again; begged Merindah with sad inquiring eyes. Suddenly she vomited, heaving up sea water and lumps of half-digested seal skin. The horrible smell made everyone in the boat gag as the foul mess spread into the filthy water in the bottom of the boat. Muller ordered Jacob and Rebus to bail it out; they both added to the mess with the contents of their own stomachs.

'Bloody dogs,' Muller yelled. 'We'll have to throw them over soon if we can't get water.'

'We may as well all jump overboard, if we don't get water soon,' Bill Bryant muttered.

Merindah squeezed milk from her breast into an open hand; she held it for Inta to drink. The pup eagerly lapped up the nourishment, then settled down against her keeper.

Cloudless sky. Winter sun. A cold south east wind. Another day.

The two small boats followed the giant cliffs; a great angry step from sea to land. There was no place to take the boats in there. The men had to keep rowing; going east and keep away from those cliffs. Another night; they had swallowed the last of the water.

Merindah became concerned for William as she was thirsty herself; he was unsettled and she knew that he needed more milk. The sailors complained bitterly about his constant whimpers. She tried to get him to suck on a biscuit, dampened with the dew on the canvas.

As the sun brought another day, they all sponged dew off the canvas with rags, and taunted their thirst with the damp shreds. Those cliffs still disturbed them; What if they had rowed past a place during the night where the boats could have landed?

'Not a chance of that,' Captain Harris told Muller as his boat came alongside.

'We need to keep going, I think it's still some distance to a break in these cliffs. We can't just stop; we would be taken into those rocks. There's no choice, you must keep going. Let other men steer, you and Bryant will need to take a turn at rowing.'

Jacob, Merindah and Sally all took turns. With the boat so crowded, it was difficult to move about and change places when the rower's swapped position. They had now been over twenty hours without a substantial drink of water. The sun was low in the west when Levi noticed that the cliffs headed away from the coast.

Levi shaded his eyes with an arm, 'Look! A beach! I can see land between the cliffs and the shore.'

They all scanned the low sandy stretch of coast.

'Move in closer to shore,' Captain Harris yelled across the water. 'Find a place to get through the surf. We must land before dark.'

'That's going to be difficult, yes, difficult,' Bryant said as they pulled away from the other boat. Everyone was exhausted from rowing, and thirsty.

As the sun set, Levi noticed a small open cove. He pointed it out to Muller.

'That may be our best chance.' Muller pulled the big steering oar across. The boat made a desperate course for the beach. The men in the Captain's boat had seen them turn, and followed.

Merindah held onto William as white breaking surf lifted and tossed their boat. The overloaded boat neared the shore.

'Row you bastards! Keep her straight.'

Suddenly a larger wave picked up their boat and drove it crazily along, like a twig on a raging river. It was impossible to steer. The wave captured the boat and rushed it forward, turned it sideways. Too heavily loaded to turn over, it swamped and quickly filled with water. Anything able to float lifted from the bottom, ropes, skins, oars and empty kegs. It was all this floating collection of objects that the men, Merindah and Sally desperately tried to grab as the boat sank under them.

Captain Harris watched helplessly as his boat swept past the mess of tangled debris, people and dogs struggling to stay afloat.

A wave dumped the Captain's boat onto the beach. Men hastily dragged it up and away from the breakers.

There was nothing they could do to help the others.

Chapter 18 – On a Hostile Shore

In the water! Ropes, oars, casks, skins.
Dogs panicking.
Men panicking.

With the Captain's boat safe on the white sandy beach, the men looked back to the rolling surf where the other boat had disappeared. All they could see were tumbling waves, debris from the boat, and an occasional glimpse of a body moving in the breakers.

As water rushed into the boat, Merindah held William tight; she called Inta, and encouraged the young dog to follow as she kicked away from the sinking whale boat. Merindah grabbed an empty cask as it floated out of the hull and placed William across its high side. She held him there while she moved away from the chaos of ropes and canvas. Sally and Jacob soon appeared alongside her in the water, hanging onto an oar which helped them keep afloat. Dina knew which way to go; she was already paddling towards the shore.

The men from the boat desperately grabbed anything that floated. Oars and casks could help them, but ropes and canvas were more a hindrance. Merindah, Sally and Jacob kept together as they slowly headed for the shore. Inta kept alongside Merindah who still had William held on top of the cask. As they neared the beach a wave gathered them up like dead flowers in a wind storm and they landed in the wash on bright white sand. Merindah stood, and with unsteady shaking legs, carried a screaming William out to dry sand.

Merindah quickly studied the beach and the low land behind it. As she scanned higher the sun disappeared over the edge of the great cliffs that headed inland leaving the narrow strip of land flanking the beach. Soon it would be dark; Merindah was cold, wet, and thirsty. Above all it was the thirst that she felt most and knew that William would feel the same.

Sally and the two dogs stood alongside of her. Jacob sat shivering on the sand.

'Where's Rebus?' Merindah asked Sally. They looked each way along the beach. Rebus lay face down in the wash of the waves, exhausted. Sally went to help him stand and he staggered out weakly and collapsed onto dry sand. Bill Bryant lurched out of the waves and quickly checked on his crew. Some were already ashore further down the beach and others followed him out of the waves. All the men from his boat eventually struggled ashore, saved by hanging onto bits that floated out of the boat.

They all had trouble finding their balance after being squashed in that boat for days, unable to stand or walk. Men from the Captain's boat came and helped them back to his boat. The Captain's woman, Sarah, brought some almost dry skins to help the other women keep warm. Merindah crouched down in the shelter of the boat; she knew that it would be a cold miserable night. After feeding William as much as she could provide, she placed him down on a skin between Dina and Inta's warm but damp bodies.

'Stay there,' she said firmly to the two dogs. 'Look after the baby. Stay.'

Merindah walked back down to the beach, searching for her skins and anything that may have washed in from the swamped boat.

Bryant joined her; he stood shaking his head, 'What a bloody mess, bloody mess.'

'Our skins!' Merindah said. 'We'll need our skins.' She sorted through debris that had come in with the waves, and what men had held onto as they floated to the beach.

'There'll be more stuff washed in in the morning, woman. But we won't get that boat back,' Bill Bryant uttered in disgust. 'Bloody madness, too many people, bound to happen, bound to. No more tobacco, a man might as well have drowned.'

'Just another bloody shipwreck,' commented second mate Muller, as he struggled to find his feet on the sand. 'I'm getting too old for this bullshit. Seems I just can't drown.'

The Captain had sent Hugh Byron and some men to find wood for a fire; they returned with a few dead branches.

'There is very little here to burn,' Hugh Byron told them. 'There's no decent growth of any sort nearby; it's difficult to find any useful timber to burn. We'll have to go further inland.'

By the time the last man had been brought shivering to the wretched group standing and resting around the Captains boat, it was dark.

Stars shone through a sky of skimpy clouds. Somebody lit a fire with a flint from the Captain's boat, and a few dry leaves from a dead bush close by. There was no water to drink, only a few salty dry ships biscuits to eat. Drained, anxious faces glowed in the flames as the dry branches flared, but soon dwindled to a few long skinny red withering coals in the sand. Merindah, William, Sally, Jacob, and the two dogs crowded together, as they had been on the boat. Only damp old shirts covered the women, they shared the few skins that Sarah gave them, their own animal skins lost somewhere out in the waves.

It was going to be a long miserable night. What would they find in the morning?

Mist! They had encountered patches of mist or fog when in the boats, but that first morning at the cove was eerie calm, with a heavy mist drifting in off the ocean.

Merindah woke cold, hungry and thirsty, hearing the ever-present noise of waves. No matter how calm the sea seemed to be, there were always waves slapping onto the beach. When she peered through the mist toward that sound that was all she could see; waves tipping over and hissing up onto the sand. Beyond that, only mist.

Low down she noticed a smear in the haze, trying to be red, or yellow. She knew it was the sun, but it would not warm her yet. William woke and she put him to her breast.

'How long can I make milk for him, when I have nothing for myself?' she murmured. 'I must find water and food today.'

Neither Sally nor Sarah had ever lived off the land like Merindah had. They came from a camp at Van Diemen's Land, taken away when they were just young girls. Much of their limited native knowledge had been erased by years with the white men.

'Merindah must find us some food and water here,' Sally told Sarah. 'If she can't I'm afraid we will all die.' Dina snuggled against Sally, with questioning eyes. 'I know you want a drink, let's see what's here.'

Men stood around the boat, wiping up dew that had formed on the canvas, sucking the moisture from rags. Blankets of mist drifted in from the ocean, making it impossible to distinguish the cliffs that were visible the previous evening. Even nearby, small bushes were just ghostly shapes.

Men went to get firewood, they returned with more of the small dead branches.

'We need better wood,' Hugh Byron said.

'Can't see a bloody thing, I only found my way back because I heard you talking,' one of the men declared.

'Just light that up and keep it going, small until you can find better wood,' instructed Hugh. 'This mist must lift soon, surely.'

Frustrated, they waited. There was no water to drink, but it virtually floated in the air. Small green bushes had moisture dripping off their frail leaves and the dogs cautiously tried to lick off the drops. Patches of mist sluggishly drifted away from the cliff face in the west.

Merindah wondered if water was there amongst those rocks.

She left William with Sarah and Chief. Sally and she took the dogs and walked towards the cliffs which rose two hundred and fifty feet above them. In small cavities they found water which had collected from the morning's moisture, enough for a small drink for them and the dogs. But not enough to fill a cask to take back to the rest of the stranded people.

'We need more than this, and soon,' Merindah said.

Back at the camp by the boat, the mist was clearing away; men had gone further and found bigger pieces of dead wood. A group stood warming themselves by the fire.

Bryant had been scouting around. 'Miles of sand heading east,' he told the Captain. 'The cliffs head inland and this coastal plain appears to get wider as it goes east, but there is only small bush here close to the coast. I think somebody should climb up the cliff to see what's there.'

'Yes, I'll get Hugh and some other men to do that. You take your dog and find something to eat,' Captain Harris told him. 'And that woman of yours, she may be our only hope of finding water. The men are desperate; they're swabbing moisture off the bushes. That won't keep us alive.'

Many items had washed up along the beach from the swamped boat. They recovered the piggin and bucket, ropes, the boats water breaker, canvas and skins. There was no hope of salvaging the boat; although not out far, impossible to recover. Nobody had mentioned or talked about the next action or effort to go east. They needed water and food urgently.

When Merindah told Bryant that she had found only a little water, he became anxious.

'You must find water today, I'm sure Dina will find food, but you must find water.'

'This is not my home place, it's all different.'

'What about those cliffs?' Bryant waved his hand west, 'You could search further along there. Like you did back at that big island.'

'I've been, there are only wet patches in the rocks. We need a lot of water for all these people. It's cool now but it will get hotter, then what?' Merindah asked.

'I don't know how long we'll be here,' Bryant told her.

'How can we go anywhere now?'

'Walk,' Bryant said.

'Walk where?'

Bryant shrugged his shoulders as he began to walk away. He expected Merindah to find water; he turned and glared at his young woman. 'Go back to those cliffs; take a cask and the two boys. Find water soon.'

Merindah fed William and left him with Sarah and Chief again. Sally, Merindah, Jacob and Levi walked west towards the cliffs, Inta eagerly followed Merindah. They carried two casks between them.

'Even if we get these full, that won't last long,' Jacob commented.

'You can bring other men back and get more if we find water,' Sally said.

They returned to the edge of the cliffs where the beach ended, the giant precipices soared up towards the sun. In places overhanging rocks jutted out, making moving shadows on the waves that surged right into the cliff base. It was impossible to walk between the base of the cliff and the sea. They turned back and following the cliff east; the coast became further away.

Merindah could see animal tracks coming from the coastal sand hills and bushes, leading into channels and gaps on the edge of the escarpment. 'Wallabies; there must be water here somewhere, animals need water.'

She pointed to the large fissures and gullies. 'When rain comes, water would pour down those, But I don't think it rains here very often.'

For hours the two women and two young men walked and climbed along the cliffs; the rock all white, and in many places loose and crumbly. Inta ran and sniffed, looking for water too. In small rock pools hidden in shady crevasses they did find water, one pool barely enough to give them a drink. They used a metal cup to fill the two casks with clear water from three more pools.

'There will be other places here like this Levi, but the hot days will dry them out quick. We'll take this back to the camp and see if men have found any,' Merindah said.

There was food at the camp, Bryant and Dina had caught a wallaby, men had found bird eggs on the beach; only one meal for twenty-five hungry people.

'You'll need to do better,' the Captain told Bryant.

Hugh Byron had returned from his expedition to the cliff top. He reported to Captain Harris.

'Just miles of low small trees inland, sheets of white rock, no sign of water or creeks. This coastal sandy plain gets wider to the east, lots of sand and small bushes. It all looks very desolate.'

'Doesn't sound good,' Muller said. 'Perhaps this will be my last shipwreck.'

The Captain gave him a dark glance. 'We will get out of this.'

Merindah and her group walked in with the casks of water. She had caught two lizards; food for the women. When everyone had drunk their fill, the casks were empty.

'Jacob and Levi can take some men back to where we got this, and get more, but won't last long. It's probably just moisture from that thick mist this morning, and other mornings.' Merindah told Bryant. 'I'll look further tomorrow.'

The Captain marvelled at the young black woman's observation. As Merindah walked away, back to her baby, he went up to Bill Bryant. 'If anyone gets us out of here alive, it'll be that woman. She can talk and understand English so well too. She's picked it up quickly, didn't she come from a black man, and before that no contact with whites?'

'Well that's what he told me, but there is something else about her, that I haven't found out. Perhaps I shouldn't bother to ask. She's certainly worth having around,' Bryant answered.

The second night at the cove was more comfortable. Most of their skins had washed in from the sunken boat, the fire kept burning with better wood and everyone had eaten a little and drank water. But they all realised that the next day needed to be more successful or they would all perish amongst the small bushes and sand.

Next morning, William seemed to be brighter; perhaps her milk improved with the water and little food. Merindah left him with Sarah again. Just her, Inta and Sally went off to find more water. They walked further along the cliff face as it went back inland. Again they found more small pools amongst the white rocks, only enough for themselves.

William would need feeding. The women arrived back at the camp at midday, bringing more lizards, and Inta had sniffed out a family of small possums, only the size of mice, but food.

Bryant returned to the beach with two wallabies. 'These wallabies aren't as tame as those on the islands, I needed that dog.'

Merindah smirked; she had seen the signs, she knew why the animals were wary.

Jacob, Levi and the men that went with them returned with two casks barely full.

'That's just ten gallons,' Muller said.

'There won't be any more there until another damp morning,' young Jacob told the Captain.

'Well, there's twenty-five people here,' he said. 'We need at least ten gallons every day.

'Another damp morning? How many of these mornings are we going to get here? If it was summertime I think half of us would be dead by now,' Hugh Byron said.

Bryant agreed.

Merindah remembered places where she and Yara went with their people. Sometimes they went to areas where water seeped into shallow wells. She walked east along the beach. There were sand hills below the cliffs; there were hollows and peaks. *Would there be water in those hollows amongst the sand?*

That evening she walked off on her own with Inta. Crisscrossing the area, she checked the vegetation at each depression amongst the sand hills. That night Merindah slept with an idea on her mind.

West wind had dried up any dew the next morning at the cove. Men returned to the rocks along the cliff face searching; they would get a little water even if it was stagnant and smelly.

Merindah approached Bill Bryant, she had spent time with him the previous night, but now she was asking him something that surprised him.

'Can you get men to help me dig?' she asked.

'Dig what?'

'Dig in the sand, we may find water.'

'What, just in that white sand?'

'Yes I think it's worth a try,' Merindah told him.

Merindah had picked a spot in a hollow back from the beach. She had recognised the plants that grew there; gullies led into the area from the great escarpment to the northeast.

She was nervous, but quietly confident, *Water must run into this depression, and soak into this sand.*

There were no shovels, only the buckets from the boats. Designed to scoop up water from the bottom of a whaleboat, a piggin was ideal, men used them, and buckets, to scoop out sand.

Hours passed; Bryant had taken Inta with him to help Dina run down more wallabies. It was a sunny winter's day, not hot, but the men digging where Merindah had indicated were desperate for a drink.

'We need a drink,' one of them uttered. 'Are the others back yet with water?' 'He glared sceptically at the tall young Aboriginal woman. 'There's none down here.'

The others returned with less water than the day before; a little for the men digging; none left for the camp that night. Muller was there, and he urged them to keep digging into the sand. A mound of sand piled up around the edge as the hollow steadily deepened.

'We're over six feet deep, it's no different,' a man from the bottom of the hole yelled out. 'This is hopeless, just fine white sand.'

'It's getting firmer,' another man said, as he passed up a bucket of sand. 'Shit, this lots damp.'

Suddenly the men became excited; they hastened their scooping with the wooden buckets. There was moisture, another foot, water.

Water; at first cloudy with sand. They stopped and let it seep in; tasted the clear, clean, fresh water. They carefully dug deeper and let the water settle again. Men eagerly passed buckets of water up the slope to be poured into casks at the top.

Everyone felt more secure at the camp that night.

Bill Bryant was proud of his woman. He took her away from the fire and spent time with her alone. The Captain and Sarah also left the group for some time together.

When Merindah returned to the camp and William slept soundly in his skin, the Aboriginal women and young men sitting around their fire began to sing once again. Merindah did not know what the others said in their songs, but that did not stop her, she just followed the rhythm. After the others stopped singing, Merindah softly sang alone in her own language. She related a sad story about a young girl who had met a young man from a distant clan. After the two young lovers spent time together, there was a baby that they could not keep. They parted, and their baby had to be given away to someone else. No one else sitting around the fire understood what Merindah related in her song, but they all listened and sensed the sadness.

Jacob sat by the fire talking quietly with Levi, the two young men discussing their short lives back in Van Diemen's Land and Sydney. They talked about their future prospects and their present predicament.

The coals had squirmed and fizzed into white ash; all the men seemed to be sleeping. The moon crept silently out of the ocean and shone a path across the waves into the beach. Sally decided that it was time to develop her relationship with young Jacob. At last she could be in control of a man. She moved quietly alongside of the young white man. He woke and she took his arm to lead him away from the camp.

'Come with me. I have some things to teach you.'

In a secluded place clear of bushes, Sally stopped. She took off her old shirt, and then she pushed her naked body into Jacobs. Soon he removed his shirt and trousers, and she quickly pulled him down onto the sand. Jacob learned more in that short time then than he had ever dreamt. The older woman enjoyed taking him. Jacob soon released his urge, lay back on the soft sand and wondered why he had waited so long. But it was different than how the other men talked about it, more fulfilling, and gentler. He nuzzled once again into the woman's breasts. This would not be the last time, they both knew that, but said little to each other.

Later Jacob took wood back to the camp, put pieces on the fire and sat thinking about what had happened. He was not sure if Bryant knew of the relationship; he wondered if he would care. *I will keep it to myself.* He needed to be very discreet, *Did anyone see me leave the fire with Sally?*

Merindah's well provided them with water. Bryant and his dogs got meat. Merindah and the other two women found plants to eat. They would survive there, but what next?

'What now? Do we go east, back west, or stay here?'

'Staying is not an option,' the Captain declared. 'Can we keep going east with most of us walking?'

'I don't think we can go east,' Hugh Byron said. 'I've seen what it like, and it's a long way back to those islands that we sailed past after Flinders Island. And what's there? We don't know. We would have to get back to Flinders Island, which is even further.'

Muller agreed, 'We can't go east now,'

'Well, we'll stay here for a few more days,' Captain Harris told them. 'I want you two to organise some fit men to go back to the top of the cliffs back west. We need to check out the country up there before we decide to move.'

'Move where?' Bill Bryant asked.

'I haven't decided yet, let's just see what it's like up there. I mean water and food. Perhaps there's natives there who may help?'

Hugh Byron would organise some of the fittest men. He would take food and water; spend two or three days looking at the country back toward the west. Although Bryant thought Merindah should be the person to do that; he did not suggest it. *Wait and see what they find.*

The camp at the cove became more established, bushes and bigger branches from further away from the beach used to make reasonable shelters. Men placed sticks and branches around the bottom of the well to stop sand falling in. The women with Inta, and Bryant with Dina, found food, they all realised they could not stay; they would need to shift soon. No one would find them there.

In the bushes amongst the sand one morning, Inta saw movement.

'Get him Inta,' Merindah yelled. 'Chase him out'. The pup dug under the bush, then another movement. Suddenly Inta backed out yelping.

Merindah had seen the distinctive pattern on the lizards back. 'No Inta, get away!' she yelled, as she too jumped back away from the bush. The lizard sprung forward toward the pup. Merindah picked up a large stick and quickly killed the lizard. She went straight to the young dog.

Merindah feared for the dog. 'Did it bite you girl, or did you scratch yourself on the bush?'

'That's not a lizard,' she told Sally. 'It's different; see its small head, no legs, fat body and skinny tail, and stripes around its body. You will die if that one bites you.'

When the pup seemed fine a short time later, Merindah relaxed.

'It must not have bitten you girl, or you would be going stiff by now. We must be careful of them. BAD,' she said with fear in her voice. Inta seemed to know that the lizard was different, she looked at it, dead on the sand; she could sense Merindah's fear. Merindah picked the adder up with a stick and carried it back to the camp. When she showed it to the others and told them of its fatal bite, they became anxious. They were alarmed again when she told them she had seen brown snakes, and they were nearly as deadly.

But, she said: 'We can eat them when I catch them.' But she was not going to eat the death adder.

Merindah now had free time to investigate the area, she walked along the beach carrying William in a skin sling around her neck; Inta trotted eagerly by her side. She noticed many birds similar to those back at her mother's beach; the same gulls and small runners feeding in the seaweed on the sand. Other familiar birds lived there. She noticed there were no big pelicans. 'No rivers here.'

A sea eagle soared in the sky, and she could see its nest high up on the sea cliff when she walked back that way. Above the cliffs another eagle circled higher in the sky; she watched it majestically swoop and soar along the edge of the cliff, then plummet with its claws ready to strike.

Merindah talked in her mother's language to the pup; she pointed into the sky. 'It has a great big nest somewhere. Look at it. No, now there are two of them. They could show us the way out of here.' The pup gazed into the young woman's eyes; she turned her head to the side, lifted an ear and whined softly. Merindah patted the young bitch's black head. 'Where would we go girl? Out of here to where?'

Hugh Byron picked out four men and expected to be away for three nights.

'I'm fairly sure what we'll find,' Hugh said. 'I've been up there, remember; didn't seem too good.'

'You need to be sure,' Captain Harris told Hugh. 'We have to get away from here soon. Can't just stay here.'

Bill Bryant heard this conversation.

'I wonder what he's got in mind,' he said to Muller, as they watched the Captain walk back to his shelter. 'I'm kept busy with my dog, getting us food. Now, do you still think it was wrong to bring the dogs?'

'No,' Muller answered. 'But it was wrong to leave that island;

we should try to go back.'

'I agree, I agree,' Bryant said, reverting to his Irish way of repeating things. 'That's what I want to do, want to do, even if he wants to keep going east. Perhaps we could walk back and somehow get out to that island again. We know those sealers are there, a ship might come back to pick them up. And Ned, or whatever his name is and his rough group are there somewhere; perhaps they would find us and help.'

'Those sealers perhaps, but I would rather keep away from Ned and those other bastards. And yes, a ship may turn up eventually,' Muller replied.

Bryant nodded. 'Yes, and now I have to go and find more for you to eat. That's all I do here now, but it's getting harder to find. I have to walk further each day, and I'm taking two men with me today. Perhaps we'll need to climb those cliffs soon to get wallabies, but I am not sure how bare feet are going to handle that.' He walked off.

The Captain had good knives and needles in his boat. The women had been scraping the wallaby skins clean, but there was no time to dry them properly. Merindah knew how to make water carriers out of the skins. She showed the others how to skin a wallaby without cuts.

'Keep the skin in one piece and then there's less to stitch up,' she explained. 'Leave the meaty side on the outside,' she instructed them. 'The furry side goes in, that will not make the water rotten. These will be easier to carry than those casks.'

Rebus had learnt some sewing skills despite Addis's mistreatment, and he sewed the bags; a slow process but it worked. Once again Captain Harris marvelled at the young woman's skills.

Hugh Byron and the four men returned after only two nights.

'It's worse than I thought,' Hugh reported to the Captain. 'There are wallabies and other animals, not many but we saw their marks and their droppings. They must find water somewhere, but we didn't find any. You can't walk without boots, terribly rough on our feet. Sharp white stones, not much dirt, just stone.'

The next morning Captain Harris called everybody together.

'We need to leave,' he said. 'Some of us should keep going east in the boat, while you others walk back along the coast and try to get out to Middle Island again. That's one option; the other is for all of us to go back to Middle island, some in the boat and the rest of you walking.'

'Sounds like you're going to be on the boat either way,' Muller replied.

'It wasn't my boat that sank, don't you remember?'

'Yeah okay, but you heard what Hugh said it's like up on top of those cliffs. How are we going to handle that?'

'You need to prepare,' said the Captain. 'Take lots of water, you still have yours, and you can take our water breaker, they are easier to carry than the casks. You can take the cook pot; we won't need it on the boat. Make some boots for your feet, there are plenty of skins here now, see what you can stitch up, or just wrap your feet up in them. You can't just stay here.'

'So which way are you going in the boat?' Muller asked.

'Well, I think it would be best if I took about seven men in the boat and go east. I could send a ship back to Middle Island or near there to pick up the rest of you; that's if you get back there.' The Captain seemed to have decided to go east. 'With only eight of us in the boat there will be room for more water and food. I think we would have a good chance of getting back. Remember Captain Bligh?'

'Well, if you're comparing yourself with Captain Bligh, don't forget that his men pushed him off his ship, he didn't run it into a sand bar,' Muller said.

'Now that's getting a bit low man, you were in charge of the ship when we went aground. You'd better be careful what you say; I'm still the Captain here.'

'Okay, let's not carry on like this,' Hugh Byron said. 'Can't we work this out, to give us all a chance of getting out of this mess?'

The decision was made for most of the group to walk west. Preparations began. The Captain still considered that it would be best if he took the boat and some men east for help.

Chapter 19 – A Long Walk Back

Another short trip, on a long journey.

Merindah reached the top of the cliff; she turned around and reflected on the scene where the group had lived for the previous few days. She understood that people could live there permanently.

People did live there somewhere, the signs were plain. She had noticed their old camp fires, and once when she and Inta had walked further east along the coast, Merindah had found a well in the sand, and recent human foot prints. She did not tell the others. She knew they should leave the well alone. *We would not be welcome here, this is their place, they know we are here, and would not want all these people using their well.*

As she gazed across the coastal plain widening in the east, Merindah saw smoke, just two wispy spirals drifting up into the cloudless sky. She told no one; turned and watched the last of the group reach the top of the cliff.

It took most of the first morning for the entire group to get to the cliff top; they carried little food, confident they would find more. Water was their big concern, the casks would be difficult to carry; they went with the boat. Now they carried the two water breakers, two buckets and the skins that they had prepared, all full of water; enough for three days if they were careful. They all wore covering on their feet. Although her feet were tough, Merindah prepared, wrapping skins around them. There would be more skins when they killed more wallabies.

That first day they walked west along the top of the cliffs. Walking in the sky, so far above the sea. They stared back down to waves rolling into rocks that were hidden from their view far below the edge of the vertical cliff. Men shuddered; they knew what would have happened if they came ashore there in the whaleboats.

Their tinder box had been lost when the whaleboat foundered coming into the cove. Sally carried a fire stick; a smouldering coal wrapped in green leaves. When they had used the water from the bucket, she placed sand in the bottom and carried the fire in there; not the usual custom but much easier to carry. Then she added a few dry twigs to keep the fire going. She had sacrificed a little water to dampen the sand to stop the wooden bucket catching alight.

Many hands helped carry water in the skin bags, buckets and two breakers. Even the cooking pot was full of water when they left the beach. That night they camped amongst small trees back from the cliff edge; they had not seen any animals. There was no sign of water, just rocks and more rocks.

Captain Harris had reluctantly decided to go west in his whaleboat. He would follow the coast keeping safely away from those great cliffs, and would go ashore and wait at the first safe place. Possibly near the last island where they stopped on their voyage east; or possibly at the western end of those great cliffs.

As he studied his chart, Captain Harris had told the walkers. 'It's over a hundred and twenty miles to the end of the cliffs. We'll meet you there, or even further west.'

They all realised that the boat could not come into the shore before the break in the cliffs, but even at that place large waves may make a safe landing impossible. Surf had swamped their other boat; they were now very cautious.

They had loaded the boat with water, dry meat and some plants that Merindah collected. Six men left on the boat with the Captain and Hugh Byron. With fewer men aboard, the boat was more stable.

Sarah walked with the other two women. 'I think he's given me up now,' Sarah told them. 'I'm staying alongside you and the dogs.' They all remembered what happened to the man with a nasty scab on his arm and scratches on his back.

The group walking sighted the Captain's boat out in the sea that first evening, but it was not there in the morning. It was going to be impossible to be in touch with each other until they reached the end of the great cliffs, or even further west.

'If they need to row, we may keep up,' Muller said. 'They'll wait anywhere they can pull in, but we know that's almost impossible for a long way. They have enough water for six days; it should get them back to that island, even if they need to row all the way. But they'll be hungry before then.'

'We can't help them and they can't help us,' Bill Bryant said. 'Let's just worry about our own skins now. We're on our own now, on our own.'

The group packed up and walked west, Sally had a new coal smouldering in the bucket. They walked away from the cliff, eager to get some animals for food. The man leading stopped at an opening in the ground. As they all came up to the spot, a gush of wind and a deep rumbling noise rose from the rocky cavity. Eventually they recognised that waves two hundred feet below them rushing into a crevasse at the cliff face caused the sound and rush of air. Air rushed up to the surface of the plateau. They saw more blowholes on their trek along the top of the cliffs.

Food and water. They needed to find both and seventeen people would need a lot of water. Even though late winter, it was windy and dry. They walked constantly. The skins wrapped around their feet made walking difficult, sometimes they went barefoot, as the sailors always did. But the relentless stones cut and bruised their feet, no matter how tough they were. Even Merindah's feet had not felt rocks like this.

The second night the dismal group camped further inland; they had lost interest in the boat. They were on their own, had used more than half of their water and they needed to find more food.

Merindah heard small animals scurrying about in the night, but could not find their tracks amongst the stones in the morning. Her and Sally ate the two lizards that she caught.

'We'll eat the last of the cold singed wallaby,' the men told her.

Sarah found berries; she was sure they were safe to eat.

Bryant and Jacob took Dina and left the camp early to find food. They soon came to a small depression.

'Might be wallabies here,' Bryant said, but they only found more broken rocks and gaps between. 'Hard to walk on; no sign of water or animals.'

'This is different than the sandy area along the beach where we came from,' Bryant told Jacob. 'Wallabies probably won't live here; there'll be kangaroos, like back at the Bluff.'

They found the others walking west.

Walking to what? Bryant wondered.

All day the group walked west together, meandering through small stunted trees and white rocks. They sat around a fire that night without anything to cook.

Muller held up an empty water skin, 'We need to drink less, it's going too fast, we have to make it last longer.' He realised then, had it been summer, they would never have got that far. Although the water in the skins tasted rancid, it would keep them alive. But they had to find more soon.

Merindah saw water containers being emptied and sensed that food would be difficult to find. She wondered if she should have tried to get help from the Aboriginals that she knew were back at the cove. Was now the time to seek help? Could she get help at this place? She knew that people would be here somewhere.

They may come to this place now in the cool time. But there would be little water here in the hot season. Then they would go back to the coast like my clan does.

Merindah began to look for signs of people.

On the third night of the westward march they camped again without fresh food. They crushed seeds that the women had collected and made a type of bread, more like a paste, but it did not even provide a mouthful for each person. Merindah killed a brown snake, but only the women and Levi would eat it. Next morning Bryant and Jacob left the camp before sunrise, taking Dina to hunt.

Smoke! Early in the morning Merindah could smell smoke as she walked through the stunted trees. The flat featureless plateau above those great cliffs did not change. Occasionally small low rises showed the way ahead.

There she spotted it, a small cylinder of smoke drifting towards them with the wind. *Other people are here.* She did not tell the others; and glimpsed the smoke again during the day as they walked west.

Bill Bryant and Jacob walked into a small depression with grass and small bushes. Three red kangaroos were grazing peacefully. The men walked forward carefully. These large and powerful animals would be a match, even for big Dina. The bitch was hungry. When she spotted them, Bryant could not restrain her; she bounded over bushes and tore after them. The large kangaroos jumped away, too fast for Dina, but two joeys fell from their mothers' pouches.

Two joeys the size of wallabies, a taste of paste made from crushed seeds was the meal that night. A small drink of water for each person and the two dogs, and no extra for Merindah even though she still nursed her baby.

In the morning Merindah had seen a thin spiral of smoke in the west again. But some men did not want to go on; they approached Muller and told him that they wanted to return to the cove.

'We know water is there, and food. We'll die if we keep going west, there's no sign of water here and we barely have enough for one more day. What do we do then?' one man said.

Others agreed. 'Yes, we should go back.'

Muller and Bryant went across to talk to Merindah, who sat with the other women.

'Are we going to find water?' Muller asked her. 'We must soon, those men want to go back, perhaps we've come too far.'

'Yes, we've come too far,' Merindah agreed. 'Water is ahead

somewhere, we just need to find where.'

'What makes you so sure that there's water ahead?'

'Other people are here,' Merindah said.

'What do you mean other people? Have you seen them?

'There are people here; they'll have water.'

'No one else is here, and we need water today,' Muller grumbled as he walked away shaking his head. 'The woman's gone mad.'

Bryant knew that his woman had not gone mad.

'Why are you so sure other people are here?' he asked.

'Smoke from their fire, they are here.'

'Well, you must find them; or their water soon, yes, soon,' he said. 'Today!'

Sunshine on their backs and a dry westerly wind in their faces, the group moved on. They had a small drink of water each that morning; after their next drink they would be carrying two empty water breakers and dry skin bags. The three women took turns carrying William in his sling. Many of the group walked on cut and bruised feet, both Sarah and Rebus did not want to walk on.

'You must keep walking,' Merindah told them.

Sarah struggled; Rebus wanted to stop, his soft feet had the most damage, Merindah retied the skins around them and he limped on in tears, hungry, thirsty and tired.

She had seen the smoke again, but the same distance away.

They must be moving; like we are, the same direction. We may not catch them. Later that day they were walking along a more defined pathway, narrow like a worn animal pad.

This is their path. Merindah did not find water that day.

Sally still carried fire in a bucket; that night they sat around a small fire without food and drank the last of the water. Bryant and Muller came to Merindah and asked about those other people, and water. She came from a place where water and food was never a problem. Now these men expected her to find both, in a place, almost as strange to her as it was to them. *The animals that live here must get water from somewhere, perhaps from the plants.*

A misty morning provided moisture in the air and damp leaves. The dogs licked the leaves, men tried to copy them. People and dogs fought to lick small patches of moisture in hollows in the white rocks. Soon the sun and the wind sucked up any sign of moisture.

Bryant urged everyone to move on. Muller grumbled, swore and fell behind the main group of walkers.

Merindah walked away from the group leaving William with Sally. She knew that they must be near the place where she first saw the smoke. The path seemed to have vanished, but those people had been there somewhere. She followed indistinct vague tracks through the rocks and trees. Inta followed, sniffing and exploring the new places. Any tracks that they found disappeared on the sheets of stone. As she walked toward the cliffs Merindah heard the sound of the waves become louder. She found more gaping holes breathing with the waves hundreds of feet below.

Merindah watched an eagle circle far above the expanse of stunted trees all leaning away from the sea. Small birds darted amongst the branches. Ants and beetle scurried about.

'How can all of this life be here, but we are going to die?' she asked herself aloud.

'No, I have William, the others and the dogs I must help them.' As she walked back away from the cliffs, Merindah sighted the rest of the group in the distance, struggling along. Their lives depended on her.

She found another track; following it led her back further inland from the direction the others were walking. Soon the track became more pronounced. Ashes lay in the shelter of a large bush and a wider path led to a depression. She noticed a large gap in the rocky ground; the ground had collapsed.

It had. Merindah stared in amazement; trees grew down in a basin their tops level with the surrounding ground. The bushes were greener and small fresh plants grew amongst rocks. Merindah climbed down. She found a small cave and could smell moisture. In a small rock hole she found water. Smooth edges showed where animals or people had stood, knelt and drank, black damp fissures stretched above into sheets of rock. There was still water draining into the rock hole, a small amount each day. Merindah could see gaps in the sheets of stone under her feet.

'Water runs into this place,' Merindah muttered in her mother's language. 'Most goes down into the rocks below ground, some seeps into this well, but it may soon be just a damp place, perhaps even dry. This small well is one place where those people get their water. They have chipped rocks away to make it hold more.'

Merindah only carried two dry water skins. She was not sure if they would still hold water. She drank, then dampening the skins outside and in, to moisten them before filling them with water. The group walking were now far ahead of her, but Merindah found her way back to the track and found them before dark. William was crying out for her.

Merindah went straight to the other women and her baby. The women were chewing roots, but becoming concerned.

Bryant was anxious. 'Where have you been? Did you find water? These people can't go any further. The men were desperate for a drink; some unable to speak, their mouths dry and lips cracked. Merindah passed him one skin of water, the other she gave to the women first. They all shared the water that Merindah brought them in the skins, but she did not drink; she had hers at the native well. She let the two dogs share her portion.

Muller approached Merindah, 'We should all go back to that place where you found that water.'

Merindah pointed west, 'No we will go that way, there will be more places, people use them.'

'You may never find them. I think we should go back to the place where you found that water.'

Bill Bryant stood close listening. 'We should do what she says.'

'I'll decide what we do,' Muller said.

'Well I am going to follow her and go on tomorrow. You can go back to that water, if you can find it, which I doubt,' Bryant said firmly. Muller stormed off. The exhausted group slept, some dreaming of water.

Awake before day break, Merindah soon found a higher place among the scrub, climbed up the biggest of the small trees. There, as the sun rose behind her, she stood looking west at the low scrub seeming to continue on forever. Once again, a small twist of smoke. She carefully searched for a landmark, but saw none, only an expanse of the same small trees. No hills, no belts of bigger trees to show a water course. The only mark to use was the edge of that world, where it dropped abruptly into the ocean. She noted the distance the smoke may have been from the cliffs, and then tried to estimate the distance from where she stood, to that smoke.

Is that their next camp after the well I found yesterday, or is there one between here and the smoke? Where the smoke came from was where the wells would be. There would not be a lot of water in each well, but even a light fall of rain would add more. Her mission was to find those places.

Merindah understood why the people were moving, the hot time was coming; the wells would soon be dry. It had been the cooler time, shorter days; occasionally rain would add water to the wells. That's why the people were there, they moved with the seasons. Like her mother's clan, they moved back to a more suitable place for the warmer season; permanent water and different food.

Muller wanted to go back to the place where Merindah had collected the water.

'There's water there, but we don't know if there is any on ahead,' he insisted. 'If we go back and it rains, there will be more water. If we go on we may not find water, rain or no rain.'

Three men wanted to go back with Muller. The women and Bryant trusted Merindah's judgment; they were ready to go on.

'Well if you are going on, tell me where to find that water. I'm going back,' Muller said. Merindah tried to explain where she had found the well.

'But there are no tracks,' she said. 'It's all stones, no marks.'

'But you found your way back to us yesterday,' Muller insisted.

'It was not easy to see your marks, but I knew which way you were going, and just kept coming this way until I found you.'

Muller was determined to go back to that well.

'It's in a small hollow,' she said. 'The ground's fallen in; the well is in a small cave.' She waved her hands about trying to show Muller where to find the water.

'That sounds easy to find, three men are coming with me.'

'We'll mark the track that we take on ahead,' Bryant said thoughtfully. 'You'll be able to follow us.'

'You do that,' Muller agreed. 'It might help you find your way back to where I am going. I'll mark my way back to the well.'

'Broken branches will be the sign,' Bryant told him. 'Now, I'm going to get food for us. Where's young Jacob?'

Muller and three men left to find the well, only taking one empty water bag with them. The rest of the group headed west to an unknown fate. They left marks to show their trail. This would also help Bryant and Jacob catch up with them with any food they could get with Dina.

Merindah's eyes searched for any signs of the people who had made the smoke. She was certain they were moving west, but she was not sure if she wanted to catch them. *No, I just want to follow them. I know where they are going now, and that's where we need to go.*

Rebus was falling behind again. 'I want to stay here in the shade of this tree,' he told Sarah. 'I'm hungry, my stomach hurts. I need a drink of water, leave me here.'

Merindah went on ahead; walking twice the distance as the others as she weaved amongst small trees searching for another cavity where water would collect. She wanted to find animal or human pads amongst the stones. 'The animals find those places; their tracks should lead me there.'

Her breasts were firm, William needed to be fed; she stopped for a rest, expecting the others to catch up. When no one came, Merindah retraced her path back to where they were stopped and waiting for her water. William was crying out for her.

'Some of the men say they can't go on,' Sally told her. 'Their feet are bad, the skins are torn to pieces, and now their feet are being hurt.'

As Merindah fed her baby she decided what to do. She told Sally, 'You stay here, mind William and Inta, I'll take Levi. He's not the strongest, but he seems to handle things better than the other men and his feet are as tough as mine. We'll take four of those skin bags and bring back water. William will be hungry, but you'll just need to give him something to suck on. Get a good fire going. Bryant may have food when he catches up with you.'

Now Merindah had to find water soon, she led Levi forward. 'You keep that side of me,' she told him, 'Don't lose sight of me; keep making a noise so I know where you are. If you find a path, or a small ditch, no matter how small tell me. Look for a dip in the tree tops; that will mean a place where the ground has collapsed.'

Hours later Merindah sat exhausted, it was almost sunset.

'What can I do now?' She sobbed. It would be dark soon and it was already too late to find their way back to the group that night. She had not found water. The lives of the people and William depended on her. All the people from the shipwreck were now split into four, perhaps five groups. The Captain and seven other men were somewhere out there in the boat, trying to go back to the end of the cliffs. Muller and three men were going back to a well with only a little water left in it. The main group was behind her without food or water. Bill Bryant and Jacob could be still away searching for food. Merindah shed tears; she had not found the water that she promised them she would.

'We will all die scattered along these rocks,' she told a bird as it sat on a branch next to her. 'Where do you get a drink?'

The sun slipped into the scrub in the west; they would not go back to the others that night.

'William needs me,' Merindah wept. 'But what can I do?'

Levi had walked ahead. He found a small rise where he could see further across the tops of the small trees. He turned and ran back past her. 'This way Merindah!'

Chapter 20 – Just One Boat, Eight Men

One small boat; the giant cliffs now on their right.
Should we go this way?

Captain Harris was not sure he had made the right decision. He was going west but he remembered what Hugh Byron said he had found behind those cliffs. 'No sign of water, just rocks and more rocks, small bushes, trees further inland. Doesn't change for miles, why would it? The coast is the same all the way.'

Harris feared that all his people walking would perish. 'Why am I going this way, they will all die. With his west we would be a hundred miles east by now.'

'Look up at those cliffs,' Hugh Byron told the Captain as they rowed west the second morning. 'We won't catch sight of the others for days, there's no way we can stop anywhere here.'

'It's about a hundred and twenty miles to the next beach,' the Captain said. 'I don't think we'll ever see them again. They'll die up there.'

Now Hugh Byron also doubted the decision to go west. 'Well, why are we going this way? Perhaps we should go east again. At least we may get help there.'

'Help for what; help for dead people?' Captain Harris said. He sat quietly staring at the giant cliff. Hugh thought he was going to turn around. But Captain Harris pointed west.

'No, I've decided. We'll take the boat to the end of the cliffs and wait for them, if they don't turn up, we will get water and food, and go back east.'

'How long will we wait?' Hugh asked.

'I don't know, we'll talk about that later, we have to get there ourselves yet. If this wind keeps blowing from the west, we may not get there either. We barely have six days water, and not enough food.'

They changed rowers and drank water sparingly.

Captain Harris sat in the stern considering his predicament. Soon he would be expected back at Granite Island; those men would have whale oil and seal skins waiting for him, and would be ready to leave. And the men left at Flinders Island would be expecting to see the ship any day.

'This is a mess, many men are depending on me, while I'm here rowing along this desolate coast, going backwards. I must sort this out.'

'There's not much you can do about it now,' answered Hugh Byron as he pulled on an oar. 'We just need to try our best to keep alive. What are we going to do about food?'

'There's still a harpoon in this boat, I wonder if we could spear one of those dolphins?'

'What, and eat it raw?' Hugh asked.

'You will if you are hungry enough.' Captain Harris said; the other men agreed.

'Let's get one,' one man said. 'Why not?' said another.

'What about seals? Must be seals on those rocks.'

'We're not going near those rocks,' Captain Harris told them. 'Not until the end of these cliffs, then we'll get a seal to eat, and more water, I hope. Let's get past these bloody cliffs as soon as we can. Could we try the sail now?'

After four days of rowing and occasionally sailing back and forth, without much forward momentum they had eaten all their food. They were all watching for a dolphin, and ready.

'They are too fast,' a man said, as he pulled the harpoon back in empty.

'We'll try again,' Hugh said. 'You others keep rowing.'

Bryant had told them that his dogs had eaten wallaby skin when they were on the other boat. The Captain told his men to cut some into strips and chew it. When they tried to swallow the fur made them choke.

'Bloody hopeless,' a man said. 'Can we catch some fish?'

'Ok, drag a line but we're not going to stop,' the Captain told them. 'Keep rowing, we'll get to the end of these cliffs in two more days.'

Hugh shook the last cask of water. 'We'll be out of water in two days. We need east wind, so we can sail.'

The small boat made its way slowly west. They had not seen any sign of the others, and did not expect to, perhaps not ever.

Six days from the cove; at last they could see white sand hills in the distance.

'We should get there by morning if you keep rowing,' Hugh said. 'We'll kill a seal first, probably the only food there.' The men rowing were too weak to talk, they had swallowed their last water, and had to get to the beach the next morning or perish.

Hugh wondered if they would find water on the beach. The Captain seemed to have lost interest; he sat in the stern holding onto the big oar, his eyes glazed; he seemed to be in a trance.

I'm the one who has to get us out of this now, Hugh told himself.

*   *   *

As Merindah desperately searched for water for the group walking along the cliff top, the Captain and the men in the whaleboat rowed against a strong west wind for days. Neither group could see or make any contact with the other. It was very likely now that one or both groups of the Belinda's survivors would perish.

*   *   *

James Miles worked with the whaling men at Granite Island. The men there expected the Belinda to return soon. They regularly brought whales into the beach. Aboriginal people helped with the boiling down of the whale blubber.

Yara still lived at the camp with the outcast Aboriginal women; that was now her home, she had become one of them. Yara's baby girl did not look like the other children who lived there, with her shiny dark skin, different facial features and a mop of tight black curls.

There was no doubt that Alinta was James's daughter, her fair hair and blue eyes much like his, but each time he saw her, James remembered her mother; the tall girl who had saved his life. He visited the women's camp often, spending time with Yara and the baby girls. Although Alinta was Merindah and James's baby, Yara embraced the baby girl as her own. James took things to Yara and the babies to make life easier.

James did not know of Bill Bryant's plan to remain somewhere sealing. When the ship left taking Merindah away, he wondered if she thought about him, as he did about her, or had Merindah disregarded their time together. Whatever her feelings were, he did expect to see her again when the ship returned.

Men from his group went to spend time with the Aboriginal women on the mainland. There were available women at the exile women's camp, but each time he visited there and talked to them, he recalled the time with Merindah and wondered if they would ever be together again.

James and the other men at Granite Island did not know that the Belinda lay wrecked in the sand at Middle Island. Nor could they imagine the crew's desperate attempt to survive.

Surviving on the desolate coast was now Merindah's life. For many days she had been finding water and food for the group walking. They expected to find Captain Harris and the men in the remaining whaleboat waiting for them at the end of the huge cliffs.

Chapter 21 – Eight Desperate Men
Against the West Wind

Why won't the wind blow the right way?
Our lives depend on it.
We can't go back now; row or die.

Mist provided moisture for the men's lips, they sponged it off the canvas; sucking the damp dirty rags refreshed each man. As the sun burnt the mist away, they could still see the cliffs on their right. But ahead in the distance there appeared to be a thin line of white sand. The sight of that beach gave them encouragement.

Hugh Byron urged the rowers on. 'Just a few more miles and we'll be able to take this boat ashore.'

'Are you sure we'll find water there?' a man rowing asked.

'We'll have to, won't we?' Hugh answered. 'If it wasn't for this bloody west wind, we would have been here days ago, still with fresh water in the boat.'

'What about natives?' another man asked. 'Will there be any here?'

'There'll be natives here somewhere, and we certainly won't be welcome if Ned and Addis have been here,' answered Captain Harris, who had revived a little after his sip of water and the prospect of getting ashore.

'I don't think they would come this far east,' Hugh said. 'Although you can be sure they'll be stirring up trouble back by those islands. If there's natives here, they probably haven't seen white men. Those islands are a hundred miles away.'

'News travels, even in these places,' Captain Harris remarked. 'You may be surprised how the Aboriginals converse over long distances, we should be wary.'

The whaleboat rode a wave onto a sandy beach. A sailor's legs buckled as he carried the anchor onto the beach and jammed it into the sand. Seven other thirsty men staggered ashore carrying two casks, and a pannikin. They left the boat in the wash of the waves. Water was the only thing on their minds. They forgot about Aboriginals; forgot about the other Belinda survivors, dead or alive up behind those cliffs.

Wary eyes watched the boat as it appeared out of the mist that morning, eyes of people who knew where the water was. In the past, these people had seen ships with sails far out from their beach.

Although they had heard about white men coming ashore in small boats further west, this was the first time they had come to their beach. They kept well out of sight as eight bearded men struggled ashore. What did these strangers want? Why were they here?

'Where would water be?' a man asked Hugh.

'I've no idea man,' Hugh answered angrily. 'I don't expect we will walk straight up to a well or a keg of water. We may need to dig, or if we're lucky, find a native well. I bet there's one here somewhere.'

Hugh could see that this area was similar to the place where Merindah had found the water at the cove. 'Perhaps water's under this sand somewhere, but I don't know where to dig. If Bill Bryant's young woman was here, she'd find water. But she's probably dead. Anyway, I doubt if any of us are capable of digging now.'

'If any of them are still alive back there, it will be that woman,' Captain Harris said. He glanced back at the cliffs which had prevented the boat from coming ashore for the last six days. He wondered about the group and where they might be. He had left his young woman with them. *Is she still alive?*

Hugh was still thinking about Bryant's woman; she would find a place to dig. 'A native well, that's our only chance, we must find one today. Fire places; find a place where there's been a fire, somewhere near the fire will be water. Not necessarily alongside of the water but it won't be far away.'

They spread out as they walked amongst the low scrub above the beach where they left the boat. Assuming that they would find water without difficulty, two men carried an empty cask each. There were tracks through the bushes leading up to the larger trees further from the beach. A startled wallaby bounded away from the men. 'Food!' a man yelled.

'We need Bryant's bitch to catch that,' Hugh Byron remarked gloomily.

They all stood still, thinking briefly about the others who walked, or were still walking toward that place at the end of the cliffs, but their urgent thirst focused them on the task of finding water. They had walked up and then back along the coast away from the beach. None of them noticed the tide rising.

Hugh Byron saw the ashes first; the fire pit in a sheltered spot behind a sand hill, out of the persistent west wind.

'This is where people camp; now we need to follow the right track to find where they get water.'

'Which track?' A man asked,

'I bloody well don't know, you stupid bastard, or else I wouldn't need you to find it,' Hugh answered, getting sick of dumb sailors.

It was just a small well, a soak in the sand. The reeds growing around it should have led them to it earlier. They had walked past the place several times in their searching. Seven more men rushed up to the water and shoved the one who found it aside. They all pushed in to get at the water, damaging the well in their impatient rush.

Hugh Byron was wild 'Shit! Now we need to clean the sand out before we can fill these casks. Somebody go back to the boat and get a bucket.'

It was almost dark. They had not noticed the afternoon slipping by as they searched for water. Neither had they considered their boat and the rising tide.

The man came running back without a bucket.

'The boat!' he cried out. 'It's sideways in the waves. All our stuff's washing up along the beach.'

The whaleboat was half full of sand, water washed in and out with each wave. Buckets, oars, casks, skins, and most of the rest of the contents of the boat, spread along the shore. Tangled amongst water and sand, still attached to the whale boat, ropes and canvas sail washed about.

The Captain was furious. 'Why did you leave the boat here like this?' he accused Hugh Byron. What could Hugh say, they were all at fault, but he would take the blame.

As darkness came they started bailing water out, with every bucket full of water they threw out, the next wave brought another and more sand over the side. Two men went along the beach recovering the things that had washed out of the boat, the easy task. Getting the sand and water out of the boat became impossible with the tide still coming in.

Hugh Byron could see it was hopeless. 'We need to wait until the tide starts going out.'

The Captain glared at Hugh. 'YOU, will need to hope those waves don't damage the boat. Has anybody seen the tinder box? We need to light a fire.'

'It was still in the boat,' Hugh said awkwardly, he knew where it was before, but even if he found it now, it would be covered with sand and sea water; ruined.

'There'll be no fire tonight.'

They waited in the cold, on the beach until the tide turned and then by the light of moon began clearing the water and sand out of their boat. Waves had packed sand hard into the boat; they needed to loosen it with an oar before a bucket could scoop the sand out. The work was exhausting, when they finished, they did not have the energy to drag the empty boat further up the beach.

'Now, we need to wait until the tide comes in again,' Hugh said. 'The boat must be above the high water mark; that will take hours.'

Some men slept; others waited. They all shivered.

In the early morning the boat floated again. They all worked together to get it safely up the beach away from waves. Now their focus returned to food and water. Whatever food they found would have to be eaten raw. No fire; they hadn't found the tinderbox, perhaps they had thrown it out with a bucket of sand.

'Would be ruined anyway,' the Captain said, sneering at Hugh. 'Fire is one thing, but we need water right now. Let's go.'

They walked through the low bushes back toward the well, carrying the casks again. One man carried a bucket to clean out the sand that they had pushed into the well when they clambered for a drink the previous evening.

The well had been cleaned out.

'Who the hell did that?' Captain Harris asked. 'Somebody has been here, we're not alone.'

In their haste to fill the casks they damaged the well again. They left it and returned to the boat.

They gathered shell fish at low tide. 'Can we eat this raw?' a man asked.

'You just watch me,' another said as he broke open the shell and swallowed the meat, and everything else that came out of the shell.

Morning sun glistened on waves that teased the men. 'Look at the sea now,' Hugh Byron said. 'It's almost calm; I wonder how often it's like that.'

'Not often I reckon, but that's how it needs to be when we're ready to leave here,' Captain Harris said.

'When will that be? Are we going to wait for the others?' Hugh asked

'I don't know yet, we'll see what we find here.'

A pod of dolphins swam past close to the shore; the men

enviously gazed at the dolphins swimming back and forth.

'They're rounding up fish and catching them,' Hugh said. 'There's food here, but we can't get any.'

Captain Harris gestured toward the point where the great cliffs bent and curved back into the land. 'Might be seals on those rocks, and maybe some flint to light a fire.'

'We can't take the boat near there, even when it's calm like this,' Hugh said. 'Too many reefs; we'll have to walk there. If we can't kill a seal, there'll be more shellfish; we'll go now. Then we'll fill those casks with water in the morning.'

Two men and Captain Harris stayed by the boat. Hugh Byron and the other men walked toward the rocky point, taking the harpoon from the boat, a knife, and a bucket. Surf pounded into the point, spray blowing backwards as the waves crashed into the rocks.

*   *   *

On the cliff above the beach the men who had repaired the well stood watching. Their clan had been using that well for generations, it was important for their survival. They only took enough water for their families' needs and treated their wells with great respect. Their women and children were at a camp on the plateau, well behind the cliff. There was still water in wells there that their forbears had hacked into the stone. When those wells dried up, and the warm season started, the families would move closer to the coast and then they would need that well in the sand hills.

*   *   *

A small seal, more shellfish, food at last. But still no fire.

The Captain was still angry about the lost flint box. 'It's going to be raw seal meat.'

They filled their stomachs with raw seal meat and shellfish, then sat or lay freezing in the cold wind with a few stunted bushes providing scanty shelter. Fire, Hugh smelt smoke.

'There's a fire up there,' he said pointing up to the edge of the inland cliff. 'People are up there, perhaps they know we're here.'

'Of course they do; they've been watching us all day,' the Captain said. 'Who do you think fixed up that well? I saw men up there when you were around at the point, just a glimpse, but I saw them.'

They were all cold and miserable, 'Shit, I'd like to get some of that fire, I'm bloody freezing.' 'We all are, you stupid bastard, and I am sick from eating raw meat,' another man uttered.

'And there would be women there too, one of them would keep me warm for a while,' a third declared.

'You are not going to touch their women,' Captain Harris ordered.

The man almost spoke; then held his tongue. *Well you have, or perhaps you had one, where did you get her from?*

'We'll see if we can get fire from them in the morning,' Harris said. 'And more water from that well.'

Another cold misty morning; they needed more water. Hugh took four men with him. He did not see through the low bushes until they walked into the reedy place where the well was.

They all stopped suddenly.

Six Aboriginal men stood between them and the well, alert and armed with long threatening spears. Clearly, they were not going to get water that day. Hugh backed away and led the men back to their camp by the boat.

'What do we do now?' he asked Captain Harris. 'No more water, no fire. They've got both. All we've got is raw bloody meat but not enough water to leave here.'

'Go back and try to talk to them, make a sign that you need water.' the Captain ordered. 'And get fire from them.'

The native men were still guarding the well when Hugh Byron and the four men returned later that day.

Hugh made signs. 'Water,' he said. 'Water,' putting his hand to his mouth and pointed to the two casks his men carried. The Aboriginal men brandished their spears and stepped boldly toward Hugh and his men.

Hugh hesitated; these men were angry, 'Looks like we're not getting any more water from here. We should back off.' In their haste to leave Hugh's men dropped the two casks.

That night they shared a little water and ate more raw seal meat while the smell of meat cooking and smoke came from a fire at the well.

'Bastards are still there,' a man said.

Fire and water, without those two things the eight men could not survive. They felt sick eating the raw seal meat.

'As soon as the sea is calm we will get the boat back in the water and move further along the beach?' the Captain told Hugh.

'Yes, but we may not find a well. Even if we do, there may be another group of natives, and then we'll need food. Here we can still get to those rocks at the point where we can get more seals. There are no rocks further along this beach; that means no seals. We need to get help from those natives somehow.'

Another morning Hugh tried again: he took four men with him to the well.

He would show the Aboriginals that he was desperate for water.

The men carried another cask, but it was the same as before, they were not allowed to go near the well. The native men became even more hostile and agitated. They stood waving their hands angrily pointing to the two casks that Hugh's men had dropped the day before.

'They want us to take those two casks away,' Hugh said. 'Pick them up.'

'Well I'll be buggered,' a man said as he bent to pick up a cask. 'They've filled it with water. Shit, both are full, I wonder if they will fill this one.'

'Don't push your luck,' Hugh said. 'I think that's their way of telling us to take that water and bugger off. Let's move, bring those two full casks.'

'How long can we survive on raw meat and little water?' Hugh asked Captain Harris.

'We've been saving a little water. If they won't fill this other cask, we'll only have enough for four days; enough to go back east to that beach where there's water and food. No Aboriginals.'

'What about the rest of our people?' Hugh asked. 'Sounds like you've given up on them. This is where we agreed to meet them.'

'We can't stay here without water or fire; we've waited long enough. They're not coming. As soon as the wind changes so we can get the boat through those waves, we'll get out of here.'

'West or east?'

'I haven't decided yet,' the Captain said. 'Although if the west wind comes again like we rowed against, it would only take two days to sail back east to that cove. Remember, food and water, no Aboriginals. Perhaps the others may have returned there too; or those who are still alive.'

'What if we keep going west to the island where we all stayed for two days?' Hugh asked. 'You remember, the first island in the group; then try to get back to Middle Island. We know there's water and food there, and no Aboriginal men, just those six sealers and their women.'

'Well whichever way we go, we'll need more food. Try to kill another seal tomorrow.'

Wind blew off the land as the sun rose the next morning.

'Shit! Look how calm it is this morning; let's get out of here while we can.'

*   *   *

Merindah and the group walking west were still days away from that beach and searching for water. Aboriginals watched the boat leave, but that day they received a message about another group of white men walking toward their area. They were wary and stayed close to their water.

Chapter 22 – Levi with his Good Eyes

Why let go, when you have climbed so high, gone so
far?
There are so many people depending on me.

Nimble Levi climbed a tree. They had walked past it, but now he
saw the depression.

Trees grew there, but their tops seemed to be lower, shorter or
was there a hollow?

'This way Merindah,' he called as he ran past.

Merindah followed the skinny youth. She knew he had found
the place.

The bushes were fresher and greener, exactly what she asked
Levi to find. A section of collapsed ground; a large area, like a
sunken rock garden.

Even though Merindah had no word for garden, she realised
that it was a special place where people gathered. There were many
old fireplaces and ashes nearby. Already as evening came birds
began to settle in trees nearby. Animal pads led toward the hollow
and over the edge.

'There'll be more water here Levi, thank you for finding this.'
Merindah was relieved. They climbed down and soon found water
in a shaded well amongst the rocks.

'A little water may seep into this well during the hot season, but
only enough for the birds; not enough for a group of people,' she
told Levi. 'There's more here now, because it's been the rainy

season. Other water has gone underground; see these gaps in the rocks. I think that caves are under here, and there would be more water, but we can't reach it.'

After drinking water and nibbling some berries, Merindah and Levi put water in the skin bags.

'These have dried out,' she told him. 'This water will make them softer; they will hold the water better to take back to the others in the morning.'

It was too late to find their way back to the others and her baby. Merindah's breasts hurt, but now she knew that she would take water back and feed William in the morning. They found a sheltered place away from the well and watched as small birds flew into the water. A flock of large noisy white parrots circled and landed on a dead tree nearby.

'Look Levi, those birds will show us where these wells are, each evening and each morning they'll be here.' Merindah told Levi and reassured herself. 'We need to watch for these signs, Levi. You can help me each day.'

Stars still hugged the low trees and an arc of orange glowed in the eastern sky when Merindah woke Levi. They took the four skin water bags to fill from the well. After drinking themselves, they sat away from the area for a short time waiting for more light. Birds moved, chattered; small animals scurried about on the stony ground.

Suddenly the birds stopped; there was no movement or sound.

A dingo walked past, stopped, sniffed the air and glanced arrogantly in their direction. This was the dingo's territory; it knew that there could be scraps here, or an animal to grab. The wild dog drank from the well. As it left, the dingo walked closer to Merindah and Levi without fear, turned and merged into the scrub.

The mingled exchange of bird conversation resumed. Spears of sunlight stabbed through narrow tree trunks.

Dawn revealed the track. 'This way Levi. Let's take this back. Quick, we'll run.'

William needed her; her tight breasts told her that.

Merindah sensed Sally's fire before she found the camp. Bill Bryant and Jacob were there. Dina had caught a female kangaroo and her joey; the group had all eaten meat, but wanted water.

'Marvellous,' said Bryant as Merindah passed around the water. 'You've saved us again.'

'No,' Merindah said, 'Levi found the well.' She rushed to her baby and relieved the pain in her breasts, and her heart. Many of the group were suffering after walking for two days without water. Rebus would need help to struggle on to Levi's well.

Muller and the three men who went with him had not returned.

Bryant thought someone should go.

'Who feels fit enough to go back to tell those blokes that there's more water ahead,' Bryant asked. Although Levi had walked far the day before, he was the only person able to go. His feet were undamaged, and he was young and agile. 'I'll go back.'

Only one bag of water remained, and that would be gone soon.

'No save that,' Bryant told the group. 'Levi; take this water, find those four men, tell them to come this way because we have more water now. The track should be easy to follow. Jacob and I will wait for you here.' He hesitated. 'If you can't find them today, save the water for yourself and be back by dark, we will wait, and go on in the morning with or without them. Does that make sense lad?'

'Yes Mr Bryant, I'll go as soon as I've eaten a piece of that meat you've saved for us,' replied Levi. He was a skinny lad, wiry and smart. He did not know who his father was, nor did his mother, who sealers had cast aside. Captain Harris had found him wandering, begging at Hobart Town and took him aboard the ship.

Levi had found the water and possibly saved all those other people's lives. Now the lives of four more men depended on him.

Bill Bryant, Jacob and the dog, Dina, would wait for Levi.

'Don't forget we'll only wait until the morning,' Bryant told Levi. 'Then we'll go on. You'll be on your own. Be careful with that water, save some for yourself. I'll expect you back here tonight or early in the morning.'

Levi ran off carrying a bag of kangaroo meat and the skin full of water. It was easy to follow the track that they had marked. He soon found the place where Muller turned back to find Merindah's well.

Muller and the three men had not marked their track clearly, but Levi was smart, he carefully followed any marks they and the others had made. After midday he found the first man lying under a stunted tree. At first the man appeared dead, but only a little water revived him.

'Steady, not too much at first,' Levi told the man. He let him drink more and left him eating a small piece of meat. He found the next man walking towards him in a delirious state. Levi gave him a little water and helped him to the first man. More water and a small piece of meat each revived the men slightly.

'Where're the other two men?' Levi asked them.

'Back there somewhere, we couldn't find the well.'

'You two wait here, I'll go back and find them; and perhaps the water. I'll need to take the water bag with me. Wait here.'

'We won't be going anywhere until you bring us back more water,' the stronger man said. 'I think you may as well leave it for us anyway, they'll both be dead by now; were half dead when I left them. No water, no water.'

'They could still be alive. I need to see for myself.'

Levi left them and walked alone, *How am I going to find them if they've wandered off this track?*

There was not really a track, but he knew roughly where the group had walked through two days before. Soon he realised that he had gone past the place where he remembered Merindah coming from with the water. *I've come too far, now what do I do?*

Levi remembered how he had climbed a tree to look over the surrounding scrub; that's how he found that other well. He ran to a slight rise and his keen eyes searched from the tallest tree.

There was no change; he would never be able to find the two

men, without something to show him where they were.

What would show him? *Birds, I remember the birds. Merindah said they would tell us things. Where are the birds?* He studied the afternoon sky. A wedge tail eagle circled high.

'What can you see?' he asked the great bird floating a mile away.

Levi needed a sign. *Now, if I waited here till sunset, I may see birds going to the well that Merindah found here, but I can't wait, I must find those two men first, and then the well.*

Large black birds noisily circled in a gang nearby. *They're watching or waiting for something; over there.*

Levi soon found Muller and the other man.

The crows would have their eyes first, next the other soft pieces of flesh. That night the dingoes would tear into the meat. Next day the eagles and crows would scrap over the rest, and then would come the blowflies and their maggots. Last would be the black ants, and within a few days there would only be white bones spread around the scrub. These two men had white skin, and their bones would be white. So would the bones of a black man be white, if he were to die there, as no doubt some had.

The two men were not dead. Not quite! Muller lay unconscious; the other man sat next to him rambling about water and a 'bloody black woman'. Water soon steadied him, but old Muller was worse. Levi dragged and sat him up against a skinny tree trunk; a little water dribbling into Muller's mouth choked him, but roused him and he swallowed the next trickle, then a little more.

Muller sat and became aware of Levi helping him; the other man improved and started to eat the meat that Levi brought. Both men recovered slowly, but Levi realised Muller would not be walking anywhere that day. The water would be gone soon, and so would the daylight. There was no sign of Muller's water bag.

'The well,' Levi said. 'I must find Merindah's well. The birds, they will show me where it is, it must be here close.' The two men took no notice of the youth.

As the sun set, large white noisy parrots showed him the way to the well. Levi watched from a tree top; then ran quickly to the spot. This well was smaller than the well he had found, but there was still water there. Enough to fill the skin water bag, a large drink for himself; still some left for the birds. He knew it would be only be a damp patch in the rocks soon. *Even these birds may need to go somewhere else soon.*

When he found Muller and the other man again, it was almost dark. Even if there was moonlight Levi would not be able to find the track. They had to stay the night.

The other two men would be waiting for Levi and more water. Further on Bill Bryant and Jacob would be waiting for Levi, and they had no water. Levi hoped Muller would be well enough to move first thing in the morning.

The walkers remained split up along that track where Captain Harris was sure they would all die. Young Levi was not going to leave anyone behind. As soon as he could see through the bushes in the morning, he gave Muller and the man more water. 'I'll be back soon.'

Again Levi ran; not for his life, but the lives of the four men. He ran down the track that he now knew well. The first two men were still there where he left them the day before, they wanted more water, and emptied the bag.

'You can walk now, go on and you might find Bill Bryant and Jacob waiting,' Levi told them. 'If they're not there, just keep following the track, it'll be easy to find now. Tell Mr Bryant that I have the other two, but Muller is in a bad way.' Levi melded in the scrub with the empty bag.

A little water remained in the well for the birds after Levi had filled the bag again and drank himself. He stopped for a spell.

'You can have the rest,' he told the birds. 'I won't be back.'

Levi found the man and Muller where he had left them. 'Here, drink. Now you must get up and walk or else I will have to leave you here to die.'

'Where'd you get that water?' Muller asked. 'That bloody black woman didn't want us to find it, she wanted us to die.'

'Why don't you get up and walk. Then you can tell her that yourself,' Levi said, thinking that would get him going. 'She told you not to come back here; we've found more water now. You can't stay here; I'm not going to run back and forth anymore.' He knew Muller was strong enough to walk; but how far?

Bryant and Jacob were thirsty, but they waited until mid-morning before they prepared to leave.

'We'll go now, Jacob. There's nothing we can do here. Levi's on his own now, and the other four are probably dead. Let's go.'

Just as they were walking out a man yelled out.

'Hey wait for us!' Two men approached.

'Where's Levi, and the other two?' Bill Bryant asked.

'Back there somewhere. Levi said that Muller's in a bad way. Have you got water here?'

'No, but there's water ahead, let's go.'

'What about Levi and the other two, Mr Bryant?' Jacob asked.

'We need to get to the water boy, and these two will need our help. I'm sure Levi will be okay. The other two will just have to come on, or die. Don't forget they wanted to go back.'

The main group had settled at Levi's water hole.

Merindah had seen the smoke again in the west early in the morning.

'They're still there,' she told Sally. 'Moving every day, stopping at a well, we just need to follow them.'

'This water won't last long with all these people using it,' Sally said.

'No; and we're not all here yet, there may be less of us now. I don't think Muller would have found that other well. I told him not to go back.'

Bill Bryant, Jacob and two weak men walked into the camp after midday.

'We can't stay here for long,' Merindah told Bryant, 'Although this well's bigger, we'll soon use all the water.'

'You go on in the morning. Take all these people with you; I'll wait for Levi and the other two.'

'But I need Levi to help find the water, his eyes are the best.'

Jacob was near, he had heard them talking. 'I'll take water back to meet Levi.' he said. He left soon after, carrying water back along the now familiar track.

'More meat, we need more meat. Come, Dina,' Bryant said as he went and found a fit man to help. They returned after sunset empty-handed.

'We'll try again early in the morning.'

Merindah had made sure that they camped away from the well. 'The birds and the animals; they need the water too. This is an important place for them, and we must give them space,' she had told them that first night at Levi's well.

Levi walked into the camp before sunrise.

'Jacob will help those two men now,' he told Merindah. 'I'll go on with you and help find the next water.'

'You drink and eat the last of that meat.'

'But the birds, will be leaving the water soon; they'll will show us where.'

'It's too far to see birds, but I've seen smoke and I know which way. We'll leave soon.'

Bryant, Dina and a man left at sunrise to find more food.

'We'll catch up,' he told Merindah. 'You should all move today, there are too many people drinking this water.'

'Yes I know; we will leave soon.'

Sally carried the fire in a bucket. Others carried skin bags, water breakers, the cook pot and a bucket, all filled with water. The group moved on, trusting Merindah and Levi to find the next well. Once again it was up to Merindah and Levi to guide the group, find the water and get them away from this desolate place. Find where the Captain would be waiting with the boat.

But they had been walking for days. How long would he wait for them?

Chapter 23 – Wait for Us

Here is the beach, where is the boat?
Are we on our own now?

Merindah and Levi went on ahead, leaving the others to follow with all the water skins and the two breakers full of the precious water. Sally and Sarah were confident which bushes grew the edible berries; they gathered food as they travelled.

Merindah followed a path that had been used regularly, or perhaps seasonally. She crossed other paths, most of those led inland.

'There have been more people in this area,' Merindah told Levi. 'I think we're getting close to more permanent living places, where there is more water.'

The main path took them further away from the cliffs than they had been for the entire trek. The trees grew closer together, making it difficult to see any distance ahead.

More tracks; Merindah hung a broken branch on a tree, and then another as she turned yet another corner; that would show her the way back. Her only guide was the sun, birds flew and hopped about, they knew the way, and teased her as they talked.

'Keep with me,' she told Levi. 'We could lose each other in these trees.'

Merindah pointed to stones that stood up across the path. 'That's a sign, they mean something.'

More corners and stones kept Merindah alert. 'This leads to something special.'

Suddenly Merindah stopped walking, she hesitated, looking down at treetops in front of her; Levi came and stood beside her. They stared in amazement at the huge area many feet below them.

White sheets of rock jutted out above the tops of trees, guarding the greener trees below, holding them in. They made shadow and kept away the drying wind.

Merindah and Levi followed the track down into the sink hole. Amongst the green bushes, below the surrounding plain, they stopped and listened. They stood, anxious; something felt different, eerie. Wind moved and rustled the trees, but no bird sounds came.

Where was the water? They cautiously entered a large cave under overhanging sheets of white rock. Dust covered things that did not seem natural. Objects lay as if placed by people; personal possessions and tools, left or discarded, or perhaps put there on purpose. Then the bones; they had not been dragged there by animals; clearly, somebody had placed them there without flesh and skin.

Merindah knew they were human bones. Now she understood what this place was.

'We have to get out Levi,' she said quietly, turning away. 'We are not going to get water from here.'

Levi knew why, he did not speak. They climbed out to the surface. In their haste to leave they took a different path and walked into an open area where skeletons of small dead trees refused to collapse onto the stony ground.

Regiments of black ants marched busily in rows. A squadron of large black birds sat in a tangle of bare branches. The ants marched on, but the crows rose in annoyance as the two stepped into the clearing.

'No! Don't, Levi,' Merindah cried.

Of course he looked up, and gasped.

'That's what they do with their dead,' Merindah said. 'Afterwards, they put their bones in those caves.'

Neither spoke as they turned and walked back along the track until Merindah found the mark that she had made on the main path.

They met the main group walking.

'Have you found more water?' Sally asked as Merindah sat quietly feeding William.

'No.'

'What's wrong with you?' asked Sally, 'And Levi, he hasn't said a word.'

'We won't find water today,' Merindah muttered without lifting her head. 'I don't feel well.'

Bill Bryant caught up with the walkers later in the day. He had a large joey that Dina had run down, he told them that Jacob had brought Muller and the other man up to the last well. They would come on later. Jacob would find the path.

'Where's the water tonight,' he asked Merindah?

'We have enough for tonight,'

'Yes, that may be, but you have to find more.'

'In the morning,' she answered quietly.

'Well, what's wrong with her, with her?' Bryant grumbled as he walked off.

When the group stopped that night, Merindah walked on ahead, she found the best vantage spot to see westward.

Three spirals of smoke twisted into the sky next to the setting sun. *Soon we will meet those people. I wonder what's going to happen then. Do they know that we are coming? Are they waiting for us?*

Early the next morning Jacob came into the camp bringing Muller and the other man with him. For the first time in days the group was together again.

'Let's all keep together,' Bryant said, he seemed to be in command now. Muller was sullen, and he avoided Merindah.

Levi and Merindah found small wells each day as the group walked west. Merindah knew that there were more Aboriginal people in the area. Only she could see the subtle signs; the wells were closer together.

When Merindah was alone with Bill Bryant, she told him, 'The country will change soon, I think we'll meet other people; perhaps at that long beach.'

Bryant became eager, 'You mean we'll meet the Captain and the others?'

'No other people, perhaps the Captain, but there will be other people there.'

Bryant fingered his pipe that had been cold for many days. 'Well whatever. Whatever. I'll send Levi towards the cliffs in the morning; he may be able to judge how much further they go.'

'Not far now, we will find things different.' Merindah said.

'What do you mean?'

'Just different!'

'Well we must not go past the place where Captain Harris will be waiting.'

'Will he be waiting?' Merindah asked. 'What will we do if he's not there?'

'He'd better be. Yes, better be.'

Levi had seen the long sandy beach in the distance from the cliff top. They all became aware of the change in the landscape as they came to the place where the cliff turned back inland.

At first the beach still lay hidden from their view by trees and the cliff. Suddenly they walked out of the scrub; in front of them stretched miles of beach.

In the distance, small spirals of smoke drifted into the blue sky.

Sarah pointed, 'Look Merindah, is that smoke from Captain Harris's fire?'

'No I don't think so. It's too far inland, and there's another fire over there.'

*   *   *

Other people carefully watched the Belinda survivors as they followed a well-worn pathway along the cliff top overlooking the beach.

The Aboriginal men kept out of sight; they were wary of this new large group of strangers who would threaten their precious water supply. They studied with unease, the chain of strangers walk, hobble and limp along their ancient pathway. Whiskery ragged white men, walking with their feet wrapped in animal skins. A large dark skin man with little facial hair. Some younger dark skin men or boys. Three Aboriginal women, taking turns to carry a baby. A young dog and one huge dog more than twice the size of their small yellow dogs.

* * *

Different pathways led inland, but the group followed one down the face of the escarpment into the low scrub that grew on the sandy coastal plain.

'We'll find different food here,' Sally said. 'Maybe wallabies.'

Bill Bryant gazed anxiously along the stretch of white beach, 'Yes, but where's the boat?' he queried. 'This is where they should be waiting for us.'

Muller scanned the beach for signs that sailors had been there recently. 'There's no recent campfire place here. Maybe they haven't got here yet… or didn't make it.'

Nobody replied to that possibility.

Close to the beach they made camp; seventeen people, one baby and two dogs. The dogs followed Merindah straight toward the sea. She carried her baby and sat him in the wash where small waves hissed along the sand. Sally came and sat next to the baby. Merindah threw off her old shirt as she ran into the waves and swam.

'Look at her,' Chief said. 'She's half fish.'

'Some bloody fish!' a man said, as he and the others gaped at the tall young Aboriginal woman walking naked back to her son.
Sally tipped coals from her bucket to light small pieces of wood that men had gathered.

'Only small stuff here,' a man said as he threw down an armful

248

of branches.

Bill Bryant took Dina and Jacob to find food.

An unsuspecting animal lay under a bush. Dina sneaked up with her nose to the sand and the wallaby bounded away. Aboriginals watched in amazement as the huge dog effortlessly pulled the animal down. They kept well out of sight as Bryant carried it back to the fire at the beach.

Merindah and Sally set off to find water. 'I know water will be here somewhere,' Merindah told Sally. 'People come here, people live here.'

'Yes they do,' Sally said as she turned a corner on the path; in front of her stood four native men standing guard over a well, threatening with spears. Women and children were at the well, filling skin bags similar to the bags that Merindah had made.

The Aboriginal men stood firm, they made it plain that they were not going to let the two strange women near their well. Merindah and Sally stood their ground. A woman from the well walked past the men. She approached Merindah who had William in the sling around her neck; pulled at Merindah's shirt, then touching William she smiled and spoke in a strange language that neither Sally nor Merindah understood. The woman took a water skin from Merindah, carried it to the well, and held it while another woman filled it. She returned it to Merindah.

But the next message was clear. 'Now go away,' she gestured. 'Go away.'

'Aboriginal people live here,' Merindah told Bryant. 'But they won't let us have their water.'

'What do you mean their water?'

'It's their well, and it's their water.'

'If there's water here we will get some, we need it. I'll take men up there in the morning with our breakers and bags, and we'll fill them.'

'I don't think you will,' Merindah said, as she returned to the fire and the other two women.

Wallaby and shellfish, the group ate well, and drank all of that water. Many of the group collapsed and slept, while others sat and pondered where Captain Harris and the others were in the boat.

Bryant studied the beach in the morning. 'They haven't been here, you're right Muller, ours is the first fire on this beach for months, the Aboriginal's fires are up there along the bottom of the ridge; you can see them there now. No, Harris and Byron did not get here, or they went straight past without stopping to wait for us.'

'Well, do we wait here or go on walking?' Muller asked Bill Bryant.

'Get water and walk west.'

Bill Bryant organised six men to help him get water, but he needed his young woman.

'Leave the baby with Sally; show me where this water is.'

Aboriginal men watched every movement that the Belinda survivors made; they could see that there were many more people in this group; twice as many. Their well had never needed to provide for this many extra people. They were not going to let these strangers near their water.

'Is this the path?' Bryant asked Merindah who walked behind him.

'Yes, the well is just around this big bush.'

Bryant suddenly froze; six black men with long spears stepped in front of him as he approached the well. Women were there, and more men.

'We need water,' Bryant said as he held up a water bag to show the Aboriginals. He tipped the empty bag toward his mouth. 'Water.' The black men shoved their spears at Bryant. Bryant stepped back, but remained next to the other six white men.

Nobody moved; the groups eyed each other intently. Birds fluttered and jumped in the bushes. Bryant stood, sweating as he stared at the determined Aboriginal men; he realised then that he was not going to get water. The same woman came away from the well, walked past her own men and took a water bag from Bryant. Once again she held it while another woman filled the bag; then she took it back and gave it to Merindah; not Bryant. The woman waved her hands, the black men shook their spears.

'Go away, go away.' The message was clear.

'What are we going to do now?' Muller asked when Bryant told him they only had one more bag of water.

'Move on,' Bryant said. 'What else can we do?'

'Move on to where? To another place where there's no water, or more Aboriginals?'

'Well, I don't know. Don't bloody well know,' Bryant said. 'All we can do now is keep heading west along this beach. Hope to find more water, I'm sure I can get food, wallabies live in this sand hill country.'

'But we need more water today. Get that woman of yours to find some.'

'Why can't we dig our own well?' Bryant muttered as he walked away. 'Why not?'

He found Merindah with the other two women. 'Where can we dig our own well?'

'They won't like that either,' she told him. 'We should leave.'

'No we have to get water first, we know water is here and we will dig our own well, yes our own well. I want you to show me the place.'

Bryant followed Merindah through the sand hills below the ridge.

'That's the best place she said.'

'Where?'

'Over there, where the native well is.'

Bryant became frustrated, but knew that she was probably correct. 'Cheeky bloody woman. Well, is there any other place?'

'Maybe over there,' Merindah pointed to a hollow closer to the beach.

Twelve thirsty men taking turns with wooden buckets did not take long to dig down six feet into the sand. Only a little water seeped in, and the sand kept collapsing into that water. They needed to let the water settle before filling every container. Bill Bryant felt pleased with himself as he helped carry water back to the camp. They were all very thirsty and used half that night.

'We'll fill everything again in the morning,' Bryant said, 'and then move.'

They did not fill everything with water the next morning. When Bryant and six men walked back to their well, it had been filled in. Aboriginal men with spears stood there, and others blocked the path to the native's well.

'What now, Bryant?' Muller asked.

Bill Bryant shrugged his shoulders and gazed at the beach heading west. 'We walk.'

The group of scruffy white men, dark boys, a large black man with those different features and three black women, one with a baby, walked west along a wide sandy beach as the waves rolled in from the Southern Ocean.

The Aboriginal women watching from the ridge above realised that they had met other Australian native women. But they did not know that they had come from two different places, so far away.

Chapter 24 – The Long Beach

Walking along a barren beach, no timber for fire, only
bushes and sand.
Sand heaped up in no particular pattern, like an ocean
in turmoil.

Sally still carried the fire in the bucket, but as they walked west she
could see that there was no solid wood to keep her fire going. In
front of them stretched a wide sandy beach with only small
miserable bushes growing between the beach and the edge of the
great uplift; which was those great cliffs curving inland. These
eroded cliffs became a steep sloping escarpment leading up to the
higher country. The group walking supposed that up there, the
country would be the same as they had been walking across since
they left the cove where their boat had been swamped.

'We should stay within sight of the sea,' Bryant told the group.
'Captain Harris may turn up in the boat. Also, there's more chance
of finding water here in these sand hills.'

It was a relief to be able to walk on the sand. They all nursed bruised
feet, and cuts from the never-ending rocks. Merindah and Levi's

toughest feet had travelled many extra miles searching for water.

'Walk in the sea water,' Sally told them. 'That'll fix them up, quick.'

Since Muller had been badly dehydrated and humiliated by his turning back, Bryant had taken command.

'How far are we going today?' Muller asked him.

'As far as we can; away from those Aboriginals. Find another bloody well, one they are not guarding.'

Merindah spoke quietly, 'You won't find a well that's not watched.'

'Yes we will, we'll find another well before the local natives see us coming.'

'That won't be possible.'

'Of course it will,' Bryant snapped. 'By the time they realise that we're there, we'll have all our water bags and our bellies full.'

'No, we won't be able to get water from their wells,' continued Merindah firmly. 'They know we're coming, they'll be waiting for us.'

'How'll they know?'

'Runners or smoke. They knew we were coming here days ago. They may have been watching us since the day we arrived at the cove in the boats.'

'Shit! You didn't tell me that before.'

'You didn't ask before.'

Bryant became frustrated. 'Cheeky young black bitch! Well, how do you think we can get water then?'

'Dig our own well again; that's what we'll have to do,' Merindah answered.

'Right-oh, right, you just show me where, we need water before dark tonight.'

'And wood for the fire,' said Sally, who was alongside Merindah. 'There's no wood on this beach and I'll need more soon to keep my fire going. There's not even bushes here now, and these sand hills are getting wider.'

Bryant saw the sand in front and the inland cliff two miles away.

'Shit! You're right, bare sand a mile wide and getting wider, just miles of crazy heaped up sand.'

A small fire smouldered in Sally's bucket.

Bryant panicked, 'Damn! You can't let that fire go out; I haven't got a tinder box; we lost it when the boat sank. Can you make fire?'

'Women aren't allowed to.'

Bryant shrugged his shoulders. *What the bloody hell do they mean by that?* He was getting more frustrated, and impatient. 'Well, keep the bloody fire going then, that's your job, your job.'

'I need wood,' Sally told Bryant. 'See for yourself, there's none here and nothing in front of us. We should head across to those sand hills toward the cliffs, there will be trees or bushes over there. If we don't get something soon, the fire will be gone.'

'That can't happen, can't happen,' Bryant said. 'We'll have to leave this beach now, or some of us will have to find wood.' He hesitated, 'No we can't get split up like we did before, we must all keep together.'

He stopped everybody from walking. 'We are going to head across these sand hills toward the cliff over there,' he pointed. 'There may be food, animals or plants, there's nothing in front for miles; you can all see that. We need firewood and water; you can see the trees from here; and water, well we just have to hope we can find water there.'

Sally smiled at Sarah; in their language she said, 'That's what I told him we should do.' Merindah understood the meaning she giggled with the other two women.

'What's wrong with you three now? What's so bloody funny?' Bryant asked as he led them away from the sea toward the inland cliff.

Merindah found Levi amongst the walkers. 'It's up to us to find water again, let's run on ahead and find somewhere suitable to dig before its dark.'

'What would they do if we weren't here?' Levi asked.

'Die! Come on Inta,' Merindah said as she ran off. 'Come with me girl, we'll find water.'

The young dog bounded along, excited, with Merindah and Levi through the mass of sand hills. Heaps of wind-blown sand spread like a boiling ocean, a maze of small knobs and crazy scattered gullies.

They finally came to an area with low vegetation. 'There's wood here for the fire,' Merindah said. 'And we'll find food amongst these plants, perhaps even wallabies. But I can't find any places where water could be, no hollows and no patches of those reeds.'

Inta sniffed around under the low bushes.

'No girl, we can find food later, we need water first.'

Merindah searched for places where the gullies on the cliff face would funnel water into a sandy hollow.

The rest of the group arrived at the place where the low trees grew; Sally quickly put light pieces of wood on the coals in her bucket.

'Should be food here, but where's the water?' Bryant said.

He found Merindah. 'Where can we dig for water then? We need water tonight, show me where.'

'I don't know yet.' She looked at her son, grizzling in the sling around Sarah's neck. Her baby and all the others relied on her to find water, but she knew that would not always be possible.

Bryant had another fear; he wanted to stay at the beach in case Captain Harris came with the boat, but now they were two miles away. He sent two men onto higher ground to keep a lookout to sea.

'We need to get back to the beach as soon as we can,' he told Muller. 'If they come past in the boat and don't see us, they won't come back.'

'Should I organise men to go back there in the morning?' Muller asked.

'I don't like to split the group up again, but perhaps we may have to if these sand hills keep going like this for much further.' Muller was still weak from the days that he had spent without water. Although he was the most senior man in the group, he let Bryant make the decisions now.   'Yes, best to stay together, but keep a lookout to sea,' he agreed.

It was almost dark before Merindah found a patch of reeds like her mother used to make baskets with. Remembering her home beach brought back memories of her family, Yara, James, the wrinkly man's camp, the exile women's camp and her baby girl Alinta. She clasped the pendant that hung on her chest under that old shirt; then remembered her mission.

'Levi,' she said. 'I need to go back to feed William. I'll send men to dig. You stay here, show them this place.'

Bryant was still away with his dog. The men did not like the young black woman telling them what to do, but they needed water, and she had picked the right places before. They took the two buckets and went to find Levi. Bryant brought only one small wallaby back to Chief's fire; that would not be much meat each for seventeen people. Chief had used the last water to boil some plants in the cook pot.

'We're all still going to be hungry tomorrow,' Muller complained.

'This will at least keep us alive,' Bryant said; he glanced at Merindah. 'Well, where's the water?

'Men are digging now.'

'I'll go and look for myself. You women skin and help Chief cook the wallaby; we need to save some for tomorrow; that means not much each tonight.'

Bryant had left to find the men digging; Sally was restless.

'I'm going to get more wood, come and help me Jacob.'

They took a long time to get a little wood; Merindah guessed why. She helped Sarah and Chief cook the wallaby and some berries that Sally had gathered. The men and Bryant returned with two buckets full of clean, but brackish water which they were only just able to drink.

'We can't live on this briny stuff, woman,' Bryant complained. 'You'll have to find better than this.'

It's all up to me then, is it? It was; Merindah sat on the sand; the moon had not risen; only those bright stars that she knew so well shone in the dark sky. She sat gazing into the fire and quietly hummed her sad song. The other two women and Levi beat out a rhythm with pieces of wood, a quiet but haunting melody.

Merindah slept, with William against her body, she dreamt of being on her mother's beach; she was with James and they had Alinta with them. Merindah was sketching designs on the sand, drawing groups of stars. She drew the sun with sun rays beaming across the surf as it rose out of the sand hills at the end of the beach. She made other symbols on the sand as James sat watching intently. Merindah dreamt of leaving Alinta with Yara, and how Yara lived with those outcast women. Women who relied on the whale meat and did not know what their future would be, living so close to all those white men.

Merindah woke when her baby moved; she pushed fresh sticks onto the dull glow of ashes. A bird moved in a tree close by. The moon had appeared; its dull light revealed the jumbled forms of sleeping miserable men groaning and snoring. As she fed William, Merindah gazed up at her moon and stars; they were her comfort wherever she travelled.

Too soon it was morning.

'Now,' Bryant told the group. 'We'll fill everything with that foul water, that's all we have. I want us to head back along the beach as soon as we can. We don't want to miss the boat if it does come.' There were groans of doubt. 'Well if we're not on the beach, they won't see us, and go on without us,' he explained. 'I want two men back along the beach now, take some of that water, the rest of us will meet you further along, that's the best we can do.'

The main group walked on between the crazy sand hills and the scrubby cliff. At the well of brackish water they filled their water containers and even the cooking pot and carried it between two men. Muller said that the terrible water would make them all sick. But even the dogs drank it, they had to; there was nothing else.

As they walked further west the sand hills became smaller and the low scrub was closer to the beach. When they met the two men who had walked along the beach, Bryant was anxious for any news of the Captain's boat.

'No boat,' they said. 'Just waves. A boat would never get in through the surf anyway.'

'Let's keep walking,' Bill Bryant urged them all. 'That's all we can do now, walk. I remember the Captain's chart; this beach is about seventy miles long before we will come to a bay. That island where we stopped is out from there. The Captain may be waiting there if there's still water in those rocks. He should be there somewhere now if they have not drowned or died of thirst. We might too if we keep drinking this bloody water.'

Other people watched them walking along that lonely beach. The message had been sent on ahead. Merindah knew people would be watching them; they would be plain to see. She kept looking for signs of water or tracks. A track coming down from the ridge would show where Aboriginals came down to a well.

They walked mile after mile between the ocean and a large area of bare plains and a few scattered low scrubby sand hills. Men were always scanning out to sea hoping to see a small whaleboat; Merindah gazing ahead searching for another place to find water, or an unattended native well.

'I don't think we'll find water here,' she told Bryant. 'We're a long way from the ridge, that's where water may be. Other people are there, I have seen their smoke over there and up on the ridge top.'

'Yes,' Bryant agreed. 'It's a long way across there now, and I don't want to leave this beach. There's wood here and probably food, let's go as far as we can today and then dig for water again.'

The three women recognised edible plants; some with berries, some with roots that they dug up and chewed. Various succulent plants grew around lakes or places which flooded with water briefly after rain, or perhaps a high tide. Some of these plants were very sappy and could be squashed to get juice, but the men tended to avoid eating those.

'These may keep us alive.' Merindah told them.

'Alive for what?' asked a man. 'For how long?'

Walking and collecting bush food, the group travelled a long way that day drinking the brackish water. They did not catch any wallabies; birds teased them and the dogs. Merindah was not confident when they dug for water that night. They found grey dry sand and then ground too hard to dig into. They set off the next day thirsty and hungry, walking further west, the weaker ones started to lag again. Muller and Rebus, the oldest and the youngest struggled.

Muller stopped the group. 'This is hopeless, we have no water left, and it looks like we can't find any here. It's useless walking until we die, we should go in towards the ridge to find water, either dig, or fight those bloody black men for it.'

Bryant had to agree, they left the weakest six men at the beach; Muller and Rebus were among them. Bryant wanted to leave Sarah there, but she refused to stay with those men without the other women and Dina protecting her. The six thirsty men sat in the shade, Bryant told them to keep looking and signal by waving a shirt on a pole if they glimpsed the Captain's boat.

'And keep the bloody fire going,' Bryant instructed as he left. 'We'll be back tonight or first thing in the morning with water.'

Merindah wondered about Bryant's confidence in forcefully taking water if they had to, but she knew they were desperate now; they had to get fresh water soon from somewhere.

'You must find water today,' Bryant told her. 'Have you seen their smoke again, are they still there?'

'They're always there,' Merindah answered. 'They'll probably watch us die'.

Chapter 25 – An Exchange for Water

Beg for water.
Make a fair deal.
What is a woman worth?

Merindah led the group across a sparse plain toward the ridge; there were bigger trees ahead. Dina ambled with her long nose against Sally's side. As always, Inta trotted alongside Merindah. A wallaby bounded away from a small clump of low bushes. Sally called Dina back.

'Well, we know food is here, but we need water right now,' Bryant said.

As the group walked toward the trees the ground inclined toward the ridge.

'When it rains, water would run down those gullies,' Merindah told Bryant. 'I am sure, if you dug there you would find water.'

'Yes but where? Anyway, we haven't the time to dig for it. You need to find a well.'

'We could make trouble.'

'We'll be prepared for them this time.'

When they reached the place with trees Bryant and his men found weapons; strong long sticks.

'Now show us where the wells may be.'

Merindah called to Levi to help her find paths. It was obvious people came there; the signs were plain for her to see. Because of the barren nature of the area, Merindah understood the natives would be in small groups, possibly just one family in each group. But she knew they would still be very defensive of their water.

It was evening before Merindah followed a path leading to a low-lying area, the reedy hollows made her sure there would be a well. There was, and at that well waited a group of Aboriginals; Women, children and six men with lethal looking spears.

'This is what I expected,' Merindah told Bryant. 'We won't get water here.'

'We must have water tonight. Talk to them, show them the baby that you are carrying, show them that we are desperate. I don't want to fight them for it unless we have to.'

The men with Bryant held their sticks ready for a fight. Dina stood to her full height, alert, she could feel the tension. The size of the dog amazed the Aboriginal men, but they stood defiant with their spears held ready and had more spears at their feet.

Apart from her little song, Merindah had rarely spoken her Mother's language since she had left the beach of bones. She held William up, and pointed to her breasts, begging for their help, but her words did not seem to impress the native men; they merely stood and brandished their spears.

Merindah spoke again. Nobody there understood a word of her speech. Nobody would for over one thousand miles.

But her pleas seemed to have affected the oldest Aboriginal man. He stood still, staring at Merindah with piecing dark eyes which hid under his white scruffy eyebrows. His thin white hair and beard lifted in the evening breeze. Merindah examined the many scars across the leathery skin on his chest. The yellow stained bone piercing his nose moved as he twitched his top lip.

The old man moved forward, took her water bag; he passed it to a woman, then pointed to the well as he spoke to her. When the woman had filled the water bag, the old man passed it back to Merindah and indicated with signs that she should drink.

Merindah drank.

He spread his hands, palm up in a silent question.

'Yes,' Merindah said in English. 'Good.' She nodded her head.

The old man took five water bags back to the well and had them filled. He handed them to Merindah, Sally and Sarah, but not to the white men.

Next, he proceeded to look carefully at Merindah and Sarah, but not Sally, he ignored her. He walked around the two young women, stopped and studied Sarah; he touched the headband that she wore tight around her forehead and short curly hair. Then he approached Merindah and spoke to her, becoming very animated. He pointed at the well and the white men's breakers and buckets. Next, he pointed to Sarah.

Merindah quickly understood what he was asking her, and what the old man wanted did not surprise her. She understood the way Aboriginals kept their small groups sustainable with new women from different places.

Merindah turned to Bryant. 'He'll let us fill all these things with water,' she said, pointing to the breakers, the other bags and the two buckets.

'That's good,' Bryant said. 'Let's fill them and get out of here fast.' He moved forward; the spears were pointed straight at him.

Bryant stopped. 'What's wrong now?'

'He wants an exchange for the water.'

'What does he want? What have we got?'

'He wants Sarah. He wants to exchange the water for Sarah.'

Bryant stiffened, he had not expected this; he glanced at Sarah. *Well, why wouldn't he? She is a fine-looking woman, and young.* But could he do that? 'Shit, bloody hell, what do we do now?' he asked.

They all looked at Sarah, then at Bill Bryant. Young Jacob spoke first. 'I think we should take these bags that they've filled and see if we can get out of here.' He held up his piece of timber and pointed it at the angry men; they aimed their spears back at him.

Six strong Aboriginal men stood firm with spears, facing thirsty, weary white men with sticks, and one fierce dog. It was not an even challenge. The native men had sharp spears in hand, and more at their feet.

Bryant was thinking fast. He knew that once again they all

needed his young woman's ingenuity. 'That's not gonna happen, not gonna happen. You must try to tell him something to make him relax. We need to get out of here before this gets nasty.'

Sarah stared at Bryant; then glared at Merindah. Merindah walked boldly up to the old man. She pointed at the setting sun, she pointed to the east, at Sarah, at the well and then last the empty breakers and buckets. She spoke forcefully in her own language waving her hands and pointing back at Sarah. The old Aboriginal man seemed to understand, he talked to the other men in his group, and they relaxed and lowered their weapons.

Merindah led the group back toward the beach.

When they were all away from the well and danger, Bryant stood in front of Merindah. 'Well, what did you tell him?'

'I told him that we would come back and make the exchange in the morning.'

Chapter 26 – Contact with the Boat

There is somebody on the beach.
We can't get in through these breakers.
Together, but apart.

That evening while Merindah made the deal with the old black man, Muller and Rebus rested on the beach by the fire; the other four men gathered fire wood. As the sun set Muller sat looking out to sea, longing for his pipe and tobacco.

Suddenly, he jumped to his feet, yelling. 'Is that a sail out there? Quick Rebus; get a long stick, tie your shirt to one end and hold it up high. That's the Captain's boat!'

Although Muller had only noticed the flash of a sail in the fading light, he knew that it had to be the Captains boat, there would be no other.

Sarah did not speak as they walked back toward the fire. Merindah worried; had she done the right thing? Although she did not intend to exchange Sarah for water, it seemed the only way to get the group away from the Aboriginals without bloodshed. Merindah knew that Sarah was terrified.

She took her aside. 'I had to do that. It was the only way to get away from them, we won't go back. I won't let them take you.'
Sarah walked on alone with her head down; she did not look up at Merindah. Tears still fogged her eyes. 'What if those men come for me in the night?'
Merindah put her hand on Sarah's arm. 'We'll be far up the beach

before they realise we've gone.

Bryant grabbed Merindah's arm, and turned her around to face him. 'What have you got us into now girl? What will we do in the morning?'

Bryant's young woman took control; she looked him straight in the eye, 'We won't go back there.'

'What do you mean?'

'We should keep walking. Give everyone a drink of water and keep walking, get a long way up that beach before morning.'

'Who is running this show? Now she's telling me what to do?' Bryant muttered to himself.

Rebus ran to meet them as they approached the fire.

'Mr Muller thinks he has seen a sail. Must be Captain Harris looking for us.'

'Well I'll be buggered,' Bryant said. 'Perhaps they are still alive and searching for us after all.' He went to talk to Muller. 'What did you see?'

'Only the glimpse of a sail, then it was too dark, but I'm sure it was a sail. Rebus waved his shirt on a stick, they would have seen it if they looked this way.'

'Right, okay, must be them.' Bryant said. 'We'll make a smoky fire in the morning. They'll see that if they're still out there somewhere.'

Merindah spoke firmly, 'No they won't. 'We won't be here.'

'What do you mean woman? We need to show them we're here.'

'But we won't be here; we'll be a long way along this beach. Gone.' Merindah knew they had to leave straight away, they could find their way, even without moonlight.

Bryant became agitated. 'What do you mean, gone?'

'We'll leave now; get far away before those men come to get Sarah. I won't let that happen. Neither will you.' Now she was in control.

Bryant hesitated, considering their position. Although they all had water, they had very little food. He remembered those fit looking black men with their sharp spears, and realised they could travel a lot faster than his group of tired hungry people.

'Yes, you're right,' he said. 'I think we should move tonight. Yes, move, now.'

'That's just what I said,' Merindah told Sally as Bryant walked away to talk to the rest of the group.

'If the men in the boat are looking for us,' Bryant told everyone, 'they'll find us even if we are further along the beach, we have to move now.' Some men were unhappy; they had already walked to the base of the ridge and back; now he wanted them to walk again during the night.

They all walked on. Sally with her fire in a bucket and Dina's nose against her leg. Merindah with William in his sling, Inta at her side. Sarah walked on nervously, occasionally looking back. She wondered how that old man would have treated her.

The group walked all through the night. At daybreak they stopped and Bryant allowed each person a small drink. It was another misty morning, once again water hanging in the air. They tried to get moisture from the damp plants; every little drop saved the water in their water bags which was diminishing too fast.

'Keep walking,' Bryant told them. 'Young Jacob and me will take Dina and get meat; anything.'

Walking along the beach was relatively easy, they had covered a considerable distance during the night, but they were not well. They had been walking for many days with little and strange food, with little or poor water. They were all tiring, some beginning to stumble.

Muller had to stop, 'We must stop,' he told Merindah.

'Yes, we're all tired,' she said. 'But not here where those men can spot us from the cliff top, we can rest up ahead by those trees. Perhaps they haven't seen us walking yet because it's still misty. I hope they're still at their well waiting for us.'

Bryant's young woman was telling the old sailor what to do, but he saw her logic.

'What if the Captain comes past in the boat? We must show him that we're here.'

'Just keep men looking, be ready to signal, only use the fire then.'

'They've been looking, but it's all misty. I'll let them rest when we reach those trees.'

That's what Merindah had suggested.

As they rested, most slept, a few men kept looking out beyond the misty waves, searching for the boat. The mist lifted slowly; late winter sun sparkled across the blue sea. Those waves never stopped, they rolled, turned, splashed and ran up the shallow beach.

'That boat'll never come in through those waves,' a man commented as he sat looking intently out to sea, trying not to fall asleep.

*　　*　　*

While Merindah made the deal with the old Aboriginal man late in the afternoon the day before, Hugh Byron sat in the Captain's whaleboat looking toward the land for hours.

Hugh and four other men had water and cooked seal meat aboard the boat. They rowed and sailed along the long beach searching for any of their crew mates who may have survived the walk along the cliff top and reached the beach. The surf rolling into shore made a haze against the background of the ridge in the distance, but Hugh noticed something different above the waves.

'Drop the sail,' he ordered. 'I'm sure I spotted something on the beach. Get the oars out; we'll circle here for a while.'

By the time they had pulled in the sail and circled back it was almost dark, they could not make out the shore line, just a red glow where the sun had descended into the land.

'I'm sure I caught sight of a flag or something! All we can do is keep sailing along the coast and come past here again in the morning. If they are there, we'll see them on the beach.'

During the night Hugh Byron sailed the whaleboat away from the shore, but in the hazy morning he steered back towards the land. In the distance above the mist he noticed the end of the cliffs where they had left the beach in the Captain's boat days before. He knew they were not that far east the previous evening when he had glimpsed something on the beach. With the men rowing, he steered south west keeping well out, away from those never-ending waves and their danger.

*   *   *

Muller told Sally to make the fire smoky.

'Smoke would be the most obvious sign for a boat looking for us,' he told Merindah when she glared at the smoke and frowned at him.

'And it's the best way to show those Aboriginal men where we are.'

'We walked far last night,' Muller said. 'We don't want the boat to go past us. Aboriginals may not notice this small smoke column, but men in a boat will, if they look this way.'

'A sail,' a man yelled, 'I can see a sail.'

Soon there were three shirts fluttering on three long sticks that they had saved from the fire.

'That must be the Captain,' Muller said. 'But he won't bring the boat in through those waves. Let's start walking again.'

Although tired from walking all night, the site of the boat gave them encouragement; the entire group walked on.

Bryant returned. Muller was excited. 'We saw the boat again,'

'Must be them then, but I have no food,'

Now the group were desperate. They each drank a little water that the old Aboriginal man had given the women. They had eaten little for two days and walked many miles.

'We must get food,' Merindah said. 'We need to eat something tonight; Sally and I will find food.'

Bryant agreed. 'We'll rest while you're away, take both dogs.'

Although they had seen the boat again, and certain that it was the Captain's, Bill Bryant realised they were still on their own. The boat would not try to come into the beach through those waves.

'They may have food and water on that boat, but they can't get it to us.'

He looked across at the inland cliff, now even further away; then at the ragged group lying and sitting on the sand.

'You'll need to start walking again soon,' Bryant told them. 'We'll rest again tonight. I'm afraid there's no food, and that is the last water. I think one day of solid walking will get us to the end of this beach. That's where islands are, rocky ones close to the island where we stopped with the two boats. There's a sheltered bay there, and the boat will be able to come ashore. We need one last push to reach that bay, and then we can rest.'

'Sniff him out, Dina!' The large lizard ran, and the dogs chased it under a bush. Dina barked, the lizard ran again, heading for a dead tree, but it was too slow.

'That's food,' Sally declared. 'Let's find more.' Merindah picked up the monitor; they walked on and came to a large bare area.

Merindah remembered catching lizards with her family. 'Let's walk around the edge of this. Lizards lay in the warm sunshine. There's one! It's different from the lizards at my beach but its food.'

The lizard did not see Inta coming and soon it was in her mouth. 'Good girl, Inta, that's the way; find another one,' Merindah encouraged the young dog.

Merindah and Sally quickly caught the group. They stopped at sundown where there was timber for the fire. Chief had no water to make a proper stew; the women squashed juicy plants, berries and roots into the cook pot. The result was a sticky mash, but food. Merindah cooked the monitor and smaller lizards in the coals. A small meal for everyone.

One last sip of water and their water bags were empty. As the walkers settled for the night, they sighted a sail again. 'Was that the Captain's boat?'

A low bank of clouds began to pile up in the southwest sky. Merindah woke when William stirred; she sat on the sand feeding him. Sleeping people who lay around her had forgotten the Aboriginal man who wanted Sarah; they were all exhausted from walking.

Merindah talked softly to her baby in her Mother's language. 'What is going to become of you my boy, if we get away from this place? Where will we be?'

So much change, so much uncertainty. Although she was smart and clever, the young woman had no control over her own, or her baby's, life. White men controlled her life, but they could not survive without her.

Merindah cradled her baby as she looked into his dark innocent eyes. 'Nobody will take you away from me.'

The sky was black; no stars; no moon. As she laid William back close to Inta, rain started. Gentle, but rain. She quickly covered the baby with a skin.

Merindah soon found everything that would catch the steady rain, the cook pot, the two buckets; she laid out some skins that they had been carrying so that they would collect a little water. Jacob woke and helped her.

Bryant and the other men had woken and were drinking water as it fell.

The sun did not warm the cold miserable morning on that lonely beach. An occasional scud of rain drifted in from the south. The group moved, at least walking kept them warm and wet, not just wet. They took off wet shirts and squeezed water into the bucket; a little more water, mixed with weeks of body sweat and dirt.

When the showers cleared they noticed a sail again; always out beyond the surf.

'They're still there. How many in the boat? Are they all still alive?'

Bill Bryant walked on, his blue eyes searching for a change, a landmark.

'Surely we'll come to the end of this beach today,' he said to young Jacob and Levi.

Levi spotted it first. 'There's an island!' he yelled.

'That's one of those rocky reefs out from the sheltered bay. We'll get there tonight.' Bryant was relieved. 'You two lads come with me, we'll take Dina away from this beach, let's look behind this scrub. If it's open country, there may be kangaroos or other game.'

The rain had refreshed the walkers, and the site of the island and the boat spurred them on.

Bryant, Dina, Jacob and Levi walked and came to more open country. Dina stopped, she stood still, watching; it moved again. Dina had seen the emu before the bird had seen her, and she had a small start. The emu ran amongst stunted trees then out onto the salt lake; a mistake, this was not a puny dingo chasing him, but a huge hungry dog.

The emu was heavy for the three men to carry back to the walkers on the beach; they cut it into pieces to share the load.

Bryant was pleased. 'Now we've got food, but we always need water. The rain helped,' he glanced at the sky, 'but it looks like that's all we are going to get.'

Muller saw the sail moving west.

'They are going on; they must be going to wait for us at that sheltered beach.'

Bill Bryant was certain that the walk was coming to an end, perhaps the boat would take them out to that island where they had found water and there were seals. No Aboriginals! *But what happens then?*

Merindah knew they needed more water. *I should look for a well, or find somewhere to dig.* They were coming to a rocky point; a place where there would be shellfish and places to build fish traps. 'People will live here,' she told Sally. 'They will have wells.'

'I think we should stop here tonight, eat that emu and try to find water.' Merindah told Bryant.

'What about the boat? I want to get to it tonight.'

'The closer we get to that point, the more chance of meeting Aborigines. We won't be welcome there, remember last time. They won't let us near their normal water places, we should be prepared.'

'Yes, that makes sense. Makes sense.'

'I've seen many paths, if we follow them there'll be wells, perhaps we'll find one they are not at, or not using.'

'Yes,' agreed Bryant. 'I'll get men with sticks, that's the only weapons we have.'

Merindah knew that sticks would be useless against the black men's spears. 'They'll be watching us now, but perhaps we can find a well and get water quickly, then get away before they stop us.'

Merindah left William with the other two women. She, Dina and Bryant went with eight other men armed with long sticks and carrying the two breakers and skins. Aboriginal men watched as the young black woman led the group of white men along the ancient paths. These Aboriginals had seen white men before, and they had experienced their weapons, they were cautious and kept out of sight.

Merindah found a well. As the men finished filling the skins eight Aboriginal men appeared brandishing their weapons.

'Just back out quietly,' Bryant ordered. 'Don't stir them up.' The black men looked at Merindah; she stood out amongst the group of white men.

'There's something different about these men, they're cautious, they're not sure if they can attack us.'

'We're not going to let them attack us. We're leaving,' Bryant said as he led his group away.

The emu meat was delicious, and the water revived them all. But the knowledge that Aboriginal men were there somewhere made them watchful.

'If there were less of us I think they would attack,' Bryant said. 'We should be careful tonight, only half of us will sleep at a time the rest keep guard, keep those sticks handy. They seemed to be wary when we pointed the sticks toward them.'

Next morning there was no sign of the native men.

'They'll still be watching,' Merindah told Bryant.

'Right. Let's move, and find that boat.'

Bill Bryant led the walkers around several rocky points; they came to a calm sheltered beach. Captain Harris's whaleboat lay anchored in the bay. Only four men rowed the boat to the shore.

'Where's the Captain, and the others?'

'They're all okay; they are out on an island. Are you all here? Looks like it. How the bloody hell did you all survive?' Hugh Byron had many questions.

Bill Bryant had questions too, but he wanted to get away from that beach.

'We should move,' he told Hugh. 'Black men followed us all the way here this morning. They seem to be fairly stirred up.'

Hugh had seen the Aboriginals, 'Yes, they're still up there. Could be twenty men, have you seen any of their women?'

'No women or children here, only men,' Bryant answered.

'I know why,' Merindah told him.

'Why?' Hugh asked.

'Women are keeping away, because white men came here before, and took women. Don't you remember the Aboriginal women with those sealers? Other white men have been here.'

Hugh thought about Ned and his pistols. 'Yes, well if bloody Ned's been here with those guns, these men would be cautious and angry. Perhaps they're just waiting for an opportunity. I reckon if there were less of us they would attack.

Merindah understood, 'Yes, they don't want you here; they will wait until you are tired, hungry and thirsty.'

Bill Bryant and Hugh Byron did not doubt her.

Chapter 27 – Escape to an Island

An island can be a refuge - or a trap.
How many people can stay on this small Island?

'So what do we do now?' Bill Bryant asked Hugh Byron. 'We all survived a terrible walk to get here, and now we seem to be still in a hopeless situation. These Aboriginals seem very agitated.'

'We need to get out to the island where the Captain is,' Hugh answered. 'There's seals and water there.'

'How far along this coast to Middle Island?' Bryant asked Hugh.

Hugh had thought about that, 'It's about another fifty miles along the coast to the place opposite Middle Island; you could keep walking to there and we could take you out in this boat.'

'I don't know if these black men will leave us alone now.' Bryant commented.

'Wouldn't you be angry if men came and took your women,' Muller said. 'We've got to get out to the island where the Captain is, somehow.'

'How far; how will we all get there?' Bryant asked Hugh. 'And then what?'

'I don't know how far, it's past those reefs and smaller islands, but we can't take the boat near them.'

Bryant fiddled with his pipe; 'You got any tobacco left?'

'Don't be bloody stupid,' Hugh said. 'Well what do you think, are you going to keep walking?'

Bryant pointed out to the sea. 'Well, can you get us all out to this island where the Captain is?'

'Probably only manage one trip a day; three trips to get you all out there,' Hugh answered. 'We don't want to over load the boat again.'

'No! Yes, but that means less men left on the beach, we'll be more vulnerable to attack, and without water. This is all we have, and yours is low.'

They decided that the next morning the boat would take five of them to the island and bring back water. That would leave twelve people on the beach.

'Twelve of us may scare the Aboriginals; keep them away,' Bryant said. 'What about after the next trip? Then there will be only five or six left here, and they may be attacked. But there's nothing we can do about that.'

As they nervously sat around the fire that night the discussion moved to their future on the island.

'How long can we all stay there?' Muller asked. 'The water may not last during the summer.'

'The Captain talked about going back to Middle Island,' Hugh said. 'There's permanent water, and a chance of a ship calling in there.'

Bryant considered that they should never have left Middle Island. 'Yes, that sounds good, good to me, yes good idea. But how the hell are we all going to get back there?' It's a long way; we have just one small boat.'

'We've done it before,' Hugh said.

They ate the last of the emu; Hugh Byron and his men were very pleased to eat something different than raw, dried, or rotting seal meat. There was little water left.

Merindah sat gazing into the small fire. She wondered about the Aboriginal people close by; the women and children. She knew that their culture was being unsettled just like at her home beach and the Bluff. Merindah looked up at her stars, hummed and tapped on a stick as the Belinda survivors sat and marvelled that they had all lived to get to this place.

Early the next morning the six weakest men climbed aboard the whaleboat along with Hugh and his men.

'We may be back tonight,' Hugh assured Bryant as men pushed the boat out into the waves. 'If we can use the sail, it may be sooner, but if we need to row both ways, we could take a lot longer.'

'You better get back, we don't feel safe just sitting here.'

Muller and Rebus went on the boat. Bill Bryant considered who he would send away on the next trip. The women would not go without Dina. The Aboriginal men concerned them there, but the white sailors also worried them, they were vulnerable either way. If Bryant sent another six men on the trip to the island that would leave him and the women exposed to the angry Aboriginals. He decided to send the women, Jacob, and the dogs on the next trip in the boat. That would leave him and five or six men on the beach.

Bill Bryant had time to reflect, *I hope that idea of mine that I talked to Hugh about works. It may be difficult here with only a few men.*

Hugh Byron's men rowed into a steady south east breeze most of the way to the island that morning, but sailed back to the mainland before dark.

'I brought back more water,' he said. 'Now how do these look?' Hugh had found some stubby sticks on the island, and as they sat in the boat sailing back to the mainland, men used knives to shape the sticks like pistols.

'Like pieces of sticks to me,' Bryant said. 'But from a distance it may fool those angry bastards. Not that I blame them from being angry, I would be too.'

'We should make them black?' Hugh suggested. 'Hold them over the fire for a while.' The wooden 'pistols' were soon black.

Bryant admired the pistols. 'Now rub on some seal fat you have in the boat; that will make them shiny.'

Hugh waved his oily pistols toward four men returning with firewood; they paused;

'Bloody hell; where did you get those pistols from?' a man

yelled.

Hugh Byron laughed. 'There you are. It fooled them.'

'Well it may work, at least worth a try, pity we haven't got something that would make the right noise and smoke.'

The crowded boat followed the moonlight path out of the bay in the early morning. When they passed the group of islands sheltering the bay, Merindah felt the power of the swell as the whaleboat lifted and fell. As her familiar moon climbed into the morning sky, the stars gradually faded, and the sun lit the ocean in the east. After midday the boat pulled into the sheltered beach that she remembered from weeks before.

'Do you remember this place?' she asked William. 'You've grown since we were here; we all know you have because we have been carrying you for weeks.'

The other women and Chief smiled and agreed.

The Captain stood waiting on the beach. 'I can't believe you are all still alive,' he said. 'And the baby is well; what did you eat?'

'Plenty of food for us,' Sally said. 'But these men wouldn't eat some of it.'

'How did you light a fire each night? You had no flint; how did you cook the meat that the dogs caught?'

'I carried the fire all the way in a bucket,' Sally told him.

'How did you stop the bucket from burning?'

'Wet sand in the bottom.'

'They told me that you had no water at times. How did you keep the sand wet when you were not by the beach?' the Captain asked.

'It's not just water that's wet,' Sally told him, giggling.

The Captain told them about his boat being washed up, and losing his tinder box.

'We had no fire for days, we only ate raw seal meat, and some shellfish, until one of the men lit a fire here with two sticks.'

Hugh headed straight back to the mainland that afternoon.

Merindah and the other two women searched the island with

the dogs.

'There must be more than seals here. Look at these small tracks; something small with claws on its feet.'

The afternoon sun brought an unlucky snake out for an early spring warming; it would get warmer on the fire that night. The women returned to the place where the Captain and his men had built a rough shelter.

Sally beckoned Jacob aside. 'Come with me, we will find some shellfish to eat with the snake.'

But Sally did not only want shellfish. Away from Bill Bryant, the worry about food and water and away from angry Aboriginal men she felt relaxed and confident; she would have her way with her young man.

Jacob went willingly. This chance would not pass him by; and they did find shellfish.

Sally and Jacob returned to the camp and found Merindah alone with the dogs.

Captain Harris had taken Sarah away. He had not expected to see her again.

'Did any of those men touch you?'

'No; but I almost stayed there with an old black man. Would you swap me for a drink of fresh water?'

'What do you mean?'

'Doesn't matter, Merindah saved us all.'

'I'm not surprised. She's a smart woman.'

When Hugh Byron left the beach in the dark that morning, Bill Bryant and the five men with him felt defenceless.

At daylight the Aboriginal men saw only six men left on the beach.

'They're still there watching, and coming closer,' one man said.

'Make the firewood last,' Bryant told them. 'We can't get any more today, we must stay together.' The six white men sat or stood close together on the beach, anxiously looking out for the boat to return. Their eyes were also scanning the beach where a group of Aboriginal men looked more menacing.

'What are we going to do if they attack us?' a man asked Bryant. 'There's nowhere to run, and I can't swim.'

'Bluff them; that's all we can do.'

As the sun crept toward the west, the Aboriginals moved closer.

'Pick up those sticks and be fierce,' Bryant told the men. Six long sticks and six ragged white men did not frighten the native men with their sharp spears.

'They are still moving in slowly,' a man said, 'doesn't look good. They're braver now that there's only six of us.'

'I'll try this,' Bryant said as he pulled the two short black greasy sticks from his belt, and pointed them at the Aboriginals; they hesitated and backed away.

'Well, I'll be buggered,' Bryant declared. 'It bloody well worked, and that tells me something. That bloody Ned has been here with his pistols, and he's used them. How long will this bluff last though? Where's that bloody boat?'

As the sun slid into the west the Aboriginal men were still there.

'Will they come when it's dark?'

'I don't know,' Bryant answered. 'Merindah said they'll wait until we get weaker. I'm bloody hungry; and getting weaker. It'll be dark soon; then we will be vulnerable.'

Bryant walked away from his group, pointed both pistols at the black men. A loud cry; the Aboriginals moved back a little further.

Hugh Byron sailed into the bay.

'Here's the boat,' a man yelled.

'Let's get out of here,' Bryant told Hugh.

'We can't go out through those reefs in the dark, we need to wait till the moon comes up; that'll be hours,' Hugh said.

'I think that we should all get in your boat and row around in circles or anchor until the moon rises. We can't stay on this beach any longer; my pistols have run out of powder.'

Hugh laughed as he helped them all aboard the whaleboat. But the laughter did not last. As they all sat in the boat and the rowers got organised, a group of yelling Aboriginal men rushed down the beach. Bryant pointed his wooden pistol at the native men; they hesitated briefly before surging forward with their spears ready to throw.

'Let's get out of here!' Hugh told the rowers as a spear hit the side of the boat.

While they sat in the boat circling, waiting for the moon to rise, Hugh told Bryant why they did not wait at the end of the cliffs. He explained that a suitable wind and showers of rain made it possible for them to sail the boat to the small island.

'But we still had no fire, there's hard stone on the island, we tried to light fire by hitting stones together. We made lots of sparks but everything was damp. After two days the sun-dried things out, and a man started a fire by rubbing two sticks together. Shit, it was good to have fire and cooked meat.'

'Those women carried fire all the way for us,' Bryant told Hugh.

'Yes, I've heard all about your trip from the others, sounds like you would not have made it without those women of yours, especially that young one. And her baby still looks fit, bloody amazing.'

'Yes she's smart; and useful.'

'In more ways than that, hey Bill?'

'What? Oh, yeah!'

When the moon rose four men rowed the whaleboat while Hugh used the large steering oar to carefully skirt past hidden reefs. Angry white waves smashed into the rocky island that protected the bay where the men had kept warm slowly rowing in circles during the night.

Captain Harris met Bill Bryant as he stepped out of the boat onto the small island.

'Shit, Bill, I'm amazed, I assumed you were all dead up above those cliffs.'

'Yes, Hugh told me. We were expecting you to be waiting at the end of the cliffs with the boat. Hugh said that you couldn't wait.'

'No, the natives wouldn't give us any more water. We had no bloody fire, and then when the sea became calm for a few hours, we took the chance to leave.'

'Yeah, Hugh told me about the trouble getting water from the native's well. Trust me, we know all about that. And he told me how you lost your flint; that's why we didn't see any ashes. Lucky you got to light a fire here. So, what happens now? Are we staying here?'

'No.' Captain Harris said. 'There are seals to eat here, I'm already sick of eating them. The women found shellfish again and they've eaten a snake. They're sure there are other animals here. But this is only a small island, the food may not last, and the water probably won't last either when the hot weather comes. A few light showers have put water in the rock holes, but they won't last through the summer.'

'So what are you suggesting?'

'We need to go back to Middle Island. There's better food; remember the wallabies. There's permanent water. Another ship may turn up there some day. Men know about that place, they'll come for the seals and whales.'

'Well let's stay here for a while, we need rest. How do you think we are all going to get back to Middle Island? It's a long way, isn't it?'

'Yes about fifty miles, but we can all go in the boat; same as Hugh brought you all out here; take four trips.'

'Shit what a bloody saga,' Bryant pronounced. 'That'll take weeks.'

'Well, I reckon we've got plenty of time,' said Hugh, who was listening.

'Rats!' Merindah said. 'That's what white men call them.'

Inta had found the nest under a mound of sand; she grabbed the native rat, shook it violently and proudly took it to Merindah. She went back, used her nose to follow a tunnel in the sand and soon caught another. When Merindah and Sally took the two rats and another snake back to the camp, the men refused to eat either.

'Well it's food,' Merindah told them. 'We're going to eat this, and get more tomorrow.'

Although she was unsure if Bryant knew about her liaison with Jacob, Sally would be in control while she could.

Young Jacob was confused. 'Why do you take me? You won't let those older men near you.

'Because it's my choice,' Sally told the young man. 'For the first time in my life, I am choosing who I'll go with. I hope you don't end up like the men who abused me and killed my babies.'

'I have heard about babies being killed. That's bad.'

'I've seen some terrible things. Things I don't want to talk about. I've seen women jump over the side of the ship to drown with their babies. The sailors just get another woman.'

'Shit, some men are awful. I'm afraid I'll get bashed if they find out I've been with you.'

'Yes, just enjoy it while it lasts, our time together may be short. You'll have other younger women, and you'll be kind to them. But you won't forget the time with me, will you?'

'No, I won't.'

'Good, now let's get shellfish; that's what we're supposed to be doing.'

When Bryant took Merindah away from the camp, she was relieved that he did not rush her. He took his time and stayed with her when he had finished. He had not asked her again about the piece of metal that she wore around her neck. Merindah was always conscious of the heavy ornament that never let her forget the time with James, or lose the memory of their daughter Alinta.

Captain Harris decided it was time to move back to Middle Island.

'Each trip will take two or three days,' Hugh Byron said. 'We'll have to watch the weather, the first half of the trip is in open water, no protection from islands.'

'We must make the effort before the weather warms up,' the Captain told them. 'I want you to get the boat ready with water and dry seal meat. You never know how long the trips will take.'

'What if I get those sealers to bring back their boat and help?' Hugh suggested.

'They may be gone now, or joined up with Ned and his mob. God knows what you'll find, but we can't stay here forever.'

After much discussion they decided Captain Harris would go with the first group back to Middle Island, with Muller, Rebus and three lighter men, plus the rowers.

'If there's a west wind when I come back,' Hugh said. 'Perhaps I'll sail the boat with only two other men; that would leave more room for the next trip. Maybe do it in three trips, not four.'

'I don't think you can handle the boat with less than four men if you need to row,' Bryant warned him.

'Yes you're right; three men and me. We may still do it in three trips,'

'Sarah is light,' the Captain stated. 'She can come on this first trip, and leave one space on the next.'

Sarah was reluctant to leave the other two women; she knew there was always the chance that the boat would never come back for them. After the trials of the last weeks she felt she belonged with them. There were many tears as the women parted; they now had a special bond.

Merindah watched the small boat being rowed away from the island. As it cleared the last point she saw the ocean swell pick it up, then only the top of the short mast showed as the boat slid into a trough. She knew that the wind was blowing water into it, and men would be bailing it out.

Once again the small overloaded boat headed out into the ocean. They carried just enough water for two days. Men rowed, and swapped places nonstop, keeping close to the mainland and passing several islands that gave brief periods of shelter from the ocean swell.

Chapter 28 – Return to Middle Island

We can't stay on this small island.
Where else can we go?
Will someone find us here before we all die?

Early in the morning of the third day, Middle Island was in their view. The drama of the shipwreck returned to the Captain's mind as they rowed past the collapsing hulk of the Belinda. When they had pulled the boat safely away from the waves they could smell smoke coming from amongst the island's vegetation.

The Captain wanted to get to their old camping place, and light a fire. 'Two men go and see those sealers; take the bucket and bring some fire back here.'

Captain Harris waited on the beach until the two men returned, one carried burning coals in the bucket. 'No men here,' he said. 'They've gone, but four black women and two children are still here.'

'What about all those skins?' The Captain asked. 'Are they still there?'

'No, I didn't see them; a ship must have been here and taken the sealers and their skins away. Their whaleboat's gone too.'

'Or Ned's mob came back,' Hugh uttered. 'Killed the sealers, or they may have joined in with him, we'll never know. I wouldn't be surprised if Ned has a hiding place close by, on another island.'

'Well what about these women?' Captain Harris asked the men. 'Do they seem well?'

'No, but they're women. There's not many to choose from.'

'Well you please yourselves, god knows what diseases they've got,' Hugh alleged. Suddenly there was much discussion amongst the men.

Captain Harris wanted his men away from the women. 'Let's get to our old camp site, and we need food, a seal or a wallaby. Today.'

His men had other ideas. 'We won't get a wallaby without Bryant's dog. I bet those women have got seal meat, probably all they eat, and shellfish.'

'They would be finding things that you wouldn't eat.'

'If Ned was here, why didn't he take those women? Perhaps he got younger ones from the mainland.'

'You haven't seen these women yet. I think you'd leave them here.'

The Captain glared at Hugh implying that he should discipline the men.

'Okay you men,' Hugh ordered. 'Muller and Rebus can get wood, and get a fire going at our old camp, the rest of you, go and get a seal off those rocks, we need meat. Forget about those women.'

'He is just as randy as us,' a man said as they walked toward the rocky end of the island. 'Perhaps he wants to get at them first.'

'I told you, you haven't seen them yet,' the other man who had found the women alone said.

'Shit, they must be rough, if you reckon they are. How long since you had a woman? Let's get a seal, let Hugh check them out.'

'What about old Muller? He might be interested?'

'No, he's forgotten what it's for.'

'Bullshit. Never!'

Captain Harris took Sarah with him to try to talk to the four Aboriginal women; he wanted to know what had happened to the six sealers.

The women's language was totally different to Sarah's, but in very broken English they explained, 'Other men come, drink rum, big fight.'

'Which men come?' Captain Harris asked. 'Was it a big ship?'

A haggard woman held up two fingers. 'Boats like yours. Big fight, women hide. Three men dead, others take boat and skins.'

Hugh sucked air through his dirty teeth, 'I'll bet it was Ned, he'll have those skins hidden somewhere, and he would have taken all the gear that we left here.'

'Yes,' the Captain said. With difficulty, he got the women's attention; pointed at the mainland and waved his hand. 'Do you want to go back there?'

The only response to that question was an incomprehensible babble as the women walked away, ignoring him.

'Those women don't look well,' Hugh said. 'I wonder if it's illness, or just a lack of good food. I'm sure there were five women here before. I wonder if one's died or if Ned took her away.'

'Well they are not really our concern. Although I can see them causing trouble with the men, you should take them back to the mainland.'

'We don't know where they come from. Anyway, the way I've heard it, they are not welcome back after they've been with white men. Probably best to just leave them here.'

'Yeah okay, leave them alone. We've got our other people to bring here yet. What's happened to those men getting food? I'm hungry, but I suppose it will be another bloody seal.'

As three men walked back across the island without a seal, small wallabies jumped away in front of them. There would be no food at the camp that night.

'Shit, where's Bryant with his dog when you need 'im?'

'One of those sealers told me that when they first came here you could walk up to those wallabies and club them with a stick. They've learned to keep out of the way now. Bloody hell, I'm sick of eating seal meat, I think I'll eat snake or rats soon.'

That night there was nothing to cook; not even shellfish.

'We need those women, and Bryant's dog to feed us,' Hugh said; they all agreed.

Next morning most of the men went hunting. Hugh decided to stay on Middle Island for another day, resting and hoping food would help regain his strength.

'The seals have got cunning like the wallabies,' a man told Hugh when they returned with only one seal.

When it was cooking on the fire, Hugh reflected. 'That's the only meat we'll get without Bryant's dogs. Or his women.'

The following day a steady south-west wind blew. If it kept up they would get there in one days sailing. Hugh Byron decided to take only three men with him back to the small island. The boat felt different loaded with only four men and two casks of water. But he was confident now, and sailed straight for the small island, keeping further away from the coast.

He sat in the stern steering with the big oar. *How many more miles am I going to do in this small boat?*

Levi spotted the sail and he waited on the beach with Bill Bryant for the boat to pull ashore.

'I am starting to remember my way around these islands,' Hugh told Bryant. 'Perhaps I'll stay here and join Ned,' he grinned.

'Aren't you looking forward to going back to Hobart Town and your family?'

'There were times recently, when I began to believe that would never happen. Anyway we're not out of this mess yet. Those sealers have gone from Middle Island, I think there was trouble. Sounds like Ned came back.'

'A ship will turn up there one day. Probably American, but I don't think I'll get on it. I want to go back east,' Bryant stated. 'What about those Aboriginal women, are they still there?'

'Yes, four and two children.'

'Shit, that'll cause trouble; you should take them back to the mainland.'

'I don't think they want to go anywhere, they seem happy to stay on the island. Don't know what to do with them,' Hugh said. 'But I reckon you're right, there'll be trouble.'

'Bound to be, bound to be,' said the Irishman. 'Did those sealers leave any tobacco behind?'

'Of course not you mad bastard, they had none before; remember? Just the little we gave them, and now they're probably smoking salty stuff they picked up on the beach from our wreck.'

'Yeah, just wishing for a smoke.'

Next morning, the whaleboat was once again overloaded with people; including two women, a baby, two dogs, Jacob and Chief.

'Right,' Hugh told his passengers. 'There's no more islands for about thirty miles, and then a fairly large one closer to the mainland. Although we can't land on that one, it'll give us shelter if we need it.'

The men rowed away from the island and followed the coast south-west. Toward the end of the first day they were still out in the open sea, but could plainly see the mainland coast and the large island.

Hugh Byron noticed dark clouds forming in the south; the wind had changed.

'Quick! Get that sail up,' he ordered. 'The wind's changed. I think we can sail straight to that island. That one, see it there.'

The wind increased and water foamed around the bow. Wind blew water into the boat; two men bailed continually to keep it out. The boat sailed fast toward the island, its speed saving them from foundering in ever worsening conditions.

As the worst of the storm hit, the boat rounded a point of the island which protected them from the strong wind.

'Now! Pull the sail down and get out those oars again,' Hugh urged the men. 'We need to stay here behind this island until this clears.'

They rowed the boat back and forth, and in circles for hours, in the protection of the rocky island, but away from rocks and out of the ferocious wind.

The sun did not set that evening; it merely disappeared behind a black mass of cloud low on the horizon. A rain squall moved across the sea under the black mass, and above it all, packs of white clouds held the storm in.

Once again the two women, the baby and Jacob sat in the bow. Merindah clutched William against her chest, Inta pushed in under her legs. The young dog trembled and whimpered each time lightning cracked and flashed.

As the strikes flashed violently through the low clouds they all caught brief glimpses of the rocky shore. They knew they were rocks, but with every tremendous clash and brilliant flash of blinding light, the shapes and shadows changed.

Shadowy monsters urged the small boat and its helpless occupants to come closer. They all sat in terror, with every eye looking into the gloom between each strike waiting for the next glimpse of the terrifying rocks, changing shape with the moving shadows.

'We don't want to get too close,' Hugh told them. 'That's a wild shore, I've seen it in daylight and I know what it's like. We need to stay this side to keep out of the wind, but I'm not going to put the anchor out here, it would be sure to get snagged on rocks. We can't afford to lose it.'

At last the sun rose into a washed, gleaming, blue sky. Although the wind had gone, the swell still rolled in as always and sunshine glinted off wet rocks and white spray. The storm had cleared the air and Merindah marvelled at the bright, clean, new day.

Seeing the island of jagged rocks that could have smashed the boat and the people to pieces in the storm's darkness, they were awed by their lucky escape. Hugh's leadership and the rugged island's protection that night had saved them from foundering or being blown into the mainland where they would certainly have been wrecked.

As they rowed west again Hugh contemplated, 'If it blew like that when we rowed along those cliffs a few weeks ago, we would not have survived to see that storm. There weren't any islands to protect us there.'

Merindah and Sally had brought cooked native rats with them. They took them out of a small skin bag and offered some to the men.

'You can just pull the skin off and use your teeth to get the meat off the small bones. The guts are all shrivelled up inside, you don't have to eat that.' Merindah demonstrated.

The men declined, preferring the little seal meat they had; the women shared the rats.

They rowed on, flanking the mainland; long sandy beaches and rocky headlands. Merindah wondered about the people who lived there. *Have white men been there too? What changes are happening?*

Dina sat close to Sally, and Inta snuggled up against Merindah and William. Merindah scratched the young dog's ears. 'Look at the land over there girl; imagine the wallabies you could chase.'

The young bitch gazed expressively into Merindah's eyes; she was part of the family. The dogs crunched the rat bones and chewed on the skins, then drank water that Merindah had poured out of a skin into the bailing bucket.

The boat sailed past many more small rocky islands before they came into the bay at Middle Island late on the second day and passed the wreck of the Belinda.

Sarah tearfully ran to greet the other two women when they walked into the rough camp.

'We thought you would never survive that storm,' Captain Harris declared. 'Where were you when it hit?'

'Behind an island, holding on and bailing out water,' Hugh answered. 'I'm not sure if I want to do that trip again, certainly not in a storm like that.'

The two dogs bounded along the beach the next morning; pleased to be off the little boat again.

The Captain found Merindah early. 'Could you take that bloody dog and get a wallaby, I'm sick of damned seal meat; cooked, raw, salted, or rotten.'

Merindah laughed. She and Jacob took both dogs and walked across the island. Normally the small wallabies only came out toward evening, but the dogs picked up their scent and found them hiding amongst bushes and rocks.

Chief used the wallabies and berries to make a thick stew, a welcome change that night, but two wallabies shared amongst almost twenty people only allowed a small portion each. Merindah and Sally ate the lizards they had caught.

As the men sat eating their small portion, one commented, 'Well, we've got food and water; there's no black men. If I had some tobacco I don't know if I'd want to leave here.'

'What about women?' another man said. 'And rum.'

'Yeah, I've been thinking about that.'

'What! Have you been thinking what I've been thinking?'

'Trouble!' Muller had heard them talking.

Merindah realised that it was going to be difficult to find enough food for thirty people on the island; especially when they would not like to eat seals continually. 'These men will need to eat lizards, snakes, and rats if they're going to survive here,' Merindah told the Captain. 'The wallabies won't feed them all, and they'll soon be all gone if we don't eat other things.'

Jacob was not by the fire, and Sally was missing too.

Merindah settled William down by the dogs and grasped the pendant around her neck as she drifted off to sleep. She dreamed of places and people far away.

Muller woke when the yelling began; he knew at once what was happening. When he and Captain Harris got to the camp where the Aboriginal women lived, they found it was the men who were yelling. The women had been expecting them and protected themselves with a variety of weapons. The men would have won eventually if the Captain and Muller had not been there.

'Get back to camp,' the Captain ordered. 'Only come here if they invite you to.'

'Oh, well, I would ask,' a man said sarcastically. 'But I'm getting desperate and I can't speak their language.'

'We could use sign language,' another man sniggered as they sulked away.

'What about Bryant's two women? He's not here. Where are his two women tonight?'

'His bloody dog is here; it sleeps with them at night and won't leave their side during the day unless Bryant takes her hunting. I met that dog when she was angry and she would've killed me if Sally didn't get her off me.'

'Why did she attack you?'

'Why, do you bloody well think? We had Sally; well we would've, if that dog wasn't there.'

'Young Jacob; he's always with those women. Him and Sally, whad'ya reckon?'

'No! She's old enough to be his mother.'

'Perhaps she's teaching him things?'

'Nah, he's just a lad.'

In the morning Merindah went to see the other Aboriginal women. Their language was strange to her, but they were able to converse in fragmented English.

She noticed their children. 'How did these women hide their children from the sealers? They must have been here before.' The Aboriginal women still kept the poultry that had been rescued from the ship. The women gave Merindah fresh eggs, and she understood the signs that the eggs were for her and William, not the men.

Merindah and Sally were expected to find extra food on the island. Men killed seals relatively easy, but they needed, and wanted different food. The women found many plants that could be eaten; berries and roots; plants that were able to be eaten whole or boiled in a cook pot. The women and Chief tried different things, but the men would not always eat the things they prepared. Most of the men eventually ate lizards and the occasional snake. But they left the rats for the women.

Hugh Byron needed to make one last trip back to the small island to collect the remaining men. Again Hugh took three men with him and sailed east. 'Now I'm just a ferry man,' he said as the boat sailed toward the small island.

After one day's good sailing they arrived, Bill Bryant and the other men helped to pull the boat up above the high tide line.

'How the hell did you survive that storm?' Bryant asked Hugh.

'I'd rather not talk about that right now,' Hugh said, 'but I guess it filled your rock holes with water.'

'Yeah, but I feared that you hadn't survived that storm, and we'd never see you again.'

'Take more than a little rain squall to drown me,' Hugh ribbed the Irishman.

After one last night on the small island the busy little whaleboat was once again overloaded and rowed away. Bill Bryant, Levi and the other men watched the island slowly sink into the waves behind them. They had not expected Hugh Byron and his whaleboat to return; they had expected to be marooned on that island and die of hunger and thirst. Then the rats that they wouldn't eat would gnaw on their bones for months.

Two days later Merindah watched the whaleboat sail into the sheltered beach at Middle Island. All the Belinda survivors were together once again; able to look at the hull of their stranded ship slowly breaking into pieces.

'What now?' Hugh Byron asked the Captain a few days later. 'Have you got another plan to get off this island?'

'Yes, one good plan,' Captain Harris answered.

'What's that then?'

'Stay here and wait! We should have done that before. It's bloody amazing that we all got back here alive. A ship will turn up here one day, this place is known; someone will come here looking for seals, like we did.'

'Yeah, perhaps you're right,' Hugh said. 'Now we need to wait and survive, but I'm afraid some of these men are going to cause trouble with those Aboriginal women.'

'Yes, but there's not much we can do about it. It could be better to let them sort things out amongst themselves.'

'I'd take those women back to the mainland, but for some reason they don't seem to want to go. Maybe they don't even come from over there,' Hugh said.

'Perhaps not. Bryant's women can't talk to them so we don't know where they come from, could be anywhere.'

Weeks passed. The men did sort out their own arrangements with the Aboriginal women. Some men were not interested; others sorted out their dealings with the women, and after more weeks passed, those men wished they had not.

'Those bloody sealers,' a man said. 'They left something behind with those women and now I've got it too.'

'What the hell did you expect? That's why I've kept away from them,' another man replied.

Weeks became months. Each man or woman had their own tasks.

Bryant caught the small wallabies, but they became harder to find. Jacob and Sally collected shellfish. Merindah and Levi gathered plants that could be eaten, and with Inta's help caught rats, lizards and sometimes a snake. One day Inta had flushed out a big monitor lizard that was as big as two wallabies. Some men collected water; others built shelters or collected fire wood. The food gradually became harder to find. Middle Island was not large, and over thirty people took a toll on its resources.

It was summer. Merindah watched as big birds flew back to the adjacent small island each night.

'They've been nesting there,' she told Bryant. 'There'll be chicks.'

A short trip in the boat and soon the food resource on that island was also being used and depleted. The half-grown chicks were easy to catch; few chicks would survive that year.

The hot months had come; William crawled around the camp. During the day everyone stayed in shade of shelters, or trees. Sun gleamed and flashed off the water in the bay, the sand on the beach and the sheets of rock burnt their feet. The waterholes would soon be dry depressions in the rocks.

Once again Bryant's young woman took the initiative.

'We must cover the water,' she told Bryant. 'That will slow down the drying up.'

Sticks and branches kept the sun and drying wind from sucking away their precious water. Merindah and Sarah struggled to find enough plants for Chief to cook in the pots. The situation became more desperate as the summer reached midpoint.

Each day the water became harder to find; the island was not going to support them all indefinitely.

'We need to start rationing the food,' Captain Harris told them. 'There are too many of us here, even the wallabies are getting scarce. There are always seals, but even they are wary of us now.'

'We can take the boat and get seals from other islands,' Hugh Byron said. 'But the water here will soon be the problem. The only solution is to move to the mainland or another island.'

'Would it be wise to go to the mainland?' Bill Bryant asked. 'Don't you remember those Aboriginal men? We have to hope it rains here soon to put water back in those rock holes.'

Merindah knew they needed better food. Just seal meat, and not eating plants would not be healthy. She kept trying different roots and any plant food that she could find. She saved the freshest parts of plants for William to chew on. Gradually they all became sick from eating mostly seal meat and rationing the water.

The island was virtually all rock, there did not seem to be anywhere to dig for water. Even a slight shower of rain or mist would cause a little water to run off the sloping rocks; that was the water that they survived on. Merindah suspected that the wallabies, rats and lizards must have got moisture from plants, or even from sea water.

The Captain told them all. 'If it doesn't rain within a few days, there'll be no water, we'll need to move, find somewhere else.' This was a new crisis. Once again all of their lives depended on them getting water and food.

Merindah knew the long hot days would soon become shorter; she waited for sunrise and took note of where it came out of the sea. The two dogs trotted off to the sloping bare rocks in the mornings, searching for any dampness from the early morning dew. Merindah and the other two women walked along the beach early each morning with William and the dogs. As the sun rose out of the ocean Merindah would swim. Then the women would sit quietly, watching waves washing over reefs; they watched the geese fly off the island close by and head toward the mainland.

'If we could fly like them we could leave here,' Merindah said.

'Yes; but where would we go?' Sarah asked. 'Those people over there may not want us, we don't belong there.'

'Those men may want you,' Sally told her. 'But not an old one like me.'

'Or a baby,' Merindah said as she picked William up. 'Let's walk.'

They walked without talking, each with their own emotions. Merindah searched the sky in the south and west. Often clouds built up closer to the landmass but would disperse before they reached the island. She knew that rain would come eventually, but would it too late?

Merindah watched another storm moving across the mainland.

'We need one of those storms to come this way,' she told Sally.

'It's not just the water,' Sally said. 'There's too many people on this island.'

'Will we ever go back to my place, Sally?' Merindah asked the older woman. 'What will become of us? Will I ever see my other baby again?'

'Do you want to go back there?'

Merindah remembered the beach of bones and the wrinkly old man. She thought about Alinta; but she was Yara's baby now.

'Bryant told me that if we go back that way, I must leave William behind, and stay with him wherever he goes. No, I want to keep William with me, better to stay somewhere safe away from lots of white men and perhaps even our own people.'

'What about Bryant's plan, will that still happen if we ever leave here?' Sally asked.

Merindah looked back down the beach toward the place where the rough camp was. 'We can't all stay here much longer. I heard the men talking about going to another island or the mainland.'

The three women turned and walked back to the camp; the dogs bounded on ahead.

The camp was spread haphazardly amongst low windswept trees and bushes beyond the white sand of the protected beach. Crude shelters made from branches, timber from the wrecked ship, seal skins and pieces of sailcloth. The shelters stood or leaned away from the wind. They huddled up against a hoax of a hill; just a higher bare sheet of the same hard rock that covered most of the island.

Small trees with white bark grew in groups and seemed to hold each other up as they leant away from the wind. Low bush grew amongst these trees. Many people moving about and collecting firewood had made the area around the camp bare. Fine dust blew when the wind swirled around the vegetation. There were small fire pits where groups of men would sit each night, but one central place where Chief prepared a meal each evening out of whatever the men or women found that day.

Merindah gazed at the camp as she walked to the women's shelter. 'No, we can't stay here,' she told the other two women. 'But I don't want to go back to the beach of bones; I will keep this boy. I'll stay with Bryant.'

Chapter 29 – Waiting for a Ship

No sign of a ship.
When will they return?
How long do we stay here?

James Miles worked with the whaling teams at the Bluff. The Americans did not return that season. Three teams worked from Granite Island, but they processed the whales on the mainland beach. Aboriginals still helped the white men; they relied on the abundant whale meat.

Extra experienced men had come on the Belinda to supervise the camp which could now be called a whaling station. The white man's presence became permanent as the whaling and the sealing operations became more established.

'This may be the last year we will camp on the island,' the man in charge said. 'I'm sure that when a ship comes back from Hobart Town at the start of the next whaling season, we'll set up a permanent base on the mainland.'

'That's next year, but where is our ship?' someone asked. 'The whaling season is almost over and the Belinda hasn't returned. There are barrels full of whale oil and stacks of seal skins. We're waiting to go back to Hobart Town.'

The whales left; the season had finished.

The Belinda lay breaking to pieces on the beach at Middle Island, but the men waiting at Granite Island had no way of knowing that. They waited expectantly for their ship to return. James had become an important part of the team working there; a valuable man on the whaleboat. Next season he would be the man standing at the front of the boat, the one who threw the harpoon into the whale.

Older men encouraged James. 'A couple more seasons; you'll be the headsman.'

Often during the winter James visited the outcast women's camp. He took more things to Yara that would help her and the babies. James enjoyed watching the two baby girls grow, and he spent time at the camp with Alinta whenever he could.

Yoola worked with the whalers at the beach of bones, but he still lived with the outcast women.

'Come and work with me on the whaleboats,' James suggested to Yoola. 'When the whales leave you can help with sealing and take food back to your camp.'

The other men working with James would tease him about his time away in the scrub.

'We know what you've been doing,' they would say when he returned.

Some of the men did not need to go far to get their women; just to the beach of bones. It had become a beach of many bones and a permanent community where many Aboriginal people camped. Sometimes white men spent days there. Aboriginal control of the area weakened and fragmented as different groups mixed.

James witnessed the friction and unrest around the whaling settlement; he talked to Yara and the other women at their camp. 'You must move away from here,' he told them. 'It's never going to be like it was before. You and your children would be happier living away from here.'

Wandura and Yara agreed with James.

'Yes, it's all changed,' Wandura said. 'We need to be near water and food, but if we move too far, we'll be in another clan's area. We may not be welcome.'

'Seems to me that the clans have lost control of their areas,'

James tried to explain. 'You should look further away. I'll bring more things to help next time I come; then you can show me where you are going to go. If I go away for the summer, I'll need to be able to find you next winter whaling season.'

Yara and Wandura understood. They agreed with James, they were keen to move away, even if the other women did not go with them.

'We are going to have another baby soon,' Yara told James. 'I want to leave here before then.'

At Granite Island the whales had gone and there was still no sign of the ship. Now the men killed seals whenever the weather allowed. Their stores of flour and other supplies became low.

'We'll be eating like those natives in there soon,' a man said. 'Our stock of tobacco and rum is almost gone. Where's our ship?'

The man in charge became very concerned. James worried about Jacob, Merindah and the men that he knew,

Spring passed and summer began and still they waited.

Another month passed and the men at Granite Island grew desperate, with only a little flour left, the rum casks empty and no tobacco. Over thirty people were camped on the small island, and now that it was summer they needed to bring their water over from the mainland. All the timber had been cut down for fire wood. After only a few years the small island was bare and disordered. Seals were hard to find without going far along the coast, and the colony of small penguins was almost destroyed.

'We won't be able to camp here next winter,' the headman told them.

'Looks like we'll still be here,' a man said.

'I think the ship must be in trouble,' the headman said. 'Maybe it's never coming back.'

They all realised the dangers of sailing a ship, especially into unknown waters. It was possible that they would never see the Belinda or her people again.

James fears increased; he went off to his own camp with fresh uncertainties.

A ship sailed across the large bay, coming from the east. It carefully moved into the anchorage in the shelter of Granite Island. James recognized the Southern Sky with a new coat of paint, new rigging, and of course a new crew. The Captain of the ship told the men at Granite Island that he had been sent to find the Belinda. He would take away the whale oil and seal skins. When they told him that they had not seen the Belinda since she left there early in the winter, the Captain understood their fears.

'Well, who's coming back to Hobart Town with us?' he asked. Most of the men wanted to leave, but at least one sealing gang would stay there for the last of the summer months. Six men decided to stay; two of those men had women with them.

'Only if you leave us some flour, tobacco, and rum.'

'That's easy,' the Captain told them. 'Let's get the oil and skins loaded, I want to get back and report that the Belinda is missing. But what can they do? She's probably lost with all her people.'

James volunteered to stay at Granite Island; he wanted to see Yara and his daughter again. He also wanted to be there in case the Belinda returned. And with it Merindah.

The Southern Sky left with the oil, the skins and most of the men, with their destruction and filth left behind. The men remaining did not work hard on getting seals; they casually made the best of their time alone.

'Perhaps now is a good time to move to the mainland and set up there somewhere,' James suggested. 'By that small river, somewhere away from the Aboriginal's camp.'

'Good idea,' the others agreed. Only the two women who originally came from Van Diemen's Land were unsure about living on the mainland, close to the local natives. Those women did not have a choice, the small group moved.

James went to Yara's camp and helped that group shift to another place further east; actually close to Yara and Merindah's original home. There they became settled and started a small community away from the whaling beach, and the disruption. James arranged for Yoola to come back to the new white man's camp, and during the next few months he became an important part of James's sealing team.

But still the Belinda did not return.

Yara and Wandura had another baby girl. James spent more time at their camp.

Chapter 30 – Rescue

Too many people on this island.
Is there a way to leave?
Will this ship take us back East?

Captain Harris had kept a rough record of their time since the ship wreck. Although he lost his journals, himself and Hugh Byron had been making marks on the side of their remaining whale boat.

'It must be early January,' he told Hugh Byron. 'The days will continue to be hot and dry. Do you think the water will last?'

'No, not unless it rains soon,' answered Hugh. 'There's probably water under these rocks. The women assume the wallabies drink sea water if they have to, or very little water, perhaps that's how they survive here in the dry summer months.'

The water situation became desperate; Bill Bryant organised men to dig a well.

'Must be water under these rocks somewhere,' he told the Captain, 'but we haven't got the tools to dig through the rock.' Their only tools were the single axe that they had salvaged from the ship, one hammer and four small wood chisels. After one day of chipping at the rock, they knew it was hopeless.

Merindah and Levi found only small damp patches at the bottom of sloping rocks; some damp enough for the dogs to smell and lick.

Merindah watched the dogs sniffing. 'There's water under those rocks, if they could dig through them.'

They walked to the highest point on the island. Levi looked west. 'There's still no sign of rain.' He turned and looked east 'A ship! Merindah! There's a ship!'

They ran to find the Captain.

'Make the fire smoke. Quickly!' Captain Harris ordered. 'Put the boat in the water, Hugh. Go out and make sure they see you. Show them the way into the bay, keep them away from that bloody sand bar though.'

The ship was the Nereus; a brig like the Belinda. Her Captain was Captain Thomas he told Captain Harris why he had been sent there.

'We're here to kill seals and check this place out for whaling.'

'That's why we came here, and we can tell you a lot about this area now,' Harris told him. 'We've been all around it in our whaleboats, or 'whaleboat' it is now. We lost the other one.'

He told the other captain about his ship being wrecked in the storm and their effort to return east in the two boats. He explained how they had lost one boat in the surf, the arduous walk along the cliff and the struggle to get the survivors back to Middle Island, with just the one boat.

Captain Thomas had little sympathy for their situation. He had come there to obtain seal skins; not rescue marooned sailors.

'We could take some of you back east,' he told Captain Harris. 'But will I get recompense for taking your people back? Perhaps it would be best if I report your situation to your superiors, and they can send a ship back here to collect you.' Captain Harris wanted himself and his crew to be taken off the island.

'We can't stay here any longer, there's very little food left on this island and virtually no water here until it rains again. My people can't just live on seals, even they will be scarce here soon if you kill too many.'

'Well,' insisted Captain Thomas. 'I've come a long way to get seal skins, and that's what we are going to do.'

'If you take us back, and call in at an island where we have left other men, there'll be many seal skins waiting to be collected. We could do a trade,' Harris told him.

'Well we'll see; first we will get skins from here; that's why we came.'

Harris was frustrated but could hardly argue with their best chance of survival.

'Well, what about water, can you spare a little water for us? We are struggling to find enough here until it rains.'

'If your men can help mine get seal skins, we can bring water in from our ship; that seems fair to me.'

'Sounds fair,' agreed Captain Harris. 'But I still need you to take us all off this island when you leave.'

'What, all of you? There's got to be more than thirty of you here!'

'No, some of these women here are not from our crew,' Captain Harris explained. 'They don't want to go.'

'Well, how many do you want me to take on my ship?'

'There are about twenty-five of us from the crew of my wrecked ship.'

'Shit, is there that many men, I presume those women, boys and children all come from the mainland over there. They will all be staying here. I presume your lot's finished with them.'

Captain Harris did not answer that question, he had a problem. Three of the women came on his ship, and those older 'black boys' were part of his crew. He knew that he could not, and he did not want to, leave them on Middle Island.

Men brought drinking water to the island from the Nereus and in return Captain Harris sent a group of his men to help get seal skins from the adjacent islands. Soon there were many skins drying in the summer sun, treated with salt from the large dry lake.

'These seals that we're killing,' Bill Bryant told Merindah. 'They're our food if that ship leaves us here, soon there will be no seals left around this island. Then what are we going to eat? We seem to have taken most of those small wallabies, even your lizards seem to be getting scarce. We will not survive here now, even when it rains.'

Sally and Jacob had spent time together again since getting back onto Middle Island. Now that the new ship had arrived Sally assumed that she may not get a chance to be with him again

Sally knew that it would be difficult to spend time with Jacob alone now. She needed every opportunity. 'We want different food than just seal meat,' Sally told Bryant, as he left to help get more seals. 'Come and help me Jacob, we will look for lizards and shellfish.' They had been picking over the shellfish for weeks, they were harder to find; it would take time.

Sally wanted more than food; she would be in control of her own life now. 'Come here to me young man,' Sally urged Jacob. 'This may be our last time together, and I want it to be special. You will have other women, but I don't want you to forget me. This has been my choice, perhaps I don't care if I never go with another man. I choose you and you did not force, or hurt me. Will you remember me?'

'Of course I'll remember,' Jacob replied uncomfortably. 'I won't forget you. Anyway, this may not be our last time together; we don't know what is happening yet, or where we are going.'

Although Captain Harris spent the night with Sarah, it remained impossible to block other things from his mind. Even if he could get all these people back to safety, what would his future be? Would he be held responsible for the wrecking of the Belinda? Would they give him another ship? He wanted to get all his people off the island, including the three Aboriginal women and the baby. What would he do with his woman if the ship owners did not give him another ship, or a position on a ship that allowed Aboriginal women? Would he pass her onto another sailor, or dump her back at Hobart Town to whatever life she could scrounge? He was well aware what that would be.

'What's troubling you?' Sarah asked.

'Oh, many things, I've got a few problems to sort out. Come here let's try that again!'

The next day Captain Harris took Merindah, Levi and four other men to the small island in the bay. They would get more chicks and perhaps adult birds to eat, but the Captain had another plan. When they pulled the whaleboat up onto the sand at Goose Island, Captain Harris sent the men off to look for birds.

'Not you two,' he told Merindah and Levi. 'You come with me; there's something else to do here, you can help.' The Captain wanted to find the stash of gold coins that he had hidden on the island, but he had lost his rough map when his whaleboat had been swamped on the beach months before.

'I think that the box with the instruments is buried around here somewhere. It's wrapped in a wallaby skin, and I made a sort of a mark with stones,' Captain Harris told them.

He pointed to the area feeling, 'If they don't find those coins, they may have to stay on the island. That box may be their only ticket out of here.'

There were no trees on the island; no shade. Loose dry sand puffed up as they walked in the hot sun amongst small spindly bushes. Merindah wanted to be back with William. Every small bush was the same, and between them the ground and stones had been scratched and moved by the hundreds of geese that flew in every night. Without any particular landmark, Captain Harris could not remember the place. He realised that it could be impossible to find. They rowed back to Middle Island later that day with no chicks or birds.

'The ones that we missed have flown to the mainland with their mothers, or perhaps we have taken them all,' a sailor told the Captain.

'Now don't you two tell anyone else what we were looking for today,' the Captain ordered Merindah and Levi. 'I don't want anyone else to know about that box off the ship. It's not much really, but may be enough to help us all get off this island together.'

Captain Thomas was on the island the next morning, looking at a pile of seal skins being salted and dried.

'These look good,' he commented. 'If we spend time here, we

would get a lot of skins.'

'If you keep taking them like this, there will be nothing left here on this island to eat,' Captain Harris told him.

'What will that matter if I take your men back? And you'll take those black boys and women back to the mainland before we go, won't you? I've counted your men, there are less than twenty of you, the rest are young black men and seven women. They won't be coming on my ship,' he declared.

'Shit,' Harris muttered under his breath as he walked away. 'How can I sort this out?' He went to see Bill Bryant.

'Bryant, we have a problem,' he said when he found the Irishman skinning another seal. 'Come with me I need to talk to you.'

When they were alone, the Captain told Bryant about his dilemma. 'That bastard doesn't want to take our women back, or those young black boys. They all came here with us but he thinks we took them from the mainland here, and we, or his men will take them back there before we leave with him'.

'But that's bullshit, they're all part of our crew,' Bryant protested. 'What are you going to do about it? Only those four women that the sealers left will stay, and I don't think they come from the mainland here either. Christ knows where they come from, could've been hundreds of miles away. My women have talked to them and it seems like they want to stay here on this island.'

'I have only one plan to convince him to take us all. Remember those coins that your woman recovered from the wreck. I need it to get us all out of here. I could tell my bosses we lost the money in the shipwreck. We just need to get all those who know that we recovered it to keep their mouths shut,' explained the Captain. 'But there's a small problem.'

'Did you put the coins in anything?' Bryant asked when the Captain told him about his dilemma.

'I wrapped the box up in one of those wallaby skins and buried it, but I'm buggered if I can find where now. Those bloody birds scratching have changed everything. Even if I still had the map I made it would be useless.'

'Well,' Bryant told him, 'there's a chance we still may find where you put the box.'

Another night with Merindah convinced Bill Bryant that he would not leave his young woman, or any of the crew, on that island.

'Will we be leaving here soon?' she asked him. 'Where will we go?'

'Yes, we'll all be leaving here soon,' Bryant assured her. 'But I am not sure where we will go, back to Flinders Island if I can have any say. But it may be difficult to persuade the Captain of this new ship to stop there; we need to convince him that he will get many seal skins. He cares more about seal skins than he does about us.'

Merindah did not understand all of what Bryant told her, but she understood enough to know he would take her and the others away with him.

'Those other women here,' she asked. 'What is going to happen to them? I think they want to stay here, they can't even tell me where they came from.'

'Yes, I think we should leave them here, but we've taken most of the food off the island, and used all the water. I will try to convince that Captain to leave a barrel of water here.'

'I think they will survive here,' Merindah said, 'but they'll need rain soon. Can we leave those hens here for them?'

'Yes, the poultry can stay here, at least they will get eggs from them, now let's stop this talking; that's not why we're here.'

Next day four men rowed the whaleboat across to Goose Island again to get more eggs. Bryant and his young Aboriginal woman and the two dogs were also on the boat.

Captain Thomas watched as the boat went past the Nereus.

'They must like those geese eggs,' he commented to a sailor, 'but why have they got those dogs with them? They told us there were no wallabies on that island.'

'Perhaps the dogs can catch geese,' the sailor answered.

Bryant took a wallaby skin on the boat with him. He wanted the dogs to find another wallaby on the island, or at least its skin, which had been there for about four months, wrapped around a box of gold coins. Bryant sent the four men off to look for eggs. Merindah took Bryant to the area where Captain Harris had buried the box.

Bryant let Dina smell the wallaby skin that he had taken to the island. 'There are more of these here,' he told the bitch. 'Go find them. Go.'

Both dogs ran off with their noses to the ground. All Merindah and Bryant could do was watch and wait.

Later that day Captain Thomas stood on his ship as the whale boat returned to the bigger island. Merindah sat in the boat with the two dogs.

'Why do they keep those bloody useless women and those bloody useless dogs?' he asked the sailor next to him. Although he did not realise it; those bloody useless women and their dogs had saved the lives of all the Belinda's crew, and now they may have found the means to get them all back east.

Captain Harris convinced Captain Thomas that there would be seal skins on Flinders Island, and Thomas agreed to sail soon.

'If you take salt back, they'll trade that for seal skins,' Captain Harris told him. 'My crew will help to bag up salt from the lake here, that's one thing this island has; plenty of salt.'

'Yes, we'll take salt with us. And your whale boat, there's room for it on my ship; you may need that boat if I leave you somewhere. While we're sailing back, your men can help work on the skins that we have got from here. Better be skins at this island of yours, I don't want to stop there for nothing, although, that may be a good place to leave some of your crew of oddballs if I'm sick of them.'

Captain Harris knew from that remark there would be little chance of persuading his counterpart to pick up the people left on Flinders Island; certainly not Jilly and her two boys.

'There'll be skins,' he assured him, but he did not mention the other men on Flinders Island.

The two captains watched men loading the Nereus with salt and seal skins.

'We'll leave in two days. Are you going to take those blacks over to the mainland, or are you going to leave them here?' Captain Thomas asked.

'Four women will stay here, because they were here when we arrived. The other women and boys are from my ship, and I want you to take them all back east.'

'But they're Aboriginals, and I gather you took them from this mainland. I don't want them on my ship.'

'They're all part of my crew, and I want you to take them.' Captain Harris showed him a handful of gold coins. 'Would this change your mind?'

'Where the bloody hell did you get that? Shit, are those black's worth that much?'

'They are worth more than you'd ever know! Now what is your answer, are you taking all of my crew?'

Merindah, Sally and Sarah were not happy to leave the other four women and their children on Middle Island. But the women wanted to stay; possibly because they had been taken there a long time ago and would not be welcome back at their home place; wherever that was. The poultry from the Belinda had been spared, even when over thirty hungry people struggled to find enough food. The hens were breeding; the women would always have eggs and sometimes chickens to eat. Monitor lizards were the hen's only predator, and when the women saw them, they killed and ate them. Merindah knew the poultry would help the four women continue to live there; they seem to have understood that. They had not killed any. 'They seem to be part of the little family, and their chickens are pets that children play with.'

'When sealers and whalers come here,' Bill Bryant said, 'they'll find poultry and eggs, it'll make a change from seal meat.

'And something else will be here for them.' Merindah said when she thought about other men coming to the island.

Chapter 31 – Still an Uncertain Future

She was only worth a dog.
Now she is worth a handful of gold coins.

As the Nereus sailed out of the bay at Middle Island, Captain Harris and his second mate Owen Muller stood at the stern.

'This will become an important place for whaling men and sealers. That will be the bay where they will set up a base,' Captain Harris told Muller. 'But I don't want to come back here.'

He was looking at the wreck of his ship trapped in the surf. It was gradually being destroyed by the relentless action of the waves that washed gently through its bones. But occasionally bigger waves smashed those bones apart and threw them up onto the beach.

'No, I'll never be coming back here, I don't think I'll survive another ship wreck,' stated Owen Muller. 'How did you convince him to let the women and those boys on the ship?' he asked. 'Only a few days ago he told me that he wouldn't take them. They are worthless, he said, and he seemed definite. Something has changed his mind. Did you offer him your woman?'

'No, we came to an arrangement, let's just leave it there,' Harris answered. 'As for the value of those women and boys, I think each one of them is as valuable and important as any one of us. More! Without them and Bryant's bloody dogs, we would all be just white bones up on the top of that cliff, or laying full of spears in the sand on a beach.'

'Yes, I agree.'

A sailor smirked at Merindah, Sally, Sarah and William as he showed them to a hatch that led into a hold half full of seal skins. He threw a wooden bucket down after them. The skins were still green, still greasy and smelly. In the confined hold it was hot and steamy. Blow flies buzzed through the cracks in the deck, and laid their eggs in any damp spot amongst the skins.

'Well, we'll have maggots to eat in a few days,' Sally told the other two women.

'That may be all we're going to have to eat,' Merindah said. 'Oh! And those rats, but I would like to cook them a little first.'

'Yuk!' Sarah said. 'This is a little different than the Captain's cabin and helping Chief in the galley.'

All three women laughed, sat and hugged; then they all cried together.

The Nereus's first mate directed the Aboriginal boys to the hold where the bags of salt were. He reluctantly showed the rest of the Belinda's crew to various places where they could keep out of the way.

'You will have to pay for the food your people eat,' Captain Thomas told Captain Harris. 'Who's going to cook and take them food?'

'Let's wait and see how many seal skins you take from my island,' Captain Harris said. 'My cook, Chief will help with the food, if your man will let him.'

'What do you mean your island?'

'Well, we have a base there now, and we're going to keep it there,' Captain Harris answered. 'And as far as paying for the food that little hand full of incentive I gave you will more than cover a bit of food.'

'Those coins you gave me are not recorded anywhere in the ship logs, it never happened, did it?'

'No, and you keep it like that. There are few who know about it, and that's the way it should stay. But I'm expecting you to look after my people on this ship, including those women and dark boys.'

'Right,' Captain Thomas reluctantly agreed. 'Take your cook to see mine, and get some food organised for your people, but keep those bloody dogs out of the way.'

'Well, that's got that sorted,' Captain Harris said to himself as he walked off looking for Chief. 'It'll be an interesting voyage.'

Later, Chief's smiling face appeared in the open hatch; he climbed down the ladder with a basket.

I have this food for you ladies And I want to talk to my favourite sailor.' Chief put the food down and picked William up. 'I may have found something special for my young sailor,' Chief gave him a fresh ships biscuit to suck.

Merindah and the other two women were below in the hold with the seal skins as the ship left the island. After they had eaten and William lay sleeping on a skin, they climbed up the ladder and sat next to the hatch. Sitting together quietly, the women each reflected on their lives as they watched the sun setting in the sea next to Middle Island far in the west.

'We left here once before,' Sally said. 'But we came back. I wonder if we will come back this time.'

'No, not this time,' Merindah said. 'But now those women are alone, I worry for them. How long before another ship comes? Another lot of men will share them, and what will happen to those children?'

Now the three women realised that although they were leaving the island, they did not know where, and what they were going back to.

'What will happen to us now?' Sally asked. 'Where are they going to put us off this ship? Will they just leave us on an island like those other women? We have no ship, no camp.'

'Bryant's plan?' Merindah asked. 'Is that still going to happen?'

Merindah had decided; she did not want to return to the beach of bones. Although Alinta was there, she was Yara's now. James would be there, but Bill Bryant had a hold on her now; William; she was not going to give up her son. Bryant had told her that if they returned to the Granite Island camp, she was to leave the boy there and stay on the ship with him. The other plan of Bryant's was that they would stay on an island together; that would allow her to keep William with her and not return to the beach of bones and the disruption. But what about James? Would she ever see him again if Bill Bryant kept her on an island?

Suddenly Sarah gasped! 'Now my man has no ship, what will he do with me? Will he give me to another man, or will he take me with him wherever he goes? No, he will not keep me if he goes back to Hobart Town, he may just dump me there. Perhaps he only needed me when he was on the ship.'

With their lives affected in different ways, and as it had always been, without any choice of their own, the three women sat without talking, each looking vacantly into the waves as the ship sailed further east to their future.

Sailors on the ship watched the women with other ideas; now they had time to consider how they could get with them. As they discussed their chances, a large dog sitting close to the women's hatch watched and quietly growled.

As the Nereus sailed across the Great Australian Bight, each one of the crew from the Belinda had time to ponder the events of the previous four months. They all knew that it was a miracle that they had all survived their ordeal. Now each one of them from the Captain at the top, to the Aboriginal boys at the bottom had time to consider and wonder where their journey in life would lead them next. Captain Harris worried about his future after the loss of the Belinda. Chief pondered if he would go on another ship.

The ship sailed east; fresh seal skins covered the deck during the hot days as men worked cleaning and salting. Clean and salted, but needing to dry more, sailors stacked the skins in the hold.

Although it was hot on the deck of the ship during the day, without ventilation below it was even hotter, almost unbearable.

Even the black blowflies just sat, only reluctantly rising, buzzing, annoyed when they were disturbed. There would be many more flies; maggots were in every damp crease of the seal skins; the rats lived and nested in the bundles of skins. The ship's cats got fat on baby rats.

Sailors' eyes became red and their faces were wind and sun burnt from working all day, looking up at the rigging and the sails, with the bright sun in their eyes. Men who had been holding the wheel looking ahead into the shimmering sea and up at the sails, came off that watch still seeing red spots in their tired eyes.

Each night a fresh breeze would push the ship faster through the sea bringing cool relief to everyone aboard.

Merindah enjoyed those nights on the deck of the ship as it rose and dipped through the swell. She no longer felt seasick, but she did not enjoy staying in the hold, sleeping or sitting on a pile of stinking seal skins. Whenever possible, the women sat on the deck close to the two dogs and the hatch which led into their place on the ship. They kept away from sailors and trouble.

One of the mates of the ship had instructed them clearly when the women came aboard that first day.

'You women are not to move from this area, just stay on the top here by this hatch, or down in there. You can only go to the side of the ship to empty your bucket. And the Captain told me if I found you with any men, ours or yours, I was to throw you over the side.'

'Well, what about the man you find us with?' Merindah wondered. 'Will you throw him over too? I don't think so; no, it would be our fault!'

'And keep that dog shit cleaned up every day, or else I'll throw those useless bloody things over the side too. Do you understand me?'

Sally looked straight into the man's face and nodded as if in agreement, but in a language only she and Sarah understood she told the man. 'You are the most useless bloody thing on this ship, and if I could, I would throw you and a lot more like you over the side.'

Although the mate did not recognise a word she said, he assumed that Sally understood.

'That's good, I'm pleased you understand me,' he replied as he walked away.

'What did you tell him?' Merindah asked.

'I told him he was the best-looking man on the ship, and if he came back here tonight, he can choose any one of us.'

The mate frowned when Sally and Sarah burst out laughing.

'No I don't think you told him that,' Merindah replied. 'But he would if he could.' All three women agreed and laughed.

The man sneered. 'Useless bloody black women,' he said to a sailor next to him. 'Why the bloody hell are they on this ship?

The ship kept clear of the coast of long sandy beaches and the huge blocking cliffs that the Belinda's crew knew so well. After ten days sailing with a favourable wind islands were on the port beam.

'Now, how far to this island that you reckon is yours?' Captain Thomas asked Captain Harris.

'It's well past these; you'll find it on Flinders chart if you've got it. Flinders mapped these islands too, but a Dutch fellow found and named this group a hundred and fifty years before he was here. The Dutch didn't like the look of the country and never came back. Although perhaps they did sometimes accidently, and some of them were probably wrecked here.'

'You would know about shipwrecks, wouldn't you?' Captain Thomas sarcastically remarked.

'Yes, well, it may happen to anyone of us, especially if you don't know the area. You may get your turn one day.'

'I agree. It certainly is a risky business. How will you get on with the owners?'

'I've no idea, but I imagine they realised the risk of sending a ship to an area for the first time. The storm that caught us would have wrecked any ship exposed there at the time. If we had got around behind that island, I'm sure we would have been safe.'

'Well, you'll need to explain that to other people, not me,' Captain Thomas stated. 'And now we have sailed back here in this ship, across the Bight, don't you think you were a bit too optimistic to even consider sailing back here with twenty-five people in those two boats?'

'Sometimes you make decisions which on reflection may have been wrong. But at the time I simply wanted to leave the place where every day I could see my ship being torn apart in the waves.'

'I can understand that,' Captain Thomas replied. 'But to try coming back here in those two boats was extremely brave, or foolish. I can't understand how you all survived the trip back to that island.'

'Well,' Captain Harris said. 'What you call those useless black women over there, without them most of my crew would've been dead in the first few days on the mainland. Now, let's get back to the present,' Captain Harris continued. 'This island of mine, it's further south, you'll find it on the chart, called Flinders Island. It's the bigger one of the group.'

'What! Did Flinders name it after himself? That's a bit vain, isn't it?'

'No, he named it after his brother Samuel, who was on the ship with him.'

'Right, well, we'll be there in a day or so, I'll need you then. I want to see these seal skins and then move on.'

Captain Harris left the other captain and went back to talk to his own mates. He needed to discuss a plan with them; he wanted to mislead and do a deal with the other captain when they got to Flinders Island.

Bill Bryant kept away from the place where the women were living in the ship. He had heard the Captain's warning that there was not to be any contact with the women while they were on his ship. He sat on a hatch cover close to the dogs after he gave them some seal meat and bones from Middle Island. The dogs would protect his women, he would not go closer.

Bryant had scrounged tobacco from a sailor, and he rammed it into the old pipe that he had carried with him along that cliff top and beach. As he lit the tobacco, Merindah recognised the familiar aroma once again. She watched the blue smoke rise into the cool evening air. She looked past his long scraggly red hair and his untidy bristling beard, but did not look past him; she saw his shock of hair and whiskers and his bright blue eyes.

What plans has he for me and my baby? What will our future be? And then past those intense eyes, past the man who would decide her future, Merindah noticed the islands toward the mainland and she knew that things were going to change. *Soon, I may be saying goodbye to people that have become very close to me, and I may never see those people again.*

Chapter 32 – The Beginning of Another Journey

Is this where we will stay?
An island home.

'There's a ship in the bay,' Jilly's oldest boy shouted to his mother. 'Is that our ship?'

'I don't know, looks like it might be. Quick fetch Olath, he's working with the other men.'

The skinny, naked, half-caste boy ran and found the men scraping and salting seal skins.

Argus stood at the water's edge barking, Olath and the other men watched the ship.

'No, I don't think it's our ship,' Olath said. He studied the masts and the outline of the ship sailing across the bay. 'No, that's not the Belinda, but they're going to stop here. Look, the sails are coming down as the ship turns into the wind.'

Captain Thomas had been very cautious as he brought his ship past the enormous rock that soared straight out of the water on the east side of Flinders Island. Captain Harris guided him past those strange craggy cliffs protecting the two bays to the south. He pointed out where a series of large waves rolled across the first bay.

'Keep away from there,' he advised. 'Must be a reef under there, see how the waves lift and run into that little bay between those cliffs.'

'Shit, I hope you know your way around here,' Captain Thomas said. 'Your recent record isn't too sound,' he commented.

'We'll be fine, just keep well away, and then go straight ahead, you can anchor in there. That's where our ship was for about two weeks. The only wind that may force you to shift will be an easterly. Then you could shift to the other end of the island until the wind goes back to the south or west. It always does.'

The Nereus dropped anchor out from the small protected cove. Sailors lowered the well-travelled whale boat that had carried most of the crew of the Belinda many miles, and them all back out to the relative safety of Middle Island.

Olath and the other men recognised Hugh Byron, Owen Muller and Bill Bryant as the whale boat neared the beach.

'Where's our ship?' they all asked. 'Where have you been? We've been waiting months.'

'The Belinda's been wrecked,' Hugh Byron told them. 'We'll tell you all the details later, but now I've got instructions from Captain Harris, you must act quickly. I presume you've got a lot of seal skins.'

'We certainly have,' Olath answered. 'But we thought you were never coming back to get them. Or us!'

'Well we're back, but there's something you have to do now.'

Olath and the men worked quickly. All the rest of that day and into the night, they took all the best seal skins inland and hid them. They stacked the smaller seal skins and some wallaby skins at their camp. The unsalted fresh skins were in a different pile. Any salt they had left, they hid in the bush. They took any of the kegs with water in them away or emptied them. Only a little water remained in small casks.

'I can see that you have things fairly tidy and comfortable here,' Hugh Byron said. 'But now I want you to make it look untidy, as if you're struggling to keep alive. I don't want the place looking attractive.'

Before sunrise the next morning, Jilly and her two boys left the camp and had taken the three goats far into the middle of the island.

'Stay away until the ship has gone,' Olath told Jilly.

Captain Thomas and Captain Harris came in on a whaleboat to inspect the seal skins. There was a reasonable stack of skins, but it was just a fraction of what was there the day before.

'Well that's not a great lot. I imagined there'd be more here,' Captain Thomas said.

'Well to tell you the truth, I expected more,' Captain Harris said, looking puzzled. 'Perhaps it's not so good here.'

'I would need most of them to exchange for that salt,' Captain Thomas bargained.

'Tell you what I'll do. These men have told me they are running out of fresh water here; some of them want to leave. If you take most of these men back to Granite Island with you, I'll let you take all of these skins, even though its six months' work here.'

'Done, sounds all right to me, but I don't know why anyone would want to stay here if that's all the skins they got in six months, and now the water's scarce.'

'Well, I have good news for you, you can leave two of those bloody useless black women and one of those black boys here and perhaps a couple of men,' Captain Harris sarcastically told the other Captain.

'Right sounds good to me, I will get my men to bring the salt in here and we'll take all of those skins. And one thing's for sure, I won't bother coming back here again, I'll sail straight past this island.'

'That's exactly what I wanted you to think,' Captain Harris said to himself as he walked away up the beach to congratulate his mates on the deceitful little job that they had done the previous night.

The plan had worked, there would be salt left there and most of the men would be taken off the island. The Nereus would call into Granite Island and some of the Belinda's crew would stay there, while the Captain and most of his crew would be taken back to Sydney or Hobart Town.

Captain Harris was pleased with himself. 'Well perhaps something good has come out of this mess,' he told Bill Bryant. 'You're going to get your island, and enough salt until I send a ship back here to pick up the rest of the seal skins, and more. And that captain won't bother coming back.'

'Who's staying?' Bryant asked.

'Well, it'll be Olath of course, and his woman and her two boys, and Levi, he's happy to stay. What do you think? Would two other men do you for now? I'll get Hugh to ask the men if two will stay.'

'Sounds good to me, that's enough men to keep getting seals, and the women can help. There aren't many seals here anyway, are there?' Bryant said smiling.

'No,' answered Captain Harris, laughing as he went to talk to Hugh Byron.

When the two Captains were back aboard the ship which was preparing to leave, Captain Harris had another deal to put to the other Captain.

'How's that ships log of yours going? Do you want to do another little deal that need not be in there?'

'The log can remain closed, what have you in mind?'

'Well, these men of mine that are going to stay here, they'll need flour, rum and tobacco. What's say you lose some of yours from this ship? You'll be back at Sydney soon. You must have more than you need. I imagine you could make up a story, how it became spoilt or stolen.'

'What are you offering?'

'Will this be enough for you to make up that little story for your bosses?' Captain Harris asked, as he handed over more gold coins.

'Yes, the bloody bindings in the hold came lose, and some rum casks broke and spoilt the flour and tobacco,' Captain Thomas said as he accepted the gold coins.

'How did you get that tight arse to give you this?' Bill Bryant asked when the Captain took the rum, flour and tobacco into the island camp.

'Well, let's just say that the box your dog found on that island held more coins than I thought. You remember; the box with the instruments that you recovered from our wrecked ship?' Captain Harris slapped Bryant on the back. 'Good luck Bill, I hope your little venture here works out. I don't think I'll come back. You look after that smart young woman of yours. She'll be the princess of this island. She's your Princess Charlotte; that's what she is Bill.'

The Captain returned to the ship.

The Nereus lay at anchor. Men rowed boats back and forth loading skins and taking salt into the beach.

Jacob had not talked to Sally since their last time together on Middle Island. They had one last opportunity to meet briefly and say their goodbyes.

Jacob blushed when Sally told him that she would remember their time together, and she hoped that he would remember her fondly.

'I was your first woman,' she said, 'and I know you won't treat any women like many other men treated me.'

'I may come back here on a ship one day, and we'll see each other again,' Jacob comforted her.

'You might, but then we'll only be friends. I want you to find a younger woman, and be kind to her.'

Jacob shuffled his feet and stared at the sea. 'I have to go now.' He left her standing on the deck.

Sally went to find Merindah, William and Sarah.

Merindah stood alone at a rail, gazing out across the water towards the mainland. Although close to the island it seemed far away. But she realised that it was even further back to the beach of bones, Alinta, Yara and James.

Merindah stood dreamily holding her pendant when Sally walked up. 'When I hold this in my hand,' she explained to Sally, 'James and Alinta are with me, or perhaps I'm with them; this is how I stay with them. Should I talk to Jacob again? We have said goodbye, but I wondered if we should tell him about James and Alinta. We could ask him to tell James where we are, and what has happened.'

'No,' Sally said. 'We should keep that our secret, yours and mine. Jacob will tell James about you, and where we are. There's no need to tell him why James would want to know.'

'I suppose you are right. Perhaps they'll both come here one day on another ship.'

'I'm sure they will,' Sally assured Merindah.

Merindah and Sally were in tears as they prepared to leave the ship; not upset to be staying on the island, but sad to be parted from Sarah. The three women sat and howled. They had been together through many traumatic experiences, and now they would be parted. They knew that it would be forever. Sarah would go back to Sydney or Hobart Town. She had no idea what would happen to her then, and she did not want to think about it. Was she just another woman who had been used, now to be passed on to a different man?

Chief was upset that Sally, Merindah and William were leaving the ship; he was very fond of William.

'There's always comes a time when I have to part with someone,' he cried. 'It's always so sad, so sad.' His giant arms hugged Merindah. 'Maybe one day I'll come back on a ship. Then I'll see my little sailor again.'

Many tears and hugs later, Merindah passed William down to Sally, who was sitting in the whaleboat with Bill Bryant and the two dogs. Merindah climbed down the ladder and stepped in. Sarah and Chief howled as Bryant, Levi and two other men rowed the boat away from the ship.

Early the next morning the wind filled the Nereus's sails. With a steady north-east wind she moved away from the cove and sailed south along a rocky shore where seals climbed out of the waves and lolled in the sun.

Jilly, her two boys, and the three dogs were there with Sally, Merindah and William on the beach, watching the ship sail away.

Merindah turned around and looked at the sand, the trees and the cliffs; she held her baby tight and thought about his future there on that island.

'Will we be safe here?' she asked Sally.

Sally did not answer. She stood in a daze, thinking of all that had happened since that day months before, when as they sailed out past the Bluff she had tried to comfort Merindah. But that had been just the start of Merindah's remarkable journey; and she had many more journeys yet to travel.

www.ingramcontent.com/pod-product-compliance
Lightning Source LLC
Chambersburg PA
CBHW072021110726

47910CB00005B/1824